How to Tempt a Rockstar

Arabella Quinn

Copyright © 2023 by Arabella Quinn

All rights reserved.

No part of this publication may be reproduced, distributed, or transmitted in any form or by any means, including photocopying, recording, or other electronic or mechanical methods, without the prior written permission of the publisher, except as permitted by U.S. copyright law.

If you purchased a copy of this eBook, thank you. Also, thank you for not sharing your copy of this book. This purchase allows you one legal copy for your own personal computer or device. You do not have the rights to resell, distribute, print, or transfer this book, in whole or in part, in any format, via methods either currently known or yet to be invented, or upload to a file sharing peer-to-peer program. It may not be re-sold or given away to other people. Such action is illegal and in violation of the U.S. Copyright Law. If you would like to share this book with another person, please purchase an additional copy for each recipient. If you're reading this book and did not purchase it, or it was not purchased for your use only, then please purchase your own copy. Thank you for respecting the hard work of this author.

The story, all names, characters, and incidents portrayed in this production are fictitious. No identification with actual persons (living or deceased), places, buildings, and products is intended or should be inferred.

Dedication

In loving memory of my dear mother,
The one who championed my writing journey,
These books stand as a testament to your never-ending belief in me. As my biggest fan, your encouragement was unwavering throughout the years I spent writing this book series. Though you're not here to see the culmination of my efforts, I know you are watching over me, cheering me on from a place where love transcends all boundaries. Your absence is deeply felt, but I carry your love and support within me, inspiring me and giving me the courage to chase my dreams.
You are forever in my heart.

Contents

Chapter 1	1
Chapter 2	9
Chapter 3	15
Chapter 4	21
Chapter 5	31
Chapter 6	35
Chapter 7	44
Chapter 8	50
Chapter 9	57
Chapter 10	71
Chapter 11	90
Chapter 12	104
Chapter 13	116
Chapter 14	130

Chapter 15	137
Chapter 16	143
Chapter 17	159
Chapter 18	167
Chapter 19	175
Chapter 20	187
Chapter 21	193
Chapter 22	201
Chapter 23	207
Chapter 24	218
Chapter 25	233
Chapter 26	251
Chapter 27	262
Chapter 28	273
Chapter 29	279
Chapter 30	293
Chapter 31	308
Chapter 32	315
Chapter 33	321
Chapter 34	331
Chapter 35	336
Chapter 36	347
Chapter 37	354
Chapter 38	363

Chapter 39	373
Chapter 40	378
Epilogue	385
Next in Series	410
Arabella Quinn Newsletter	413
Bad Boys of Rock Series	414
Also By Arabella Quinn	417
Other Novels by Arabella Quinn	419
About the Author	422
Excerpt	423

Chapter 1

Bash

D EBAUCHERY WAS ON THE menu tonight.
It didn't matter that it was a Monday night; in fact, most nights I partied my ass off. But the knowledge that I didn't have practice at our rehearsal studio tomorrow ramped up the level of this party a hundredfold. There was no doubt in my mind, tonight was going to get very ugly. I'd been drinking steadily for hours, and I'd already done too many bong hits to count. I was in the mood to take a hit of something even wilder, but my little sister was here.

My sister, Kaylie, had an apartment within walking distance of my own. While I loved that I could keep an eye on her in Los Angeles, sometimes, like tonight, she cramped my style. She partied with us a lot, usually bringing her wannabe actress friends with her.

I shouldn't complain too much, because tonight one of those friends pulled me into Sid's bedroom, even though my bedroom was only one door further down, and gave me a blowjob. It was sloppy, but it did the trick. If Sid had walked in, she would have blown him too.

I had to be careful of the wannabe actresses because they were all about social media. They loved nothing more than to be plastered all over it. From experience, I knew that if they could link their name to a rock band, all the better for them. The wilder the scandal, the more these girls benefited, no matter how shitty it could turn out for me and the band. Our label had warned us to keep our image squeaky clean after a bit of malicious gossip about us recently hit social media, so I was extra cautious of them.

When a new group of girls showed up, the party got even wilder. A few hours later, I was stumbling around and slurring my words, almost completely wasted. It was to the point where I knew I should grab a few girls and head to my bedroom so I could fuck them until I passed out. Of course, that's not what I did.

I wasn't exactly clear on how it all started. One of our roadies, Ben, who looked more like a member of a motorcycle gang than a sound engineer, was running his mouth, bragging about how good he was at eating pussy. The next thing I knew, I was being roped into a pussy-eating contest. Two girls volunteered to be the subjects, and Sid and I were pitted against each other. I was confused as to why big-mouth Ben wasn't a contestant considering he was the one making all the ridiculous claims, but I was too wasted to figure it out.

I chugged a beer someone handed me and glanced around the room. It was packed full of outrageously drunk people. The music was blaring, and people were dancing, spilling drinks, and snorting lines off the coffee table. A few couples were fucking in the corners; they knew that if Sid or I found them in our bedrooms, they'd never be allowed back here. That threat seemed to work most of the time.

Sid was saying something to me, but I wasn't listening. He shook my shoulders, and I tried to focus on him. Sid was like a brother to me; we'd been friends since we were 13 years old. Our band, Ghost Parker, was the fourth and hopefully, last band we'd be in together. Our second album was in production and, by all accounts, it was going to be huge.

Sid's lips turned down in a frown. "I'm not doing this, man. You can't either. You're totally wasted."

"I'm fine." My head was spinning wildly, but I felt pretty damn invincible.

"You're not fine. And Kaylie is here. You can't do this in front of her."

I looked around the apartment, searching for Kaylie. I'd forgotten about her. "What the fuck is she still doing here? Tell her to go home."

Sid ran a hand through his hair. "You know she's not going to leave. And I'm not eating some girl out in front of her. You're not either, asshole."

Ben sidled up to us and slapped his meaty hand on Sid's shoulder. His voice boomed above the music, "What the fuck, Vicious? You can't puss out. I have a hundred bucks on you. No way this pretty boy can beat you."

Sid, who was called 'Vicious' by most of the people that worked with the band, shook his head. "It's not happening, Ben. Bash won't do it either."

"What are you? His old lady?" Ben was always instigating trouble. Problem was that I somehow always ended up in the middle of it. The fucker knew how to push my buttons.

Ben turned to me and started trash-talking. "What's the matter, Bash? You afraid you're going to lose? I tell you what; I'll make it easy for you. How about Dylan? You think you can beat Dylan?" He started getting in my face aggressively. "Or are you just a little bitch?"

I scoffed. "Dude, I thought you were the world's greatest pussy eater. Now you're getting Dylan involved? Look who's a little bitch now."

"Oh, shit." Ben laughed. "Is that a challenge? I could beat you with both hands tied behind my back. Let's do it, fucker. A hundred bucks says I can take you."

God, I wanted to wipe that smirk off his face so badly. "There's not a pussy on this planet that doesn't shrivel up in fear when it sees your ugly mug coming at it."

Our trash talk had gathered a lot of attention. The crowd around us began laughing and heckling Ben at my idiotic insult.

Ben shook his head and laughed. "You fucker! Alright, you and me. Let's go. And, let's make it $200."

Everyone was listening now. I was too drunk to even consider that I could lose this bet. "Fine, $200. When I win, you have to pay it to the poor girl who has to put up with having your ugly face between her legs."

Another round of raucous jeering broke out. I vaguely noticed Sid shaking his head in disgust, but then he was gone and I was being dragged over toward the couch.

I'd never been in a pussy-eating contest before. Hell, I'm not sure I'd even heard of one before. Ben was making a big show of getting his hands tied behind his back while another roadie was laying down the rules. I realized I was really drunk when I could barely focus on what was happening. Two girls were reclining on the couch, legs spilling over the front, in the middle of the party. One was sliding her panties off from under a short skirt. The other girl was already bare from the waist down and her legs were boldly parted, giving the crowd an unimpeded look.

Someone had turned off the music and almost everyone had gathered around the couch. The roadie who was acting as the judge — I think his name was Garrett — had everyone's attention. "The rules are simple. The first one to get their girl to cum wins. I'll be the one to verify the orgasm, so ladies, raise your hand when you orgasm, so I can check. Ben, you are only allowed to use your mouth, but Bash, you can use your mouth and your fingers."

Fuck, this should be a piece of cake. I would attack her clit with my mouth and her G-spot with my finger and have her coming in seconds flat. For a split second, I thought about not using my hands — to make the competition even — but then disregarded it. I was drunk, and I wanted to win. I absolutely did not want to lose to this asshole.

Ben held his hands behind his back as they got tied. "Which girl do you want? You pick, Bash."

I looked at the two girls. The girl with the short skirt looked uncomfortable. She couldn't even look me in the eye. When the other girl smiled at me, I pointed to her. "I'll take her."

As we knelt down in front of the girls, the crowd got rowdy, chanting our names and grunting and hollering like a bunch of zoo animals.

Ben smiled at his girl. "Hike your skirt up a bit, honey, so I can get in there real good."

My girl looked unfazed that I was about to dive between her legs in front of a crowd of onlookers. I picked the right girl; she was definitely less uptight.

Before I could form another thought, Garrett began a countdown. "5, 4, 3, 2, 1 ... Go!"

I wasn't concerned about finesse, just speed. I parted this girl with my fingers, secured my lips around her clit and slipped two fingers inside her, immediately searching out her G-Spot. Working hard and fast, I wasn't sober enough to know if anything I was doing was actually turning her on, and I didn't really care.

I was going to town for a while when the crowd suddenly erupted with cheers. I lifted my head for a moment to see that the other girl had raised her hand. Ben was dancing around in celebration, while Garrett was supposedly inspecting the girl's orgasm — however the fuck that worked.

My mouth dropped open in disbelief. "That's bullshit! That was like … not even a minute."

Ben was wagging his tongue like an insane clown. "That's all it takes when you've got it, brother."

Garrett pulled the girl with the short skirt up from the couch and raised her right arm in the air like a champion prizefighter. "Folks, we have a winner!"

"Pay up, bitch." Ben approached me with his hands still tied behind his back. "That'll be two hundred fucking bucks."

I wiped my mouth with the back of my hand. No way that fucker won. They must have cheated. "You'll have to take an IOU."

I remembered taking a good amount of ribbing after that, which did nothing for my mood because I hated losing. I looked for Sid, but he was nowhere to be found. Suddenly, I wanted everyone out of my apartment.

♫♪

The next thing I knew, I was waking up to an annoying noise. Shit, it was my cell phone. I grabbed the phone off my nightstand and looked at the screen. Kaylie was calling.

I pulled the phone to my ear and croaked out a greeting. "Hey, Kay."

When I rolled onto my back, I realized I wasn't in my bed alone. I suppressed a groan when I caught a glimpse of the girl I was in bed with. Sadie. Fuck.

I hated this girl. Sadie was hot with her pretty eyes, plump lips, shiny black hair, and luscious tits, but I never liked her 'emo' personality. She was always lurking in the periphery, glowering like she was ready to flip tables or frowning as if her puppy had just died. Talking to her was a huge chore because she was always so whiny and negative. Perhaps the creepiest thing about her was that I felt her eyes on me all the time, watching from the shadows like I was her prey. I'd made the mistake of kissing her once before, at a party. It had taken me months to shake her after that.

What the fuck was I doing naked in my bed with Sadie, the girl Sid and I secretly called Satan? She opened her mouth like she was going to talk, so I put my finger over her lips to shush her.

Kaylie's voice came through the phone. "Did I wake you up? I'm not surprised; you were pretty drunk last night. You were gross."

Fuck, I couldn't deal with Kaylie right now, especially not when Satan was naked in my bed. "Did you have a reason for calling?"

I heard her sharp inhale of breath. "I'm pissed at you, Sebastian. You were out of control. Do you even remember what you did last night?"

"Not particularly," I mumbled. But, shit, it was all starting to come back to me.

"Does a certain contest ring a bell? Of all the disgusting things you've ever done, Sebastian, that's probably the grossest. You have no respect for women—"

I could not deal with this now. "Kaylie, we'll talk later. I've got to go. Bye."

She was still speaking when I hung up. Damn, the pussy-eating contest — the memory was really fuzzy. Apparently, Kaylie knew all about it. I hope to God she didn't actually witness it. Could this day get any worse?

I turned to Satan and groaned as I flicked a finger back and forth between us. "Did we?"

She shrugged like she didn't have a single care. "Like bunnies."

I may have winced.

She reached out and stroked my arm. "Want to do it again?"

Chapter 2

Sidney

It was 10 o'clock when I rolled out of bed to use the bathroom. Thank God the girl I'd been with last night had taken off without a word about a half hour ago. I didn't know much about her, but I'd seen her arrive last night with Lacey. She'd just recently started hanging out with some girls who were part of our local groupie gang. Alyssa was her name. She was okay looking, but the sex had been less than stellar. We were both drunk, so maybe that was the problem. At least she hadn't taken part in the pussy-eating contest.

Christ. What was Bash thinking? I clearly recalled the look of absolute disgust and horror that swept over Kaylie's face before she'd run from our apartment. I wanted to chase after her, just to make sure she got home safely, but I was too much of a coward. My stomach twisted with revulsion.

I slipped a pair of sweatpants over my boxers and threw on a

T-shirt before I stumbled out of my room and weaved my way into the kitchen. It smelled like a frat house in our apartment. The seedy smell of old weed clung to the fabrics. Beer bottles, containing various amounts of liquid, were scattered everywhere. I hit a few damp spots on the carpet as I crossed the room. A red solo cup that had once contained a mix of beer and cigarette ashes was overturned on the coffee table.

I stopped in my tracks. There was a naked man on our couch. I squinted in an attempt to identify who it was. Probably one of the roadies. And, fuck, there was a spent condom lying on the floor next to him.

I was just sick of everything. Between the pussy-eating contest in my living room, my less than pointless and unsatisfying hook-up last night, a random naked and sweaty ass touching my couch cushions and now a jizz-filled condom lying on my nasty beer-stained rug, I was pretty much done.

It was hard to be philosophical about existential matters when I hadn't even had my first cup of coffee yet, but there had to be more to life than this. Right? My friend and bandmate, Ryder, had been banging the same girl for months now. He was happy as hell now that she'd moved to California to be with him. I guess I just hadn't found the right girl yet, because I couldn't imagine settling down with one chick.

An image of a girl with wavy, dark hair and big green eyes flashed in my head. Scowling at my rogue thoughts, I pushed the image from my mind. No, I definitely hadn't found that sort of girl yet.

I made a cup of coffee and began surveying the damage. I just didn't have the energy to clean anything up right now. Plus, Bash would probably invite people back here again tonight and it would just get trashed all over again. Maybe I should take off and leave the cleanup all to him this time. It would serve him right.

I had a trash bag half filled with empty beer bottles when Bash emerged from his room. I glanced over my shoulder to see who would come out with him and about choked on my tongue when I saw Satan trailing behind him. She was dressed head to toe in black, as usual, and her heavy black makeup was smeared around her eyes.

She was one of those goth-type girls. I'm not sure who she was friends with, but she showed up around here like a bad penny. Bash looked miserable, and it was the funniest thing I'd seen in a while.

"Well, good morning, you two." I snickered. "Did you have a good time last night, Sadie?"

I'd never seen her smile, and she didn't crack one now. Her voice was always monotone. "It was ... underwhelming."

A burst of laughter, which I tried to disguise as a cough, escaped from me.

Bash frowned. "What do you mean by that?"

She shrugged. "Not what I expected."

He grabbed a mug from the cabinet. "Me neither, believe me."

No one spoke after that. Satan just stood in our kitchen watching us. I felt an overwhelming urge to hide the knife block. Why did she have to be so creepy? She was a cute girl, but so weird.

Finally, Bash sighed loudly and turned to her. "Do you need a ride home?"

"No." She didn't move.

Bash caught my eye, but I just shrugged. He was the dumb ass that hooked up with her. She was his problem.

When the atmosphere got too heavy for me in the kitchen, I headed out to the living room and saw the naked guy again.

I yelled into the kitchen. "Bash, come help me get this guy out of here."

I'm sure Bash was eager to escape from the kitchen. He was at my side in seconds, staring down at the naked guy.

"I think his name is Garrett. He's coming on our next tour," he said.

I started looking around for his clothes. "Well, wake his ass up and get him out of here. He better not have pissed on the couch or anything." I toed at a lump of material on the floor and discovered a hoodie. "Bash, it's fucking disgusting in this place. I'm getting sick of it."

"Yeah, yeah. You've told me." Bash shoved at the guy a few times. "Get up, Garrett."

Garrett finally stirred and then sat up and let out a long groan as he ran his face through his hands. "I feel like hell."

I threw the hoodie at him. "Time to hit the road, Garrett. Maybe you can share a cab with Sadie?"

I turned to the kitchen to look for Sadie as I said the words and jolted. She was right fucking behind me. Standing less than a foot away. I almost had a heart attack.

Satan, I tell you.

Garrett got dressed and then stumbled out the door. At least some people got the hint. Satan was still hovering.

"You want to collect the beer bottles?" I thought I might as well put her to work if she wasn't going to leave.

She looked at Bash for a long moment. "No. I gotta go." With that, she turned on her heel and walked out the door.

Bash let out a pent-up breath. "Thank God."

I studied his pale face. "What the fuck were you thinking? Hooking up with her? Remember after you kissed her?"

He closed his eyes. "I don't remember hooking up with her. She says we fucked, but I don't even remember bringing her to my room."

I shook my head like a disappointed parent. "You were so wasted.

Do you even remember the pussy-eating contest?"

I didn't get to hear his answer, because our door opened. Satan returned. She was carrying something big and bulky by its handle. It looked like a baby contraption. With a baby in it.

What. The. Fuck.

Satan put the baby carrier down in the middle of our living room floor. "Someone left this outside your door for you. There's a note."

She left without a backward glance.

Bash and I stared at each other for way too long without talking. I had no idea what he was thinking because my brain was too busy short-circuiting.

Bash spoke first. "It's a baby."

Okay, we were getting somewhere.

I slowly made my way over to the bundle, my heart beating a mile a minute. The baby's eyes were closed. I imagined it was sleeping. A folded piece of paper rested on top of its small blanket. Bash joined me at my side as I bent down to gently pick up the note. I opened it and read the contents to myself, with Bash reading over my shoulder.

> I'm so sorry, but I can't do this anymore.
> I'm leaving town. My boyfriend doesn't want us to take the baby.
> I should have told you sooner, but I wasn't sure what I was going to do.
> You're the father. Please take care of our baby.

There was nothing else.

Bash finally spoke. "Holy fuck! That's so messed up. You're a fucking father!"

My eyes about popped out of my head. "Me? What are you talking about? This can't be mine. I always practice safe sex."

Bash scoffed. "And I don't?"

My voice started rising in consternation. "You can't even remember fucking Satan last night. Give me a fucking break, Bash."

"What about that time when you fucked that chick and the condom broke?" He shot back at me.

"What?" I said incredulously. "That was like a year ago."

Our voices grew louder as our argument grew even more heated. "Exactly. The timing fits, Einstein."

The baby scrunched up its face, let out a strangled gurgle, and then started crying.

We looked at each other.

"Oh fuck. What do we do now?"

Chapter 3

Bash

T HIS WAS NOT HAPPENING. I wanted to crawl back into my bed and wake up in a few hours to no crying baby. The noise was splitting my head open. I dug my fingers into my scalp, trying to get relief. "Why won't it stop crying?"

Sid squatted down and began rocking the baby basket thing by its handle, but the baby only cried louder. "I don't know what to do." He sounded panicked. "Search it on the internet."

"What?" I pulled out my phone. "How to make a baby stop crying?"

He kept rocking the baby. "Yeah, hurry."

I quickly typed it into my phone. "This looks good: Top 10 ways to make your baby stop crying."

I impatiently waited for the page to load. God, I couldn't even think with all the racket. The page popped up, and I scrolled past the boring introduction and baby pictures to get to the list. I read out loud, "Number 1. First, check to see that all of baby's basic needs are met. Change baby's diaper if she's wet or soiled. Feed baby if she seems hungry."

Sid stared up at me with panic in his eyes. "How can we do that?"

Shit, we definitely didn't have diapers, and I was pretty sure this baby wasn't hungry for beer and stale pizza.

I glanced back down at my phone. "Number 2: Gently rock baby."

Sid frowned. "I'm doing that. It's not working."

"Okay. Calm down. We've got eight more. Let's see, number 3: Swaddle baby."

Sid ran a hand through his hair. He looked as agitated as I felt. "What the fuck is that?"

I skimmed through the description. "It's basically wrapping the baby in a blanket."

"It's already wrapped in a blanket. This list is shit!" He growled.

"Hold on." I consulted the list. "Sometimes a change of scenery helps. Take the baby for a walk outside in the stroller. Or a ride in the car."

Sid stood up. "Well, we don't have a fucking stroller or a car seat. Let's bring it into the kitchen. That's a change of scenery."

I followed behind as he carried the baby in the basket thing into the kitchen. The baby didn't care. It kept crying.

"Fuck!" Sid looked like he was about to cry.

I took a deep breath. "Maybe you should stop cursing in front of it."

"Fuck, you're right!" Sid answered and then immediately winced at his language.

"Okay. Where are we? Number 5?" I scrolled the page down. "Sing to the baby."

"Sing?" Sid looked around the room in a panic. "I can't think. What song? What song?"

He suddenly started belting out the chorus to our band's lead single, *Day of Fire*. The little screamer toned it down a bit. It was only wailing at half the decibels now.

"Hey, I think he — or is it she? — likes it. But you need a better song. Something for a baby. I can't think right now. What did your mom sing to you when you were little?"

As soon as the words came out of my mouth, I wished I could take them back. Sid spent his childhood in foster care. He was already 13 when he was placed in my next-door neighbor's house where he stayed until he was an adult.

Sid stopped singing and glared at me. Crap. The baby's cries ratcheted back up to full throttle.

"I'm sorry, man. All this crying — it's getting to me. Try something like *Twinkle, Twinkle Little Star*." Under all this pressure, it was the only song I could think of for babies.

The baby calmed a bit. Why wouldn't it stop? I checked my phone while Sid belted out *Twinkle, Twinkle*. "Number 6: Offer baby a pacifier. Nope, we don't have that either. Number 7: Keep the baby close and feeling secure. Use a baby sling to keep them near your body."

Sid rubbed his eyes. "A baby sling? What the hell ... heck is that?"

The second Sid stopped singing; the baby started screaming again.

Oh God, my head was pounding. "Maybe you should pick it up? Just hold it so it feels secure or whatever."

He looked like I'd just asked him to scale Mount Everest.

I rolled my eyes. "Fine. I'll do it. Anything to make it shut up."

I bent down, but he stopped me. "I'll do it."

He slid his hands under the baby and gently tried to pick it up from the basket thing. "I think it's stuck in there."

At my wit's ends, I grabbed a water bottle from the refrigerator and rummaged through the cabinets for an aspirin. "I can't freaking think." I popped two pills and then downed them with half the bottle of water before scrolling through my phone again. "Number 8 is to try white noise. Use a white noise machine or run a vacuum cleaner. What the fuck is running the vacuum cleaner going to do? Let's see, number 9 is burping them to see if it's a gas build-up. Um, okay. And number 10 is that the baby might have colic."

I silently read the part about colic. "Shit, I hope the baby doesn't have that."

Sid looked at me helplessly and then ran to the entry closet and pulled out our ancient vacuum cleaner. He dragged it into the kitchen, sat it a few feet from the baby and then unraveled the long cord. "I'll fucking try anything at this point."

"Language."

"Right." He plugged the vacuum in and then turned it on.

The baby's arms flailed at the initial sound, but then a miracle occurred. The tiny little package with the biggest set of lungs I'd ever heard finally quieted down. Sid looked at me, shock plastered all over his face.

"Thank God! I thought it would never shut up. We need to call someone. Social services or something. Maybe the police?"

Sid looked stricken. "What? Why would we call them? This baby belongs to one of us."

Had he lost his mind? "We don't know that! And even if it did, we can't take care of a baby! You're fucking insane if you think otherwise. This baby was abandoned by its mother. We need to call the police."

He grabbed my arm in a tight grip. "No. They'll place it in foster care. I know there are a lot of good foster parents out there like Shari was to me, but there are also a lot of bad ones. Bash, I spent 13 miserable years getting shuttled back and forth between different foster families before they placed me with Shari. I was considered 'difficult to place' so they passed me off to whoever the fuck would take me in. A lot of those people only did it for the money. I was treated like shit by them. I told you some of it, but it was so much worse — brutal at times. There's no way I'd ever abandon a child of mine to that. No. Way."

I couldn't believe my ears. "So, what? You want to take care of it? Keep it? How the fuck are you going to do that? What kind of life could you give a kid? Do you think a kid should be exposed to," — I waved my hand around the trashed apartment — "all this? Drinking, drugs, sex, rock and roll? This lifestyle is not something a kid should be around."

"I know that." Sid was pissed. "I wouldn't expose my kid to this shit. No, I'd change. I could be a good father."

Sid wasn't thinking right. I was starting to panic. I had to convince him. "You'd change? Just like that? If a day ends with the letter 'y' you're doing at least one of those things. You party like a fucking rock star. Getting shitfaced or high. Fucking a new girl or more than one. I know exactly what you do with girls; I've witnessed it firsthand how many fucking times? And what about Ghost Parker? You're just going to give all that up?"

He folded his arms across his chest. "Stop saying the F word in front of the baby. And yes, I'll give all that up if I have to."

"No, you won't." I shook my head in denial. "And what if this baby isn't yours? What then? What if it's neither of ours? Or what if the baby is mine? What then, Sid? Are you going to take care of it?"

"Maybe."

Fuck. He was stubborn. I tried to keep my voice even and reasonable sounding. "You'd have no say in the matter if it wasn't yours. And you just can't keep a random baby that shows up on your doorstep. We need to do the right thing. After I hide all the bongs, let's call the police."

Sid growled at me through clenched teeth. "Don't call the police, Bash. I'm warning you."

When Sid wanted to, he could look like a vicious mother-fucker.

Chapter 4

Sidney

The baby finally passed out to the sound of the vacuum cleaner. I didn't dare move the baby, so I left it in the kitchen with the vacuum running and moved into the living room. I desperately needed a few minutes to think.

I began picking up the room, tossing beer bottles, stray caps, red plastic cups, cigarette butts, a pair of lace panties, and other garbage. I used a paper towel to pick up the used condom and tossed it.

Bash was right. This was no place to take care of a baby and I had no business doing it. I knew nothing about babies. I could cut down on the partying, maybe even get my own place, but what about the band? Ghost Parker took up a lot of my time. We didn't have the exact dates yet, but we'd be on the road touring soon. We were away for nine months during our last tour. This one could be longer, especially if our new album was as big of a hit as we thought it would be.

The thought of that baby being mine was like a sucker punch to the gut. I'd had some really bad experiences growing up, but that never stopped me from wanting a family of my own someday. Actually, I wanted it a lot. I wanted my own family, and I wanted to foster-parent some kids, too. Maybe even at-risk kids — older kids that had been rejected as much as I had been.

Those dreams had always been at the back of my mind. It was always something for the future. Maybe when Ghost Parker was a huge band and I didn't have to worry about money any longer. After I'd sown my oats. Maybe in my forties. I certainly wasn't equipped to handle a baby right now.

Wait.

Pressing my lips tightly together, I berated myself. I wasn't exactly a helpless sixteen-year-old child; I was almost 30 years old. If this baby was mine, I had a responsibility. I had resources. What kind of man was I if I abandoned my own child?

Come hell or high water, I was going to protect this baby at all costs.

♫♫♪♪♪

Bash was sitting on the couch looking completely lost. I knew I had to start making some decisions quickly, before he picked up the phone and did something stupid, like called the police.

"I think we need some help right now. Who can we call that knows about babies? Lacey?"

Bash snorted. "Lacey? Are you kidding me? I'll call Kaylie. She used to babysit all the time."

"Kaylie?" My head snapped up. "No. Not her."

Bash pulled out his phone and looked at me strangely. "Are you okay? You look like you're about to puke."

"It's, it's just..." I was a stammering mess. "I don't want this to get out on social media. Or in the press."

"It's my sister, dude."

He was already pulling up her number. I couldn't stop him. What was Kaylie going to think? My heart was pounding. Fuck.

Bash threw down his phone. "She's not answering. I think she's still pissed at me for last night."

Relief washed over me. It was stupid. She was going to find out eventually. It was time to let go of the weird feelings I had for Bash's little sister. He had warned me off her years ago. He'd also warned off all the guys in the band when she'd moved out here and started hanging around us.

None of us were good enough for his baby sister. He knew us all too well. He knew all our degenerate secrets; in particular, mine. And this baby proved that he'd been right about me all along. I was a fuckup.

"How about Talia? You think she knows anything about babies?" I asked.

Bash nodded. "She's a hell of a lot more wholesome than Lacey. Christ. You think she can keep quiet about it?"

Talia was Ryder's girlfriend. I didn't think she'd do anything to hurt the band. "Yeah. But then Ryder will know. We'll never hear the end of that shit."

Bash cocked an eyebrow. "Everyone's going to know sooner or later if we keep this baby here. You realize that, right?"

I sighed. "Yeah. Let's worry about that later. Just call her."

Bash looked at his phone. "I don't have her number. I guess I'll just call Ryder."

He called Ryder and then put the phone on speaker. It rang a few times before Ryder answered with a chuckle. "Hey, Bash. What are you doing up so early?"

"I need to ask Talia something. Can I get her number?"

"She's right here ... underneath me." Another chuckle, and then, "You can talk to her right now." We heard Talia laughing as we heard some muffled sounds of movement in the background. I felt a sharp stab of jealousy. Ryder was in love. I'd never known him to be so deliriously happy.

Bash rolled his eyes and shook his head.

Talia got on the phone. "Hey. What's up?"

"Uh..." Bash paused for a moment like he wasn't sure what to say. "Sid and I have some questions about babies."

"Babies?" she asked. "Don't worry, Bash. No matter what you guys do together, even if it's supposedly 'accidental', you two can't make any babies with each other."

I sighed when I heard Ryder snickering in the background.

Bash pushed on. "Did you ever babysit before? Do you know how to make them stop crying and stuff? Take care of them?"

"Sure. Why? What's going on?" She sounded curious.

"Would you be able to stop by our apartment today? Actually, can you come over right now?"

I cringed. I thought he'd beat around the bush a bit, but he barreled straight in.

The phone was silent for a long beat. "Well ... Ryder's going surfing, so I guess I could come over. I'm not going to regret this, am I?"

"You might," Bash answered.

Jesus. I stepped closer to the phone. "It's nothing bad. We just need a little help with something. Some advice. Please, please come over and help us out."

"Sidney. Hi. Now you've got me intrigued. I'll see you soon. Bye." She hung up.

I handed my garbage bag to Bash. "Help me clean up this place before she gets here."

We only got in 15 minutes of cleaning until the baby woke up again. I followed Bash into the kitchen and shut off the vacuum cleaner. It had been driving me crazy, anyway.

I knelt down and looked at the squirming baby whose face had gone all red. "Maybe it's hot?"

I pulled open the little blanket and discovered a few things. First, the baby was strapped into the carrier with a harness-like belt. That's why I couldn't lift it out before. Second, there was a baby bottle filled with milk, two diapers, and a pacifier tucked under the blanket. Why hadn't we checked before?

I unclipped the buckles as fast as I could. I couldn't get this squawking baby quiet fast enough. There was something primal about its cries that froze my blood and induced a panic. I just knew that I needed to protect that baby.

It took us forever to slip its tiny arms out from the harness straps because we were so terrified of hurting it. Bash slapped my fumbling hands aside and picked up the tiny thing.

"I know exactly one thing about babies. You have to support their heads whenever you hold them. They're not strong enough to do it themselves. I picked up Kaylie when she was a baby and her head flopped back. My mom wasn't happy."

The baby settled down a bit. Bash awkwardly maneuvered the little bundle so that it was resting in his arms and began pacing around the kitchen. Finally, the baby stopped crying.

Was that a twinge of jealousy I felt that he'd been able to stop the baby from crying? What if this was my baby? Shouldn't I be holding it? Comforting it?

This very well might be Bash's kid. I didn't even want to think about that. What would happen to it then? Who would protect it? Fuck, this was insane.

♩♫♪♪

Bash was holding the baby, swaying back and forth, in the kitchen next to the running vacuum cleaner when I heard the knock at the door.

Talia was grinning when I opened the door. She was a beautiful girl and really fun to be around. Bash and I had flirted with her enough, but she had it bad for Ryder. Which was a really good thing, because he was a complete mess when they'd broken up. Luckily, Ryder had gotten his shit together and won back the girl.

"C'mon in." I stepped aside and closed the door behind her.

"What's all this about babies?" she asked.

I led her into the kitchen where Bash was singing *Take Me Out to the Ballgame* to the baby. Her eyes widened comically. "Someone left you two in charge of a baby?"

Neither of us answered.

"What's with the vacuum cleaner?" She reached over and turned it off.

The baby started fussing in Bash's arms. "Put it back on. It likes it."

"It?" Talia's eyes narrowed at us.

Bash shot an accusing glance my way. "We don't know if it's a boy or girl."

Talia turned to me. "What in the world is going on here? Spill it."

The baby let out a screeching wail. It drove me crazy. It needed something and my every instinct was to help it, but I didn't know how.

"We'll tell you, but first, can you help this baby?" I begged. "It's been crying like this and nothing we do seems to help."

She gently squeezed the baby's foot. "When's the last time he ate? He looks hungry."

"He? You think it's a boy? But, he's not wearing any blue." Bash was studying the baby.

I was growing frustrated. "Does that matter?" I turned to Talia. "You think he's hungry? How can you tell?"

"He's rooting," she answered.

Bash's furrowed his brow. "Rooting? What the fuck, I mean heck, is that?"

"See how he's turning his head into you? He's looking for your nipple. That's rooting."

"Oh, Jesus!" Bash gasped. "He can't have my nipple."

I ignored the idiot and picked up the baby bottle that was still in the carrier. "We don't know when he ate last, but he came with this."

I could see the questions burning in Talia's eyes, but she held them for now. "How long has this formula been sitting out?"

I tried to think about when the baby could have shown up at our door. People had been coming and going from our apartment all night. Plus, the girl I was with left around 9:30. He must have been dropped off after she left. "I think about one to two hours tops."

Talia took the baby from Bash's arms, supporting its head like a pro. "Give me the bottle."

She pressed the bottle nipple to the baby's lips, and he chomped on immediately, sucking like his life depended on it. Finally, there was silence.

Bash stretched his arms and neck. "We should have popped that in his mouth long ago. Damn. Poor little guy likes his nipples."

Talia spun to us. "So, is someone going to tell me what's going on? Whose baby is this?"

I watched the baby as he ate. He looked so peaceful now. "He was left at our door with a note. His mother took off and abandoned him."

Talia frowned. "Oh, my God! Bash! What are you going to do?"

Bash stepped back a pace. "He's not mine!" He looked horrified. "He's Sid's baby."

Talia whipped her head around to me. "I'm sorry. I just ... when Bash was holding him, I thought..."

I glared at him questioningly. We didn't know for sure who this baby belonged to. Why was Bash doing this?

I almost corrected him, but then thought about it. If I took responsibility, no one would tell us to call the cops and turn the baby over to foster care. Until I found out who this baby belonged to through a paternity test, I wouldn't let that happen.

"Yes," I croaked. "The baby's mine."

"Oh, Sidney." Talia looked at me pityingly. "And you don't even know if it's a boy or girl? Did the mother leave any information? A birth certificate? Medical records? Do you even know who the mother is?"

My face heated with shame. "No. She just said I was the father. I don't have any other information."

"What are you going to do?" She studied my face.

"I'm going to keep him."

Bash's jaw clenched with frustration. I'm not sure why I said it. I wasn't sure the baby was mine. I couldn't decide anything until I got solid answers from a paternity test.

Talia nodded, her face softening as she looked at me. "Come over to the couch with me. I'll show you the proper way to feed a baby, so they don't swallow a lot of air. And, I'll show you how to burp him, too. That's really important."

We moved out of the kitchen to the couch with Bash trailing behind us. The bottle was half done. Talia pulled it from the baby's mouth and demonstrated how to burp him. After the baby let out a surprisingly loud burp, she put him in my arms, helping me position him correctly before she handed me the bottle.

The baby was staring back at me as he gulped down the baby formula. I felt a tightening in my chest. This could be my son. I swallowed the lump in my throat.

Talia was talking about how often I should feed him and how much he should drink and when I should change his diaper, but I'd missed most of it. The responsibility was overwhelming.

I looked up at Bash. "Make yourself useful and get some paper and a pen. Write all this stuff down for me. I'll never remember it all."

Bash grumbled, but then left the room in search of paper. Talia put her hand on my arm. "I know your head is probably spinning, but you're going to need a lot of stuff to take care of this baby. And a lot of help. But, I know you can do it, Sid."

Her encouragement meant a lot. When Bash returned, Talia repeated the feeding and diapering information while the baby finished up the bottle. I delicately maneuvered him over my shoulder the same way Talia had done earlier and patted his back. This time, along with a burp came a mouthful of stinky formula all over my shoulder.

Bash wrinkled his nose with disgust and made a gagging sound.

Talia frowned at him but smiled reassuringly at me. "Spit up is normal. That's why you should lay a cloth over your shoulder before you burp them. Like I said, you're going to need a lot of stuff."

Talia took the baby while I went to change my shirt. When I came back, she had a towel spread on the floor with the baby lying on top of it. "Now, I want you both to watch how I change his diaper, so you can do it later. I don't smell anything, so I think we're safe for now. Bash, add baby wipes to the list. Unscented. You should probably pick up a case of them. And a case of diapers. This guy doesn't look like a newborn size anymore. I would guess size 1."

Bash scribbled on a piece of paper. "Case of unscented baby wipes. Case of size 1 diapers. Got it."

She unbuttoned a million tiny snaps on the baby's clothes and then worked his feet out of the footies. "Slide the clothing out of the way so it doesn't get dirty when you change him."

She opened the velcro diaper tabs and pulled the diaper off and then grinned up at me. "It's a boy! Congratulations Dad."

There was that strange feeling in my chest again.

It took her only a few seconds to roll the old diaper up and secure it with the tabs, unfold the new diaper, and put it on the baby. It looked pretty easy.

She redressed the baby and then handed him back to me. "Now, we've got about three or four hours until he's hungry again."

"What do we do now?" I asked.

"We finish our list and then you give me your credit card. You're going to need a lot of stuff right away." Talia began ticking things off on her fingers. "Formula, diapers, clothes, a crib, a car seat, a stroller at a minimum."

Bash wiped his brow nervously. "You're going to leave us alone with him again? What if he starts crying?"

Talia glanced my way. "You're going to have to get used to taking care of him eventually, but I can watch him while you go shopping if you want."

I looked down at the little baby in my arms. How was I going to do this? Panic skittered through my veins.

"Tell me everything that we need. In detail."

Chapter 5

Bash

WE'D BEEN WALKING AROUND the gigantic store for over an hour and we only had the diapers and wipes in our cart to show for it. There was still a lot on our list to go through, but neither of us knew what we were doing. We were staring at about a hundred different types of bottles. Talia hadn't specified exactly what type we needed.

Sid couldn't make up his damn mind, and it was killing me. "We're wasting too much time. Just pick one. Talia said we needed to be back before his next feeding. We're running out of time."

"How come you told her that he was my baby?" he asked.

I flinched. "I just panicked. I'm not really sure we're doing the right thing here, Sid."

He visibly stiffened. "But you won't call the cops, right?"

"No. Not yet, at least." I really didn't understand him. How had he taken so quickly to the idea of having a baby? This was my best friend. Sid 'Vicious' Anderson. Not some baby whisperer. "I need time to think this through. This has been a complete mind fuck."

Relief crossed his features. "I know. But this could be my son we're talking about. Or yours. We can't abandon him. We owe him so much more."

The way he talked about this was making me nervous. "Maybe giving him up for adoption or whatever would be the better thing for him in the long run? What kind of life would he have with us? I can't even believe that you're contemplating it."

Sid scowled at me. "We're taking too much time." He pulled a baby bottle starter kit off the shelf. "You said we didn't want him to have colic right? These say they're anti-colic, so they must be good. What's next on the list?"

I sighed. "Pack and play."

"What's that?"

I shrugged. "Beats me."

After wandering around the store aimlessly for ten more minutes, we flagged down an employee who helped us with the rest of our list. We showed her the photo Talia had us take of the baby carrier, so she could help us get the correct car seat base for it. The pack-and-play turned out to be a playpen/crib/changing table combination. We picked one that was in stock, added the sheets for it to our cart, and then moved on to the stroller. For that, we chose the one with the nicest wheels that was compatible with the baby carrier we already had. Then, the friendly lady led us to the clothing section. We picked out clothing for the kid, bibs, burp cloths, and two blankets checking off the list. Finally, we bought ready-to-feed formula as recommended by the lady.

My eyes were popping out of my head at the price total that rang up on the register. Sid didn't even hesitate before he handed over his credit card.

"What are you going to do with all this shit if the baby isn't yours?" I asked him as we wheeled all the crap out to my car.

He didn't seem fazed. "I guess I could donate it."

"You're really going to keep this baby?" I couldn't help but ask him again.

"We are. He might be yours. Don't forget that." We reached the car and started packing it with all the shit. "We're going to need a nanny."

Fuck. How could I convince him that this was insane?

The baby was sleeping in Talia's arms when we got home. She had me go sterilize the new bottles (which I had to look up how to do) while Sid set up the pack-and-play. I felt bad for Sid because she was giving him all kinds of instructions about the kid while he was working. It was all so complicated.

When the bottles were drying, I helped Sid out. It took us forever to figure out how to strap in the bassinet section of the pack-and-play. "I'm starving. When do we get to eat lunch? And what about tonight? How are we gonna watch this kid?"

Talia gave me a stern look. "Baby's needs always come first. And, no more parties here. No threesomes. No girls. No drinking. No drugs. It's going to be a big adjustment. I've got to get going soon, but call or text me anytime if you have any questions about the baby."

I shot Sid a look. Why wasn't he saying anything? "You're gonna leave us?"

She stood up with the kid. "Ryder's already been texting me. He wants to know why I've been here so long. Is this baby thing a secret?"

Sid cleared his throat. "I know you're going to tell Ryder. And he'll eventually tell Knox and Ghost. But, let's keep it to a tight circle for now. I don't want it to get out in the media."

"Okay." She agreed. "How about Kaylie? Does she know? Maybe she could help you a bit until you get some hired help."

We needed help. As soon as Talia left, I was going to try calling her again. "I tried calling her earlier, but she didn't pick up. I think she's mad at me."

Talia gently laid the baby down in the bassinet. "What are you going to call him? He needs a name."

"Yeah, he does," I agreed. "All the celebrities name their kids weird names. Like one of Michael Jackson's kids is named Blanket. And Elon Musk named his kid some weird symbol."

Talia snorted. "You two aren't exactly big celebrities."

Sid scowled at me. "Yeah. You're just the drummer. No one even knows the drummer."

"You're just the bassist!"

"Well, we're not going to saddle this kid with some weird ass name, so it doesn't matter, anyway."

Talia looked between the two of us. "It's like two men and a baby."

"Huh?"

Just then, the baby started to cry.

Talia smiled. "Play with him a bit and then give him a bottle. Remember, he'll probably want to eat every three to four hours. I've got to run. Good luck!"

She scurried out the door.

"How do we play with him? He doesn't do anything?" Sid wondered.

"How do we make a bottle?" I added.

Fuck.

Chapter 6

Kaylie

I got off the bus and started my three-block walk home. My feet hurt from standing all day. I worked part-time as a customer service agent at a department store. My primary job was to deal with customers, a disappointingly huge number who were trying to scam the store with ineligible returns. In those cases, my job was to pretend I didn't understand what they were doing, yet still deny their requests with a friendly smile. That rarely went over well.

The last thing I felt like doing when I arrived home was making myself dinner, but I was starving, so I didn't have much choice. My roommates weren't home, which wasn't unusual, so I decided to go with a simple yet tasty standby. I started whipping up a prosciutto and spinach grilled cheese sandwich on whole wheat bread while I scrolled through my e-mail.

I'd been to every open casting call I could manage in the past two years and had submitted to hundreds of online casting calls. Only a handful of those had led to callbacks or auditions, and so far, I'd only eked out a few minor roles. In between, I'd been taking acting classes, attending seminars, schmoozing and networking, maintaining my personal actor's website, and actively following every director, casting director, producer, writer and interesting project on social media. It was exhausting. Would I ever progress from an aspiring actress to an actual working actress?

I put down my phone and flipped the sandwich over in the pan. Every day I checked my e-mail with bated breath, hoping for that special e-mail that said they wanted me, and that I'd be absolutely perfect for the role. Constant rejection was so demoralizing.

While I ate my sandwich, I flipped through social media, making witty and profound comments wherever I could fit them in without being obnoxious. It was a fine line to walk, especially when I excelled at talking to people face to face far more than online brown-nosing.

Satisfied with the amount of social media footprint I'd left behind for the day, I closed my apps. I noticed I had a few new phone call notifications. Bash had called again but hadn't left a message. When I was on my lunch break, I saw that he'd called twice earlier in the morning, but I was in no hurry to call him back. He'd hung up on me this morning, and after what he'd done last night ... I couldn't even deal with him. I'd let him stew a bit, letting him squirm knowing he pissed me off.

I had a few new texts — my roommates, an actor friend, a silly group text I was in — nothing unusual. And then I saw the texts from Talia. We texted from time to time, mostly checking in on parties the Ghost Parker boys were attending. It was nice to have another friendly female in the ranks. This set of texts was more cryptic than the usual stuff we shared.

Talia: Answer your phone next time Bash calls.
Talia: Or just call him!
Talia: Better yet — get your ass over to his apartment. ASAP!
Talia: And call me after you go over there. I need someone to talk to about this development!

What in the world was going on? Was Bash that butt-hurt that I wasn't talking to him, that he'd recruited Talia's help? Nah, it didn't make sense. I was friends with Talia, but he really wasn't. Plus, the silent treatment I was giving him was less than a day old. And, he'd never let that bother him too much in the past; I was usually the one who cracked first, even when our argument was invariably his fault.

Something was up. Despite how crazy tired I was when I got home from work, suddenly I was feeling more awake. I wanted to go over to Bash's and see what was going on. Who was I kidding? It was the perfect excuse to see Sidney.

Hating myself for being so weak, I groaned. I headed to my bedroom and peeled off the demure work outfit I was wearing. Then, I slipped on my favorite pair of dark wash jeans that made my ass look amazing, switched out my utilitarian bra for a lacy black push-up and tossed a pink, deep V-neck fuzzy sweater over my head. I touched up my makeup, brushed my hair until it was shiny, and then spritzed some fragrance mist into my cleavage.

Perfect.

I was ready to see Sid. Uh; I mean... I was ready to confront my brother.

I slipped on a pair of running sneakers, not the sexiest shoes a girl could wear, but they'd have to do. I had a couple of blocks to walk and my feet were still aching. It wasn't that cold outside, but it might be cold later, so I brought a jacket with me.

I had a lot of time to think while I walked to Bash's apartment and, of course, I spent it daydreaming about Sid. He'd moved in next door to us, back in Georgia, when I was 8 years old. I didn't realize I'd had a huge crush on him until I was about 12. He was 17 then, a grown man in my eyes and a total heartthrob.

For all the time he'd spent at our house with Bash, he never paid me any attention — no matter how obnoxious I acted. I was a little actress even back then, so I cringed when I recalled just how obnoxious I was. I was like a yapping dog begging for scraps of food.

When he and Bash graduated high school, they were gone. Traveling with their current band, making music, and pursuing their dream. I didn't see much of Sidney at all after that until that fateful night seven years ago when I was 16. It was the night I spent 7 minutes in heaven with him. I'm pretty sure he didn't even remember that now, but I remembered every last detail. And it's haunted me since.

That night had reignited something that I had long since brushed off as a stupid childhood crush. The feel of his lips on mine, his hands on my skin, the taste of his tongue, the euphoric dizziness being near him created — it was all burned indelibly into my mind.

It went from an innocent crush to blinding obsession, but he was gone from my life without a backward glance. From then on, I compared every experience I had with other boys to that one experience with Sid. No one could ever come close to making me feel like Sid had. I didn't lose my virginity until I was twenty, despite plenty of opportunities with handsome and decent men my age that I dated, because I had been secretly waiting for Sid to come back and claim me.

Eventually, I had to grow out of my obsession. I didn't see Bash much anymore beyond holidays, let alone Sidney. I earned an associate's degree in theater and performing arts back home and then headed to Los Angeles, eager to prove myself. A few months later, Bash and Sidney, along with the rest of Ghost Parker — Knox, Ryder, and Ghost — moved out to L.A. to establish a home base for the band that was rapidly growing in popularity. My brother, with his roommate Sid, relocated just two blocks from my apartment.

That was two years ago. And since, I'd been back in the tortuous limbo of being so near to Sid, but not having him. But this time, I saw him much more. It made my love life miserable. Dating was impossible. I found fault with every man I met.

Just like when I was little, I hung around Bash as much as I could, vying for any scrap of attention Sid threw my way. I never hooked up in front of them, putting men off pretending it was because of my brother, but in my heart I knew — I was still secretly waiting for Sid. Why couldn't I get him out of my head?

You would think these past two years would have cured me. I knew Sid and Bash tried to behave when I was around, but they would get drunk ... I'd seen that stupid sandwich trick too many times when I'd watched in agony as the two of them would lead a girl into one of their bedrooms. I'd heard all the threesome jokes thrown their way. It destroyed me that the guy I'd crushed on forever was having threesomes with my own brother involved. From the jokes, I knew that Bash and Sid weren't 'together'. They just liked to share and watch girls with each other. Or whatever else that was involved in that type of a threesome. I wouldn't know. I was a strictly one guy / one girl person, as vanilla as they came. And Sid wasn't. He was in a rock band. Duh.

I couldn't exist in this limbo any longer. If Sid and I weren't meant to be, I needed to know. I'd spent years hung up on him when he hadn't offered me any hope. Last night, I'd planned to force the issue. I'd planned to either seduce him or walk away forever if that didn't happen. It was time to let him go. I needed to focus on other men. Myself. What I needed.

I'd gone to their 'party' with a plan. Lines that I'd meticulously prepared and rehearsed until perfected. A seductress — the biggest role of my lifetime. I wasn't a shy person, so I was going to lay it all out in the open. If he rejected me, so be it. I just couldn't do this anymore.

As soon as I walked in, I knew the party would get out of hand. Some of the roadies present there were hardcore. Then, Lacey showed up with an entourage of women that were dressed for action. I've tried to be a sex-positive person, but let's face it, some women were just slutty. Let's call a spade a spade. When Whitney pulled off her skirt (of course she had no panties on under there), jumped on the couch, and spread her legs wide in front of the crowd for a pussy-eating contest, um ... sorry, she's slutty in my book. Not that Bash and Sid and the other guys weren't just as slutty.

True, I had seen Sidney glancing at me nervously and trying to stop the sickening contest, but I was still mad at both of them. They were both immature man whores, not ready to grow up yet. Why the hell was I wasting my best years mooning after him?

The funny thing was that Bash had warned me of this. He was always a protective big brother. He claimed it was because he knew just how dickish guys could be. He knew how they acted. What they thought. He was one of them.

'Not all guys are assholes, Sebastian. Not all guys act like that.'

'Too many do. I'm around it all the time. I see it all the time.'

'Like the guys in your band?'

'Especially the guys in my band.'

My pace must have matched my hectic thoughts, because I arrived at Bash's apartment sooner than I expected. Climbing up the steps, I felt a shiver of trepidation. I was afraid of walking into their apartment unannounced. I'd never just shown up before. Who knew what I was walking into? A freaking orgy for all I knew.

I almost turned around, but then stopped myself. It was still early. If they were up to nonsense this early on a Tuesday night, then that was a sign. A bad one. Albeit, only one of the hundreds of bad signs I'd noticed for the last two years.

Maybe, if I caught them during downtime, it would be good. I could lecture Bash on his disgusting behavior and maybe suss out if Sid showed anything other than brotherly interest in me. If I got Sid alone, maybe I could launch into my spiel. I should have done a few shots before I'd come over. Hell, I wasn't about to seduce Sid in front of my brother's watchful eyes, but maybe I could ask him out. Ask him not necessarily for a date, but something innocent sounding — for a coffee. I felt my cheeks heat. Why was this so hard?

I made it to their apartment door and knocked. There was no answer. I listened carefully. I didn't hear any loud music, but there was some kind of noise. What the hell was that? What were they doing in there?

I knocked again, louder this time, with my fist. Nothing.

I almost left. I had a key, but I was chicken to use it. What would I be walking in on? I had almost consigned myself to the thought that I would eventually have to walk away from my crazy infatuation with Sidney, but I certainly didn't want to do it with devastating images in my head. What the hell was that noise? What kind of kinky shit could be happening in there?

God, I was such a coward. Giving myself a mental pep talk, I took out the key and opened the door.

Holy shit.

A pair of icy blue eyes connected with mine.

Sidney.

He was holding a...baby?

What?

I stood motionless, not knowing how to react. I glanced over at Bash sitting on the couch with his head resting on the back cushion like he was exhausted.

Bash jumped up. "Kaylie!"

His eyes shot over to Sid. They exchanged a long look I couldn't interpret. It was like they were having a conversation without speaking. A flash of guilt, a subtle shake of the head, a widening of the eyes.

My eyes flew back to Sid, and my heart lurched in my chest. He looked amazing. I always thought of him as a Viking because he was built like one. He stood over six feet tall, about six foot, three inches, I guessed, and had loads of muscles. His dirty blond hair was always on the longer side and perpetually looked messy. He had piercing blue eyes and enough tattoos to make my lady bits clench with need. There always seemed to be a bit of scruff on his face, but I could tell he hadn't shaved in weeks; he'd gone beyond the sexy stubble phase to full facial hair. He'd never looked more like a Viking warrior than right now.

Except for the baby in his tatted arms.

I looked around their apartment in a daze. The living space was crammed with new stuff. Baby stuff. A portable crib. A stroller. A case of diapers spilled out onto the floor. Baby clothing draped over a chair.

And that loud droning noise ... why was the vacuum cleaner turned on and just sitting in the center of the room?

Bash turned off the vacuum cleaner. I still hadn't spoken a word since I'd entered the room. My mouth hung wide open. I couldn't make words exit my mouth, but Bash must have seen the question in my eyes.

He flashed a brief apologetic look at Sid before turning to me. "This is Sid's baby. He's the father."

Chapter 7

Sidney

Kaylie looked like she was going to hurl. I felt like I was going to hurl. And I wanted to kill Bash. Fuck me.

I didn't want to hide this baby like a shameful secret, but Kaylie was the last person I wanted to know about this. And lying about the paternity was fucking weird, but I was going along with it for my own selfish reasons. The fact was that we didn't know for sure who this baby belonged to.

"Sidney?" Kaylie turned her confused eyes to me.

"Uh..." I had no idea what to say to her. "This little guy showed up at our door this morning."

She was staring at the baby. "And you're sure he's yours?"

I was horrified at how fucking upset she looked. I glanced at Bash, silently pleading with him to tell his sister the truth.

Bash looked nervous. "He's going to get a paternity test, of course, but the mother left a note. She said the baby is his."

Kaylie still hadn't moved from her spot. She turned anguished eyes back to me. "How could this happen? How could you do this?"

Bash actually flinched at the censure he saw in his sister's eyes. "Things happen, Kay. The condom broke. The girl told him she was going to get a morning-after pill, but obviously, she didn't. He had no idea until this morning that he was a father."

My gut twisted. I knew in his mind that Bash thought he was defending me. Everything he said was technically true, but we didn't know if any of that applied to this baby. I knew Bash was afraid of disappointing his sister and his entire family if this was his baby. Until he was sure he'd own up to nothing, but he was using me to shirk any possible responsibility right now. I wasn't sure I liked it at all.

Kaylie had finally broken out of her frozen shock. With each new revelation out of Bash's mouth, she'd taken another step backward until her back was up against the closed door. She wanted to flee, and I couldn't blame her. A regret so acute settled in my gut, but I had no time to examine it. I didn't want her to go. I had to explain this to her somehow. Make her understand. Jesus, make her not look at me like that — like I was the world's biggest fuckup.

Her hands twisted on the doorknob behind her back.

Thank God Bash said what I couldn't manage to get out. "Kaylie, don't go. We need your help."

Her eyes darted to him and then at the baby stuff scattered all over the room. "This is crazy. Where's the baby's mother?"

Neither of us spoke for a long, uncomfortable beat. Finally, Bash spoke, "She left the baby at the door and took off. The note said she left town."

Kaylie's hand clutched her chest, and she was looking everywhere but at me. "What else did the note say? Can I see it?"

Bash shifted from foot to foot. "Um, I threw it away when we were cleaning up, but it barely said anything. Just that she's leaving town and that Sid's the father. She didn't even sign it, so we don't technically know for sure if the broken condom girl is the mother."

Her eyes shifted to me, anger flashing across her face. "So you're not really sure who the mother is? And let me guess, the possibilities are what? In the dozens? More than that?"

God, I wanted to kill Bash. This time it was me that couldn't meet her eyes. I stared down at the baby in my arms, resting peacefully.

"Easy, Kaylie," Bash replied. "That's not helping. Give him a break right now. This is really stressful."

Kaylie sighed loudly. "So, you just heard some crying or something and you opened the door and there he was? With all this stuff?"

"Well, no." Bash looked my way. "Actually, Sadie found him this morning when she was leaving."

Kaylie's head whipped back toward me. "Sadie! Oh my God."

I winced, but luckily Bash spoke up. "She was with me."

Kaylie's shoulders sagged. She looked pale and uncertain. "Bash, I haven't forgotten what you did last night. That contest ... thing. And then, Sadie? I thought you couldn't stand her? But I can't even think about any of that right now. Where did all this baby stuff come from?"

I cleared my rusty throat. "Talia watched the kid for a couple of hours while we did some shopping. She made us a list of things we needed right away. Then she gave us some tips, but neither of us knows what we're doing at all."

Kaylie took one tentative step forward. "What do you need help with?"

Thank God she hadn't gone screaming out the door. "I think I smell something ... not right. With the diaper. I think he needs to be changed and we haven't done that yet."

She crossed her arms over her chest. "Okay. Show me what you've got and I'll watch. I'll let you know if you do anything wrong."

I looked down at the baby. I hated even moving if he wasn't crying. "Maybe we should wait."

"No." She shook her head. "You can't let him sit in a dirty diaper. He could get a rash or something and then he'll be miserable. Plus, the poop can be really soft or runny, so the longer you wait, the greater the chance it will start getting everywhere or leaking out of the diaper."

"Okay." I looked down at our nasty carpet. The first thing I was going to do when I had a free moment was get new flooring. I shuddered, imagining the baby crawling across the stained carpet. And we needed a new couch. "Bash, can you get it set up for me?"

Bash grabbed the towel we'd used earlier and spread it out on the floor. Then he ripped open the case of wipes and pulled out a plastic rectangular container. We had already opened the diapers even though we hadn't worked up the courage to use them yet, so he just scooped a new diaper off the floor. He placed the items next to the towel.

Kaylie lifted an eyebrow. "Why are you changing him on the floor?"

"Uh?" Bash and I shrugged at each other.

She rolled her eyes like we were two morons. "There's a changing table on the pack-and-play."

"Right."

She marched over to the crib and pointed to the contraption on top. "This is where you can change him. Do you have a changing pad? No? Okay, bring the towel over here. This could get messy."

Bash laid the towel out on the changing station. "What are the straps for?"

She pushed the straps aside. "This baby is still little. You'll need the strap when he starts to wiggle more. For now, just keep it out of the way, so it doesn't get dirty. I just realized that I'm going to have to teach you both all kinds of safety lessons — like never leaving the kid unattended on this thing. Ugh, there's so much stuff you have to learn to keep this little guy happy and safe and you two are like dumb and dumber."

Bash looked panicked. "Why do I have to learn all this stuff?"

I was grateful when she didn't even hesitate to answer. "Of course, you have to learn. Don't be such a big baby, Uncle Bash."

Bash laughed and nodded. "Uncle Bash."

Kylie might be deeply disappointed in me, but at least she hadn't taken off. She was willing to stick around and teach us things. I was relieved that she was still talking to me.

Changing his diaper was a disaster. Kylie made me and Bash do it while she watched. This kid had taken a big dump, and it had smeared everywhere inside the diaper. The smell was horrific, and Bash kept dry heaving. We went through at least twenty wipes and still the baby's parts didn't seem fully clean. The baby was screaming his lungs out (Kylie said because we were taking too damn long) and that just upped the pressure a thousand-fold. We had to change his entire outfit because we managed to get poop on it somehow so that just added to the fun.

He was finally clean and settled down, and I needed a Valium. My nerves were shot. Kylie was walking him around the apartment in her arms, murmuring soothingly in his ear. I couldn't take my eyes off them.

After she walked us through how to heat a bottle and test its temperature, she watched over while I fed the baby. Halfway through the bottle, I stopped the baby's feeding to burp him. I felt a buzz of pride when she smiled approvingly at me. When he fell asleep in my arms after the feeding, she helped me slowly lay him down in the pack-and-play bassinet.

A knock sounded on our door. Bash had ordered a pizza right after we'd finished changing the baby and it had arrived.

"Thank fuck. I'm starving." He went to answer the door.

I shrugged at Kylie. "We haven't eaten today. It's been ... hectic. Do you want to stay for some pizza?"

She shook her head. "No thanks. I'm gonna head home now. I'm not working tomorrow, so maybe I'll stop by to see how you're doing. Goodnight, Sid."

She made her escape. Her absence left a gnawing sadness in my gut. I'd fucked up everything.

Chapter 8

Kaylie

I DIDN'T GO TO see how the boys were doing the next day. My thoughts were too jumbled. I did eventually call Talia. I had to talk to someone, and she was one of a tiny number of people who knew about my stupid infatuation with Sid.

Talia had recently moved to California to be with Ryder and was living in Greyson Durant's house on the beach in Huntington Beach, while Ryder was currently living on Knox's couch. Grey was the leading man in the long-running TV series, *Devious*. I'd only met him once at a party that Talia had brought him to, but I hoped maybe Grey could open some industry doors for me in the future.

Talia answered the phone, sounding out of breath. "Hey, Kaylie. I've been waiting for your call. How're you doing?"

"Argh," I groaned. "I went over to Bash's yesterday and found out about the baby, obviously. I think I'm moving out of the shock and denial phase and moving into anger today. I can't help it; I'm so angry with Sid right now. How could he be so stupid?"

Talia was quiet for a few moments. "I'm sorry. This must be upsetting for you."

I laughed bitterly. "That's an understatement. The worst part is that I had just decided to admit my feelings to him and then this happens."

"Yeah. This may not be the best time for that now."

"I'm not going to tell him at all. In fact, I'm done lusting after him." I was furiously pacing the floor. "He's a father, Talia. He has a baby! It's just … unbelievable."

"That doesn't mean you can't have a relationship with him. It doesn't sound like he's interested in the baby's mother. So maybe there's still a chance?"

"Oh, please!" I huffed. "He doesn't even know who the mother is. No, I asked for a sign from the universe the other day and this is a sign. A big sign. I have no choice but to get over him. I knew he was immature with all his partying and stuff, but this? It's so irresponsible!"

Talia spoke to me in a soothing voice. "He may have made a mistake, but he's trying to be responsible. He wants to keep the baby and be a good father. Maybe he's growing up?"

"Well, I'm not getting involved with that," I countered. "I'm just 23. I just wanted some sexy times. Or a relationship of some sort. I'm not ready for whatever he's got going on now." My declaration brought a sting of tears to my eyes. I'd told myself the same thing over and over since I'd found out about the baby, but it still hurt to affirm out loud.

Talia sighed. "I hear you. It's just a shame."

I pushed aside my feelings and continued in a cheerful voice. "Still, he's my friend, and he needs a lot of help. You should have seen him and Bash trying to deal with a diaper explosion. It was comical."

"I can imagine."

"I didn't even tell them that the baby needs a bath soon. That would just freak them out. It seemed like too much all at once. Their sink is just nasty. They need a baby bathtub and so much other stuff."

Talia agreed. "Yeah. I just sent them out for basics just to survive a few days. They could probably use one of those baby swings, too."

"So, I was thinking," I paused for dramatic effect, "we should throw Sidney a surprise baby shower."

"Oh, my God!" Talia exclaimed. "That would be perfect. Then he'd know we're all here for him and the baby."

"It would have to be soon. I'm thinking this Saturday. Do you think we could pull it off?" I asked.

She thought for a moment. "Yeah, we'd have to keep it small, anyway. Sid doesn't want it to get out beyond his circle of friends. And we could have it here at Grey's house. You or Bash would just have to get him and the baby here without telling him somehow."

"Okay. We'll figure something out. I'll send out the invites. I'll stick to his close friends, so it'll be co-ed." I snickered. "I doubt any of these guys have ever been to a baby shower before."

"The guys won't know what Sid needs for the baby. I was with Ryder in a baby store for his nephew and, my God, he was so clueless."

She had a point. "I'll assign presents for everyone to buy to make sure he gets everything he needs. I'll send out the invitations with gift assignments today since we don't have much time."

"I'll take care of decorations and party games, and I'll put Ryder in charge of food and drinks." She paused and then added, "I'll supervise him so we don't end up with just beer and cocktail weenies."

The plan was coming together. The boys might grumble about attending a baby shower, but I was sure everyone would be happy to support Sid. They might be a bunch of rock and roll degenerates, but they always had each other's backs.

I was sliding firmly into the friend zone with Sid. Right where I should be. I buried my feelings by diving into the planning of the baby shower. The rest of my day off from work was filled with phone calls. The baby news had not spread beyond Bash, Ryder, Talia, or me. I had to fill in everyone, deal with various levels of shock, and swear them all to secrecy. While everyone was pretty shocked, Ghost was mostly amused by the whole thing and Knox was surprisingly nonchalant about it. Donovan, the band's manager, spent five minutes cursing before he finally calmed down. Everyone I invited said they would attend and agreed to buy the gift I'd assigned them. The rest of the evening I spent catching up on social media and looking for acting leads.

The next day, as we'd planned, Sadie picked me up in the morning to go shopping for our respective baby gifts. I'd invited her to the shower since she was apparently the one who'd found the baby in the first place. She already knew about Sid's baby and she promised to keep it quiet. I knew she had a big crush on Bash and that my brother didn't really care for her. She was a nice girl, and I felt a certain connection to her with the whole unrequited love thing even though I'd never tell her about my pathetic thing for Sid. Plus, it'd annoy Bash if she were there. It served him right for having sex with her.

After shopping, I worked a shift at the department store. On the bus ride home, I texted my brother.

Me: How's it going with the baby?

I stared at the screen and waited when I saw he was responding.

Bash: It felt like that little demon was up all

> night long last night. During the day he needs
> food or a new diaper non-stop.
> **BASH:** I'm exhausted.

Taking care of a baby was so unlike Bash. I was proud of him for helping.

> **ME:** It is really hard. I'm glad that you're helping Sid.
> **BASH:** I can't keep helping him. He has to figure out for himself that he can't do this. Keeping this kid is crazy.

I frowned. I had the distinct impression that Sid was firmly resolved to take responsibility for his child and wanted to raise him. He didn't know who the mother was, so what other choices did he have? Give the kid up for adoption?

> **BASH:** He won't listen to me. Maybe he'll listen to you? Tell him how insane this is.

My stomach churned. Bash's words made me nervous.

> **ME:** It's his choice. Don't be so selfish, B.
> **BASH:** We should call off the baby shower. That will just make him think we all support this.

A lick of anger flamed in my gut. What the fuck, Bash?

> **Me:** Everyone does support this. I will back up whatever Sid chooses to do because I'm his friend. I thought you were, too?
>
> **Bash:** I am. That's why I'm not lying to him about this.

I knew Bash was probably scared. He didn't want his lifestyle to change. He didn't want to lose his best friend and didn't want the dynamics of Ghost Parker to change, but he was thinking very selfishly. This was a baby who needed a parent and very possibly Sid felt bonded to the baby already. I understood that. I would never be able to give up my own child for a matter of convenience. Maybe in other circumstances I could, but in this, I could understand Sidney's point of view.

I might write off Sid as a romantic partner because I wasn't ready for kids, but I'd never write him off as a friend. Then again, Bash wasn't really writing Sid off as a friend. He just wasn't ready to be a co-parent either. We were quite the pair.

> **Me:** I'm on the bus heading home. I'm gonna stop by so I can talk to you about this.
>
> **Bash:** I'm out. Went to Knox's for the night. Need sleep.

Bash was bailing out on Sid. I wasn't surprised. After all, he'd already spent two nights in a row not partying.

I made up my mind. On my phone, I pulled up the menu from

the Chinese restaurant I passed on my walk home to my apartment and placed an order for pickup. Within an hour, I'd picked up the food, gone home and changed clothes, and then headed over to Sid's apartment.

Chapter 9

Sidney

SOMETHING STIRRED ME FROM sleep. Kody was sleeping peacefully on my chest while I sprawled out on the couch. I had thought about placing him in the pack-and-play, but I hadn't wanted to give him up. I loved holding him, especially when he seemed so content.

Just as I began drifting off to sleep, I heard the noise again. I struggled to keep sleep from pulling me back under. Was it my neighbors banging on the walls? God knows it would be poetic justice considering the number of times they had complained about us disturbing their peace.

My apartment door opened, and for a moment I thought I must have been dreaming. Kaylie stood in the entry, her eyes fastened on my own bleary ones. Since I'd seen her last, her presence had invaded my mind more and more despite my attempts to banish it.

She stepped further into the room. "I didn't mean to wake you."

She really was here. I kept Kody clutched to my chest and sat up. "Hey. What are you doing here?"

Her nose wrinkled as she looked around the room. This time it was baby stuff messing up the place. Instead of empty beer bottles lying around, it was dirty baby bottles. The remnants of whatever food I managed to make myself in between baby duties littered the coffee table. The kitchen was an even worse disaster.

Her eyes flicked to the baby. "I can't believe Bash left you here alone."

Kody shifted in my arms and I planted a kiss on his head after he settled. "Don't blame him. This shit is hard. He needed a break."

"Uh-huh." She didn't look convinced. "When's the last time you ate? I brought Chinese food. Do you want me to fix you a plate?"

I groaned. "Yeah, that'd be great. I am so hungry."

While she went into the kitchen with the food, I moved Kody to the pack-and-play. He fussed for a few moments but went back to sleep after I gave him his binky. He would probably sleep for another hour.

My stomach growled loudly when Kaylie returned with two heaping plates of food. "I'm not sure what we have to drink. Would you like a beer or some wine? Or water..."

"Water is fine."

When I returned with two water bottles, she had cleared off the coffee table for our food and had settled onto the couch.

"Is this couch new?" she asked.

I sat next to her and scooped up a forkful of food before answering. "It was delivered yesterday. The old one was so disgusting. I didn't want Kody anywhere near it."

"Kody?"

"Yeah. It's short for Dakota. Bash wanted to go with Axel. I won rock, paper, scissors, so I got the final say." I shoveled in another mouthful of food. I was ravenous.

"Dakota Anderson." It slid off her tongue. "I like it. And Kody is a cute nickname."

After that, we ate in silence mostly because I was scarfing down the food. She was still working on her first plate when I finished my second large helping. It felt so good to feel full.

When I'd finished eating, I sat back on the couch and noticed the yellowish stain on my T-shirt. Baby spit up and drool was all over me. I hadn't showered in days and I must have smelled awful.

I groaned as I pulled at my shirt. "I must look like shit."

She laughed. "I've seen you looking better."

I ran my hand through my hair. "It's been crazy. I don't know how single moms do it. I haven't showered, because I'm scared to leave the baby alone. Even for a few minutes."

"You'll figure it out." She slapped my arm playfully. "Why don't you go take a shower while I'm here? I'll keep an eye on him."

I'd purposefully been trying to keep my eyes off her, but I couldn't help but glance her way when she touched my arm. I don't know what exactly set me off — her sexy body so close to mine, the subtle scent of her feminine perfume, the way she brushed against my arm or the Cupid's bow of her luscious lips that I couldn't drag my eyes away from — but I felt that telltale tightening in my pants. Within moments I had a rock-hard cock tenting my sweatpants that was quite visible. Thank God Bash wasn't here; he would kill me if he saw.

Before Kaylie noticed, I hopped off the couch, making sure to twist away from her view. "Thanks. I think I'll take you up on that offer."

Showering felt like an absolute luxury. I could usually get in and out in under 5 minutes, but this time I savored every minute that the hot water ran down my skin. Knowing Kaylie was just in the other room while I was naked didn't help my hard-on any. After I was clean, I let my imagination run wild while I took care of my dick, so I could be around Kaylie without pitching a tent.

I grimaced as I wrapped my hand around my dick. Kaylie was Bash's little sister. I really had to stop thinking about her like that.

Why the hell did she affect me so much? Sure, she was attractive — okay, make that sexy as fuck — but I'd been with plenty of hot women. Ever since we kissed that one time when she was a teenager, I'd had this unexplainable hangup with her. Sometimes I wondered if it was because she was off-limits — making the forbidden seem more attractive, but I genuinely hadn't recognized her when we kissed. And my reaction to that mostly innocent kiss had been explosive. So much so that it shocked me.

Right now, my dick was straining just thinking about it. My fist pumped my dick faster as I remembered the underaged minx slipping her hand into my pants. It happened years and years ago, yet I still remember it so clearly.

Fuck! I tried to focus on something else. I conjured up an image of the threesome I had with the two hot blonde chicks last month. Those two had been kinky as fuck, but the memory didn't even get my dick to twitch.

I was a sick bastard because as I pumped my cock, I was imagining Kaylie's hands touching me. I remembered that day with her years ago. That fucking innocent kiss. It worked me up like I was starring in my own personal porn flick.

It all started because Curtis dragged me to that lame high school party...

Downward Spiral turned out to be a really prescient name for our band. We'd started out on a high note - four high school kids who loved to play music, forming a heavy metal rock band. For a foster kid who'd bounced from home to home, forgotten and unloved until I was 13 years old, the attention the band brought me was a potent aphrodisiac. We weren't the 'top of the food chain' jocks in high school, but the band gave us lots of cred, maybe not with the cheerleader types, but definitely with the bad girls. We had our own bad-boy category, and we owned it.

Flash forward to that day, and I sensed we were close to the very bottom of that downward spiral. Rock bottom would be the death of our band. We were almost there; I just hadn't admitted it to myself yet.

Curtis had called a band meeting. We hadn't had one in months, mainly because we had nothing much to talk about. We played gigs about 2-3 times a month, usually at the same college bar where we had a small following.

One of my co-workers at the auto parts store dropped me off at O'Malley's Pub where I was currently nursing a beer across the booth from Curtis.

"Where's Bash and John?" I was getting tired of watching Curtis fiddle with his phone.

He didn't even look up. "Bash can't make it. John's gonna try to meet us."

"You get any hits with our demo?" I knew the answer, but I asked anyway.

Curtis looked around the room nervously and began tapping his fingers against the table. "No bites yet. I'm looking into some new leads though."

For some dumb reason, we'd made Curtis our 'manager'. None of us had the time or inclination to do the job. John and I worked full-time hours at shitty jobs, and Bash worked part-time and went to community college. The four of us lived together in a small apartment, but only three of us contributed to the bills.

Curtis slept on our couch and ate our food. He was the epitome of a human leech. Somehow, he managed to wrangle free shit from everyone around him. Since he had the most free time, we'd left him in charge of advertising our band, booking our gigs, and orchestrating our big break into the music industry. To say it was failing would be a huge understatement.

When I'd graduated high school, my foster mom, Shari, had wanted me to go to a community college like Bash or to mechanic school to learn how to work on cars. I enjoyed messing around under the hood of a car, but I enjoyed playing bass guitar even more. I wanted to make money doing something I loved. Shari had reservations about my choice, but she supported me in the end. Now that I was facing a lifetime of being a clerk at an auto parts store, things weren't looking so rosy.

I chipped at the label on my beer bottle. "We have any new gigs lined up?"

His leg was bouncing a mile a minute under the table. "Tequila Hut on Saturday. Nothing next weekend, but the Hut again after that. Thursday and Saturday." He took a drink of his beer and then returned his attention to his phone.

I knew he didn't want to talk about it, but I pressed. This was supposed to be a band meeting after all. "What about those clubs you mentioned at the last meeting? You were going to contact them?"

His hand tightened around his phone. "They've got no openings right now. I'll try back again in a few weeks."

"Did you even call them, Curtis?"

He took a long gulp of beer and then brought the bottle down onto the table with a distinct thud. "Fuck off, Sid. If you think you can do a better job than me, then have at it."

I was quickly losing my patience. "If there's nothing new, then why did you call a fucking band meeting? I've got better things to do than stare at you all night."

He couldn't sit still; he was bouncing agitatedly. Wiping his brow, he looked around the room again. "I don't know. We haven't had one in a while. I thought maybe we could all hang out. You know, have some fun. You remember what that is, Sid? Fun?"

"It's hard to have fun when I work full time and I can barely make rent."

"Oh fuck. Not that again. Would you get off my fucking back?"

That hadn't meant to be a dig at him. It just happened to be true. I took a deep breath and bit back the angry reply I was about to make. Curtis was already on the edge about something. He couldn't contain himself. If I didn't know any better, I would say he was tweaking, but I lived with the guy. I would know if he were on meth.

I finished up my beer while something seemed to catch his attention on his phone. He was texting back and forth with someone. After a few minutes, he got up. "I gotta roll. I'll see you back at home."

"Hey," I stopped him. "I don't have my car here. I need a ride home. Drop me off?"

His lips twisted into a frown. "I'm going the opposite way and I can't be late. See if Bash or John can pick you up."

Unbelievable. "Jesus, Curtis. You're just going to leave me here?"

He stood and slid out of the booth. "I have to meet someone at this party over on Maple Street. You can come with and then I'll drop you home."

Maple Street wasn't far from here. It'd probably be quicker just to go with Curtis even though he was being a dick.

I squared the bar tab Curtis opened for us not even bothering to ask him to contribute before I followed him to the parking lot.

He walked over to a beat-up Ford Crown Victoria. It had to be at least 20 years old. "My buddy Vinnie's car." He chuckled. "Used to be a police cruiser."

I slid into the passenger seat wondering how the hell Curtis always managed to have a car to use, no matter how crappy it was, without ever spending a penny. He turned up the radio, blasting out some rap music, while we headed toward the party on Maple Street.

He didn't tell me anything about the people he was meeting, and I didn't ask. We pulled up to the house in the middle-class neighborhood. Parked cars lined the street, so we had to park and then walk back to the house. I could hear sounds of music spilling out of the house as we approached. There was definitely a party in progress, but we didn't go to the front door. I followed Curtis as he led me to the back of the house and entered a back door that led into the kitchen.

There were about five kids in the kitchen, drinking out of red solo cups. They definitely weren't legal drinking age — probably high school kids.

Curtis addressed the guy filling up his cup by the keg. "Is Caufield around?"

The kid nodded. "Yeah, man. He's upstairs."

Curtis turned to me and rested his hand on my shoulder. He flashed me a friendly smile. The fucker could be charming when he wanted to be. "Sid, I gotta go talk to someone. It shouldn't take too long. Why don't you grab a beer while you wait? Check out the party?"

Curtis was heading out of the kitchen before I could reply.

The kid by the keg tilted his head. "You need a beer?"

"Thanks."

Fuck. I was stuck at some high school party while Curtis took off upstairs probably to score some drugs. He'd always been a recreational user, but I'd seen some signs lately that made me think he'd become more than that. Chances were good that he'd stick around up there and smoke whatever they offered for free while they made their deal. I should have stayed at O'Malley's and waited for someone to get me. Who knew how long Curtis would take?

I accepted the plastic cup full of beer that the kid handed to me and took a sip. It tasted like cheap ass skunked beer. The kind I drank in high school.

A girl sidled up to me. "Hey, my name is Aimee."

Two beers later and Aimee was getting a little too friendly with me while a tall skinny guy was shooting daggers at me from the kitchen table. I'd already texted Curtis a few times, but he wasn't answering. When Aimee gave me the full-body press up against the counter, I decided it was time to check out the rest of the party.

I followed the sound of music toward the front of the house. At least twenty kids were hanging out drinking. It was a fairly mellow party, most of them were grouped into small clusters playing drinking games. If anything, these kids looked even younger than the kids in the kitchen.

There was a group of about eight kids arranged in a circle to my right when I walked into the room. A pretty blonde girl jumped up from that group and grabbed my arm. "Well, hello there. You're exactly what we needed. Want to play?"

I glanced over. A brown beer bottle lay on its side in the middle of the circle. What the hell? I guess these kids were playing Spin the Bottle.

I shook my head. "Nah, I don't think so. I'm not staying long."

The bubbly cheerleader type wasn't going to give up that easily. She was still tugging at my arm. "C'mon. You have to! Brad just left with his friends. We need more guys in the circle."

I glanced over at the circle of kids and then back at her. "How old are you?"

She chuckled lightly. "I'm 18." She quirked an eyebrow and tilted her head mockingly. "How old are you? Eighty?"

Touche.

I was twenty-one, ostensibly only three years older than these kids, but the age difference seemed much greater. She looked like she might be 18, but some kids in the circle looked much younger.

"What's the matter? Are you too chicken?" She rolled her eyes. "I promise we won't bite."

For fuck's sake, I wasn't scared to kiss a girl. I was just too old for these stupid games. But somehow, blondie was already pulling me into the circle.

Reluctantly, I sat down next to the blonde girl. She pressed my shoulder with hers. "New player starts the round. Spin the bottle."

Jeez. I'd already allowed myself to be pressured by a bunch of teenagers, no way I was going to wuss out now. Nonchalantly, I gave the bottle a spin.

I hoped the bottle would land on Blondie. I'd give her the kiss of a lifetime until her toes were curling. Show her a taste of what a real man with experience could do. I was nothing like these adolescent, skinny runts sitting around the circle. I had my suspicions that she may have exaggerated her age and I could tell she found me attractive. So did the other girls, whose eyes swept imploringly back and forth between me and the spinning bottle.

The bottle slowed, and for a moment I panicked. It looked like it would stop on a guy. I didn't know what rules the kids played with this game, but there was no way I was kissing a dude. No matter how uncool it made me look. But thankfully, the bottle spun a tiny bit more and landed on the pretty girl next to him.

The boy looked disgusted; I was probably about to kiss the girl he was crushing on. The girls in the circle all started shrieking and the blonde girl next to me yelled out, "K, you lucky bitch!"

The bottle hadn't landed on Blondie, but the dark-haired girl was pretty enough. She looked much younger than Blondie, which gave me pause, but it was only a kiss. I could keep it innocent enough while still putting on a show for the crowd. I wanted these kids to think I was as badass as they thought I was. Why the hell did I care? I had no idea.

The cheerleader blonde nudged my arm.

I stood up in the center of the circle and maybe puffed out my chest a bit, but the girl remained frozen to her spot. Frankly, she looked slightly panicked. If this timid little girl didn't get up soon, it was going to make me look like an idiot.

I reached out my hand to her and when she tentatively took it, pulled her to her feet. Not giving her a second to react, I crushed her flush against my body and held her in place. Before she could think, I captured her lips and bent her body backward, giving her a pure Hollywood kiss that had all the girls screeching in unison around us.

When I straightened her upright and removed my lips, the girl seemed to be in a daze. Christ, her eyes were still closed even. It was a good thing I didn't give her any tongue or else she probably would have fainted.

The shrieking and catcalls continued while I kept my hands on her shoulders waiting until she seemed steady on her feet and I knew she wasn't going to keel over.

My job here was done. I'm a smug bastard; I couldn't keep the smirk from my face.

I sat back down in my spot next to the blonde girl.

"What are you doing?" She slapped my arm. "This isn't Spin the Bottle!"

I looked around the circle, confusion evident on my face. "What?"

"This is Seven Minutes in Heaven. Go get her, stud!"

Seven Minutes in Heaven? What the fuck was that?

Oh fuck.

♫♫♪♪♪

My hand was nowhere near satisfying enough. My dick was spent, but ready for round two when I thought about Kaylie in the next room. I wanted to sink into her so badly. The dirty little secret was that she turned me on like no other woman ever had. She wasn't a little girl anymore, but she was still Bash's little sister and she deserved my respect. She didn't need an asshole like me who wanted to fuck her and walk away. I was a father now; I needed to start acting more responsibly. Turning the water to cold, I stood under the stream of freezing water until my teeth were chattering.

After I'd dressed, I went in search of Kaylie. She'd spent enough of her time here helping me. She probably wanted to get home. On my way, I checked in at the portable crib to see that Kody was still sleeping soundly. I stopped for a moment to just watch him. My heart stirred with something almost painful. Love, I guess. I would do anything to protect this kid. To keep him safe. I wanted to pick him up and hold him at that moment, but I knew it was better to let him sleep. He'd be up shortly, and I'd have plenty of time to cuddle him.

I found Kaylie in the kitchen. Her back was to me as she stood at the sink washing baby bottles. Fuck, she was so gorgeous. Of course, my eyes strayed straight to her ass. She was wearing skinny jeans that outlined her ass so perfectly that I could trace her curves right through the material. Her dark wavy hair hung down her back to just below her shoulders and I zeroed in on her right shoulder where the wide neck of her blue and white striped sweater had slipped down exposing a delicate strip of silky skin.

I imagined my lips running over that skin, sucking on her neck until I left a mark, my cock pressing hard against her ass. The cock that I'd just managed to get back in control was stirring to life again. I needed to stop this. If she knew what I was thinking right now, she'd be disgusted with me. She'd run straight for the door and I wouldn't blame her.

She must have sensed me watching because she wiped her hands on a dish towel and slowly turned around.

Nowadays, I usually saw Kaylie at parties, where she was all dressed up in glamorous dresses, fancy makeup, and high heels. Today, standing in my kitchen wearing jeans and little makeup, she was even more captivating to me. She was tall for a girl, about five foot seven inches, I guessed, but here in my kitchen wearing her ballet flats, she looked tiny.

Her eyes flashed me a challenge, and it almost undid my tenuous grip of control. Out of all her beautiful features, her stunning green eyes stood out the most. For years, I'd heard girls endlessly comment on Bash's eyes, but I'd never really noticed the appeal. But on Kaylie, those same eyes had my stomach all tied up in knots.

I needed to break the unbearable tension that had built between us.

"You didn't have to do the dishes," I croaked lamely.

"It's no problem. Kody's still sleeping and I'm almost done. I'll just finish this last one ... and then I could really use that glass of wine you offered before."

Neither Bash nor I drank wine, but I was sure I could find a bottle or two. Usually, people brought over bottles of alcohol when they came over to party, but some brought wine from time to time.

I was confident that I could be hospitable enough to offer her a glass of wine. The question remained if I could keep my mind out of the gutter and my hands to myself in the process.

Chapter 10

Kaylie

I sat on Sid's couch wondering if I should politely decline the glass of wine I'd asked for and escape his apartment while I still had my pride intact. When I was in the kitchen finishing the dishes, I'd felt his presence behind me the moment he stepped in the doorway. I'd waited a few minutes for him to speak, but he didn't. When I finally turned around, the look he was giving me was pure heat.

Lord, he looked sexy. His hair was still damp and his henley shirt clung to him like a second skin showing off his broad chest, defined pecs, and muscled arms. The scent of his body wash filled the air, and I almost took a step toward him. He hovered in the doorway, big and manly. Desire had shot straight through me. It took all my restraint not to melt into a puddle on the floor or fling myself at him.

Now he was in his kitchen rooting through his cabinets looking for a bottle of wine because I couldn't think of any other way to break the tension before he realized I was eye fucking his body and about to jump his bones.

The way he looked at me made me shiver. There was no doubt he was attracted to me, but he'd never once acted on it. He always treated me like a little sister. I'd caught him in a few unguarded moments looking at me with a hunger in his eyes, but I always ended up doubting what I thought I saw because he'd flirt with anyone in a skirt, yet never with me.

I've wanted Sid since I was 15 years old. Here I was, seven years later, still acting like the same awkward, fumbling teenager around him. I was as bad now as when I was locked in that closet with him.

I remembered that night as clearly as if it'd happened yesterday. Bash had graduated from high school, so he didn't live at home anymore. That meant I had a little more freedom without my big brother watching my every move. My other brother, Brent, was a senior in high school, but he'd never been as suffocating as Bash was.

♫♪

I'd snuck out to a party with my friend, Sarah. So far, the party had sucked. I had two beers, but they tasted so terrible that I'd dumped most of them into the bathroom sink when no one could see me.

I joined a circle of older kids playing 7 Minutes in Heaven because Ricky Porter, senior football god at my high school, was playing. I thought getting trapped in a closet with him would be legendary. Thankfully, when he spun it, the bottle landed on Carrie Silverstein, a popular cheerleader. When they exited the closet after their seven minutes, Ricky was pulling up his fly with a decidedly cocky smile on his face.

Five minutes later, Ricky was rounding up his posse of cool boys and leaving the party. He'd never once glanced my way. Why would he? I was only 15 years old. Only an inexperienced sophomore. Blowjobs happened in the closet? It was a good thing the bottle landed on Carrie. I had no business playing this game. I hadn't even been kissed by a boy yet. Forget blowjobs.

I was thinking about how I was going to get home; Sarah's big brother was supposed to pick us up at 10, but I didn't want to stay at this party any longer. Sarah had her sights on this jerk from our biology class, so she wasn't giving me the time of day right now. I was about to get up from the circle and mill around when my heart started beating double time in my chest.

Sidney Anderson walked into the room.

It couldn't be him.

There was no way he'd be here. The three sips of nasty beer must have made me delusional.

But it was definitely him. I'd recognize him anywhere, even though he looked older. And even hotter than the last time I saw him.

I looked around nervously to see if he was with Bash, but it looked like he was alone. He was wearing worn black jeans with black boots and a T-shirt with a black leather jacket. He was insanely hot.

His presence demanded the attention of every person in the room. Of course, Carrie jumped up to accost him right away. I was jealous that she was confident enough to talk to him, to grab his arm like that.

Along with everyone else, I was watching when she lied and told him she was 18 years old. Bash was twenty-one now, so Sid must be as well. He definitely stood out from this high school crowd. He looked so cool, so hot, so much older. Even Ricky, the football player, looked like a boy in comparison.

I was still trying to get my rapidly beating heart back to normal when Carrie pulled Sid into our game circle. I felt like I was underwater when Sid spun the bottle. Everything seemed to move in slow motion. The bottle spun around and around.

This must be a dream.

Pinch me.

Because the bottle slowed down...

and stopped.

It was pointing right at me.

I couldn't move. I wasn't breathing.

I was having an out-of-body experience.

He pulled me up to stand with a smirk. Pressed me against his hard body. Dipped me and planted a kiss on my lips.

I thought I'd pass out on the spot. I was seeing stars.

Looking supremely cocky, he sat back down.

He didn't recognize me. He'd never have kissed me if he knew who I was. I'd changed a lot in the last few years; I'd grown up, filled out, and even lost the braces on my teeth, but if the lighting in this room wasn't so dim - if he'd seen my eyes - he would have recognized me. My coloring, especially my green eyes, was just like Bash's. Everyone remarked on the resemblance when they saw us together. Especially since our middle brother, Brent, had lighter hair and amber-colored eyes.

I was still in a daze when we were pushed into the front hall closet together. The louvered doors let in a small amount of light, but it was mostly dark in there. Coats, boots, and shoes, all stuffed to one side for this game, crammed into the closet, giving us very little room to stand. I was less than a foot away from him; he was so close I could feel the heat coming off him.

"Jesus, it smells like feet in here," he grumbled.

I couldn't help it; I inched closer to him. All I could smell was his cologne. He smelled like heaven. "Um, what should we do?" My voice sounded squeaky and timid, like a mouse.

"Do? We're not going to do anything." He swept his hand through his hair. "We're going to get out of here."

A tinge of panic zinged through me. "What? We can't leave!"

"Oh yeah? They can't force us to sit in this nasty closet. I'm leaving."

I was trapped in a closet with my biggest crush, and all he wanted to do was escape. Fuck my life!

"If we leave now, I'll never live it down! It'll destroy my reputation."

He sighed heavily. "That's the stupidest thing I ever heard."

I couldn't let him leave. The universe handed this fantasy to me, and I had to make the most of it or regret it for the rest of my life. It was time to use my acting skills to project a confidence I didn't have. Last year I played Betty Rizzo from Grease; I just needed to channel her personality to get what I wanted. I'd never have this opportunity again.

"It might be stupid, but it's true. We have to stay inside this closet for 7 minutes."

He shifted on his feet. "Jesus Christ!"

I swallowed down my nerves and pressed the issue. "And the bare minimum we have to do is kiss."

"I'm not going to kiss you."

I could feel the aggravation coming off him in waves. "Why not?"

"Because you're too young."

"I'm eighteen!"

He chuckled. "No, you're not."

"But you already kissed me in front of the entire party!"

"That wasn't a real kiss."

He was leaning against the back wall of the closet. I inched closer to him until I was directly in front of him. "So, give me a real one."

"You barely survived the first kiss."

So true. "You caught me off guard."

He took a deep breath. "Look, you seem like a sweet kid, but you're too young for me, and I don't even know you."

Oh, my God! He was ruining everything! "Right, you can't kiss me because you don't know me? Is that how all the 20-year-olds act nowadays? Do you do background checks and ask her to fill out personality surveys before you kiss a girl?"

"Fuck, you're impossible."

If my fantasy had been slowly deflating before, now the bubble had finally burst. He was flat-out rejecting me.

A lump of emotion lodged in my throat. "Am I that hideous that you're too disgusted to even kiss me?"

"What? No! You're really cute, it's just—"

A tear escaped from my brimming eyes and trailed down my cheek.

"Fuck! Are you crying?"

I swiped at my tear. "You can leave. I'll just stay in here."

"Don't get upset. This is just a dumb game..."

"Just go." I didn't want him to see my utter humiliation.

His rejection was absolutely soul-crushing. I wished I'd never come to this dumb party.

"Jesus. If you're going to be such a big baby about it, I'll give you a damn kiss."

I didn't want his pity. My bottom lip quivered as I answered, "Forget it. I don't even want it anymore."

"Oh, for fuck's sake. You're ridiculous." His arm shot out and wrapped around my waist. He pulled me in close until I was leaning up against him, my palm splayed out on his impossibly hard chest.

A thousand thoughts raced through my head at once.

Do I tilt my head?

Sid was going to kiss me!

Do I open my mouth? Or pucker my lips?

Sid was going to kiss me!

Will I taste like stale beer?

Sid was going to kiss me!

But then all the worry that I was going to do it wrong was swept into oblivion because he was kissing me.

I finally understood so many things that previously had been inexplicable to me. At that moment, I would have done anything Sid had asked of me. Hell, I'd be begging for more if I wasn't dumbstruck with amazement right then. I'd finally realized how passion could overcome common sense; something I would have scoffed at minutes before.

Not only had my mind been opened up, but my body was experiencing an awakening as well. I felt this kiss all over — from the crazy fluttering in my stomach to the buzz of excitement coursing through my veins all the way to the throb of desire pulsing between my legs. It was a sensation so euphoric, I'd never come close to conceptualizing it in my wildest dreams.

All my reactions were pure instinct; my tongue responded to his probing, tentatively at first and then more boldly when Sidney groaned his approval. Impossibly, Sidney deepened the kiss, making my core flood with desire. I could feel the bulging hardness in his pants between us, and it excited me. Despite my utter lack of experience, my hand which had already wandered under his jacket to explore, slid downward until it slipped inside his pants. There was no conscious thought, just a primal need to touch him. For one glorious moment, my hand surrounded his dick, and it wasn't until later that I registered how massively huge it felt.

It wasn't the right move because Sidney reacted immediately by breaking our kiss and yanking my hand out of his pants. I didn't regret it, though.

Sidney was trying to put some distance between our bodies, but I was still caught in the aftereffect of that amazing kiss. The surrounding world slowly began to intrude on my senses — the coats crowding in around us, the sounds of my rowdy friends coming to get us out of the closet — as I fought to control my breathing.

I was still in a full-body press against Sid when the door swung open. My first kiss had been epic. Sid frankly looked shocked and maybe a bit frazzled.

The smirk was on my face now. "Thanks for the kiss, Sidney."

I wasn't able to see his reaction because the pack of girls tugged me from the closet. My face must have looked like the cat that swallowed the canary because Carrie shouted, "Oh my God, K, you dirty whore!" I went along with the flow as the raucous pack engulfed me and pulled me back to the party.

It was only about 10 minutes later when I was standing at the keg in the kitchen. I was still riding a dopamine high from that kiss when I felt his presence behind me. My stomach fluttered.

"How did you know my name?" His voice sounded gruff.

I turned around and faced him. I watched his face morph from shock to horror.

Standing under the bright fluorescent lights, I knew that he'd finally recognized me.

"Oh fuck. K! Kay as in Kaylie?"

I nodded.

"Kaylie Archer?"

I couldn't hold back my smile. "The one and only."

"Oh, fuck."

On a scale of 1 to 10, that kiss totally broke the scorch meter. Sadly, I was later to learn that not all kisses were like that. In fact, I'd never experienced anything near that intense since. Kissing some guys was like kissing a dead fish — cold uncaring lips. Then there were the overly soft and excessively wet lip kisses or the darting tongue that felt gross and invasive. Sometimes a kiss produced not even one flutter, even with the cutest guy. An extraordinary kiss needed some mysterious magic ingredient.

For me, Sid possessed that magic ingredient. I was too naïve to know it at the time, but that toe-curling kiss had set me up for years of frustration.

I sat back on the couch, trying to shake off the memories before Sid came back with my wine.

Yes, I still craved Sid like an addict craved his next hit, but I was more experienced now. I understood he was exactly the type of man I shouldn't want. He was the epitome of the douchebag male that Bash had warned me about. Sid was a man whore. His only goals in life were to make music and casually fuck women. Kody was proof that he was also irresponsible on top of all that. He'd proven that he wasn't interested in commitment or relationships.

I had to forget about our undeniable physical chemistry and focus on just being friends with him. I was a strong woman; I could do this.

So, why was the first thing that entered my mind when he returned with my glass of wine — the size of his cock, which I now knew must be damn impressive?

"A red cabernet was all I could find. I hope that's okay?" He handed me the glass and then sat down at the opposite end of the couch from me.

I took a sip. "It's fine. Thanks."

Surprisingly, he was drinking a bottle of water. I didn't think the boys took a night off from drinking, but I guess with Kody's arrival, a lot of things had changed.

I searched around for something to break the conspicuous silence that had settled between us. "So, how's everything going with Kody? You didn't have much time to adjust to becoming a father."

He glanced over towards Kody's crib. "It's exhausting, but I think I'm getting the hang of it."

"You seem to have taken to him quickly."

"I always wanted to have kids; I just expected it to happen much, much later in my life."

His answer surprised me, but I kept my face impassive.

He rubbed a hand down his face. "I've got so much going on right now, I haven't been able to sleep at night wondering how I'm going to juggle everything. I'm just trying to hang on one day at a time — hell, one hour at a time. "

"So, you're going to keep him? Have you looked into other options?"

He looked over at me, startled by my question. "He's not an inconvenience that I can just throw away."

"That's not what I meant. You have options. You could give him up for adoption. There are tons of good people out there looking to adopt newborn babies."

His eyes flashed stormily, but he kept his tone even. "I'm not abandoning him."

I knew I was probably pressing him too far, but I didn't back down. "Have you taken a paternity test yet? Are you even sure he's your baby?"

"He's mine," he growled.

"Don't you think you should alert the authorities? Maybe they can track down his mom and help you confirm his paternity, so everything is handled properly?"

Sid popped up from the couch and began pacing. "If I call the police or child services, they'll just take him away from me. They'll place him with a foster family."

"They might let you keep him until you can establish paternity."

He stopped his pacing and pinned me with a stare. "No, they won't. And that's not a chance I'll take."

"What if he's not your kid, Sidney? Then you're bonding with him and — "

"His mother trusted him with me. She said I was the father. I'm not going to abandon my child, Kaylie."

That was the second time he'd mentioned 'abandoning' Kody. "Placing him in the care of professionals until the situation is sorted out is hardly abandoning him. It might be what's best for him."

His eyes blazed and his voice raised with anger. He looked like he was ready to punch his fist through the wall. "You think Child Protective Services is what's best for him? Did you forget I grew up in that system, Kaylie?"

I swallowed. "I thought Shari was a good foster mom?"

His jaw unclenched and his eyes softened. "She was. But I was 13 years old before she saved me. Those 13 years before were a nightmare."

"I didn't know." My stomach sank. "When you moved in next door, I was really young, so I guess I never considered it. I feel awful that I never asked you about it."

"I wouldn't have told you." He grimaced. "Bash knows some of it, but I haven't even told him the worst parts of it. I really rather just forget my entire childhood before Shari."

He had such a haunted look in his eyes. I'd spent so much of my life idolizing Sid in a superficial way; I'd never scratched below the surface. What kind of shallow person was I?

"I wish you would tell me about it. I want to understand what you went through. Where were your parents?"

Sid walked back over to the couch and slumped down onto it. He remained quiet for so long that I didn't think he'd answer me.

"I have some memories of my mom when I was really young. I never knew anything about my father. For all I know, he never even knew I existed. Or, more likely, my mother didn't know who my father was."

There were some definite parallels to Kody here. I was being so judgemental with Sid about Kody because I was hurt by the situation when I had no right to be. I was being a selfish bitch while Sid was dealing with everything on his plate, including his own past.

"There's no father listed on your birth certificate?"

"Nope. It says 'unknown'." He paused a moment and then continued. "When I turned 18, Shari helped me look up my records. I entered the Georgia system when I was 19 months old. My mother was investigated for neglect and child endangerment. She was a drug addict, so I was taken from my home. They couldn't find any family members to take me in."

"That's awful," I murmured.

Sid continued, "My mother's grandfather was contacted and apparently willing to take me, but they deemed him unfit. From what I could tell from the records, it seemed like his age was the only factor. There were records of his phone calls over the years checking up on me. He was told it was in my best interest if he never contacted me and that I was thriving in my current situation. It was all horseshit. I was anything but thriving. I still wonder how much better my childhood would have been if they'd let my great-grandfather take me in."

It was one of those 'what-ifs' that probably played over and over in his head and seemed to be haunting his past. "They must have had a good reason for what they did."

He laughed bitterly. "You have a lot of misplaced trust in the system, Kaylie. I don't fault you, but believe me, it's a horrible system where a lot of horrible decisions are made."

I wanted to argue that the system was inherently good — that the people involved spent their lives trying to protect children, not make things worse. But Sid was right. I had no real-life experience to back up my beliefs. I tended to look at the world through rose-tinted glasses.

I decided to drop it. "So, you were in other foster homes before you got placed with Shari?"

Sid took a swig from his water bottle. "I was in and out of foster homes and I stayed in group homes in between waiting for someone to take me in. They labeled me 'hard to place' when I was very young, so the foster homes that would take me in got rougher and rougher the older I got."

I was careful not to show any of the emotion I was feeling because Sid was watching me carefully as he spoke. I had long since ditched my wineglass on the coffee table, so I pressed my hands into my lap to hide the nervousness I had about asking the next question.

"Were you abused in some of these homes?"

Sid drew in a deep breath. "Yes. In most of them. Once I was labeled 'hard to place', I wasn't exactly sent to the cream of the crop foster parents. I was placed with the ones who were doing it solely for the money."

I flinched at his answer but quickly schooled my features. "Why were you considered hard to place?"

"Several of my foster parents accused me of stealing."

"God, that's awful." Now I was getting angry. "You'd never do that."

Defiance flashed in his eyes. "I did. I stole from them."

"Oh, Sidney."

"The fucked up part is that I did it for my mother."

"Your biological mother?" I asked.

"Yeah." He stroked his chin in thought. "I guess she was allowed visitations. She visited every once in a while for a few years when I was really young. I was probably about 6 or 7 years old. Most of the time, the social worker would prepare me for the visit, but she wouldn't show up. That fucking crushed me."

His voice croaked a bit with emotion, but then he continued.

"We'd meet in the social worker's office or one time at the park that I remember. I was so happy that day at the park. She'd always bring me a lollipop, and I thought that was so nice of her."

I prompted him to continue, "Were the visits nice?"

"When I think back on it now as an adult, they were horrific. But at the time, her visits were like Christmas Day." He glanced my way, probably trying to gauge my reaction.

"Why were they horrific? What happened?" I prodded.

"Like I mentioned, she was a drug addict. She wanted one thing from me — money." He shrugged like he was shrugging off the emotions that his insight brought with it. "She was always whispering to me how bad my foster parents were. That they were bad people. She told me to steal from them, to sneak into their purses, or search through their bedrooms looking for money or any valuables. She patiently explained to me what items might be valuable, like jewelry or watches. I should look for items tucked deep in the back of the jewelry boxes and not bother with the everyday jewelry kept in plain sight."

I was glad Sid was lost in his memory and no longer watching me because the picture he was painting was bleak. "Did you take stuff?"

"I stole whatever I could. I wanted to please her. She gushed over the stuff I'd bring her. Once, I brought her twenty bucks. She was so happy that she cried. She was hugging me so hard I thought she'd squeeze out all my breath."

Who would do that to their own son? An addict, I guessed. Thank God Sidney didn't grow up under her care. "So, what happened?"

"Eventually, I got caught. The foster parents kicked me out. Then I stole from the next home. By the time my mother was out of the picture, it was too late. I was about 8 years old and considered impossible to place permanently. I was a boy and over the age of 4, then add behavioral problems on top of that. They put me with anyone who'd take me at that point."

"What happened to your mother? Have you been in contact with her now that you're older?"

He grimaced. "She OD'd when I was about 8 years old. Nobody bothered to tell me, but it was right there in the records. She just stopped coming around."

It now made so much sense to me why he was so protective of Kody. The very people that should have protected him had abandoned Sid his whole life. I mourned for that lost little boy. I'd had such an idyllic, sheltered childhood that I'd been blinded to the struggles that Sidney had to overcome.

I wouldn't turn a blind eye anymore. "You said you were abused in some of those homes. What happened? Only if you're comfortable telling me…"

"I don't want your pity, Kaylie."

"I don't know what it'll make me feel," I answered honestly. "So far, I'm a bit disillusioned. Heartbroken at what you went through. Angry.

I feel naïve. I don't know — even ashamed that I was so unaware. Maybe I wish I could have helped you back then. Is that pity? I don't know. Mostly, it makes me want to do something now. Even if it helps just one kid."

Sidney stared at me for a long beat. He spoke quietly, "I've always wanted to foster parent someday. Even when I was going through the darkest times as a kid, I'd think that when I grew up, I'd foster some kids and be the best foster parent ever."

His confession left a lump in my throat. I'd really underestimated him. "You will someday. You've already proven what a wonderful dad you are with Kody."

He broke eye contact with me. "You want to hear about some of the not-so-wonderful foster parents I've had? I'll tell you if you want."

I didn't trust my voice, so I just nodded.

"Well, let's see. One of my earliest memories is probably from second grade. That family only gave me a few hand-me-down outfits to wear. Anything nice gets stolen in the group homes, so I didn't come to them with many of my own possessions and they didn't buy me anything new. They also didn't allow me to shower often. Usually only if they knew I had a meeting with my caseworker. Anyway, I was nicknamed 'Stinky Sid' at school. I was mercilessly picked on."

I shifted on the couch, feeling sorry for the little boy he was.

"Then there was the lady that pinched me whenever I did something wrong." Sid frowned at the memory. "If I gave her a funny look or said the wrong thing, I got pinched. If I didn't eat my vegetables or do my chores fast enough — pinch. She'd make any excuse to pinch me. I had bruises all over my body."

His fingers began tapping on the back of the couch. I reached out to touch his arm, but he didn't seem to notice.

"Other parents slapped or used a belt on me for punishment while nothing similar happened to their own kids. I was forced to eat food I didn't want. I had to sit in time-outs for hours. Once I was locked in a cold basement overnight without any blankets. Sometimes I had to sneak food because I wouldn't eat with the family and they'd forget to feed me. One of my foster fathers was a military guy. He punished me by making me do exercises for hours. That mom was really nice though, so I didn't mind being there as much. In a lot of the houses, I had an excessive amount of chores, while their own kids had none."

Agitated, he stood up from the couch and started pacing.

"That was the type of physical abuse I encountered. A lot of the families were just plain neglectful. I'd be left unattended for days even when I was really little. But none of that compared to the emotional abuse. That was the worst. I can't even describe the constant humiliation and mocking that some parents did. They were hateful people that got off on breaking kids down. It took Shari a long time to undo some of the psychological damage that did to me."

For a few moments, I was quiet and let everything he told me sink in. I never had an inkling that Sid had gone through all that. I had always judged Sid harshly for his promiscuous behavior, but maybe there was something much deeper keeping him from forming meaningful attachments.

"I'm damn lucky that Shari took a chance on me when she did." He shook his head slowly. "Otherwise, I'd probably be in jail or dead right now."

"Thank you for telling me all that," I said quietly.

"I shouldn't have unloaded all that on you. I'm not sure why I did."

I was spared from responding because Kody let out a cry alerting us that he was awake. It was a good thing; I needed more time to process everything Sid had told me.

I spent the next couple of hours helping Sid take care of Kody. It was nearing ten o'clock. Kody's diaper was changed, he was dressed in his pajamas and had been fed a bottle, yet he didn't appear that sleepy. Sid, on the other hand, was barely keeping awake.

I was walking around the apartment with Kody when I saw Sid's head drooping again. I tapped him on the shoulder. "Hey, why don't you go get some sleep? I can manage to get Kody down myself. Actually, I can stay and take the first feeding when he wakes up. That way you can get a bit of uninterrupted sleep. You look like you've been running on fumes."

Sid stood up. "I don't want you walking home in the middle of the night."

I rolled my eyes. "I've done it before."

His brow furrowed. "I don't like it. Let me call you a cab."

"How many times does Kody get up at night?"

"It's pretty brutal." He looked up toward the ceiling in thought. "Let me think. He'll probably wake up around midnight. Then he might sleep until three or four o'clock if I'm lucky. Then he gets up in the morning super early. Like 6:30."

"You can't keep doing this without any help," I reasoned. "I'll take his overnight feedings tonight. I'll sleep right here on the new couch. Then you can get him in the morning. That way you can get a pretty decent amount of sleep."

"Kaylie, you don't have to do that for me."

"I know that. But I want to help and it's no big deal. I didn't have any plans for tonight, anyway. Plus, I'm not working tomorrow morning. It works out perfectly."

A slow smile broke out on his face. "You know what? I think I'm too tired to argue with you. I'll get you some blankets and a pillow, so you'll be more comfortable."

"Could I borrow a T-shirt to sleep in?"

"Yeah."

Thirty minutes later, Kody was sleeping in the portable crib and I was ready for bed. I had changed into the Rolling Stones T-shirt Sid brought me. Little did he know, I had no intention of ever returning this shirt. I fell asleep sniffing the faint scent of Sidney on the shirt like a psycho.

Kody woke me up twice during the night. Within a half hour, I had him changed, fed, and back asleep. The first time was easy-peasy. I struggled the second time to wake up.

I heard Kody's cries again, and this time I struggled to open my eyes. Damn, this was hard; I was so tired.

"I'm coming," I mumbled.

I half-rolled, half-fell off the couch, and staggered to my feet. My bleary eyes would barely open.

When I finally got to the crib, Sidney was there lifting Kody out of it. "Good morning, sleepyhead."

"Ugh, is it really morning?"

Sid laughed. "I've got him. Why don't you catch a couple more hours of sleep? You can use Bash's bed if you want so it's quieter. Bash is staying at Knox's."

"I think I will. I'm too tired to exist right now." Sighing, I trudged off towards the bedrooms. While my eyelids drooped with exhaustion, I was not too exhausted to miss Sid's quick perusal of my sleep outfit. I was wearing his T-shirt, but I'd ditched my jeans leaving my legs bare. The shirt covered my butt, so I figured it was okay.

I was heading for my brother's bedroom when I passed by Sid's room. His door was open. Without thinking about it too much, I went into his room instead and curled up in his bed. The sheets still retained a faint trace of his body heat, and his scent enveloped me. I didn't even have time to appreciate it properly because I fell fast asleep.

Chapter 11

Bash

What the hell was that noise? It sounded like a drill boring deep into my brain. I forced an eye open and remembered that I was sleeping on Knox's couch. The heinous noise finally stopped.

"Sorry mate, did I wake you?" Knox's voice rang out from the kitchen.

I sat up on the couch. "Are you making one of your protein shakes?"

"You want one?"

I've had his shakes before. They tasted like dirt with a dash of rotten egg thrown in. "No, thanks."

Knox walked into the room carrying his green sludge. "I'm headed to the gym. You wanna come?"

I propped my head up with my hands. I should really go to the gym. I hadn't done much working out in the past few weeks. Knox, Ryder, and Ghost were really good about keeping in shape and they'd kept me and Sid from slacking off too much while we were on tour.

Today, I just wasn't in the mood. "Nah. I'm gonna go practice for a couple of hours to let off some steam."

Knox nodded. He understood that playing drums was a full-body workout. It was also therapeutic for me. For now, I could get away with being lazy. When we toured with Cold Fusion, a band at the top of their career, their drummer, who I considered a mentor, told me that inevitably as I got older I'd have to take better care of myself. Until then, I was going to enjoy the fuck out of the fast life.

Knox sank down on the couch next to me. "You didn't bring a lass back last night? I got home around one o'clock and you were already sleeping."

I groaned. "I went out with a bunch of roadies last night — Ben, that new guy Garrett, and some others. Fuck, it was a disaster."

He laughed. "What happened?"

"Nothing fucking happened," I grumbled. "Those morons scared all the decent women away. They are the biggest fucking cockblockers."

It just hadn't been the same without Sid there. "And, I forgot what it's like to pick up women at a bar without Sid. I'm so used to our routine. We always hit on girls together. It was way too much work to do it solo, especially with a bunch of horny idiots trying to shoehorn themselves into the middle of the situation. It wasn't as much fun."

Knox snickered. "Aww, you miss your BFF, Vicious."

"Yeah, I fucking do. I can't wait for the tour. Then everything will be back to normal. New girls lining up, begging to get fucked with no expectations attached. Sid won't be LARPing as a stay-at-home mom anymore—"

The sound of a new text notification on my phone cut my rant off.

Who the hell was texting so damn early? I started searching around the couch looking for it.

I finally found it wedged between two cushions. I read the text and groaned. "Fucking Garrett. He wants to know if he should give Martha my phone number."

Knox lifted an eyebrow but didn't comment. He was amused by my silly drama.

"Who the fuck is Martha?" I typed those words into my phone as I said them out loud.

I waited for his reply. "He says, 'Martha is the blonde chick that gave you a blowjob in the bathroom last night'. What the fuck? Why would he give her my phone number? Sid would never ask me something so asinine."

I typed out my answer: FUCK NO.

I saw he was replying, so I waited for the new message to pop up. "She'll give him a blowjob if he gives her my number. He's begging me. Jesus, he probably fucked her last night and I guarantee they're naked in bed right now. Fuck, I'm blocking his number. I don't need his bullshit."

Knox slapped me on the back, barely holding back his laughter. "The clarty bastard will do anything for a gobble."

"I don't know what the fuck you're talking about, Scotty." I frowned. "What's got you in such a good mood, anyway? It doesn't look like you got any luckier than me last night."

"I don't bring the ladies back here. They cramp my style. I always go to their place to have a shag, then it's easy to sneak away when I want. Live and learn, ya numpty." Knox's eyes glimmered with humor.

"I guess."

"And something you taught me," he added, "No parties here. Look what a boggin' heap your apartment turned into."

I slumped against the couch cushions. "And now a baby is living there. How fucked up is that?"

Knox tipped up his cup and drank the rest of his shake. "Well, all this blethering's been fun, but I've got to get to the gym, and speaking of the bairn, I've got to buy a gift for the baby shower."

"Shit." I sighed. "Don't you think this baby shower is a bad idea?"

"What do you mean? Kaylie said Sid needs a lot of baby stuff right away. He could use our support right now."

Was everybody on Sid's side? Couldn't they see how crazy this was? "Sid needs to realize that he can't keep the baby — the sooner he does the better."

Knox was watching me so intently, it felt like he could read my mind. "I know you're afraid of losing Sid, but you've got to take your feelings out of the equation."

"I'm not afraid of losing Sid," I scoffed. "It's just that this baby shower is only encouraging this farce to go on longer and it will eventually be more painful for Sid in the end."

"You're being selfish, Bash. You might feel differently if it was you in the same situation. What if this was your wee bairn?"

Fuck, there was no way Knox could know it was a possibility, but what he stated out loud was my worst fear. I couldn't handle it if Kody were my kid. Instead of voicing any of that, more whining came out of my mouth. "But, what about the tour? It's coming up soon. What about Ghost Parker?"

Knox shrugged. "That's something Sid will have to figure out. Whatever he decides doesn't mean your bromance is over, Bash. You'll always have your friendship, but it might need to change or adjust a wee bit."

"I don't want it to change."

His mouth quirked with a little smile. "Did you think it was never going to change? It was inevitable with or without Kody. What did you think was going to happen when one of you got married? Did you think you were going to share a woman? Two wives? Swap? It doesn't work like that in the real world."

"Well, it should."

He'd already called me out as being selfish and I guess it was true. Selfish and pathetic.

He stood up. "I have to buy a baby bathtub and an entire list of bath stuff. I don't even know what half of it is."

"Yeah, I have to buy a 'manly' diaper bag and a list of other shit. How on earth could a diaper bag ever be manly?"

Knox snickered. "Make sure it's covered in teddy bears and duckies."

I had to pick up my car if I was going to drive out to the studio space to work on my drums, and if I was right by the apartment, I might as well stop in and see how Sid was doing.

The conversation I had with Knox was running through my head non-stop. Yeah, I knew I was acting selfishly. Knox wasn't the first person who'd pointed that out to me.

I abandoned Sid when he needed my help, but we didn't see eye to eye on this baby thing, and I wasn't sure how I was going to get through to him. I thought he'd come to his senses by now.

One thing I was sure about was that he'd never do the same to me. If the shoe had been on the other foot, he would've stood by my side the entire time. He never would have turned tail and run as I did.

I wanted to be more supportive of him, but if I dug a little deeper into my head, I knew exactly why I wasn't. It was because we still weren't certain who Kody belonged to. Sure, Sid was playing along pretending he was the dad for now, but what if that wasn't the case? I had been willfully ignoring that scenario ever since I'd panicked and blurted out the lie to Talia and then repeated it to Kaylie.

Truthfully, this baby could be mine. I'd done some stupid things in my life. Irresponsible things, but I was pretty good about using a condom. I was scared about getting STDs, so I was fastidious about covering it up no matter what a girl told me.

If the baby turned out to be mine, I'd put him up for adoption. I couldn't raise him. Then what lie would we tell? Would Sid go along with the adoption story still pretending that he's the father? I wasn't so sure, and it made me nervous. What would my parents think if they found out? They'd be so disappointed and I know my mom would be heartbroken if she knew I was giving him up. Fuck! Maybe they'd take care of him so I could keep touring with the band.

This was such a helpless feeling. None of this was part of any plan I'd ever made. Sid was fucking insane making us go through all this. We should have called the police the moment we found Kody. If it were up to me, no one would have known about this.

Christ, that panicky feeling was skittering across my chest again as my thoughts spiraled into chaos. I had just resolved to visit Sid and try to be a better friend. Taking a deep breath, I pushed aside my anxiety as I unlocked the door to our apartment.

The first thing that hit me was the smell of bacon. I could hear Sid whistling in the kitchen. Christ, how could he be in such a good mood? I followed the sound into the kitchen.

"You're here just in time for some breakfast." He approached me with Kody in his arms. "Here, you take him. He doesn't want to stay in his carrier and I don't want him near the stove while I'm cooking. I keep having to pick him up and put him down and then he cries."

He transferred Kody into my arms. It was obvious he had become much more comfortable handling Kody after only a few days, but I was still tentative when holding him. I made sure to support his head while I watched Sid crack some eggs into a frying pan.

He glanced over his shoulder at me. "I'll be done in a minute. Can you change his diaper for me?"

I held in the groan that wanted to escape. Changing a diaper was the last thing I wanted to do right now, but I'd just vowed to be more supportive of Sid. I guess this meant diaper duty.

I brought Kody over to the changing pad on the crib and noticed that Sid had all the supplies organized within easy reach. Kody was wiggling around while I changed him, but he wasn't crying.

He was a really cute baby. He was kind of chubby with big, impossibly blue eyes. At first glance, he looked almost bald, but he had a soft layer of blond fuzz on his head.

When I really studied him, I realized that he looked a lot like Sid. He certainly had Sid's coloring. He didn't really resemble me at all. It set my mind at ease a bit. Maybe Kody really was Sid's baby and I could eventually learn to accept it. Things wouldn't be the same, but I'd been best friends with Sidney for years. I didn't want to lose that.

I finished diapering Kody and then picked him up. I was wandering around the room with him when I heard a door open from the back hall where our bedrooms were located.

Did Sidney have a girl stay overnight? How the fuck did he get lucky when he had Kody to take care of? No wonder he was in such a good mood. He had been busy fucking some girl when...

The girl walked out of his room. She was half-naked, dressed only in the Rolling Stones T-shirt I'd seen on Sid a thousand times, her hair was rumpled, and —

Holy Fuck!

"Kaylie!" I shouted in absolute shock. "What the fuck?"

"Bash." She looked up and stopped in her tracks. At least she had the decency to look embarrassed. "Don't yell like that. You're scaring the baby."

"What the absolute fuck is going on here?" I growled out.

Kaylie's eyes narrowed. "None of your damn business."

She placed her hand on her hip and glared at me. Unfortunately, that only highlighted the fact that she wasn't wearing anything else under that shirt. Fuck me, now I'd need some brain bleach to obliterate that image.

Sid must have heard the commotion because he came out of the kitchen. The fucker looked guilty as hell. If I didn't have Kody in my arms, I probably would have tackled him to the ground right then and there. I was about to explode with anger.

He looked at me pleadingly. "Nothing happened. She just stayed over to help with Kody."

"In your bed? Naked? You took advantage of her, you asshole," I ground out between my teeth.

Sid winced.

Kaylie gasped.

"He did not take advantage of me! It was mutual; I wanted him to fuck me." Defiance burned in her eyes.

Goddammit! Steam was about to burst from my ears. I was so pissed, I couldn't think straight. "Get some damn clothes on. I'm taking you home."

Her face had turned bright red, and she was shaking. "No. You don't get to tell me what to do. You're not my father. I'm an adult. I can do whatever I want and I can fuck whoever I want."

God, I wanted to strangle her.

Kody began to cry so Sid came over and took him from my arms. As he was grabbing Kody, he squeezed my arm hard enough to break through my angry haze. He spoke only loud enough that I could hear. "Nothing happened, Bash."

I looked into his eyes and saw the truth there. It took a few seconds for everything to click. If nothing happened, then Kaylie was winding me up for some damn reason. Probably because I'd come on too strong when I suspected the worst. Didn't she realize she was playing with fire? I would have killed Sidney if he'd touched my sister.

I took a deep breath and turned to her. "Kaylie, I know you're an adult, but I just don't want to see you get used or hurt by some dickhead."

Her eyes flashed. She was still pissed. "So you're saying that Sid is a dickhead? He's your best friend."

"No." I glanced over at Sid. He was watching our argument intently. "But I know Sid. He's got nothing to offer a girl like you. You need someone who will treat you right. A guy who's committed and caring. Someone who's respectful. And responsible."

I tried to answer as tactfully as possible, but Kaylie just rolled her eyes at me. "Maybe I'm just looking for a one-time fling. A quick fuck."

"That's not who you are, Kay. And you'd only get hurt." Sid was no longer watching me. He looked defeated; his shoulders slumped, and he was looking at the floor. It surprised me that my words hurt him. It wasn't like him, and he knew what I said was the truth.

"I hate you! You're such a hypocrite. Get away from me. I don't want to talk to you. In fact, I'm leaving so I don't even have to see your stupid face."

Kaylie was acting like a child, but I would be crazy if I pointed that out right now. She was angry and lashing out. She needed time and space to calm down, but I didn't want her to leave while she was still so pissed off at me.

"I'll walk you home. We can take Kody for a walk. Has he gotten out of this apartment yet?" I threw Kody into the mix hoping it would make Kaylie more amenable to the offer.

"I can walk home just fine on my own." She was stubborn.

"Yeah, but it would give Sid a quick break and let Kody get some fresh air. You haven't even tried out the fancy stroller we bought yet. The tags are still on it." I held my breath, hoping she'd give in.

Sid looked uneasily between the two of us. "I don't know. It's kind of chilly outside."

Kaylie's eyes softened when she turned her attention to him. "He'll be fine. We'll bundle him up."

She'd conceded. Now I'd start winning her back around, by setting up how Sid would get to the baby shower without him knowing. That would earn me points in her favor. "Oh, by the way, Ryder asked us to come out to the beach tomorrow to hang out. I told him we'd be there."

Sid's brow furrowed in confusion. "I can't hang out. What about Kody?"

"What about him?" I asked. "We'll bring him, of course. Ryder wants to see him."

I could tell Sid did not want to go.

Kaylie stepped in. "You can't keep him cooped up in this apartment for the rest of his life. And you haven't been out in days. It'll be good for you both."

With both of us working against him, he eventually folded. "Okay, I guess. But we can't stay for too long."

I took charge before anyone changed their minds. "Great! Kaylie, why don't you get dressed while Sid and I get Kody bundled up for our walk?"

Kaylie pierced me with a look. She knew exactly what I was doing, but silently went back into Sid's room to change.

Sid started changing Kody out of his pajamas and into a warmer outfit.

I began removing the tags from the stroller and positioning the carrier into it for our walk. "Dude, I'm sorry about all that. I lost my mind when I saw her come out of your room dressed like that and I jumped to conclusions."

"Nothing happened," Sid mumbled.

"I know. I know that you'd never do that to me."

Sid winced. I guess my mistrust hurt him more than I thought. "I don't think she liked how you pulled the big brother act on her. She's an adult. She should be able to make her own choices."

"I get it." Jesus, now I had to explain myself to Sid. Why wasn't anyone ever on my side? "I just don't want to see her get hurt. She might think she wants casual sex - she's been surrounded by it, which is my own damn fault - but it would end up hurting her."

Sid remained quiet.

"But, I think I underestimated her. She's too smart to get used like that. I just lost my head for a moment. That's why I want to walk her home. I need to apologize to her. Clear it up. It was a misunderstanding."

Sid was avoiding looking at me. Jesus Christ, he was just as pissed at me as Kaylie, like a little bitch.

I grabbed his shoulder to get him to look at me. "Like I said, I should have known better. You're my best friend. I trust you and I should have realized you would never take advantage of her like that. I messed up. I'm sorry."

Sid turned away. "Yeah. No problem."

♫♫♪♪♪

Kaylie bristled beside me as we walked Kody in his stroller down the sidewalk toward her apartment. The sun was out, but a stiff, cold breeze whipped about occasionally. Kody was bundled up tight, sucking on his binky. He seemed to enjoy the walk.

Finally, I broke the silence. "I'm sorry, Kaylie. I didn't mean to upset you."

She gave me the death glare. "You don't have any right to judge me."

"I wasn't judging you." Not really. I was trying to protect her.

She paused the stroller and turned to me. "So, the fact that I had sex with Sidney last night is okay with you?"

"Fuck no!" The answer was a little too emphatic, so I tried to even my tone. "Kay, I know you didn't sleep with him. I jumped to conclusions. I'm really sorry about that."

She resumed pushing the stroller again. "I really don't understand you, Bash. You're one of the biggest man whores I know. I've seen it with my own two eyes. Yet the idea of me having a little bit of fun sends you into a complete meltdown. So what if I'd had sex with Sid? Why do you care?"

God, she was going to kill me. I took a deep breath and tried to make her understand. "I care because I know his track record with women. You're too innocent for Sid. He would corrupt you. A girl like you needs someone like — like Charlie."

"Charlie?" she sounded outraged. "You know I broke up with him because he cheated on me?"

"What?" Shit, that was a terrible example.

"I caught him flirting with other girls at the place where he bartends when he didn't know I was there. Once that opened my eyes, I was pretty sure that he'd been more than just flirting on occasion."

"That bastard!"

"It's okay. After I dumped him, I wasn't even that upset. It made me realize that I never was that into him."

I never knew why Kaylie had broken up with Charlie. He just dropped out of the picture. How fucking self-absorbed was I? "What I meant is that you need a stable, committed relationship. Not a quick hook up."

"Your double standards are glaringly sexist. Men can have sex without a relationship with impunity, but emotional women will get their tender hearts broken."

"I'm not talking about all women, Kaylie. Obviously, I hook up with women who are only looking for fun all the time. That's just not you and that's okay. And guys like Sid would use you and leave you without blinking an eye."

We'd reached the concrete steps up into Kaylie's apartment.

"Bye, Bash. I'll see you tomorrow. Drop off your gift at my apartment, so Sid doesn't see it. I'll wrap it and bring it over to Grey's house. Be there about two o'clock and text me when you're five minutes away, so I can get everyone in place to surprise him."

"Okay, I will. And Kay ... I love you."

"I know." She sighed. "I think you're underestimating me, Bash. And, I think you're underestimating Sid."

She climbed up the steps and disappeared into the building.

Fuck, what the hell was that supposed to mean?

I turned the stroller and began walking back home. Within seconds, the binky popped out of Kody's mouth and he began crying.

I tried to pop it back in, but he wouldn't take it. He kept spitting it back out. His crying got louder.

What was wrong? I mentally went over the checklist. I'd just changed his diaper. He'd just been fed. He wasn't cold. We were outside - that was a definite change of scenery. What else?

I began singing. Twinkle, twinkle again. I needed to look up some new baby songs when I got home, but I couldn't think of any others under pressure.

Jesus, did he want to be held?

I unstrapped him from the harness and made sure he was wrapped up tight in the blanket before I lifted him out of the stroller. The moment he was resting against my chest, he quieted down. I positioned him so that I could securely carry him with one arm and he snuggled against me until his head was nestled into my neck.

"Okay, little man. It looks like you and I are going to take this stroller for a little walk."

I pushed the stroller along with my free hand the entire way back to our apartment.

Chapter 12

Sidney

"Slow the fudge down!" I growled to Bash from the backseat for the third time, but then immediately flashed a smile at Kody, who was buckled into his rear-facing car seat. It had only taken Bash 45 minutes of intense struggle to install it to my satisfaction this morning.

Bash let off the gas a tiny bit. "Slow the fudge down? What fudge are you referring to?"

I glanced out the window. "You know what I mean. Stop driving so fast."

He scoffed. "I'm not even doing the speed limit anymore. Little old ladies in minivans are passing me left and right. You're the one that made us late by stuffing every last diaper we had into the backpack for Kody."

"It's better to be prepared," I said in my defense. "Besides, who cares if we're half an hour late? It's only Ryder and Talia. They won't care."

I knew I was being a little obsessive, but I'd never taken Kody out before. Frankly, I didn't want to go today, but I'd been ganged up on and overruled. It was true; I couldn't remain holed up in my apartment forever, but it felt like I could keep Kody safer there.

So far, Kody didn't seem to mind the car ride. He was awake, but not crying. These past few days, I'd been figuring out all kinds of little tricks to keep him happy, but the main thing I'd learned was that he was always content when he was in my arms. Just picking him up would stop his cries. What would I do if he started crying now? I felt a trickle of anxiety when I thought about it.

"So I guess Ryder is officially shacked up with Talia at Grey's house now that you've kicked him off Knox's couch?"

"I didn't kick him out," Bash grumbled.

I shouldn't rag on him too hard. After he'd walked Kaylie home yesterday, he left to practice drums for a few hours. He came back home and showered, and then shocked me when he ordered some takeout dinner for us. He ended up spending the night at home, a Friday night, hanging out with me and Kody. Then this morning, he was up at nine o'clock, helping me with Kody again.

I wondered if it had anything to do with what happened yesterday with Kaylie? I wasn't angry with him because he'd jumped to conclusions and didn't trust me. Shit, he probably shouldn't trust me; I wanted to fuck his sister so badly.

I was pissed — no, make that upset — that he'd reaffirmed everything I didn't want to hear. That I was no good for Kaylie. That she deserved more than I could give. But just because I didn't want to hear it, didn't mean it wasn't true.

My mood had soured since that conversation. "We're only staying for two hours, tops."

"Okay. Just try to relax and have a little fun. You've been a real pain in the ... butt lately."

We were both getting better about not cursing in front of Kody, but fudge, it was hard.

When we got to Grey's house, there was just enough room in the driveway behind Ryder's truck to park the car. Bash's driving skills had never bothered me before, but I was a nervous wreck with Kody in the car. It was nice to climb out of the backseat and stretch my cramped legs.

I unbuckled Kody from the car seat so that I could hold him instead of lugging him inside the house in the carrier. I told myself that it was because Kody would feel more secure in my arms, but I think I needed him more than he needed me. He helped calm me.

Bash grabbed the bags of shit we'd brought for Kody. "They texted us to just come upstairs."

We entered the house and then began the ascent to the third floor, where the main living space was located. I crested the stairs and...

"Surprise!"

The top floor was packed with people yelling 'Surprise!' while a few party horns went off.

What the fuck? I was surprised, that's for sure. I looked around the expansive space that contained all my closest friends and noticed the decorations — blue balloons and crepe paper streamers everywhere, an enormous 'It's a Boy!' sign and tons of baby-themed items scattered about. A giant pile of presents wrapped in gift paper was stacked up in the center of the open space.

The shout of surprise had startled Kody, so I rocked him gently in my arms and gave him a quick kiss on the head while I tried to work out what was going on.

Immediately, the girls began crowding in on us, cooing at Kody and trying to get their hands on him. Lacey was begging to hold him, but I'd just gotten him settled and was reluctant to give him up. Bash must have read my resistance. He took Kody from my arms and began showing him off to the girls. He led them away like a pied piper toward the couches.

I watched after them, hoping Bash wouldn't let Kody be passed around when Knox stepped over and punched me on the arm. "Hey, don't worry, mate. Bash will take care of him. How are you doing?"

"What's going on here?" I looked around as my other bandmates came over to say hello.

Knox laughed. "This is your baby shower, ya eejit."

"Somebody get this man a beer. I think he could use it," Ghost joked.

I didn't want to drink when I was taking care of Kody, but I guessed one beer wouldn't hurt.

Greyson congratulated me next. He had become friends with Talia when Ryder still owned the house next door. Greyson Durant was a famous actor, known for his long-running role as Colton Grimaldi on the hit series, *Devious*. He spent most of his time at his house in West Hollywood, so he'd generously rented his house to Talia when she needed a place.

I shook his hand. "Wow, Grey, thanks for hosting this party at your house."

He smiled. "I didn't do anything. It was all Talia and Kaylie, but I'm happy to have it here."

Ryder came over with a bottle of beer for me. He pulled me into a bro hug and spoke low so only I could hear. "I almost died when Talia told me. Shit, man. We'll talk later. But, dude, we've all got your back."

Damn, this was almost too much. I was starting to feel a little mushy.

Our manager, Donovan, barreled in next and introduced me to his girlfriend. I didn't pay much attention to her because girlfriends never lasted long with him. This one wore a super-short and super-tight dress that did nothing to downplay her enormous tits.

Donovan didn't bother to lower his voice at all. I'm sure the entire party heard his booming voice calling me out, "Fuck, Sid. You dipshit. What the fuck were you thinking? How many times have I told you boys about this? Well, fuck, we'll figure it out. We'll talk on Monday, yeah?"

Donovan wandered away, with his girlfriend trailing close behind him. I stepped further into the room to see if I could spot Kody through the throngs of people milling about, and I almost bumped into someone.

It was Kaylie. Yesterday, when I'd last seen her, she'd been spitting fire; she was so mad. She'd been dressed in my T-shirt and nothing else, and I imagined sliding my fingers up the silky skin of those long, sexy legs.

"I hope this has been a good surprise?" she asked nervously.

I nodded. "Yeah. I heard I have you and Talia to thank for it. How did you do all this so fast?"

"I'm a woman of many talents." She laughed.

Oh God, I wish I could sample all of her talents.

She leaned into me and spoke softly. "I only invited your close friends and they all know to keep their mouths shut about this. You don't have to worry about this getting out into the media."

"I know. Thanks. I guess I couldn't hide him away forever. I don't really want to, anyway. And, everyone's been so great about this—"

"Except for Donovan. I heard what he said. Just ignore him, the jerk." She was outraged on my behalf. It was cute.

"That's just Donovan."

Talia swooped in and gave me a kiss on the cheek. "How is everything going with Kody? You hanging in there?"

"We're surviving."

She laughed and then turned to Kaylie. "Sorry, Sid. I have to steal her away. I need help with setting up the first game."

Games? What kind of games were played at a baby shower? Talia whisked Kaylie away, and I caught sight of Tommy heading my way.

Tommy was the drummer for Cold Fusion, an enormously popular band right now. He had a sick mansion somewhere up near Malibu. I couldn't believe he came all the way here just for me. He had two kids, the youngest wasn't even a year old yet.

"Congratulations, Sidney!" He slapped me on the shoulder. "I remember when Roxy was born; it was crazy, but these past few years have been the absolute best of my life."

I blinked a few times in disbelief. Was I hearing right? This was coming from Tommy, a legendary womanizer in the rock world. The funny thing was, I could glimpse the truth in his words. Kody had already filled a giant hole in my life that I didn't even realize existed. He'd only been with me a few days and already I wasn't sure I could handle it if he was taken from me.

Contrary to what Tommy suggested, these days weren't the best of my life. I was too sick with worry about things like Kody's paternity, about possibly dropping out of the band to care for him, and about losing Bash as a friend. All this anxiety was burning me up.

He patted me on the back reassuringly. "You look skeptical, brother. But listen, it's all going to work out. I've got two little ones, and it takes some juggling, but it's doable."

"Yeah. I guess. Thanks." I pasted on a smile, but it felt false. I wouldn't have someone like Livvy at home watching the kids while I went on tour. Our situations were different. I was a single dad.

The other guys crowded in around us. I was handed another beer. It was like any other day. Everyone acted the same as they usually would. It was like this enormously big thing hadn't even happened to me. It was the same as ever, but I felt a distance growing between us. I had changed. As I stood there sipping my beer, I wondered how long I'd have to endure all the stupid dad jokes before I could go check on Kody.

I didn't have long to wonder, because the party games got started. First, there was a 'Guess the candy bar' game. Candy bars were melted into a diaper to look like a pile of messy shit. I'd seen enough of the real thing in the past few days, so it didn't gross me out, but by the moans and facial expressions of the others, it was pretty nasty. Ryder ended up winning that game. His licking of the melted chocolate was accompanied by the ear-splitting shrieks of the girls, but when he won a spa gift basket, their horror turned to jealousy.

The next game was a guess-the-baby food game. I'd finally managed to get Kody back and was feeding him his bottle, so I just watched. It was a good thing. From the gagging faces everyone made, the food must have tasted horrible. Marie won a coffee-themed gift basket for winning that contest.

Despite the noise of the party, Kody was getting sleepy as he finished off his bottle. While the party got even rowdier with a beer chugging out of a baby bottle tournament, I settled Kody down for a nap in the middle of Grey's king-sized bed and surrounded him with pillow barricades, so he would be safe, even though he was too young to roll over yet.

I sat watching him sleep for a few minutes before I rejoined the party. Tommy's wife, Livvy, was running around the room doing a victory lap. From looking at the chart hung on the wall, the tournament brackets all filled in with winners, I could see that Livvy had already chugged five beers. She was visibly wasted.

The final round of chugging from the baby bottles pitted Livvy against Greyson. There was no contest. Livvy's success sucking the baby bottle resulted in Tommy having to endure lewd jokes about his allegedly small dick size, but he handled it stoically. Tommy was so chill; nothing ever seemed to phase that guy. When Livvy won a set of fancy massage oils, Tommy was not complaining.

As the guest of honor, I got to go first in the next game. It was called 'bobbing for nipples'. A galvanized steel tub was filled with water and probably a hundred of the silicone nipples from baby bottles were floating in it. I thought it'd be easy, but the nipples were damn slippery. In one minute, I'd only snagged six nips.

Marie was next, but she didn't want to get her face too wet, so she only managed to snag two. Livvy was too drunk. She practically drowned herself, so Tommy cut her off early. Sadie was surprisingly good; she snagged 13 nipples. I'd thought she would be the champ, but in the end, Ghost won with 15 nipples.

This had been a crazy baby shower so far, so when Ghost won a basket full of vibrators, I could only chuckle. Much to the girls' delight, Ghost distributed them amongst all the girls like some kind of perverted Santa Claus.

I was sitting on the couch, nursing my second beer while the majority of my friends were drunk or high. Most of the party had moved out onto the deck overlooking the ocean. Normally, I'd be right out there with them, but it didn't feel right anymore. Not with Kody relying on me.

No one seemed to notice my absence. Well, maybe Lacey did. Suddenly, she plopped down on my lap. I moved my beer to the side to accommodate her.

Lacey was the female equivalent of me and Bash — always up for a good time. She never let emotions or feelings get in the way. She owned her sexuality and felt no shame about it. I liked that about her.

We'd met years ago at a party when Ghost Parker had first settled in L.A. She was always the life of the party. Guys wanted to fuck her and girls wanted to be her. She drew attention wherever she went. She was a fearless girl, yet good-hearted.

Soon after we'd first met, Bash and I had a threesome with her. There wasn't a shy bone in her body, and if she wanted something, she went after it. Did I mention she was smoking hot? She had a body built for sin. The encounter had been sexually perfect in every way. Everyone had left, extremely satisfied. It had been the greatest sexual experience I'd ever had.

There had been no awkward parts. It was nothing like the disaster that must never be spoken about. The diametric opposite of that catastrophic threesome — the one everyone always teased us about. Thank God they didn't know the complete story. I'd only let the concept of what happened slip one time when I was drunk while we were on tour. Their teasing was bad enough, but if they knew everything, we'd never be able to live it down.

With Lacey, it was nothing like that. The sex had been mind-blowingly amazing. Incredibly, there had been no awkwardness when we ran into her after. I began to think in my head that maybe she was the perfect woman.

Then one night, months later, she arrived with her posse of girls at a nightclub Bash and I were hanging at. Bash was making moves on a girl that I had no interest in. As usual, all heads turned and eyes were glued to Lacey when she arrived. She could have had her pick of any man at the club with a crook of her finger. I stealthily watched her for a few minutes.

When I glanced over at Bash, he caught my eye, lifting his brow. I knew that look. He was silently asking me if I wanted to team up and have a threesome with Lacey again — to relive that amazing experience. I knew that if I nodded yes, he would drop the girl he was with within a heartbeat.

I shook my head no. He stared at me quizzically for a long beat and then went back to flirting with the girl.

I ended up having sex with Lacey that night, solo. I wasn't sure if that had been my intention all along. We went back to her place, and I used every tool in my repertoire to satisfy her. The sex had been extreme. And extremely good. Probably one of the top two experiences in my life, the other being the threesome with her and Bash.

After hours of fucking, I lay next to her in bed, waiting for my body to recover so we could do it again. That's when I realized I didn't want to. I didn't want to fuck her again. I felt no connection with her. It was an odd feeling, like I was floating around untethered. No connection was exactly what I wanted. Right? The longer the strange feeling persisted, the more confused I got. I panicked.

I bolted from the bed and started getting dressed without a word of explanation. Why did I have to explain? Lacey knew the drill. She knew what this was. I told myself that she didn't need her hand held as I took my leave. I couldn't even look at her, let alone speak to her.

I couldn't get out of there fast enough.

The next time I saw her, she marched right over to me. As I mentioned, she wasn't a shy girl. She demanded to know what the hell happened. I mumbled some lame excuse along the lines of 'Sorry, I just wasn't feeling it.' That was the only time I'd ever seen any vulnerability on her face. It lasted just a microsecond, but it was there. I'd hurt her. I'd hurt the tough-as-steel Lacey.

Since then, I'd gone out of my way to be kind to her. I even considered us friends now, because sometimes we had actual meaningful conversations when we ran into each other.

Today, without a second of hesitation, she hopped onto my lap, her tits right up in my face and leaned over to whisper in my ear. "Jesus, Sid, my ovaries damn near exploded when I saw you holding that precious baby."

Her ass pressed near my cock and she was wiggling to get comfortable. Her perfume enveloped my senses. Nothing. My dick felt nothing.

I chuckled. "Keep those damn ovaries away from me, Lacey. I've already got myself into enough trouble."

Her feminine laughter rang throughout the room. Her lips lingered right next to my ear. I knew exactly what those same lips looked like wrapped around my cock. I knew exactly how talented they were. Still nothing.

I grabbed her arm gently, trying to stop her endless wiggling. She practically purred in response. She was definitely tipsy. Sometimes, when she wanted to, she gave off the image of a bimbo, but she was anything but. She was smart as hell, perceptive, and loyal to her friends to a fault. Somehow, despite my missteps with her, I'd been deemed one of her friends.

I wished that I could feel something more for her. We couldn't be more sexually compatible. She'd expressed how much she'd liked my cock, and I know she hadn't been faking all those orgasms. She'd gushed about my skills when we were in bed together. It should have been a boost to my ego, but instead, I'd gone from sexual nirvana to needing to escape.

I had realized that I didn't love her. Since when had that ever been any kind of consideration before?

Her hand rested against my chest and brought me back to the present. "You really don't know who the baby mama is? That's pretty crazy."

Crazy was one word for it.

I felt it before I could answer Lacey. Eyes resting on me. I couldn't ignore it even if I tried. I glanced up from Lacey's tits and looked across the open space into the kitchen. Kaylie was watching us. Her face was perfectly neutral, but I still felt like I'd gotten caught doing something despicable. I looked away quickly, but not quickly enough. Lacey had noticed. As I mentioned, she was no bimbo; she was perceptive.

Lacey stiffened in my arms. "Oh, my God! Is it Kaylie?"

"What? No! God, no!" Her accusation shocked me, but I managed to chuckle in what I hoped sounded like disbelief, not nervous laughter.

She studied my face. "Now, that would be a problem. An epic problem, Sidney. Look me in the eye and tell me it wasn't Kaylie."

This time, I really did laugh. Her theory was preposterous. "Haven't you seen Kaylie a bunch of times over the past year? Did she look even the slightest bit pregnant any of those times?"

"True," she conceded. "I've seen her in form-fitted dresses. There's no way she was hiding a pregnancy."

"Plus, there's the important fact that I've never fucked her. She's Bash's little sister, for fuck's sake." Hopefully, that would make her drop the subject.

"Hmm. Still, something is going—"

I didn't give her time to finish her sentence. Instead, I lifted her up off my lap. "I've got to go check on Kody."

"Fine!" she huffed. "I think it's time to open presents, anyway."

Chapter 13

Kaylie

I was throwing out some empty beer bottles in the kitchen when I looked up and saw Sid. It felt like someone punched me in the stomach. Lacey was sitting on his lap, getting comfortable. They might as well have been going at it right there. Hurt, jealousy, and anger all came roaring to life, making my heart thud heavily. When Sid caught me staring, I quickly looked away. How humiliating.

I didn't have time to examine any of my runaway emotions because Talia came into the kitchen and started rummaging through the cabinets. "Hey, why don't you join us on the deck? Knox is going to do the cinnamon challenge. Apparently, none of the guys use social media, because none of them have any clue what it is. Knox thinks it's going to be no problem to swallow a spoonful of cinnamon. This is gonna be so good. You don't want to miss it. "

Avoiding her glance, I said, "I'm just cleaning up a bit. I'll be out in a few seconds."

"Found it!" Talia pulled out a small glass bottle of powdered cinnamon from the shelf and then grabbed a spoon from a drawer. "Don't worry about cleaning up. Grey is having a cleaning crew come in tomorrow."

"Okay."

Suddenly, she paused and turned to me. "Hey, I'm sorry. How are you doing with all this?"

I shrugged. "I'll be fine. No biggie."

"We haven't had time to talk. I'm busy with Ryder tomorrow, but let's set up a time sometime this week to chat. Okay?"

I smiled weakly at her. It was all I could muster. "That'd be great."

Talia skipped off. When I glanced back at the couch, it was empty. I scanned the area; Sid was nowhere to be found, but Lacey was heading my way. Shit.

I wanted to gauge her eyes out, but my anger was misdirected. Lacey was just being Lacey. If only I could be more like her.

She circled the giant kitchen island until she was next to me. "Are we ready to open presents yet?"

At this point, I just wanted this shower to be over. "In a few minutes. Thanks for helping me with the party games, by the way."

"Sure, no problem. It was nice of you to throw this baby shower for Sid." She casually leaned her hip up against the island.

"I wanted him to know that all his friends support him."

"Uh-huh."

"And he needed a lot of stuff for Kody." I tacked on lamely.

"What's going on between you and Sidney?"

My eyes narrowed at her pointed question. A flush of anger heated my skin. "Did Bash say something?"

She was watching my reactions like a hawk. "Why would Bash say something?"

Shit. Now, I'd unwittingly confirmed something. It was best to give her a piece of the truth before she jumped to conclusions. "Oh, you know." I brushed it off like it was nothing. "I stayed over at their apartment to help overnight with Kody, and Bash came home in the morning and went ballistic. He made some dumb accusations that were the furthest thing from the truth."

Her eyebrows raised. "It pissed you off."

"Well, yeah," I confirmed. "He should butt out of my love life. It's none of his business."

"Your love life with Sid?"

"No! Jeez." I spluttered my denial. "I just told you. Nothing happened! God, Lacey. Stop."

"You're in love with Sid." She said it quietly.

I shot her a disdainful look. "Are you crazy? You must be drunk or high. Or both."

She wouldn't back down. "It's written all over your face."

My heart was beating triple-time. "Please, this isn't funny."

"I'm not laughing."

"La-cey," I hissed. It was an urgent plea for her to shut up.

"Listen, hon." She put her hand on my arm. "I'm like a steel trap with secrets. Once they go in, they never come out. Have you ever heard me spill any secrets? And, believe me, I know them all."

Lacey had never spilled any secrets to me, but then again, I didn't know her very well. I did know her friend, Kristi, one of her girls, folded like a cheap suit the minute she was pressed for any information.

My hand crooked on my hip in challenge. "I recall you mentioning a few details about a certain threesome you enjoyed."

My stomach twisted; I almost barfed just thinking about it. I'd been on the outskirts of their group, a girl's night out, drinking cocktails when Lacey dropped the bomb that she'd had a threesome with my brother and Sid. The sour taste of bile filled my throat, and I thought I'd vomit right in the middle of the circle of gossiping girls.

She was praising their innumerable skills and waxing poetic about the x-rated experience. Multiple orgasms. Jizz everywhere. The massive size of their dicks.

Then she'd looked up. 'Oh shit, Kaylie, I forgot you were there.' She had the grace to look embarrassed. 'You probably don't want to hear about your brother. You look a little ill. So sorry, babe.'

Her eyes widened. "I remember that! I assumed that when you looked like you wanted to slit my throat and hurl at the same time — it was because of Bash. Now I know! Oh, honey, I'm doubly sorry. I never would have intentionally thrown that in your face. I had no clue. Kaylie, I think of you as a little sister."

I couldn't keep my frustration bottled. "God, why does everyone say that? Little sister. Like I'm a kid."

"Well, you're younger than this crew. And you give off an innocent vibe."

"I'm not that young." My retort sounded petulant.

"You're much younger than me. How old are you?" she asked.

"Twenty-three."

She nodded like my answer had confirmed everything. "Well, I'm thirty-one. Don't tell anyone."

"What?" I was surprised. "I didn't realize. I thought you were maybe twenty-six. You look so young!"

She was even older than the guys in the band. I had no idea.

"Yes, I'm thirty-one years old and I've never been in a significant relationship with a man. They don't seem to want anything more from me than my body."

That couldn't be true. I thought it was more likely that she chewed up men like a shark and then spit them back out like they were poison.

She laughed bitterly. "I'll let you in on a little secret about myself since I know your big secret. The lifestyle that might seem like heaven in your 20s can turn hellish later in life. People change. They want different things."

What the hell was she trying to tell me? That she wanted something deeper than just casual sex. That her happiness was all an act? "You're looking for a relationship?"

She laughed at the absolute incredulity on my face. "Has hell frozen over? Is it that hard to believe?"

"So, you and Sid?" A sorrowful pit formed in my stomach at the thought. Were they together? Was she Kody's mother? Oh. My. God.

She must have seen the panic in my eyes. She held up her hand. "First, let me tell you there is nothing at all between me and Sid. I like him. Maybe more than like him. But he has made it clear that he is not interested in me like that. It's a tough pill to swallow. Yes, I actually do have feelings. I've been hurt by men, but if you tell anyone, I'll have to kill you."

I breathed a sigh of relief. I couldn't imagine Sid settling down with any girls. But, Lacey? That might kill me. "I'm sorry, Lacey. I know how it feels. Believe me."

She nodded. "I hope we're still friends, Kaylie."

"Of course." She had been friendly and kind, almost like a big sister. She didn't have to reveal all that to me.

"When I was over there sitting on his lap ... It just proved to me that I had no chance with him." The corners of her mouth twitched into a faint smile, but it didn't reach her eyes. "I think he's interested in someone else."

She turned and left the kitchen.

I was sitting on the couch sandwiched between Talia and Knox. Sid was sitting center stage, with a goofy paper plate hat on his head laden with bows and ribbons. Every time he opened a new package, the girls added more to the hat until it couldn't hold one more tiny ribbon. Now they were just sticking the stuff directly to his body. The first two bows got stuck to his T-shirt right above where his nipples were, of course. He was being a good sport about it all.

Surprisingly, the boys had all gathered to watch. The gift opening was always the most boring part of a baby shower, but most of the guests at this shower were completely loaded at this point.

I'd spent some time on the deck and I'd seen more than just booze passed around. I had an interesting conversation with Ghost while we both admired the sunset over the ocean. He asked me questions, each one stranger than the last, like he was checking off questions from some kind of bizarre survey. After I told him all about my waxing routine (he asked), he checked his phone and then thanked me. It was weird.

I had a chance to talk to Greyson while I was out there. Talia always encouraged me to speak to him about acting parts. Networking was the name of the game in this business, but I felt intimidated by him. He was super successful, a Hollywood megastar, on top of being indecently handsome. Talia had told me that he was also very nice, but I couldn't fully believe it. Apparently, on the day she met him, at her behest, he spoke on the phone with her old roommate back in Ohio because she was a big fan of his. It turned out that Greyson was a genuinely nice guy. He promised to keep me in mind if he heard of any promising acting leads for me.

That alone should have brightened my mood, but I was like a sulky teenager. My emotions were all over the place.

I was antsy. It was taking Sid a long time to open all his presents. He didn't even know what half the gifts were. He received everything a baby could need: a swing, bouncy seat, diaper pail, high chair, monitor, sound machine, exer-saucer, bath, playpen, diaper bag, and tons of tiny baby clothes. The boys of Cold Fusion banded together and purchased furniture for the baby. According to the brochure, which was wrapped up in a cute box, it included a gorgeous-looking crib with a matching dresser and changing table, a rocking chair, and a bookcase.

As soon as Sid opened all the gifts, I retreated to the kitchen. I needed space. I didn't even know what was going on in my head anymore. After the talk with Lacey, I worried that I really was in love with Sid. Could it be true? Did I even know what love was? Even if it was true, it was the stupidest thing in the world. How could I let myself be so dumb? God, it couldn't be true.

I was just in lust with him. That was the mantra running through my head.

Puttering around the kitchen, pretending to be cleaning up, I half listened to Lacey announcing the next activity. She explained to the group that there was some old wives' tale that every comment Sid made opening the gifts was actually a comment that was made at the time of Kody's conception. Sadie had been taking notes as Sid unwrapped the presents, so Lacey was going to read out the results.

I'd heard this at a few baby showers before. The subtle innuendo would have all the grandmas in the audience atwitter. It was all silly fun. Until I heard the comments.

Lacey read out the usual comments that got a few chuckles from the crowd:

This is fucking awesome.
This looks like fun to play with.
How does this work?
What do you do with this?
I've never seen one of these before.
What is this thing?
What does it do?

Sidney even hammed it up when the size jokes started rolling in.

It's too big.
I'm not sure we have room for this.

I turned my back on the nonsense. This wasn't real. Nobody had said those things on the night Kody was conceived. Why was I getting so upset? Why was I swallowing down a lump of sadness in my throat?

It just hammered the point home that Sid had sex with someone that night. He'd had sex with lots of someones in the past, but that time was different. He'd been intimate with someone and created a new life.

It brought back all the shock and disappointment I'd tried to bury and fused it together into the confusing jumble of mixed feelings I had toward Sidney.

While everyone else was drunk and carrying on in the other room making sex jokes, I was holding back tears. I saw Lacey glance my way, and I knew I had to escape before she came to check on me. One sympathetic word could start an avalanche of tears.

I quietly ducked into Grey's bedroom. Kody was still napping on the bed. Someone had set up the brand-new baby monitor and placed it near Kody, so I had to be quiet. No blubbering for me.

I sat on the bed, listening to the muted sounds of the party going on in the other room, breathing in and out, trying to get my emotions under control. Watching the little guy gave me some peace. I felt calmer.

I'd been sitting for less than 10 minutes when the door opened. Sidney slipped inside the room.

He didn't look surprised to see me in here. "I just wanted to check on him."

Stupidly, I replied, "he's still sleeping."

"Thank you for this baby shower. I appreciate it so much. I heard it was all your idea. You've been a great friend, Kaylie."

Friend.

Just what I didn't need to hear right now.

It was like a pat on my head. Good girl.

God, I couldn't take this anymore.

I stood up. "No problem." I scrambled out of the room and shut the door behind me. I couldn't get away from him fast enough.

♫♫♪♪♪

The party was starting to break up. I'd seen Sid emerge from the bedroom with Kody earlier, but I'd avoided being anywhere near the two of them. Tommy had already left much earlier with a drunken Livvy. Donovan was heading out the door now with his girlfriend. I was desperately looking for a ride home.

Lacey had just announced that she had a party bus coming to pick us up and take us first to a swanky restaurant north of here overlooking the ocean and then out to hit some nightclubs.

I did not want to party tonight. I was too busy throwing myself a big pity party. There were times, if I was a little down, that I could drag my butt out the door, have a few drinks with friends, and forget my troubles. I could shake my booty, flirt outrageously with strangers, and shake the doldrums. Tonight was not one of those nights. It could only lead to ugly crying, bitter confessions, and drunken regrets. Hard pass.

I had to lie to Bash that I had work in the morning to get out of going. It was easier than spending energy that I didn't have, convincing him that I wasn't in the mood to party.

I told him I would call a cab. He knew it would cost a ton of money and was trying to give me his credit card. I was pretty broke, but I was arguing with him on principle when Sidney said from behind me, "I'll drive her home."

Bash looked up and smiled lopsidedly. "That's right. You've got to take Kody home. You can bring Kaylie home, too. Perfect!"

He might as well have said, 'Take the kiddies home to bed while the adults go out to party.'

"No," I said a bit too forcefully. "I can get myself home."

Bash scrunched his brow. "Don't be silly, Kay. Sid's heading that way."

"It's no problem," Sid added. "Actually, you'd be doing me a favor. You could sit in the back and watch Kody while I drove."

I had no good reason not to go with him. I knew I wasn't going to win this battle without looking either ridiculous or making Bash or Sid suspicious.

We packed up Bash's car with some of the smaller presents with Ryder promising to deliver the rest tomorrow in his truck. It took us forever to get home. Who knew that Sid drove like such a granny? We didn't speak at all. I kept busy playing with Kody, trying to keep him occupied, so he wouldn't fuss.

Sid parked in the parking garage down the block from their apartment where they kept their car. He asked if I could take Kody into his apartment and watch him while he made a few trips back and forth to unload the car. I couldn't decline without seeming churlish.

He entered the apartment with the last load. "Would you stay for pizza? I'm going to order."

I grabbed my purse, ready to bolt. "I've got work tomorrow."

"It's not late. C'mon, eat with me," he pleaded. "You have to eat dinner, right?"

I suddenly didn't want to go back to my empty apartment on a Saturday night. Yeah, I was giving myself emotional whiplash. Even I could recognize how foolish it would be, but being alone with Sid and Kody was comfy. I couldn't turn it down any better than an addict could turn down their number one choice of addiction.

I put down my purse. "Okay. I'll stay."

Sid put the baby swing together while we waited for the pizza delivery. After we ate our pizza, between the two of us, we got Kody fed, his diaper changed, and him dressed in his pajamas. We placed him in the baby swing, where he rested contentedly for a while before drifting off to sleep.

I was sitting on the end of the couch, my legs tucked up underneath me. Sid was on the other side of the couch, his head resting against the back of the cushion, his eyes closed and his long legs stretched out in front of him. He looked so achingly beautiful; his hair was tousled and a five o'clock shadow dotted his face. It was a rare moment to unobtrusively admire his incredible physique — the dips and planes of his well-toned muscles that were obvious even through his shirt.

When he opened his eyes and turned his head, his intense blue eyes fixed on me and my stomach lurched in reaction. With one look, my body was on fire for him.

He pinned me with his gaze and spoke quietly. "Today was amazing, Kaylie. I don't think anyone has ever done something so nice for me."

I looked away. Here I was absolutely drooling over him while he was trying to toss me firmly into the friend zone again. God, I was such a fool. I stood up abruptly. "I've gotta go."

"Wait." He sat up straight. "What's wrong? Are you mad at me?"

I was such a baby. Why couldn't I control my damn emotions around him? "No. I'm not mad at you."

"Something's wrong with you. You were mad at me at the shower, too. Please, just tell me what I did. Are you angry about what happened here the other day with Bash?"

"No," I denied. I sat back down. "Well, I'm not mad at you. I was angry at Bash. He really gets on my nerves sometimes. I mean, he of all people has the nerve to lecture me about casual sex?"

As predictable as rain, Sidney jumped to Bash's defense. "He's just trying to protect you."

I held up my hand. "Please, don't you start too. I'm mad that all of you treat me like a little girl. A helpless, fragile little girl. I'm not. Despite what my brother thinks."

"It's not like that," he protested. "No one thinks of you as helpless or fragile. We respect you. We all think of you—"

I didn't let him finish. "—like a little sister. I know you do, but guess what? I'm not your sister."

He ran a hand through his messy hair. "I know."

Time to push the boundaries a bit. "If I had sex with you..." I hesitated a moment. I didn't want to give too much away, and he looked shocked by my suggestion. "Or with Knox, for example," I hastily tacked on. Sid's shock was quickly replaced with anger. "Would it be so bad? Would Bash really care? Is it at all any of his business?"

"Of course!" he replied a little too adamantly. "You're his sister."

I slumped back against the couch cushions. "It's just so annoying! I sometimes wish he didn't live so close to me. Brent was never like this with me."

Sid pulled at the collar of his T-shirt. "Brent is a nice guy. He just assumes all guys are like him. They're not, and Bash knows that."

"No, that's not it. Brent just trusts me more."

We were both quiet for a few minutes.

I turned to look at him. "Do you remember when we played that game 7 minutes in heaven?"

"Yeah."

"Did you ever tell Bash about that?"

He cocked an eyebrow. "Of course not. He would've killed me."

"You didn't even know it was me though!"

"But you did."

I grinned. "Yeah. I knew."

He returned my smile. "Why didn't you tell me?"

"You wouldn't have kissed me if I did."

The smile melted from his face. He was staring at my lips maybe even remembering our kiss.

"What if we kissed again?" I inched closer to him. "Bash never found out the first time…"

My words hung in the air.

"Kaylie…"

I moved even closer. "How would he ever find out? I'd never tell him."

"It's a bad idea." His voice sounded scratchy.

Now my gaze was locked onto his mouth. My tongue dipped out and wetted my lips. "I was only 15 when we kissed. I wonder if it was just a fluke? Or was it really that good?"

He pressed back against the couch. "You don't really want this. You're just trying to stick it to Bash."

My eyebrow arched. "Don't tell me what I do or don't want. Maybe

I want to give casual sex a try. Who would be better to try it with than you? Someone I trust."

He shook his head. "You shouldn't trust me. I'm no good for you."

"No?" I tapped a finger to my chin like I was thinking. "Maybe I'll ask Knox, then."

That got his attention. He growled like an angry animal and then grabbed my arm. The kiss was all sorts of fucked up.

Angry. Brutal. Dominating. Possessive.

It lit up every pleasure center in my body like the fourth of July.

I was utterly lost. In big, big trouble.

Our first kiss was no fluke.

Suddenly, I did feel like a little girl, one who was playing with fire. I was going to get burned. Hopefully, I'd go out in a blaze of glory, because there was no turning back from this.

When I came out of my kiss-induced haze, Sid's hands were wrapped around the tops of my arms, literally holding me back.

I stood up on shaky legs, but the next line I delivered was worthy of an Academy Award. "Maybe I *want* to have sex with you, Sidney. Have you ever thought about that?"

I heard him groan as I made my exit.

Chapter 14

Bash

I ROLLED MY SUITCASE over the bumpy industrial carpeting in the hallway until I got to the door of my apartment. Sid hardly ever left our place now that he had Kody, unless I forced him to; he was practically a hermit — so I was pretty sure he'd be home.

I'd just gotten back from spending three days at my parent's house in Georgia. Since our new tour dates still hadn't been announced and Donovan hadn't been busting our balls about rehearsal, I decided it was a good time to visit back home. My parents had been after me to visit for a while.

I even spent a night out with my brother, Brent. Picturing the sizzling nightlife of Atlanta, I asked him to line up a fun night of partying. What I got was Brent bringing me to some local pub where we met up with a few of his work buddies.

Despite the slim pickings, I ended my no-sex streak of two days by hooking up with a cute southern honey pie that I met at the pub. Too bad she shared that shit all over her social media. She didn't post any covert dick pics, thank God, but she did snap a picture of my clothes scattered all over the floor. The hell? Along with a selfie that she snapped when she'd been sitting on my lap as proof that the clothes belonged to me. Of course, she had a prolific social media presence, so locally, that shit had spread like fire. Luckily, there'd been no nudity posted, because, yep, my mother had seen it, and I had to endure a long and ridiculous sex lecture from her.

I loved my mom and dad, but living with them was stifling. It was good to be back in L.A. I fumbled in my pockets until I located my keys and then unlocked the door.

It was quiet inside; Kody must be sleeping. It still shocked me every time I came home how different the place looked now. Baby gear crowded every nook and cranny, but today the place was picked up and clean. The nasty carpet had been ripped up and a new hardwood floor had been installed while I was in Georgia. I'd already seen the new couch, but a few side tables with actual lamps on them and a new coffee table resting on a colorful area rug made the space look more grown-up. And, shit, we had new curtains.

It even smelled different. No longer did it smell like a week-old party all the time. I could detect some weird baby scents — baby powder? — and some kind of bakery scent, sort of like fresh bread.

I plopped down on the couch and put my feet up on the new coffee table. I'd been traveling since early this morning and it wore me out.

I could hear Sid in the kitchen at the sink. I called out, "Yo, my parents say hi."

My parents didn't know about Kody — I couldn't tell them, especially after that excruciating sex lecture from my mom. I'd planned to, but could never get the words to come out of my mouth. I didn't even tell Brett. My motives were selfish even if I told myself that I was protecting Sid, in case things didn't work out. The crazy thing was what Sid and I thought of as things working out were two entirely different things, but I willfully ignored the warning signs that flashed in my brain. I felt like I was standing on train tracks and disregarding the vibrating rumble below my feet. I shook my head to clear it. The less I thought about the Kody situation, the better.

The water shut off. A few seconds later, Sid came out of the kitchen.

Except it wasn't Sid.

It was a little old lady.

Wielding a butcher knife.

What the fuck?

She was shooting me a death glare. Her voice was shrill. "I already called the police, so you better get your ass out of here before I stab you ... repeatedly."

My heart was racing. Who was this psycho? And where were Sid and Kody? Were they okay?

I held up my hands in a placating manner. "Whoa. Who the fuck are you?"

She waved the knife around. "There's nothing here to steal, you deranged meth-head. Now get the fuck out!"

This woman was off her rocker. The knife looked sharp, but she was barely five feet tall and looked about eighty pounds. I was sure I could handle this tiny grandma from hell. "Steal? I fucking live here, you demented old bat. I'm glad you called the police so they can haul your ass to jail."

"You live here?" She looked dubious. "What's your name?"

The immediate answer that came to mind was 'None of your fucking business,' but I bit my tongue. After all, she was still waving a knife around. "Sebastian Archer. Who are you?"

"We'll get to that in a minute, Sonny. You don't look like Sebastian; you look like a homeless person. Do you have any ID on you?"

I hadn't shaved in a few days, and I'd been traveling all day. True, I didn't look my best, but hardly like a homeless person. I thought about refusing to prove myself and waiting for the police to show up and take care of this old bird, but since she was staring me down while brandishing a knife, I reached into my pocket and removed my wallet.

"Hold it. Just toss the wallet over here so I can see your ID. And keep your hands where I can see them."

Grumbling, I tossed my wallet onto the floor in front of her. She picked it up and made a big show of looking back and forth between my driver's license photo and me.

"I guess it is you. You must photograph well. The real you isn't quite so impressive. Yeah, I know all about that Photoshop." She sniffed derisively, finally lowering the knife.

I took a deep breath. This wacko was really starting to piss me off. "Now that that's all settled, who the fuck are you?"

She placed her free hand on her hip. "Get your darn feet off the table and take off your shoes. I don't need you tracking your filth all over the place."

A headache was coming on. I pulled my feet off the table and then, one by one, took off my shoes.

"That's better." She looked me over like I was a piece of shit she'd found smashed on the bottom of her old lady sneakers. "I'm Josie. Kody's nanny. And you're Sebastian, A.K.A. Bash, the absentee roommate. I've heard all about you."

I groaned. This was the woman Sid picked to take care of his son? Holy hell. "Where's Sid?"

"At the grocery store. I can't spend all day yammering with you, I'm busy. Kody's sleeping, so don't make any noise." She marched herself back into the kitchen.

About a half-hour later, Sid found me on the couch. I hadn't moved a muscle. I was too tired to even take a shower and even though I was so thirsty, there was no way I was going into the kitchen with the evil nanny in there.

I tried to rub the sleepiness from my eyes. "What were you thinking, Sid? You picked a fucking psycho nanny to watch Kody."

Before he could answer, we heard a shout from the kitchen. "I've got good ears. I can hear you, little drummer boy."

I rolled my eyes. Fuck, she was annoying.

"Dude, she said she called the police on me. They never showed up, so I guess that was just a lie."

"Had him soiling his britches." Another shout from the kitchen.

Sid had the nerve to laugh at that. "She's an amazing nanny. Kody loves her."

"He's a fucking infant. He doesn't know any better." I rubbed my temples when he didn't answer. I lowered my voice so she couldn't hear me. "Did you ever see that movie? The Nanny or something? This won't end well."

He brushed off my words. "How are your parents doing?"

"The same," I answered. "Just happy to see me. Brent was boring, as usual. They asked about you."

His lips turned down in a frown. "Did you tell them about Kody?"

"No."

Something flashed across his face. Disappointment, maybe. Was he disappointed in me? In himself? Both of us? I didn't fucking know, and it didn't sit well with me.

He tilted his head, looking like an eager puppy. "You sticking around for dinner?"

I looked warily towards the kitchen. I was about to make up some excuse, probably pathetic, when Sid cut in.

He mumbled under his breath. "She leaves at five o'clock."

I glanced at my phone to check the time. If I hauled my ass in to take a shower, she'd be gone by the time I was out. I could do that.

"Yeah, I'll stay."

Sid smiled at that and then sat down on the other side of the couch. He looked happy that I'd decided to stay. Maybe he was missing hanging out with me as much as I missed him. It wasn't as awesome as a night of clubbing and hooking up, but having dinner and watching TV was better than nothing, and I was too tired to track down entertainment for myself.

Sid tapped his fingers on his leg. "Hey, the baby furniture is being delivered in a couple of days. Do you think you could help me? I'm going to have to move some stuff around to fit it anywhere. I'm not even sure where to put it all."

Just as I had begun to get that familiar happy feeling of being around my buddy, a pit of unease sunk deep in my belly.

I vaguely remembered that the guys from Cold Fusion had bought Sid baby furniture for his shower present, but I hadn't been paying close attention. "What do you mean by furniture? A crib?"

He listed out the items as he ticked them off on his fingers. "A crib, dresser, changing table, bookcase, and a rocking chair, I think."

"Where the fuck is all that going to fit?"

"I don't know. I was hoping I could use your room." He paused for a moment. "For some of it. Since you're not there that much anymore."

Fuck! Panic was gripping my insides. "I still pay the fucking rent, Sid. This is still my home. Fuck, do you want me to move out?"

His eyes widened. "No. I want you to stay. I want you to be here. But you don't want that anymore, do you?"

"Of course I do!" The words flew out of my mouth, but they lacked conviction.

"Then why are you never fucking around here anymore?"

He fucking knew why. I clenched my jaw so hard, trying to keep from lashing out at him. Instead, I spoke carefully. "What am I supposed to do, Sid? Huh? Sit around in this apartment with you day after day staring at the fucking walls? You never leave. You never go out anymore. You've sacrificed everything for Kody, including your friendship with me. And I get it. I do. But I don't think I can just sit here and hold your hand while you stew in misery."

"You're wrong." His words were a snarl of rebuke. "Being with Kody is not miserable. It's better than endless parties and fucking girls whose names I don't even know."

He didn't know how much his words stung. I'd taken a backseat in his life and I'd slowly come to accept that. But this felt different. Like he was pushing me out the door. I didn't fit anymore.

Abruptly, I stood up. "I gotta get a shower."

Out of the corner of my eye, I saw the nanny from hell fading back into the kitchen. I'd forgotten about her. She'd been listening to our entire conversation. Great. She was probably sharpening her knives right now.

I stopped by Kody's crib and peered down at him for a moment before striding down the hall to my room.

Chapter 15

Sidney

MY LIFE WAS FALLING into a predictable routine. During the week, the new nanny, Josie, showed up at 9 o'clock in the morning on the dot. Then, I rushed off to the studio and immersed myself in music. The hours at rehearsal were my only escape from baby duty. I had to be home by 5 o'clock every evening because Josie didn't like to be out after dark. Or anywhere even approaching dark.

During the evenings, my sole focus was Kody. Caring for him wasn't too difficult anymore. It was the lack of uninterrupted sleep that was killing me. Getting up every two to three hours all night long messed up everything. Some days, I felt like I was just sleepwalking through life. I was tired and moody all the time. My brain felt like it had shrunk — basic math seemed too complicated to attempt. I'd even noticed that I'd gained weight, because I didn't have any time to work out anymore.

Every once in a while, Kody slept for a four-hour stretch. I'd get excited he was sleeping longer, but then he'd punish me with a bunch of two-hour intervals in a row.

So, it wasn't surprising that even though it was only 9:18 p.m. on a Saturday night, I could barely lift my head off the couch pillows. Kody had just fallen asleep. He probably wouldn't be up until around midnight. It'd been all baby, all day for me with no respite. My brain was mush. Maybe I could watch some TV or play a video game? Or, I could get some much-needed sleep. All of those options seemed like too much work right now — even dragging my tired ass into my bedroom.

Bash had been staying at Knox's, but he showed up here from time to time, usually to hang out and watch TV. I know he deliberately stayed away when he knew he might bump into Josie. Those two were like oil and water. They did not get along. Bash was still pissed that I didn't choose a hot nanny. Josie was in her sixties, but she had been the best choice to take care of Kody by far. She was a sweet, cookie-baking grandma, but Bash somehow brought out a sassy streak that consisted of biting sarcasm and acid-dipped criticisms directed only toward him.

And she called him 'little drummer boy'. That did not go over well with him.

But Josie had been a God-send to me. While I was busy in rehearsal with the band, Josie took exceptional care of Kody. I told her right away that I had nanny cams all over the apartment. She waved that off, saying she didn't care. I was pretty obsessed with checking those cameras. At first, it was to make sure Josie was treating Kody right. Now that I knew she was, it was mainly to get a peek at him while I was gone. Just seeing him brought a feeling of inner peace and happiness to me.

When I returned home, the apartment would be cleaned up, mine and Kody's laundry folded and put away, the dishes done, and dinner cooking in the oven. I had no clue how she managed it all.

When I'd protested her making dinners for me, she claimed it was easier for her to cook on the clock while I was paying her. She would make a meal and then carve out a portion for herself to take home and heat.

This week, especially with Bash missing and Donovan absent, our rehearsals had been ending early. I'd been getting home at two or three o'clock, but Josie refused to take off early. Since I was paying her for the time, she'd stay. Instead, she'd started teaching me how to cook.

Her husband had died years ago, so she was used to cooking meals for one. She was showing me simple meals that were delicious and more nutritious than the thrown-together crap I'd been eating. She'd started giving me grocery lists, and I was more than happy to comply.

On top of all that, she was just amazing with Kody. In the short time that she'd been with me, she'd patiently taught me everything I needed to know about caring for a baby — everything from figuring out how to strap him into that sling contraption to giving him a bath. She'd even come with me when we took him to the pediatrician her daughter used for a check-up and vaccinations after his blood titers let us know where he stood.

She wasn't the hot nanny of Bash's dreams, but she was worth more than her weight in gold to me and Kody.

Today, Bash had shown up around noon. He forced me out of the house; we ended up spending a few hours walking Kody around the park. There wasn't too much we could do with a newborn.

I was trying harder with Bash after we had an argument earlier in the week. I knew I was harboring some resentment toward him, but it wasn't something I wanted to examine too closely.

He half-heartedly tried to get me to go out with the band tonight.

He suggested I leave Kody with a babysitter so I could get a break and hang out. There was no way I was going to leave Kody with some unvetted person I'd never met. It wasn't up for debate, and Bash must have known that. He gave up pretty easily.

My friends were probably all gathered together somewhere, pre-gaming before they hit all the trendy local nightspots. I didn't necessarily miss the boozing, the drugs, or the girls, but I did miss my friends, and I missed adult company. I missed feeling a part of the group.

Would Kaylie be out with them tonight? I wasn't sure, and I certainly couldn't ask anyone.

What did it matter? I doubt she was sitting at home feeling sorry for herself like I was.

It had been more than a week since I'd seen her. Since that kiss. Fuck, I couldn't stop thinking about her or replaying that crazy kiss in my mind. What she'd said about wanting to have sex with me, I repeated in my head over and over.

I knew she was playing a game. She was mad at Bash for interfering in her life. Kaylie was just being sassy; she had no idea how much she affected me. That one playful, teasing line kept me up nights lying awake, wishing I could have her.

God, I was hosting my own damn pity party. I grunted my disgust. Instead of stewing in misery, as Bash had called it, I forced myself off the couch and grabbed my acoustic guitar.

I liked messing around on my acoustic. The first Christmas I'd spent with my foster mom, Shari, was when I'd gotten my very first guitar. I'd been still settling into her place, not trusting any of it yet. Playing the guitar had been a refuge; I'd bring it up to my bedroom and shut the door. I spent hours fooling around with it, experimenting with the different sounds it could make.

YouTube was still fairly new, but I voraciously consumed any video I could about guitars: how to tune them, take care of them, change the strings, and of course, how to play them.

When my interest didn't wane, Shari set me up with lessons. When I found out that the kid next door played the drums, it was only a matter of time before we became best friends. Our first performance was just me on the acoustic and Bash on the drums at our middle school talent show.

It wasn't until years later that I started playing bass. We were starting a group and didn't have a bassist. I picked up a bass guitar and never looked back. Sure, it was like learning a brand new instrument and I had to practice my ass off to be any good, but when the sound from my bass merged perfectly, bridging the rhythm and melody of the song, the feeling was sublime — like pure drugs surging through my veins. An unbelievable high.

But, when I picked up the bass, I craved perfection. The acoustic was reserved for relaxing. Playing with sound. Clearing my head. There were no expectations of making awe-inspiring music. I just played.

My fingers started plucking chords, and I knew what they itched to play, but she was someone I wanted to keep firmly out of my head. I ignored the itch and started playing an old standby I loved to play, *Wild World*, by Cat Stevens.

I transitioned into another favorite, *Give A Little Bit*, by Supertramp, but after a while, it felt like I was singing to her. Pleading with her. Fuck. My hand slapped the strings to stop the sound.

I took a deep breath and stroked the strings until they produced the familiar opening to *Wish You Were Here*, my favorite Pink Floyd song to play. But, goddammit, that sounded just as needy as *Give A Little Bit*. Fuck, I was getting all uptight when I just wanted to relax.

It was useless denying it. I closed my eyes and strummed the guitar, filling the air with music that was bursting to get out of me. It was the song I wrote about her. The song I was still writing. The music was as familiar to me as breathing. I'd composed the melody years ago, but the lyrics were always evolving.

Yeah, the original lyrics contained thinly veiled language referencing blowjobs and sex, and I admit I still liked singing those lines. But over the years, I'd added more nuanced lyrics. Lyrics about yearning and forbidden desires added a depth that still surprised me.

Like a broken record, I played that song over and over. I made little tweaks here and there, trying out fresh sounds, but mostly I just poured my soul into it each time. I played until Kody woke up at midnight. After I fed him and he went back to sleep, I picked up my guitar and played it some more. I played it for hours, trying to exorcise the thoughts from my head. Trying to exorcise her from my head.

It was the song I'd written about Kaylie.

Chapter 16

Kaylie

I hadn't seen Sid since the baby shower — since I'd goaded him into kissing me. Again. Just like I had in the closet when I was 15. How freaking desperate was I?

Desperate.

I needed to see him badly. I couldn't get that kiss off my mind. Our first kiss hadn't been a fluke or the imagining of an inexperienced teen girl. There was just something so delicious about him — something that my whole body responded to. The kiss hadn't quenched my thirst for him at all. It had exploded it.

My real-life sexual experiences were pretty vanilla, but in the past two weeks, my fantasy sex life had been unleashed. I craved Sid so much that I diligently blotted every utterance of opposition coming from my logical brain and convinced myself that casual, no-strings sex was what I wanted. The question was: how did I get Sid to give it to me?

It was going to take some work to break down his barriers.

First things first, I needed an excuse to see him. I'd been toying with the idea of stopping by his place to return his T-shirt — the one I'd been wearing to bed every night while I imagined him doing dirty things to me. It didn't even smell like him anymore, but I'd rather barge into his apartment in my birthday suit than give up that T-shirt. I had to think of another plan.

When I got off the bus at my stop, my feet started walking toward Sid's apartment instead of my own. Stupid feet. I didn't even have a plan. It was just past three o'clock. I knew from Bash that the boys had been ending their rehearsal sessions early. It had concerned Bash, because things didn't feel like the usual lead-up to a tour. Bash couldn't wait to get back on tour with the band, but I absolutely dreaded the day they announced the new tour dates. It was coming soon, so I didn't have much time to work out a seduction plan, assuming Sid was still going on tour with them.

I could always drop by and say I wanted to see Kody. The plan was good enough. I wasn't looking my best, but I didn't think I could let another day go by without seeing Sid and finding out what was going on with him.

I used my key to get into the building but knocked on the door instead of barging right in like I had the last two times I'd been here.

"Who's there?" I heard the muffled voice on the other side of the door call out.

That must be the nanny. Did that mean that Sid wasn't even home? Maybe rehearsal had run later today.

"Hi. It's Kaylie. Is Sid there? I wanted to check in on Kody..."

The door swung open. A short, gray-haired woman eyed me up and down. "I'm Josie. Kody's nanny. C'mon in."

I stepped inside.

Josie closed the door behind me. "We don't get many visitors here. Heck, this place is like a ghost town. My mother-in-law gets more visitors at the nursing home."

I laughed. "This place used to be party central. Sid scared them all away."

"Kody just went down for a nap. He's in the portable crib if you want to take a peek."

There was nothing more peaceful than a sleeping baby. I gazed down at him. "He's getting so big. Wow!"

She stood beside me. "He's a very happy baby. Sid's a good father."

I nodded, not knowing what else to say.

"Sid texted me that he's stopping at the grocery store. He should be back soon. Come sit and keep me company while we wait. Do you drink tea? I made some German coffee cake, but I'll warn you now, it has a lot of raisins in it."

How could Bash call this woman an old battleaxe? She was the sweetest thing ever.

"Sure, I'd love some."

I sat at the kitchen table while she bustled around making tea and serving us each a slice of cake. When she finally settled down at the table with me, I took a bite of the spongy cake. "Wow, this does have a lot of raisins in it!"

It was loaded with raisins. I would consider it a pure raisin filling at this point.

She had a wicked gleam in her eye. "Yeah, Sid really likes raisins."

"Oh, my God!" I slapped a hand to my mouth and giggled. "And Bash hates raisins. He detests them."

"Oh?" She pretended to act all innocent. "I didn't know."

"No?" I wasn't buying it.

"Oh, hell." She dropped her act. "He picked out all the raisins from the first cake I made. You should have seen his face when he took a bite of this one."

Josie was showing a little spunk. I liked it.

She tapped her fingers on the table. "So, you know Sebastian doesn't like raisins? Hmm. I was thinking those green eyes of yours reminded me of someone..."

"Yeah," I confirmed. "I'm Bash's sister, Kaylie. But don't hold it against me."

She took a sip of her tea. "You're the little sister, Kaylie? The one who threw the baby shower for Sid?"

"That's me." I sighed.

"Sid mentioned you a few times. He's lucky to have such a good friend."

I grimaced for a moment before pasting on a fake smile, but I was pretty sure nothing got past Josie. I mentally shook myself; an aspiring actress should be able to mask her emotions better. "I've known Sid since I was 8 years old. He moved in next door to us when we were kids in Georgia. He and Bash have been best friends forever."

Josie leaned towards me. "Do you know the rest of the guys in the band? What is it ... Ghost Poker?"

"Ghost Parker." I couldn't help but laugh. "Yeah, I know them."

"Are they all as hot as their pictures?"

Not what I was expecting. "Uh, yeah. They're all really hot."

She lowered her voice like she was imparting a secret. "I'm trying to work out a way I can meet them all. I want to get a selfie picture with each of them to make my granddaughter jealous."

I set down my teacup. "How old is your granddaughter?"

"She's fourteen. When I told my daughter and granddaughter that I was working for a rock star, they didn't believe me. I even showed them a copy of the NDA I'd signed, but they thought I was pulling their legs; I've got a track record doing that. So, I had to get a selfie picture with Sid for proof. He didn't mind and said I could even post it on my social media. He just told me not to tell anyone that I was working for him as a nanny. I guess he's trying to keep Kody out of the media."

Subtly, I tried to remove a few raisins from my cake. "It's for the best. The media spotlight can be cruel."

"Yeah, I've been following Ghost Poker all over the world wide web. I even set up a few fake accounts so I can make comments. I like to rattle Sebastian. It's the most fun I've had in years."

Interesting. Bash wasn't kidding. Josie had it in for him, but she was giving him hell just for kicks. Oh well, I wasn't about to spoil her fun and clue Bash in. "I'm not sure Bash looks at any of that. Their manager takes care of all their social media accounts."

Josie wasn't deterred. "Did you know there's a site dedicated to Ghost Poker's-" she leaned forward and whispered, "penises?"

Eew. "I know, but I'm pretty sure a lot of those pictures are fakes. It's some kind of twisted competition that some groupies and jersey chasers get into. They chase after any type of celebrity and post dick pics on the internet for their own slice of notoriety and sick validation."

She waved off my explanation. "Nah. I'm sure the one that bends to the right really is Sebastian's penis. He gives me such a dark scowl whenever I hold up my finger and crook it slightly."

I stopped chewing and had to force the mouthful down my throat. "Gross! Can we not discuss Bash's private parts?"

"Sorry, honey. I forgot — he's your brother. That was over the line." She patted my hand. "How about Ghost? He tickles my fancy. If I were ten years younger..."

Ten years? Okay, I had to take it back. Josie wasn't quite the sweet grandma I thought, but she certainly was hysterical. "Ghost has a lot of experience if you know what I mean. He's probably good in the sack."

Her eyes opened wide. "Ooh, a real Lothario. Good to know! And Ryder?"

"He has a serious girlfriend."

"Drats. I wouldn't mind a little afternoon delight with him, that's for sure. Knox?"

I smiled, warming up to her little game. "His accent melts panties. And, he's sweet. But, also, a big-time player."

Josie sighed. "Yeah, he's on the list."

I arched an eyebrow in question. "The list?"

"Oh!" She looked at me guiltily. "Just the selfie list, dear."

"Uh-huh." I tried to keep my lips from smiling.

"And Sid? Does he make you want to drop your panties?" She eyed me keenly.

My face heated. "Jeez. He's your employer! Let's not talk about him."

"Ah-ha!" Her fist thunked the table. "I thought I detected something before, but now I'm sure. You're smitten with Sidney."

I looked at her dumbly. Or was I just playing dumb?

"Smitten," she repeated. "Enamored. Head over heels. You're in love with him."

"No," I denied. "He's like a big brother to me."

She scoffed. "No, he isn't. You're a terrible liar. Your eyes give you away."

"Okay." I took a sip of tea. "Well, let's just say, I'm like a little sister to him."

"Then you need to open his eyes."

She made it sound so easy. "It's not that easy. Besides the age gap, I'm his best friend's little sister. And Bash is very overprotective of me. He's told his friends, including Sid, that I'm off-limits."

"Age gap?" she snorted. "How old are you?"

"Twenty-three," I answered.

"You're plenty old enough to know your heart. Hell, I was pregnant with my second baby when I was twenty-three."

"Tell that to Bash," I muttered under my breath.

She scooped up another bite of cake. "And Sidney? How old is he?"

"He'll be twenty-nine soon."

"That's six years. That's no age gap." Josie shook her head. "In the end, age doesn't make much difference. My husband was two years younger than me and yet he croaked on me when he was forty-nine. You never know."

"I'm sorry that you lost him, Josie."

She cut herself another slice of cake. "I'll always love him, but I still have a lot of years to live and I don't want to be alone during them. A woman has needs. I've had plenty of male company, so don't worry about me."

"I think Sid might be interested in me, but there's some kind of bro-code with Bash going on. He holds back with me when he'd hook up with any other woman in the world."

"And you're bowing down, meekly letting Sebastian stand in the way of what you want?"

"It's not like that." I tried to explain. "I hate to admit it, but I think Bash might be right in some respects. Deep down, I'm not a casual sex kind of girl. I want a real relationship with a man, not just good sex."

Her eyes lit up. "Good sex? So, you've had sex with Sid?"

"God, no. I told you he doesn't look at me like that." I paused a moment. "Well, he does sometimes, but he suppresses it, I think.

Unless I'm completely delusional and seeing things I want to see. But, he's the only man who's ever made me get that feeling — the butterflies in the stomach, the..."

"The tingles?" She provided helpfully.

"Yes," I agreed.

"Well, that changes everything. You can kiss a thousand frogs, but if one gives you the tingles, in my experience, he's the prince. It doesn't happen very often. It's a signal. I think of it as the spark when one soulmate recognizes the other. You shouldn't ignore it."

"I don't know about soulmates." I laughed nervously. "But, there's definitely physical chemistry there."

Josie propped her elbows on the table and leaned her chin in her hands studying me like a bug. "Why exactly are you not pursuing this? This is the 21st century, so don't give me that excuse about Sebastian not approving."

I threw up my hands. "He's not the type of guy for me. I mean, he's a rock star for goodness' sake. He's into the whole rock and roll thing — the drinking, the drugs, the kinky sex. He's into the entire lifestyle and that's not me. I'm boring."

She put down her teacup. "I haven't seen him do any of those things."

"That's because of Kody. Case in point, he has a baby. He's so freaking irresponsible."

"That's funny," she spoke quietly, "I would call him the opposite of irresponsible. He rearranged his entire life to take care of Kody without a moment's hesitation. He loves that little baby and he'd do anything for him."

I stared at her. Yes, Sid had changed a lot, but Josie hadn't seen what he was like before Kody. He would be back on tour soon. The booze and the women wouldn't be out of his life forever. He'd be back to his old ways of out-of-control partying and anything-goes sex or even the freaking group sex. And, that was the Sidney that I had to protect myself from. He was the one that could rip my heart out of my chest and shred it to pieces.

"He'll go back to his ways," I mumbled to myself. "I can't risk it."

Josie patted my hand. "That sounds like a recipe for loneliness. There's always going to be a risk with any man."

I balled up the napkin that I'd been picking at. "Yeah, but soulmates can damage your heart forever."

Of course, she had a rebuttal, but I didn't get a chance to hear it. Sid had returned home and walked into the kitchen, arms laden with groceries.

Josie hopped up from her seat. "Kaylie stopped by to see Kody, and she was kind enough to keep me company, but since you're home now, I'm going to head out and beat the rush hour traffic."

Sid stood frozen to the spot. "Kaylie. You're here."

Josie removed a Tupperware container from the refrigerator and then collected a canvas tote bag from the counter. "I left a chicken and rice casserole in the refrigerator with some broccoli for dinner. There'll be plenty for two people."

Josie sent me a pointed look before breezing out of the apartment. I hoped the whole disappearing act wasn't as obvious to Sid as it seemed to me.

Sid put the groceries down on the counter and began putting them away. "She usually stays until 5 o'clock even when I'm home early."

I hadn't seen him since I'd announced that I wanted to sleep with him. My cheeks heated as I glanced his way. This was pretty awkward. "We had cake," I blurted out.

"She has a bit of a sweet tooth." He pulled a tub of cream cheese and a box of graham cracker crumbs from his bag and showed me. "She's making cheesecake next. I swear I've gained ten pounds in the last few weeks."

"No! You look great!" It slipped out of my mouth. It was the response I'd have made to any of my girlfriends who were complaining about gaining weight.

His lips curled up smugly. "Thanks."

Jeez, I was nervous around him. I decided to let my comment go before I dug myself any deeper.

He glanced my way. "You want to stay for dinner? Apparently, there's enough for two."

"I have an audition tomorrow."

I wanted to kick myself. I'd come over here with the express purpose of seeing him. Now that he was here, I was ready to flee.

"You have to eat though. Stay and keep me company."

Our eyes locked, and suddenly my brain was scrambled. That invisible pull between us was as strong as ever.

Kody began crying.

I stood up, "I'll get him."

I escaped the room and lifted Kody from his crib. He stopped crying, happy to be attended to. I said my hellos to him and stroked his sweet head as I carried him over my shoulder into the kitchen.

As soon as he saw Sid, he began squirming against me and crying. Sid didn't hesitate, he took Kody from my arms and settled him against his chest.

"Let me put your groceries away."

Sid waved me off. "It's not a problem. So, you said you have an audition?"

I sat back down at the table and watched Sid. He was mesmerizing. He was so utterly masculine with his hard muscles and inked arms and yet he held Kody so tenderly, absently rubbing his back and dropping kisses on the top of his head as he put away the rest of the groceries.

He glanced my way, waiting for a reply. I had to get ahold of myself. "It's an open audition, so they'll be hundreds of girls there, but the part looks interesting."

I was always excited to go to an audition, but I reminded myself that the chance of landing the role was low.

"Do you have to memorize lines? Or practice for it? I could help."

Did he want to spend time with me? Or was he just being nice to me because of the baby shower?

"No," I answered. "I can't do anything to practice for it."

"So then you can stay for dinner." He said it like it was a fact. A done deal. I guess I really wanted to stay because I kept my mouth shut and nodded.

We spent the next couple of hours taking care of Kody. The time flew by. It was amazing how one tiny person could take up one hundred percent of our focus. I helped Sid heat our dinner and then we ate at the kitchen table while Kody sat contentedly in his carrier watching.

Without Kody occupying our attention, the conversation grew stilted. I searched for something to say.

"How's rehearsal going?"

He shrugged. "We're kind of half-assing it. We've got all the new songs down, so that's good."

"No tour dates announced yet?" I held my breath.

Sid finished chewing before answering. "The guys are worrying. Donovan contacted our label and our rep told us they're still working out the logistics for the tour. She said it was a little trickier this time since we're the headliners, but we aren't big enough to fill stadiums yet. They want tickets sold out at all the venues, so they need to amp up a lot of publicity first. They want our new songs out and climbing the charts. The business side of all of this is pretty intense."

"You said the guys are worried?" I know Bash was jonesing to get back out on tour, but I didn't know about the others.

"We're kind of in limbo. The guys feel like we're losing all the momentum that we built up. We recorded the album, but there's been no movement on it. Not even a release date. Luckily, we trust Donovan to figure it all out because we don't know what we should be doing. Right now, it's weird that he's not even getting on us about slacking off a bit with rehearsals, but I don't mind spending more time here with Kody every day."

"So what's going to happen when they announce the tour dates? Have you figured out what you're going to do yet?"

He was quiet for a long moment. I couldn't look at him. Suddenly, I was very interested in my chicken.

Even though I had no say in the matter, I knew what I wanted him to say. I wanted him to say that he wasn't going on tour. Whether he quit the band or got a temporary replacement, I didn't care. I just didn't want to be apart from him for another year. I didn't want him to go back to his old lifestyle.

It was a pipe dream. Even if he stayed behind for Kody, it's not like we were a couple. We were barely friends.

The talk with Josie had gotten me all worked up about soulmates and fairytale nonsense, but Sid didn't feel that way about me. It wouldn't be so damn easy for him to treat me like a little sister if he did.

"I'm not sure," he finally answered. "Every day that goes by without the tour being announced, I breathe a sigh of relief. I was thinking about asking Josie to go on tour with us. I'd lease my own bus, just for me, her, and Kody. If I cut out all the extra crap, the after-parties, and drinking, I could spend a ton of time with Kody. I would be like any other working father."

"You want to take Kody on tour with you?" My heart plummeted.

"I don't want to miss any time with him. And making music has always been my passion. Ghost Parker is so close to making it to the top, I can't quit now. I need the money to take care of Kody. If I quit, what could I do to provide for him? I don't know anything else." He looked agonized just thinking about it.

"What if Josie doesn't want to go?" I asked.

"I don't fucking know."

♫♫♪♪♪

Kody was sleeping, and it was getting late. I'd spent the entire evening with Sid and he hadn't given me a single sign that he was interested in being anything other than a friend.

There were no heated looks. No lingering touches. I knew because I couldn't keep my eyes off him.

Abruptly, he clicked off the TV. "You seem distracted."

"I'm sorry. The movie I picked is boring and I guess my mind keeps drifting." I kneaded the pillow in my lap.

"You've been quiet tonight." He looked at my wringing hands. "And nervous. Is it about tomorrow?"

"Huh?" Tomorrow? What was he referring to?

"The audition?"

I can't believe I'd forgotten about that. Still, it was a good excuse for my behavior. "Oh, yeah. That's it," I finished lamely.

"This has nothing to do with what you said to me after the baby shower? Does it?" He pinned me with his gaze.

Oh God, I felt like I was going to throw up. "What?" My voice shook. "I don't remember saying anything in particular. Must not have been anything important."

Please, just drop it.

"Kaylie, you said you wanted to have sex with me."

My face felt like it was on fire. "Uh, I don't remember. I must have been joking."

I had to escape. I scrambled off the couch, but Sid was quick. He was up in a flash and grabbed my wrist, halting my escape. "Are you sure it was a joke?"

The touch of his hand stopped me in my tracks. Suddenly, we were pressed together, body to body. I don't know if I'd pressed up to him or if he'd pulled me into him, but we were close enough that I was sure he could feel my trembling.

His hand which was resting on my hip pulled me against him, and I whimpered.

He leaned down and whispered in my ear. "I haven't stopped thinking about what you said. Or that kiss. I can't get you off my mind."

A fire ignited in me.

His words. His silky voice. His lips so near my ear. His hard body pressed against me. I was drowning in sensation. My soaked panties were a testament to my arousal.

He tipped my chin with his fingers so I had to look up at him.

"Fuck, Kaylie," he groaned.

His fingers slid underneath my hair and onto the back of my neck and then he was kissing me.

Possessing. Demanding.

I was lost to that kiss. Consumed. He must have been holding me up because my knees had gone weak.

When he pulled away, I opened my eyes. His eyes were half-lidded and dark with lust. He looked like a predator ready to pounce.

"Fuck, I don't want to stop."

"No." I shivered. Desperation tinged my next words. "Don't stop."

For a moment, I thought he was going to do just that. He held back.

My hands which had been uselessly hanging by my sides jumped into action. They encircled his waist and locked together like I was latching onto a lifeline.

He let out a low rumbling growl and then captured my lips again. It was a slower kiss. Sensual. Drugging.

Then his lips were exploring the shell of my ear, my neck, and my collarbone arousing a frenzy of need so carnal and deep within me.

A strange mewling sound escaped my lips when a hand slid beneath my shirt.

His lips brushed against my heated skin. "Tell me to stop Kaylie."

It was a command, but I couldn't obey. I was too far gone, mindless with want. I pressed harder against him, needing to feel the proof of his desire for me.

When his hand slipped down the waistband of my leggings and into my panties, I sagged. His fingers slid between my folds and stroked my clit a few times before they sunk inside me.

"You feel so good, Kaylie. So wet and tight." He moaned and then added, "You're going to kill me."

I was vaguely aware that I was clinging to him, shaking like a leaf and making strange noises. An orgasm was rushing at me so fast that I couldn't breathe. I was tipping over the edge. He moved his fingers, and that did it. I was coming hard. I couldn't stand; I couldn't think. I couldn't do anything.

He withdrew his fingers quickly. "Holy fuck."

I was still coming down from the most intense orgasm I'd ever had when he scooped me up and carried me over to the couch.

He held me in his strong arms. That's where I fell asleep almost immediately — warm, safe, and cozy on his lap.

That's also where I woke up hours later. The afterglow of the amazing orgasm had worn off and panic set in.

Sid was sleeping. I had to get out of there before he woke up. He'd been so surprised when I orgasmed. No wonder, he had kissed me and then barely touched me and I'd gone off like a fireworks show.

It was embarrassing. That had never happened to me before. I acted like a complete virgin around him. The last thing I wanted him thinking was that I was an inexperienced little girl. I'd gone and proven that I was everything I pretended not to be around him: young, way more sexually inexperienced than him, and just plain vanilla compared to what he was used to.

And right before I had fallen asleep with my ear resting on his chest, the rumble of his voice roused me enough to hear his whispered regret, "Oh God, what did I just do? Fuck!"

I couldn't face him. I didn't want to hear him tell me how sorry he was. Or what a mistake it was. Or give me any platitudes meant to let me down easy.

Mercifully, Sid didn't wake up when I climbed out of his lap and I was able to slink away like a thief in the night.

Chapter 17

Bash

I STARTED A BASIC drum warm-up, but I was barely paying attention to what I was doing. Ryder was messing around with his guitar, and Sid was still sipping his coffee. Sid had strolled into practice ten minutes behind me and Ryder, but Ghost and Knox still hadn't arrived. It was already after 10 o'clock, but we'd all been slacking for weeks. Our nine o'clock start time had slowly morphed into ten o'clock and now we weren't even starting to really practice until eleven.

Sid and Ryder were laughing at something when Donovan burst into the room like his hair was on fire.

He looked around the room. "Where the fuck is Ghost? And Knox? Christ, tell me they're here!"

Ryder shrugged. "They haven't shown up yet."

"Fuck!" Donovan tugged at the hair on the side of his head.

"Richard Diamond is on his way up."

I stopped tapping my sticks. "Diamond Dick? What's he doing here?"

Donovan shot me a look of warning. "Mr. Diamond." He looked at his watch. "Get Ghost and Knox here ASAP. I'm gonna kill them. Fuck! I'll try to stall Diamond Dick for as long as I can."

He scurried out of the room while Ryder picked up his phone to call our missing bandmates.

I'd met Richard Diamond only a handful of times. He was a bigwig at our record label, Black Vault Records. The entire music industry called him Diamond Dick behind his back, but no one would ever dare call him that to his face. He was so respected — or maybe he was feared — in the industry that he had the power to make or break musicians, even outside BVR.

Usually, we only worked with our BVR rep, so this must be something important. I hoped to God it had to do with starting our tour, but my stomach soured with doubt. This had to be something else. Something unusual for the big guy to appear in person. What if they were cutting us from the label?

My heart was pumping hard with nerves. I needed this tour. I'd been impatiently waiting for it to start up and I knew something didn't feel right. And now, Diamond Dick was here at our rehearsal space. Fuck!

Ryder put down his phone. "Knox can be here in 10, but Ghost is at least twenty minutes out."

I heard Donovan talking in the hall. They were headed this way. So much for stalling. "We better look busy."

Sid nodded and then picked up his bass. I started tapping a count on the drums and then Ryder eased in with a wicked guitar riff.

A few seconds later, Diamond Dick entered the room with Donovan hot on his tail. He motioned for us to stop playing and within seconds, the room was quiet.

I'd never seen the man in anything other than a bespoke suit with expensive leather shoes and a fancy watch on his wrist. All in luxury brands that I didn't know. I've heard of Armani, Rolex, and Salvatore Ferragamo, but Diamond Dick existed on a whole other level above those.

Besides his thousand-dollar haircut, luxury cars, and a frigging yacht, Diamond Dick was a good-looking guy. I'd seen him plastered all over the media with famous models and stars on his arm. He had power in this city and wasn't afraid to wield it.

He looked at each of us. "Where's the rest of the band?"

Ryder spoke up. "They should be here in about 15 minutes."

He scowled. "Time is money. This is sloppy, Donovan."

"I'm sorry, Mr. Diamond. Can I get you a coffee?" I'd never seen Donovan acting so obsequious.

"Kombucha." Ignoring us, he pulled out his phone and made a call. "Helen, push back my meeting with Griffin for thirty minutes. I haven't seen the contract yet either. Call me when it's ready."

Donovan stood in place, looking confused.

Diamond Dick snapped at him. "Get me a kombucha. I have to make some calls while I wait." He walked out of the room.

Donovan looked like he was about to shit his pants, so I threw him a bone. "Kombucha is some kind of healthy drink. Try the grocery store around the corner."

"Fuck!" Donovan groaned with displeasure. "Don't say anything stupid while I'm gone. And, for fuck's sake, make sure those two assholes get here soon."

The three of us looked at each other after Donovan left. After a lengthy pause, I spoke out. "What the fuck?"

Sid shrugged. "Who knows, man?"

He didn't look very concerned, and that pissed me off. He was probably hoping the tour got canceled. It would solve his Kody problem.

Ryder started pacing nervously. "This can't be good." He pulled the strap of his guitar over his shoulder and set it down. "I'm going to hit the bathroom. I'll check in with Knox and Ghost and see if I can hurry them along."

Sid set down his bass and then picked up his phone. He was undoubtedly staring at his nanny cam app, hoping to catch a glimpse of Kody. He couldn't go more than an hour without checking in on him.

"You think this is about the tour?" I asked.

Sid took a deep breath. "I don't know, but I'm not ready, man."

I knew. And it made me feel like a prick for wanting the tour, which would take him away from Kody. I knew this would happen. The longer Kody was around, the more complicated things would get. Even I was starting to feel guilty about the situation. I was questioning everything. I didn't want to, but even I was getting attached to the little guy.

Lightly tapping on the drum skins, I tried to release some of the nervous energy bottled up inside me. Sid was eying Ryder's acoustic guitar which was propped against the wall near him. He picked it up and began strumming. I knew playing guitar was a form of release for him, too.

It took about two beats for me to realize he was playing *Free Fallin'* by Tom Petty. My hands started moving on their own accord and soon I was accompanying him on my drums.

He played for about a minute and then stopped. He seemed lost in thought but then began playing something new. I listened. The song was familiar, but I couldn't quite place it. My hands began moving — my mind had already picked out the best beat to lay down a rhythm.

What was he playing? It finally hit me. It was the song Sid had been fiddling around with for years. Neither Sid nor I were big contributors to writing the music for any of the bands we'd ever been a part of, but Sid had been perfecting this song for years. I'd even occasionally caught him singing lyrics to it.

I adjusted the beat for the upcoming chorus, enhancing the melody with a driving pulse that gave it some dynamism. The song had a catchy melody that grew on you the more you listened.

I loved jamming with my band, and especially with Sid. We synched together better than any two musicians could.

Sid was completely lost in his song, but I wasn't. I noticed Diamond Dick's body filling the door frame. He stopped to listen to us play, no longer barking orders on his phone.

I wasn't sure what to do, so I kept playing. Sidney was backtracking in the song, making slight changes to the verses and experimenting with different bridges, but the chorus remained the same.

At some point, he noticed Diamond Dick watching. He strummed the guitar a few more times and then dropped his hand.

Dick stepped into the room. He was staring at Sid. "What song was that? What band? I've never heard it."

The man knew every song in existence and could identify most of them within a few seconds.

Sid shrugged. "It's nothing."

Dick's eyebrows drew together in confusion, which was an emotion I'd never seen him express before. "Is it a new band? Something not out yet?"

Sid scowled. "No. It's just something I fool around with for fun."

Dick's eyebrows rose. "It's something you wrote? What's it called?"

"Nothing," Sid grumbled.

I knew Sid considered the song personal, but we couldn't afford to piss off BVR. After playing the chorus a few times, those lyrics had come back to me. "It's called *Okay Babe*."

Sid shot me an angry look, pegging me as a traitor.

"There are lyrics?" Dick inquired.

Sid remained silent, so I spoke up. "Yeah. There're lyrics too."

"You wrote the whole thing, Sidney? No one else has rights?"

Sid grimaced. "I did, but it's not a song for Ghost Parker. It's just something for me."

Diamond Dick chuckled. "Right. Let me hear it again from the top. I want to hear it with the lyrics."

Sid looked mutinous. "I'm not the singer."

Dick's face grew hard. "Yeah, well, the singer isn't here, so sing it for me." He turned around to Ryder, who was standing in the hall behind him. "Ryder, jump in when you're comfortable. I want to see what you can add."

We played it for about ten more minutes, with Sid reluctantly singing the lyrics he'd written, making changes whenever Dick made suggestions. We stopped when Donovan came barrelling into the room, holding an armful of kombucha bottles. "I didn't know which kind you preferred."

Dick crossed his arms over his chest. "Donovan, have you heard this song, *Okay Babe*?"

Donovan's eyes flickered from me to Sid to Ryder. "No. Never heard of it."

We didn't get to hear whatever Dick was going to say about it because Ghost and Knox finally arrived.

Dick looked at his watch pointedly. "Glad you gentlemen could join us."

Ghost was the complete opposite in appearance to Diamond Dick. He was dressed in rumpled clothing, covered in tats, had a few piercings, and blond messy hair that hadn't seen a pair of scissors in forever. Despite the disparity in appearance, Ghost could more than hold his own with Dick. Ghost exuded a presence and a charisma that no one could overlook, not even Dick.

Ghost lifted an eyebrow. "What's going on?"

"My hellish day has just gotten a lot more interesting. That's what's going on. But now that we're all here, finally, let me tell you why I came."

Knox shuffled further into the room and stood next to Donovan, who looked like he might vomit. I held my breath, waiting for the man to continue.

"I've already wasted too much of my time, so I'll cut to the chase. *Labyrinth* and *Disintegrated* are both cut from the album." He spoke with an air of authority. "We chose two songs that were dropped that we want you to rework for the album. We're scheduling the studio time now. Plan on three weeks from now; I'll get back to you with the exact dates."

Ghost tipped his chin up. "They're both great songs. Everyone at BVR loved them. We finalized this weeks ago."

"Not everyone loved them and nothing is final until I say it is."

Ghost's jaw clenched. "*Labyrinth* was some of my best work. What the fuck is wrong with it?"

Dick picked a piece of lint from the sleeve of his suit jacket. "It's too deep, too poetic, and two minutes too long."

Ghost scoffed. "You mean it's not mainstream enough?"

"Exactly." He looked around the room at all of us. "This is non-negotiable."

Ghost was livid and Knox looked frustrated. Ryder hid his reaction well. I could understand how they felt because these songs were like their babies. Cutting them had to be hard. I didn't care as much about which songs made our album, but it disappointed me because this was sure to delay our tour. The only person who seemed unfazed by the news was Sid.

"Now for the good news." He paused for a long moment, commanding our attention. "Sidney has been hiding a hit song."

Sidney's head shot up. "What?"

"*Okay Babe*. I want a demo by the end of the week. Ghost, tighten up the lyrics. Keep the chorus simple and catchy, but clean up the verses. Sidney, I want you singing on backup. This is the one, boys."

Sid was scrubbing a hand through his hair. "But it's not a Ghost Parker song! It's not our style."

Diamond Dick chuckled. Excitement animated his usually stoic expression. "I'm going to put this in front of one of the biggest pop music producers in the industry. In his hands, this song is going to blow you away. We'll release it as a single. If I'm right, it'll climb the charts fast. We'll have to rework your tour to get bigger venues. This is it. You'll be richer and more famous than you ever imagined."

"*Okay Babe*?" Ghost muttered. "What the fuck?"

Dick smirked at him. "Yep. Get ready. It's going to be the biggest goddamn hit. You'll be hearing it everywhere. You'll be playing it everywhere, too. It'll be your cash cow, but you'll get so fucking tired of hearing it."

Ghost sighed. "I already am."

Chapter 18

Sidney

"Something smells delicious," I called out as I entered my apartment and kicked off my shoes. It was good to be home.

Josie was sitting on the floor next to Kody, showing him a rainbow-colored plush toy. They were doing tummy time, something that Kody only tolerated in small doses.

I plopped down on the floor beside them. "Hey, Kody. I'm home, buddy."

His head wobbled on his neck as he lifted it up off the mat for a few seconds to look in my direction.

"Did you see that? He lifted his head!"

I brought my face close to the ground and called his name, trying to get him to do it again, but he began crying.

"He's getting stronger every day," Josie said proudly. "But now he wants his daddy."

That word shot straight to my heart like an armor-piercing arrow. I wanted to be Kody's father more than anything in the world. I was his father. There was no denying the unbreakable bond we had. I shouldn't even question it.

But ... what if?

I scooped Kody up into my arms, nuzzling his cheeks with my lips, which never failed to make him smile. I offered my hand to Josie, and she took it and stood up.

"You want to leave to beat the traffic?" I asked.

"No. I'll stay till five o'clock." She checked the time on her watch. "The pot roast won't be done for another hour, anyway."

Josie cooked my dinner every weekday now. She provided the grocery list, I shopped, and then she cooked. She'd asked me to buy a crock pot since I didn't have one, so I ordered the best one I could find online. For days, she grumbled about it having too many buttons, but now she couldn't stop raving about it. I had to find out when her was birthday because I couldn't wait until next Christmas to get her one and I knew she wouldn't accept a gift without a reason.

In the short time Josie had been with us, she'd become more than a nanny to me. She was becoming a substitute mother. I still tried to speak with Shari about once a month, but it wasn't the same. And I still hadn't even told her about Kody. That unsettling feeling came over me again.

Josie was folding up the play mat. "How are your new songs coming along?"

She'd become a pretty big fan of Ghost Parker. "Okay. We're finishing up our new single."

"The one you wrote?" She arched a brow. "The next big hit?"

She'd heard me ranting and raving about it the other day. I'd written the song about Kaylie for myself. I didn't want to share it with the world. And if Bash ever found out, he'd kill me. The lyrics were all about sex with a girl that I could never have. On the surface, the lyrics were PG, but the meaning behind them was explicit.

Ghost liked the explicit imagery, and he even dirtied it up a bit more. He said if BVR forced us to make a pop song, he'd turn it into the dirtiest one around. I could barely sing the backup parts without getting a boner.

I'd had to go home and write out all new lyric notes to give to Ghost so that it read Okay Babe instead of Oh Kay, Babe. Fuck, if anyone ever figured it out, it would get ugly.

I took a deep breath and answered Josie. "Yeah, that one. The changes that the guys have made to the music and lyrics all sound fantastic, though. I believe Diamond Dick when he says it's going to be a big hit. It's really catchy. I'm kind of proud of it, but nervous, too."

"What's the name of it?"

Fuck, my cheeks were heating. I stammered out some nonsense, "It's, uh, I'm not sure what we're going to call it yet. Maybe the suits will focus group it and change the name — "

She placed a hand on her hip. "Why won't you tell me? Is it something naughty? Never mind, I'll just ask Sebastian."

The last thing I needed was for Josie and Sebastian to discuss the name of the song. "It's called *Okay Babe*," I blurted out.

She wrinkled her brow and thought for a moment. "Oh ... Kay babe."

Dammit, did she just pause between the O and the Kay?

"And you wrote this song? Interesting." A wide smile crept over her features. "Can I read the lyrics?"

Hell, no. "Do you smell that? I think Kody needs a diaper change."

"Uh-huh."

I had a feeling I wasn't fooling her.

I brought Kody over to the changing table and began changing his clean diaper.

Josie followed me over. "I haven't seen Sebastian around lately. You think he's avoiding me?"

I sighed with relief that she was dropping the subject. "He usually shows up after you're gone. I think he's got stuff to do after practice."

"His sister is a real sweetheart. Too bad she hasn't visited again. What was her name? Katie? Kacey? Kay ... something?"

"Kaylie," I croaked.

"Right. Kay ... lie."

I busied myself fixing Kody's clothes.

"Yeah, she's really sweet and so pretty. Does she come by here often?"

Jeez, this woman was hard to throw off the trail. She was like a hound dog tracking a scent. "She occasionally stops by to see her brother."

Josie snorted. "Like he's ever here."

I finished dressing Kody and picked him up. "Why do you pick on him so much?"

A gleam of mirth shined in her eyes. "Because it's so much fun."

I shook my head. "You should be nicer to him. He's my best friend."

"Your absentee best friend."

I sighed. "He bolted at first, but he's been spending more time here lately. He's been helping with Kody at night, even enjoying some of your home-cooked meals."

She crossed her arms. "But he's just visiting. He doesn't sleep in his bed and he's not here in the morning when I come."

"What do you expect from him? There's a nursery taking up half his bedroom. I won't allow him to bring women or booze into the apartment anymore, so what is he supposed to do?"

The more I defended him, the more she dug in. "He's not supposed to desert his best friend."

I carried Kody into the kitchen. "He hasn't deserted me. I see him every day. And, it's not like my other bandmates are over here hanging out with me anymore or helping with Kody. Bash has been the most supportive of me."

She began preparing a bottle for Kody. "And his sister has been supportive. Kay ... lie. She threw you the baby shower. And visited to check on Kody. Don't forget her."

I almost groaned out loud. That was the problem. I couldn't forget her. I spent all day singing about her. Singing about fucking her.

I hadn't heard a single peep out of her since that night. What a complete dumbass I'd been. First, I'd confronted her about the joke she'd made about sleeping with me and then I kissed her silly, practically mounting her right on the spot because I was so turned on.

I'd been so out of control. Shaking just to get another taste of her lips. Had I just been imagining her breathy whisper telling me not to stop? Probably.

I'd had no business doing those things to her. Kissing her. Touching her. My hands had dipped into her pants. I'd just wanted to touch her. When she felt so incredibly good — wet and slick — all I could think of was getting my cock inside of her. I'd gone mindless with need.

It had only taken the tip of my finger to slide inside her and she'd come apart. She'd come so hard, it buckled her knees. And it shocked the hell out of me. I was so surprised that I didn't even know what to do.

So, I put her in my lap and stroked her hair while her ass wiggled up against my throbbing dick. Within seconds, she'd fallen asleep.

And now, everything was so confusing because she snuck off after I fell asleep. I waited a few days, hoping she'd come back to visit Kody so I could apologize or try to explain, but she didn't. Then I texted her. I debated forever about texting her; we hardly ever texted each other. In fact, all our previous texts had been about Bash. This was the first time I texted just to talk to her. I asked her how her audition went; I felt that was fairly innocuous enough, but she didn't answer.

Over the past few days, I texted her a few more times.

> **Me:** We have to talk.
> **Me:** Stop avoiding me.
> **Me:** Text me back, Kaylie.

I didn't blame her for not answering. She probably hates me. She must think I used her. I would never intentionally hurt her.

Christ, my insides twisted up just thinking about it.

"Hello? Earth to Sidney." Josie passed a hand in front of my face.

I blinked. "Sorry, what did you say?"

"I was talking about Kay … lie and then you got this weird expression on your face. Anyway, it's nice that you have a few friends that have stuck around since Kody showed up."

I winced. "Please don't say her name like that."

She nodded slowly. "So, it's true?"

I just stared at her.

"OK, I won't."

Josie tested the temperature of the baby formula on her wrist and then held out her arms to take Kody. "Let me feed him and then I'll get out of your hair."

I didn't feel like giving him up. "I can do it."

She followed me back to the couch and then handed me the bottle when I was situated. "Where's Kody's mother, if you don't mind me asking?"

I thought about making up some story, but I knew Josie wouldn't betray my confidence. Plus, nothing got past her. She'd ferret out the information sooner or later.

"Please don't tell anyone this, Josie. Not even your daughter. I don't want it getting out. Kody was left outside our door with a note. His mother said she was leaving town and could no longer care for him. She didn't leave her name, so we don't know who Kody's mother is."

"We?"

I was watching Kody drink his bottle, but I looked up at her question. "What?"

"You said 'we'." She pursed her lips and squinted her eyes. "We don't know who the mother is, not I don't know."

"So?" What the hell?

"Who is we?"

"What are you? The CIA?" I laughed nervously. "I mean, me and Bash. We read the note together."

"And you're sure you're Kody's father? You took a paternity test?"

Dammit. Here we go again. "I'm his father."

Josie sat down on the couch next to me. "Oh shit. You didn't take one. Why not?"

Anger crept into my voice. "What's with all the questions?"

Her hand touched my arm. "Hey, I'm on your side, but you have to talk to me if you want my help."

"I know you're on my side." She'd been nothing but fiercely loyal to me. "I'm sorry, Josie. It's a sore subject for me. The truth is, we don't know who the note was meant for, me or Bash. He told everyone that I was the father and I went along with it because I was afraid Bash would do something stupid like call the cops and then they'd take

Kody away."

Josie placed a hand on her chest. "Bash might be Kody's father?"

I closed my eyes. "We don't really know. And it's eating me alive."

I glanced over at her nervously, fearing what she'd say.

It took her a while to speak. "It's eating you alive because you need to find out the truth. You need to do a paternity test."

"But, what if—"

She held up her hand and cut me off. "I didn't say what we'd do with the information. We'll figure that out after we know. Paternity tests are confidential. No one will ever find out if you don't tell them. First, you need to find out."

"What if Kody is Bash's baby?"

Josie frowned. "Maybe he'd let you become Kody's guardian? Or adopt him? Who knows? But, let's not borrow trouble. Find out and then we'll plan. Even if he is your baby, Sidney, I think you need to take some legal steps to secure your rights as a father in case the biological mother ever shows up again."

I knew she was right, but as I stared down at Kody, a black fear gnawed at my insides.

Chapter 19

Kaylie

It was Friday night, and I didn't have any plans. I'd endured a long day at work with customers bitching at me non-stop, so a glass of wine and a good book sounded like heaven.

I changed into some yoga pants and a comfy sweatshirt and settled down in my room with my e-reader when I heard the obnoxious noises from the room next to mine. Martina, my roommate, was holed up in her room with her boyfriend. Luckily, they didn't spend that much time here, because the walls were paper thin. I could hear every little gasp, grunt, and moan as they went at each other. It squicked me out.

I grabbed my cell phone and escaped to the kitchen. I idly browsed through social media thinking I should make some posts, but within minutes I was staring at my text messages again. The messages Sid had sent me.

First, he'd asked me how the audition went. I'd stared at those five words forever, trying to dissect what they meant, but I was too chicken to answer. The next day he texted that 'we have to talk'. That text had sent my heart plummeting to my feet. I knew exactly what he was going to say to me and I didn't want to have that talk. Then came the texts telling me to 'stop avoiding me'. Treating me like the child I was being. I really was avoiding him.

Regret. Mistake.

Those were words I did not want to hear come out of his mouth. I'd rather pretend none of it ever happened — at least around him. When I was by myself, I relived those moments of bliss with him over and over in my head. A soul-stealing kiss and a spontaneous orgasm all in under two minutes. Ugh! Sid must think I'm such a loser. Whenever I thought about it, I always wavered between getting hot and bothered to being completely mortified.

I was still staring at his texts when my phone rang. I glanced at the caller ID which read CDX ENT before I picked up. Five minutes later, I was hanging up the phone with a giant smile on my face. I was doing a happy dance in the kitchen when my other roommate, Jill, came home.

She eyed me warily. "You're drunk already?"

"No." I stopped dancing. "I got a callback!"

Her eyes widened. "No Shit! That's awesome."

"I can hardly believe it. I've been on such a dry spell lately."

"Is it for tomorrow?" she asked.

"Monday morning, 8 a.m." I frowned. "I'll have to get someone to cover for me at work."

Her eyes lit up. "So that means we can celebrate tonight. I'll call Martina and tell her to come out with us tonight. The three of us haven't been out together in a while."

"Martina is here with Pete. They're bumping uglies as we speak." I scrunched my nose with disgust.

Jill laughed. "Well, they have to come up for air, eventually. I'll text her. I need to grab some food first and get changed. Some friends of mine were going to the Backstage later, so let's just celebrate there. It'll be like old times."

"Do we have to go there?"

"Yes, we do. It'll be crowded, so if he's working tonight, he won't have any time to talk to you. You'll barely have to see him." Her eyes narrowed at my doubtful expression, then she continued more sternly. "C'mon, Kaylie. You can't avoid him forever. That was our favorite bar."

"Fine," I concede. "But I'll meet you guys there at nine o'clock. I've got to run an errand first."

I didn't want to deal with the drama of running into my ex-boyfriend, but it wasn't like I was pining away for him. Once I suspected he wasn't faithful to me, our relationship quickly deteriorated. When I confronted him about it, his explanations were weak, so I ended up breaking up with him. He made a few feeble attempts to win me back, but I shut him down hard, especially when I realized I wasn't that upset about the whole thing. We'd been over for months, so there was no reason I couldn't go to the Backstage tonight to celebrate getting a callback.

I ate a quick dinner and then spent a significant amount of time primping. First, I showered, shaved, and lotioned until my skin was silky smooth. Then, I blew out my hair and curled it loosely. I went a little bolder with my makeup than usual — a heavier application on my eyes and a color approved by Talia for my lips.

The dress I chose for the night was purchased on a recent shopping trip with Talia. She was the queen of finding the perfect outfits despite my meager budget. For tonight, I picked a little black dress that Talia called 'sneakily sexy'. It was a body-hugging black bandage dress that enhanced my curves, pushed up my boobs, but only displayed a hint of cleavage. Long sleeves consisting of a sheer black material showed off my arms and the same sheer material tightly covered the entire dress. It was sinfully short. If I lifted my arms, my ass cheeks would be exposed, but Talia was right — my legs looked pretty sexy when paired with black high-heeled strappy sandals.

When I was satisfied with my appearance, I spritzed a liberal amount of my favorite designer knock-off perfume on the base of my throat and my cleavage. The cab I'd ordered was still ten minutes out, so I distracted myself by listening to some music. I didn't want to overthink anything and chicken out.

My plan was to stop by Sid's apartment. I couldn't avoid him forever and this way I could see him on my terms. This way, I looked fantastic and had a built-in excuse to leave whenever I needed to cut bait and run.

The cab dropped me off at Sid's building and this time I buzzed up to their room, so he'd know I was coming. Kody was in his arms when he opened the door for me.

I think I got the reaction I wanted from him. He looked me up and down, his mouth hanging open slightly and his eyes pausing in a few key areas before he shook himself from his daze.

"Kaylie, you look ... amazing."

I was playing the role of 'one prod of your fingertip didn't give me an enormous orgasm the other night', so I breezily stepped into the room and made some cooing noises at Kody.

"Is Bash home?" I asked.

"No," he shook his head. "He's probably already out for the night."

"Oh, darn. I wanted to see if he'd come out and celebrate with me."

"What are you celebrating?"

I looked up at him with a big smile. "Remember the audition I had the other day? I got a callback."

"Wow! That's great!" His smile lit up his entire face. "How did it go? Did you wear that?"

I laughed. "I just got the call tonight; I'm going back in on Monday morning. They told me I'm one of five girls and no, I'm not wearing this. You want them to pay attention to your acting, not your clothing. Usually, you wear the same outfit that you wore to the audition."

He shifted Kody. "Yeah, I can see how that dress would be distracting."

"Well, I should be going." I turned toward the door to leave.

"Wait!" he implored. "About the other night..."

I faced him, dreading his next words.

"About what happened..." he trailed off.

"Don't." I held up my hand. "I don't want to hear what a mistake it was. I'm not sorry it happened and I'm a big girl. Just drop it."

He looked conflicted like he wanted to say more, but the door swung open and Bash walked in holding a pair of drumsticks.

I caught him up on my news and then asked him to come out to the Backstage bar with me. He had other plans but readily agreed to change them.

He turned to Sid. "How about you come out too? You haven't been out in ages."

Sid frowned. "You know I can't. I've got Kody."

"Can't you call Josie? Or get another babysitter? Kody will be sleeping in a few hours. The babysitter wouldn't even have to do much."

He shook his head. "Josie won't come out this late and I don't know any babysitters. Nah, you two have fun without me."

Bash narrowed his eyes. "You know what? I'll watch Kody. You go out with Kaylie. Relax and have a few drinks. You've been cooped up in here for weeks."

Sid glanced at me for a moment and then looked back at Bash. "You're going to watch Kody? I'm not sure. Plus, it's a Friday night."

Bash held out his hands to take Kody. "I've been out every night this week. I'd rather hang with Kody tonight. And don't worry, I know how to make a bottle, change his diaper, and get him to sleep. I can handle it."

After a few more minutes of convincing, Sid finally caved. He left Kody with Bash while he went to change his clothes.

Bash had been slowly spending more time at home, so he seemed to know what he was doing when I quizzed him on baby care. My stomach was churning with nervous anticipation as we waited for Sid. I hadn't expected to hang out with him tonight, but I was sure it would be fine since we would be in public. He wasn't going to give me the 'you're like a little sister to me' speech in the middle of a crowded bar. At least, I hoped he wouldn't.

Sid emerged from his bedroom looking so hot. He had on a blue button-down shirt that matched his eyes with the sleeves rolled halfway up his forearms and a well-fitted pair of dark jeans. He had tamed his shaggy hair and had a delicious amount of five o'clock shadow. It had taken me hours to get ready, but he'd transformed into a put-together sexy hunk in less than ten minutes.

Before we left, Bash pulled Sid aside and spoke to him in a low voice. I pretended to be enthralled with Kody, but I was straining to listen. Bash told Sid to keep an eye on me and Sid agreed. I bit my tongue even though it was infuriating how they treated me like a little girl needing protection sometimes.

We took a cab to the Backstage. We chatted awkwardly about Kody and how Bash would do with babysitting him. I spent the entire ride staring out the window in a desperate attempt to keep myself from drooling over him.

Jill was already at the bar with her friends when we arrived. The place was already filling up nicely. I noticed Charlie working behind the bar, but I quickly walked across the room where Jill and some friends had a booth. A waitress came by to take our order. Both Sid and I ordered a beer, but Jill ordered two tequila shots so we could toast my callback.

Not much later, I did another shot with Martina when she arrived. Then someone bought a round of shots for the whole group. I knew my limits with hard alcohol and I was about at it. I'd learned in high school that I couldn't hold my liquor very well. Depending on my initial mood, I'd get either really weepy or really chatty when I got drunk. And by chatty, it meant I had absolutely no filter. During a post-prom party, I'd let slip my best friend's deepest secret — that she'd kissed her prom date's older brother the week before. Yeah, I'd learned my lesson, so I decided to slow down and only sipped on my beer.

I was pleasantly buzzed and really enjoying myself. Sitting next to Sid, thigh to thigh, I was aware of every single move he made and every word he spoke, even if I rarely spoke to him. I had started out playing the part of 'fun party girl', but I realized now that I didn't have to act; I really was having fun with my friends. Sid was sitting back and taking it all in, occasionally needing to fend off some random girls who hit on him from time to time. I was coming back from the restrooms when I got stopped by someone. Ugh! It was Charlie. I'd forgotten about him.

There was no avoiding talking to him without being rude. I was eager to get back to Sid, so I tried blowing him off. "Aren't you working? Don't you have to be behind the bar?"

He had two shot glasses in his hands, holding one out to me. "I heard Martina say you were celebrating something. What's going on?"

Charlie was an actor, too. That's how we all knew each other. "I got a callback for a really good part." I shrugged like I was downplaying it, but a part of me — the buzzed part — wanted to show off a little. Maybe rub it in.

"Seriously? That's awesome, Tasty Cake." He was still holding out the shot. "Take the shot glass. Let's toast to you getting the part."

I grabbed the glass without thinking while my mind focused on his use of his nickname for me. "Don't call me that anymore."

"Sorry." He clicked his glass to mine. "Cheers. To you becoming a big star."

I tipped back the tiny glass and swallowed down the alcohol. I expected it to burn, but it went down smoothly.

He leaned in close to me. "I'm glad you came here to celebrate. Did you wear that dress for me?"

There was no room for me to step back from him. "If I had my way, we'd be celebrating somewhere else."

He chuckled right next to my ear. He was crowding me. My mind was grasping for something to say to put him in his place when I felt his hand on my ass and his fingers stroking the bare skin of my upper thigh.

I slapped his hand away. "Don't touch me."

"Don't be like that, Tasty Cake." He pushed his body closer. "We were so hot together. I miss you."

I put my hand between us so I could push on his chest. "We are done. You can go be hot with one of the bimbos you were hooking up with while we were dating."

"I don't know why I even looked at any other girl. You're so hot and sexy and smart, too. I realize what a fool I was. Give me another chance, Tasty Cake. I'll prove to you how good we can be."

"Is he bothering you, Kaylie?"

My eyes popped open wide. Sid was right next to Charlie, shooting him a murderous look.

I didn't want to start trouble between the two. I just wanted to get away from him. "No, I was just leaving."

Charlie grabbed my arm to stop me. "Hold on, Tasty Cake—"

Sid was livid. I thought he'd break a few molars the way he was clenching his jaw. He grabbed Charlie's arm and squeezed it hard until he released me. "Don't touch her."

Charlie shook off Sid's grasp. "Now your big brother isn't letting you out without a guard dog?" The sneer on his face made him look ugly. "Down, boy. She can decide who she wants to speak to."

This was going from bad to worse. I had to do something before they came to blows, but the last shot was kicking in hard. Shit, I was drunk. "I don't want to talk to you, Charlie. Not now, not ever. We're done. And I've realized that I was never that into you. Just leave me alone."

Charlie scowled darkly while Sidney grabbed my hand and pulled me into him.

Charlie called me a bitch, but who cared because suddenly, Sidney and I were kissing. I wasn't sure how it happened, but it was most likely because I tried to climb him like a tree. I was planted between his legs and his tongue was doing incredible things inside my mouth. Sid's kisses were magical.

When he pulled away from me, my world was spinning. Thankfully, Charlie had taken the hint and stalked off. Sid's kiss had been dreamy and toe-curling, but now I was barely clinging to reason. I was plastered. At least I realized it, because any minute now I was going to slip into actions that were beyond my control.

"Dance with me," I sounded breathless.

Sid laughed. His arms were around me; I think he was already quasi-holding me upright. "I think you've had too much to drink."

"Did I? Did you?" Who knows what nonsense I was uttering?

Sid lifted a brow. "I just had one beer. I'm not drinking; I've got Kody to think about."

We were swaying to the music in the middle of a crush of bodies.

"I love this song. Will you kiss me again? To this song, so I can remember it?" I pleaded with him.

He was staring at my lips. "Kay, babe. You're wasted."

"Please?"

The next kiss was long, deep, and extremely thorough. It made me want to do very naughty things. I thought I heard someone yell 'Get a room' right before Sidney pulled away from my lips.

I gazed up at him, trying my best to focus. "You look so hot tonight. Both of you."

"Both?"

"Yeah, I see two of you. It's strange. Double the pleasure." Yeah, I was slurring.

He grunted. "I think we need to get you home."

Suddenly, I was in a moving cab. I didn't even remember getting into one, but Sidney was next to me, so I felt safe. I snuggled up close to him. He gently redirected my hand which had been slowly sliding up his inner thigh. Darn! So close.

"You're supposed to be this big womanizer, but when it comes to me … nada. What's wrong with me?" I pouted.

"You're too good for me, Kaylie." He tucked a stray hair behind my ear.

"If I wasn't Bash's little sister, would you have sex with me?"

He groaned. "Yes."

Climbing onto his lap, I began sliding my hands over his chest. "I'm an adult and I can do what I want. I won't tell Bash, I promise."

I felt the rumble in his chest when he laughed. "You're so drunk. You're going to be so hungover tomorrow."

I ignored him. "You're worried I'm too naïve and that I'd expect more from you. I don't. Just sex is okay. I'm not looking for more. I know you don't do girlfriends. Plus, you have Kody. I'm not wanting anything more like a relationship. Especially with a single dad. I'm only 23, jeez. You don't do relationships. That's okay. Kody and all that. Relationships suck. Look at Charlie."

He stilled my hands that were rubbing his chest. "You're rambling."

"I do that when I'm drunk. Lucky for you, I could be crying. But, as I was saying, I rather just have sex with someone I like. And I like your tattoos. And you have big muscles. Did I mention you have the bluest eyes? If we had a baby, what color eyes do you think it'd have?"

"Jesus, Kaylie. You should quit talking. You're not going to be happy tomorrow when you remember all the shit you're saying to me."

Inspiration struck. "I know! What if we blindfold each other and have sex? Then, you'll never know it's me."

He snorted. "So, we're both blindfolded? You're so wasted if you think that's a good plan."

"Can I see you naked before I put the blindfold on though? I want to see you naked."

"Fuck." Sid adjusted himself.

"You're not small down there, are you? That would be weird. Not proportional. A crime against humanity, if you had a teenie peenie or a dinky winky. Tell me, are you at least average-sized? Your penis, I'm talking about. Penis? That's such a weird word. Penis. Penis. It's not manly enough. How about cock? Is your cock at least average, Sid? Or a little bigger than average? You're pretty big. Do you have a giant cock?"

He kissed me again, probably to shut me up. It was so long and delicious; he had me whimpering and mewling and grinding against him.

He tried to still my movements. "I hope for your sake, you don't remember any of this."

The next thing I realized, I was in my room. He may have carried me upstairs. Did I refuse to walk? "I can't get this dress off. I don't want to ruin it. Do you like my dress, Sid?"

"It's very nice."

"Will you unzip it for me?" I spun around and almost fell over.

After he unzipped my dress, he deliberately looked away as I clumsily stepped out of it. I grabbed the sleep T-shirt off the end of my bed and slipped it on.

Sid held my covers back as I crawled into bed. He kissed my forehead and whispered, "Sweet dreams, Kaylie."

Chapter 20

Sidney

K ODY WAS ABOUT TO doze off. It was close to his bedtime, but I didn't want him to sleep just yet. Once he fell asleep, what was I going to do? I thought about going to bed, too. I could use the extra sleep after staying out late last night, but it felt so lame to go to sleep at nine o'clock on a Saturday night.

Everyone was out partying. It seemed like a lifetime ago, but just a month earlier, I had been going out, drinking, and partying almost every night. I'd gotten a taste of my old life last night and it had reminded me what I was missing.

Tonight, all the guys in my band had gone out to a nightclub near the shore. Tyler Matthews, lead singer of Cold Fusion, and his bandmate Tommy invited us all to join them in their VIP room. Bash asked if I could join them, but he gave up pretty easily when I said I couldn't. It stung a little, but I understood. I was already grateful that he'd given up his Friday night and babysat Kody the night before.

So, I was jealous of my friends and disappointed that I was stuck at home missing the fun. I had Kody, but I felt lonely. It felt like everyone was moving on and leaving me behind. I wasn't as fun anymore, so I was forgotten.

Even though our tour was delayed while we recorded some new songs for our album, it would happen eventually. What would I do then? I had floated the idea of Josie coming on tour with us in a separate bus to nanny Kody and she had shot it down. She'd laughed hysterically at me, in fact. As much as I didn't want to, maybe I'd have to leave the band and Ghost Parker would go on tour without me.

Could I sacrifice my entire career — my biggest passion in life — for Kody's sake?

When I thought about it, I knew I could. I would do anything for this little guy. Holding him against my chest, I rubbed his back.

I wondered what the guys were doing now. It was still early; they probably weren't even at the club yet. It wasn't so much the partying that I missed, but I missed the camaraderie with the guys. And I desperately wanted to see Kaylie again. Earlier, I wanted to ask Bash if she was going out with them, but I couldn't without evoking his suspicion. Would she be there? Dressed in a sexy as fuck dress?

She'd taken my breath away with how sexy she'd looked when she'd shown up at my door the night before. The dress hugged her curves and I couldn't help but imagine those gorgeous legs that went on for miles wrapped around my waist. My cock was stirring just thinking about it.

After last night, I'd realized that I only wanted her, not any other girls. There had been other women at the bar that I could have hooked up with, but they hadn't interested me at all. I wanted Kaylie and not just for sex. I wanted a real relationship — something I'd never had and never wanted in my life before.

She'd said a lot of crazy shit last night. There was no doubt that she was into me, but it sounded like she was only interested in sex. She'd babbled a lot of shit when she was plastered. Those shots she'd downed were like a truth serum. She didn't hold anything back.

She'd admitted that she'd never consider me as anything but a bit of fun because of Kody. That was exactly what I had always wanted from women — no relationship, just fun. And yet, that statement had gutted me to the core. I could remember her exact words. She wasn't looking for a relationship, especially with a single dad.

I knew I had to forget about her. I wasn't going to have a quick fling with her. Eventually, she'd move on. Any interest she had in me would wane. I was sitting at home on a Saturday night, taking care of a baby. She was out partying, looking like an absolute bombshell. Guys would be swarming all around her. She never lacked male attention. She'd move on just like my bandmates were.

It was like my thoughts managed to materialize her. The buzzer rang; it was Kaylie asking to come up.

This was a good time to put us back on course. We were friends. Anything more would lead to disaster.

I left my door open a crack and sat down on the couch, holding Kody. He'd be my shield, so I wasn't tempted to do anything stupid, like get a taste of her lips again.

She knocked and then strolled in. She was dressed up for a night out. Tiny dress, heels, makeup, jewelry — the whole nine. Her beauty never ceased to amaze me, but there was something missing tonight. Her eyes looked dull. They lacked their normal sparkle.

"Are you heading out? Bash already left."

"I know." She glanced around the room, not looking my way. "I ditched the party bus. The music was pounding; I just couldn't take it anymore. And I got one whiff of alcohol, and I thought I was going to hurl. I knew I was going to be miserable the entire night." She shook her head. "I don't know why I was torturing myself trying to go out tonight."

I laughed. "You're still hungover?"

She finally looked at me. "Yes. The thought of drinking right now … I just can't. Jill said I'd be fine after one shot, but I don't even want to be out right now."

"So, you came here instead?"

That had her blushing furiously. "I didn't want to go home to an empty apartment, and I figured you'd be here…" Her voice trailed off.

I knew I shouldn't. Knowing and doing were two different things. "Kody and I were just going to look for a good movie. You're welcome to join us."

She smiled brightly. The sparkle was back in her eyes. "That sounds great. I just have to text Bash to let him know I made it home safely. He made me promise."

She wasn't exactly home, but I didn't mention that. I'd make sure she got home safely.

I patted the cushion next to me after she typed out her text. She came over, removed her heels, and sat down.

She glanced over at me as I was searching through movie choices on the TV screen. "I remember you saving me from Charlie. Thanks."

"No problem. He was being an ass." I couldn't help but add, "he called you Tasty Cake."

"Ugh!" She dropped her head into her hands. "That's a stupid nickname. I used to think it was so cute."

My only comment was a grunt of disgust.

"I hope I wasn't obnoxious. I'm a terrible drunk. Did I say anything stupid?"

I raised an eyebrow. "Not stupid. Just interesting."

She turned on the couch to face me. "Like what?"

I rubbed Kody's back; he was sleeping now. "You said you wanted to have sex — with both of us blindfolded."

She looked horrified for a moment but then laughed. "You're just pulling my leg. I don't care how drunk I was, I would never say that!"

This was kind of fun teasing her. "You did. You were rambling about a lot of things."

She got all nervous again. "I tend to ramble when I'm drunk. What else did I say?"

"You were really interested in my dick size."

Her hand flew over her mouth in horror. "No!"

"You went on about it for quite a while," I informed her.

"Oh, God!" She shook her head. "I don't want to know any more. Please, just forget all of that."

"Okay."

She was silent for a moment, then she cleared her throat and spoke. "Thanks for making sure I got home safely. I remember snippets of it."

I shifted Kody to my other shoulder so I could see her better. "Do you remember me carrying you up all those stairs?"

She pinched at her lips. "Vaguely. Did you tuck me into bed? Or was that a dream?"

"I did."

I remembered unzipping her from her dress and forcing myself to look away. When I looked back, she was wearing my Rolling Stones T-shirt. My T-shirt was longer and baggier than that little black dress she'd had on, but somehow the T-shirt looked sexier on her. There was something about seeing her in my clothing that did strange things to my insides.

I hadn't even realized she still had my T-shirt. Was the shirt just lying around or had she been wearing it to bed for weeks now? I wondered if maybe she liked me more than she'd let on. She was here with me right now, not out partying. Or was that just wishful thinking? When she was spewing her drunk truths, she'd practically confessed that she was only interested in a quick fuck.

She was watching me intently. She took a deep breath and then swallowed. "I remember we kissed. And I may have gotten a bit handsy, too."

I shrugged casually. "Nothing I couldn't handle."

She giggled. "I promise I'll behave tonight. I just want to relax."

We decided on a comedy to watch. Within five minutes of starting the movie, she moved to lean against my side. Kody was on my shoulder and Kaylie cuddled up on the other.

I didn't watch a second of the movie because I was too aware of the girl in my arms. I was too busy memorizing the feel of her — her warmth, her smell, her soft hair against my cheek.

She fell asleep halfway through the movie. I didn't want to move when I was sandwiched between my two favorite people. The night had started with me feeling depressed, but now I was content. In fact, it was far better than partying with the guys. Maybe even the best Saturday night I'd ever spent in my life.

I tightened my arm around her, and she sighed sleepily into my neck. This was heaven.

What the hell was I doing?

Chapter 21

Kaylie

I wasn't Kaylie anymore. I was Sofia.

Yesterday morning, I received my audition materials — the project breakdown, the audition sides, and the character breakdown for Sofia. I was a young wife living in a middle-class suburban neighborhood. I worked at an upscale hair salon and my husband was a firefighter. Most of the TV sitcom's action took place in our home, my hair salon, or at the firehouse.

I knew my lines inside out. I practiced them for hours in front of a mirror before I even asked for feedback from my roommates. And then, desperate, I bribed my grumpy neighbor with the promise of homemade chocolate chip cookies to get a male perspective on the character. He didn't hold back. He said I sounded like a 'bitch' at times, a 'nag', and even a 'feminazi'. I gritted my teeth, but surprisingly, the feedback was invaluable. I honed the delivery of my lines until I sounded charmingly sarcastic and less bitter. Acting in a comedy was all about timing, nuance, and character interplay. I had no experience with comedy acting, but this role fascinated me.

As I'd gotten ready this morning, my mind ran away from me. What if I got the part? And then, what if the sitcom was picked up? What if it turned into a multi-season smash hit? What if I won a freaking Emmy? I was getting a bit carried away, but dreaming about the what-ifs was exciting.

As I waited for my Uber driver to show up, I took some deep breaths to center myself. Sofia would have taken the two bus lines needed to get to the audition, but I was too worried that something could go wrong and I'd be late, so I splurged for the Uber.

When the app notified me that my car was waiting, I headed down the stairs of my building. Practicing lines in my head, I exited into the chilly morning. My cab was waiting at the curb and I took a few steps towards it.

I was immersed in my head, repeating lines, so oblivious to my surroundings that the hand roughly encircling my upper arm took me by surprise. The painful grip of fingers digging brutally into my skin whirled me to a stop.

The man that stopped me was about my height, unkempt in appearance, with a menacing look in his eye.

"Let go of me." I yanked downward to free my arm, but his grip was solid.

The quick flash of anger that I'd reacted with morphed into fear.

The man pulled me to the right, forcing me to take a couple of steps before I could plant my feet.

"Let go of me! Help!" I yelled as loudly as I could.

A dirty hand clamped over my mouth.

My eyes darted around frantically. There was a man walking across the street, but he put his head down and kept walking.

My attacker forced me against his solid frame and was using his whole body to push me along the sidewalk.

"Shut up, bitch. This is exactly what you want. I'm going to fuck the brains out of you." I felt his spittle coating the side of my face as he rasped out the words.

He grunted when I dropped my body like a sack and tried to bite at his filthy hand covering my mouth, but somehow he was still moving us.

My mind was screaming, 'Fight!' I had to knee him in the junk, gouge out his eyes, punch him in the throat, or even headbutt him, but he was so strong and I was panicking.

"Get off her or I'll break your leg with this tire iron!" A man bellowed. "The cops are on the way."

My attacker paused and then let go of me. I dropped to the sidewalk as he ran off.

"Are you okay, miss?" He held out his hand to help me up.

I took stock of myself as I stood up. My right palm stung where it hit the sidewalk. The fall had abraded my skin, but I wasn't bleeding. In worse shape was my right hip and knee. My knee was very sore, and I had trouble putting my full weight on it, but at least my pants hadn't ripped.

The good samaritan stared at me, becoming slightly impatient when I didn't answer. "Do you want me to call the police?"

Dazed, I looked at him. I realized from his photo on my app that he was my Uber driver. "I thought you already called them?"

"Nah," he answered. "Just said that to scare him away. Don't have a tire iron either." He laughed.

Amazingly, I was still holding my bag containing all my audition paperwork and my phone. I dusted off my pants. "Thanks for scaring him away."

His chest puffed up. "No problem. You still need a ride?"

"Yeah," I sighed. "And I don't want to be late."

I limped behind him to the car. I tried to keep my mind blank as I touched up my makeup; his hand had smeared my lipstick. I wished I could rinse my mouth somehow because I could still taste his salty skin. I tried unsuccessfully to brush a dirt stain off my pants with shaking hands.

My knee was throbbing, and my whole body trembled with a delayed reaction. I began pushing the whole incident out of my mind by repeating the lines I'd memorized in my head over and over. That bastard was not going to ruin my shot at this role.

♫♫♪♪♪

I was sitting at a small cafe sipping a coffee while I watched people walk by on the sidewalk outside. I'd only been able to nibble at the sandwich I'd ordered, even though I'd barely eaten all day.

My audition went great. Somehow, I put the incident out of my head and focused on the audition. I read the lines just like I'd practiced. I'd been called back in several times to read, which was a promising sign. A few times, I'd stumbled in the tone of my delivery but corrected it on the second take.

The feedback I got from the producers seemed to be positive. I'd seen them nodding their heads several times as I read. I left feeling encouraged.

But now, a different scene was playing in my head over and over. The man grabbing me. Feeling utterly helpless. The words he said that I couldn't quite remember anymore, but in essence, were that he was going to rape me.

I shuddered as I thought about it. What if no one had stopped him?

It was funny; I'd lived for twenty years in Georgia without ever witnessing a crime, but a few years in L.A. and I'd seen a handful. There was the mugging I'd witnessed while I was riding the bus. I called the police, even as I saw a cop parked in a marked car less than a block away, doing nothing about it. Also, I'd seen a man breaking into a car by smashing the window and I'd witnessed a homeless man physically harassing an older woman. Shoplifting was so common that it didn't even faze me anymore.

But now I'd been a victim of a crime that could have been so much worse. I found myself evaluating everyone who passed by the window. Could they be a potential criminal? Did that man look like a rapist?

I was nervous and edgy. The thought of going back home, where that guy could be lurking, made me feel sick to my stomach.

When I'd dawdled too long at the cafe, I pulled up a map on my phone. I knew I was somewhere close to Ghost Parker's rehearsal space. I'd only been there once, but I remembered the name of the street it was on. It looked like it was a 15-minute walk from here. Before I left, I browsed the pastry selection and bought a bagful of French Crullers for the boys.

It was broad daylight. I'd never even thought twice about walking the streets during the day, but today I had to give myself a pep talk. Gripping my phone tightly, I was ready to dial 911 if needed. I studied the pedestrians closely as I walked and hurried past any alleyways between buildings. I couldn't stop myself from repeatedly looking over my shoulder.

By the time I found the rehearsal space, I was covered in a cold sweat. I signed in at the lobby and then made my way to the corner of the building where the guys were located.

The door was shut, but I could still hear the muffled sound of a song coming through. I didn't recognize the song; it must be one of their new ones. I opened the door and made my way over to the couch to watch them play.

Ghost noticed me first. He acknowledged me with a head tip, but he kept on singing. Of course, Sid had to notice me next. I cringed when he stopped playing, which quickly led to the rest of them stopping as well.

Sid frowned. "Why are you limping?"

Damn. I thought I was doing a good job not limping, but Sid noticed right away.

Bash pulled some plugs out of his ears. He had a big smile on his face. "Kaylie. You've come to watch us practice?"

Back in the day, I used to watch Bash and Sid practice with their old bands all the time, but now I rarely did. Lifting the bag of pastries, I said, "I brought some tasty crullers, but I didn't mean to interrupt you. You shouldn't have stopped."

Sid repeated, "You were limping."

Bash stood up. "Limping? What happened?"

The concern that washed over his face made my eyes tear up. "It's nothing. I just banged my knee on the sidewalk."

Sid put down his bass, took a few steps toward me, then stopped uncertainly. "You look pale. And you're shaking."

The guys all huddled around me, worry etched on their faces, while Bash circled his drum set and enveloped me in a hug.

Sinking into his embrace, I knew I'd come to the right place. I needed their strength for just a moment to bolster my own.

Bash pulled back, holding my shoulders as he looked me over. "You're trembling. Does this have anything to do with the callback?"

I smiled weakly. "No. Actually, I killed the audition. I think I might have a shot at it."

Sid ran a hand through his hair. "Then what happened?"

Bash sat on the couch with me while I told them everything. It was surprisingly cathartic to get it all out. While I felt slightly better, the guys were expressing various degrees of anger and worry for me.

Ghost rubbed his chin. "You're sure you don't want a doctor to look at your knee?"

"No. I looked at it in the restroom at the cafe. It's just a bit swollen and bruised. And a little stiff. I'm sure it'll be fine in a few days."

Ryder was pacing. "What if that asshole is still hanging around the building?"

Knox agreed. "She can't go back there alone."

"No way. She won't." That was Bash.

"Hey, I'm right here." I looked at them all. "I can't spend the rest of my life with a bodyguard tailing me."

Bash ignored me. "We've got to go to the police. Maybe they can catch this guy."

"I don't know..."

Sid crossed his arms over his chest. "I agree. And no going in and out of the building alone until they do. It's not safe. In fact, why don't you stay in Bash's room? He's not sleeping there."

I paused for a moment, waiting for Bash to object to that preposterous suggestion, but he didn't.

I shook my head. "No. I think we're making too much of a big deal out of this. It was just a one-time thing. I'll be fine."

Bash took me to the police station closest to my apartment. Before we left, each of the guys hugged me and told me they'd help in any way they could.

Sid hugged me for a few seconds too long. He whispered in my ear before he released me, "Kaylie, please, come stay with me. I'm worried you won't be safe."

We spent more than an hour there. Most of the time was spent waiting to give my statement and then waiting for them to take pictures of my bruised arm and knee.

I gave them the best description of the man that I could and all the information from my Uber driver so they could follow up with him as a witness.

The police chalked it up to a random act; and frankly, I wasn't too confident that they'd do too much to investigate it. They said they'd rotate extra patrols through the area and send out a few detectives to see if they could locate anyone matching the description in the area. I left with the officer's phone number and the order to call and report any suspicious activity or if I spotted the man again.

For as much as the incident had frightened me, the police didn't seem too impressed with it. They brushed it off as a petty crime, which in the scheme of things that they saw daily, it probably was.

Still, Bash took me home and escorted me into my apartment with strict orders not to leave tonight. I wanted nothing more than to take a hot bath and hide out in my room. He was going to drop by in the morning to drive me to work.

I protested all of this, saying it was silly, but I was secretly thankful for it. I was still scared.

Chapter 22

Sidney

I WANTED TO RIP out my hair.

Kaylie was attacked.

I paced the room like a caged lion. I was completely powerless to protect her, and that enraged me as much as it scared me to death.

Josie came in from the kitchen. "Dinner is all set. I packed up my portion and I'll head out unless you need me."

"Are you sure you're safe getting to your car?"

She eyed me for a second. "I got a great spot today. I parked in front of the building next to this one. And I keep my pepper spray handy when I'm walking. Don't worry about me. What's got you in such a tizzy?"

"Kaylie got attacked today." I swallowed down the nerves that were threatening to spill over. "Bash is at the police station with her now."

"Oh, Lord! Is she hurt? What happened?" The tough-as-nails

grannie disappeared before my eyes. She suddenly looked frail and uncertain.

After I explained what happened, Josie made some tea for us. She decided to stay and keep me company until Bash got back to us.

It was just after four o'clock when Bash came home.

I stood up. "Where's Kaylie? How is she?"

Bash strode through the room and then plopped down on the couch. He looked tired. "She's at home. I made sure she was safe, and she promised not to step foot outside her apartment until I came to pick her up tomorrow morning. She won't be alone tonight. Jill will be there soon."

He left her there alone? Jesus. "Why didn't you bring her here where we could keep an eye on her? At least we'd know she was safe."

Bash threw up his hands. "She wanted to go home. She's stubborn, man. She's already trying to downplay it after the trip to the police station."

Josie spoke up from the other side of the room. "What did the police say?"

"They took all the information and filed a report, but I don't know how much we can rely on them. I got the impression this was too small for them to bother doing much. They seem to think this was a random, one-time thing, but what if this guy is still lurking around over there?"

Anger coursed through me. "So, what are we supposed to do? Just wait and see if she gets attacked again?"

Bash scrubbed at his face with his hands. "I was thinking I'd go walk around her building. See if I can spot this dude hanging around. I heard her description of the guy. The best shot to catch him is before he changes his clothes because the rest of her description was kind of vague."

"I'll go with you."

Bash shook his head. "You've got Kody. I'm going to see if Knox will come with me. If not, I can do it myself."

Josie sat down on the couch next to Bash and laid a hand on his forearm. "Don't do anything stupid. You'll regret it, and that won't help Kaylie at all. Just call the cops if you spot him."

I could see ideas warring in his mind for a moment, but then he said, "I won't. You should see the bruises on her, though. She says she's fine, but I can tell she's scared. That bastard has to pay for what he did. And what he tried to do. He told her that he was going to rape her. If her Uber driver had turned a blind eye... Fuck!"

We all remained silent when his voice trailed off. My gut clenched with roiling anxiety, but I had to focus on keeping her safe, not on what might have happened.

Josie broke into our dark thoughts. "I'm going to get some pepper spray for her. I never leave home without it."

I let out a long breath. "Bash, can you keep an ear out for Kody? I'm going to walk Josie to her car."

Josie stood up. "There's no need. I'll be fine."

I wanted to shout. Frustration tore at me. I was angry, but not at Josie, so I forced my voice to remain cool and reasonable. "Kaylie lives a couple of blocks from here. That's where she was attacked — in broad daylight. The guy is still out there, so I'd rather not chance it."

Uncharacteristically, Josie gave in without a fight. "Okay, let me get my stuff."

As soon as I finished escorting Josie to her car, I whipped out my phone. I needed to know that Kaylie was okay. I didn't think I'd ever spoken to her on the phone before, but I wanted to hear her voice.

"Sidney?" she answered tentatively.

"Are you okay?" I knew that she was safe at home, so why did I sound so frantic?

She paused for a moment. "I'm fine. Just a little shaken up by it."

"You should stay at my place. In Bash's room." My words were tumbling out fast. "Bash can drive over and pick you up in the car."

She sighed. "I'm perfectly fine at my place. Jill will be home soon and Bash is going to pick me up in the morning. The police think the guy is long gone by now."

"But, what if he isn't?" I was squeezing my phone hard.

She slowly released a breath. "Sid, I can't hide in my apartment forever. I'm not going to let this guy take away my freedom."

A growl of displeasure scratched my throat. "Just for tonight then."

"I'm not going anywhere tonight." She sounded exasperated. "In fact, I'm enjoying a relaxing soak in the bathtub right now. I've got me knee elevated out of the water, with an ice pack on it, so..."

Her words stopped me in my tracks, right in the middle of the sidewalk, forcing people to walk around me. I didn't hear the rest of what she was saying. The visual in my mind of Kaylie soaking in a bathtub was so detailed and so erotic, that I had an instant hard-on.

Fuck! I shouldn't be imagining Kaylie like that — reclining in the tub, her perfect breasts just peeking out over the waterline and one leg raised just enough to catch a glimpse of her pussy. The same pussy that had been sopping and so damn slick with arousal for me.

A wave of desire coursed through my veins. I tried to tamp it down with the usual arguments.

Kaylie was off-limits.

Bash would kill me.

She was like a little sister to me.

It wasn't working. That ship had sailed. I certainly didn't think of Kaylie as a little sister anymore, and I was beginning to rationalize the Bash issue with all sorts of convenient caveats.

What he didn't know...

Kaylie could make her own choices.

I'd fooled myself for a while, but there was never any doubt that I was sexually attracted to her. Our few recent encounters had only fueled the fire that was raging inside me for a taste of her. The maddening need was starting to chip away at my resolve to keep my distance.

We were two consenting adults. As long as I treated her with respect, there should be nothing wrong with having sex with her. Hell, I was beginning to think that maybe I was interested in pursuing an actual relationship with her. I hadn't been able to get her out of my head. I spent all my time thinking about her, wanting to be with her — not just about all the ways I wanted to fuck her. It was more than that; I liked hanging out with her. I enjoyed our quiet nights together more than I'd enjoyed hanging out with my band at post-concert parties on tour.

I was just beginning to wrap my head around my feelings, but whenever I probed just a little deeper, I felt a stab of panic. Shockingly, I wasn't panicked about the thought of settling down, but about how Kaylie felt about me. I couldn't forget what she'd said to me when she was drunk.

She'd made it clear she wasn't looking for a relationship. At least with me. I was only good for a quick romp. A 'no commitment' fuck. After all, I was a single dad. I had a son, and she was too young for that kind of responsibility.

I appreciated the utter irony in the situation. But instead of chuckling at the universe, I felt like cursing it. In fact, I couldn't contemplate the situation for too long without feeling a tightening of anxiety in my chest.

Growing up in foster care had taught me to shun relationships and emotional attachments. It was a matter of survival. But after a decade of living the sexually indulgent lifestyle of a rock star, the appeal had tarnished. I'd experienced brief glimpses of that disillusionment through the years, but I was an expert at burying my emotions usually by burying myself deep inside my pick of a number of willing women.

Witnessing Ryder's relationship with Talia was the first noticeable crack in my carefully constructed beliefs. At first, I couldn't comprehend how Ryder could give up the plethora of sexy and willing women throwing themselves at him to settle down with one woman. I was beyond cynical about love, but to see it shining in Ryder's eyes and to witness the absolute peace and contentment it brought him began to open my eyes.

Before Kody, I was already questioning things. Ryder's relationship shone a spotlight on the hollowness in my life. Then Kody came along and forced me to reprioritize everything. I was forced to step back from the meaningless hookups with women and discovered that I didn't miss them at all. What had seemed unimaginable a short time ago was now indisputable.

With these new revelations, all the complicated feelings I'd had about Kaylie all along, that I'd valiantly tried to beat down, were now coming to the surface. And the simple truth of it was that she wasn't ready for a relationship.

"Sidney? Are you still there?"

I shook myself out of my thoughts and discreetly adjusted the uncomfortable bulge in my pants. "I'm just worried about you. Even if that guy is gone, what you went through was scary as fuck. Promise me, you'll let me know if you need me? For anything?"

Chapter 23

Kaylie

MY HAND TREMBLED AS I looked down at my phone. Another message from an unknown caller. I was scared to look, but what if this was about the audition? What if I got the part? I had to check.

Taking a deep breath, I tapped the newest voicemail message until it opened on the screen. I read the transcription, not even needing to hit play and hear the person's voice.

"Baby girl, I'm coming for you."

A trickle of fear pierced my insides. I glanced around the bus. The man in the seat diagonally behind me looked over. Was he watching me? I quickly looked away from him and closed my eyes. No. That was silly, I admonished myself. He only looked my way because I'd turned around.

These damn phone calls were making me paranoid. And who could blame me after what happened yesterday morning? Plus, I was running on fumes from having had a restless night's sleep.

I'd thought I'd put the ugly incident behind me when I was relaxing in the tub. Then Sid had called and his protective attitude chafed at me. It felt like he was in big brother mode. I hated playing the helpless female in distress. And then my actual big brother had gone and called my parents. I'd spent over an hour on the phone trying to convince them I was safe and didn't need to move back home. It was enough to make me scream. I lay awake for hours, dissecting it all in my head before finally falling asleep.

Just hours later, I awoke from a disturbing dream that quickly faded into the wisps of forgotten memory, but still left my heart pounding for a few long minutes as I sat in the dark.

Trying to keep busy so I didn't dwell on matters, I showered and got ready for work super early. I had an hour to kill before Bash was supposed to pick me up, so I grabbed my phone to check out social media.

That's when I noticed the phone calls I'd received overnight. I checked them just in case they weren't random robocalls that had made it through my spam blocker. A few were hangups. One that sounded like a bunch of grunting and heavy breathing. Blocked. One that was a deep voice rasping, "I bet your cunt is dripping while you're waiting for me. It won't be long." I gasped and then blocked that number, too.

Was it a wrong number? Or a threat? Uneasiness had flooded through me. Could it be connected with the attack? It didn't make any sense. How could that man get my phone number? He didn't know my name, my address, or any information about me. It was just a coincidence; a coincidence that I hadn't shared with Bash. I didn't want to give him or my parents any more ammunition to use against me.

But now, there were more calls. From different numbers. I lifted the phone to my ear to listen to the latest message. It was hard to tell, but the voices sounded different, too. What were the chances that different men were leaving sexual messages on my phone? One wrong number was possible. Several didn't make sense.

The bus halted at my stop and I got off. My shift had ended at 2 o'clock. Bash had told me to call him when I left work, so he could meet me here, but I deliberately hadn't called him. I thought I could prove to him I didn't need an escort, like a helpless little girl. As I looked nervously around the city streets as I walked home, I realized it was a mistake. These phone calls had completely unnerved me. Instinct was telling me that something was wrong.

I walked at a brisk pace, keeping a sharp eye on my surroundings. If I saw anything suspicious, I was going to call the police right away. My heart skipped a beat when my ringtone went off. Unknown caller.

I swallowed. I had to answer it. What if it was the casting director calling me back from a different number?

"Hello?" I answered in a friendly tone.

"Where you at, bitch?" It sounded like a young male, angry with slurring speech.

"Who is this?" I hated that my voice trembled.

A sinister chuckle. "Your darkest fantasy."

I whipped around to make sure no one was sneaking up behind me. My plea sounded desperate, "Stop calling me."

"I'm gonna do more than call you, bitch. I'm gonna wreck that cunt of yours."

I hung up. Fear pounded through my veins. I felt nauseous and lightheaded at the same time. I fumbled with my phone to block the number and then I half-ran back to my apartment, constantly looking over my shoulder and scanning my surroundings. Every person looked sinister.

I was out of breath, my pulse pounding violently in my ears when I slammed into my apartment and locked the door. I frantically searched through my handbag for the phone number of the police officer who had filed my report yesterday.

By the time I got through to Officer Adams, I was worried I might have overreacted. He politely took down the information about the calls and advised me to screen all my calls, even after I told him I was expecting an important call about a job. He gave me a few general safety tips, mostly common sense, and then said he'd get back to me.

When I finally hung up, my hands stopped shaking. I felt safe in my apartment, but I was still jittery, waiting for my phone to ring.

About an hour later, Martina came home. She had heard about my attack but hadn't gotten the details. I told her the story and then filled her in on the obscene phone calls I was getting. She'd been very sympathetic but seemed to brush off my worries.

My phone rang again when I was in my bedroom straightening up. I tensed. I let my ringtone play for a few seconds before glancing at the screen. It was the police. I let out a sigh of relief. My relief didn't last long. A woman who identified herself as an LAPD detective asked if she could come to my residence to speak to me. I consented, and she arrived within twenty minutes.

She introduced herself as Detective Doris Jenkins and told me that the officer who took my case had referred my file over to her.

"When you called today with the information about the phone calls, Officer Adams suspected something else was going on and referred the case to me. This is an area I specialize in, and unfortunately, he was right to do so."

My eyebrows scrunched together with confusion. "What do you

mean?"

"I did some searching on the internet and confirmed what Officer Adams and I both suspected. A photo of you, along with personal information such as your phone number and address, was posted to an unscrupulous website."

"What?" Shock punched cold through my veins.

She put a hand on my shoulder. "The particular site where your information is posted is a really nasty one. We've been trying to take it down for over a year now. It's international and the site owners must have some powerful people in their pocket. We've gotten no cooperation from the authorities over there."

I stared at her, my eyebrows knitted incredulously as I shook my head in confusion. "I don't understand?"

"Do you want to sit down?" she asked. "This next part, well, it's very distressing."

I collapsed onto the sofa while she remained standing.

She continued, "You may have heard of revenge porn? In this case, you got lucky in that no pornography is involved. The photo of you is just a headshot. It looks like a professional headshot."

"Oh, God." My shoulders slumped and my head dropped into my hands.

"Unfortunately, whoever posted it stated that you had a rape fantasy. I'm sorry, Kaylie, but the post reads like you wrote it and are begging strangers to rape you."

The room started to spin. I felt sick like I might vomit.

The detective knelt down and rested her hand on my knee. "Take a deep breath. Listen, in my experience, these postings usually only lead to harassment, maybe some obscene phone calls for a few days, until it dies down. The creeps quickly move on to obsess over the next posting. Very rarely does this lead to any actual rapes or violent assaults."

My head shot up. "But I was assaulted yesterday morning. Do you think it was because of the post?"

The detective's lips thinned. "It may be related."

"And my phone number is listed? And my name?" I gasped as I realized the implications. "And my address?"

"Oh my God, Kaylie!" Martina wailed from her bedroom doorway, where she'd apparently been listening to the conversation. "You're going to be a beacon for every sick fuck in the entire city. They have our address! It's not safe to live here anymore. I can't believe what you've done!"

She retreated to her room, slamming the door shut before I could even process what she'd said.

The detective droned on about the cyber team working to take the post down or trace who had put it up, but I was barely registering anything. Every bit of safety and security I'd felt in my apartment slipped away. Martina was right. I had a target on my back.

I tried to focus on what the detective was saying. "... flyers to all your neighbors in the building about not buzzing in anyone they don't know."

The detective stopped speaking when Martina stormed out of her room, pulling a suitcase. "I'm staying at Pete's and I won't be back. And don't expect any rent money from me. I should sue you! You've made this place unlivable. "

I didn't say a word as she left. Dealing with her drama was not a priority right now.

The detective turned concerned eyes on me. "It might be a good idea for you to stay somewhere else tonight. Until we get a handle on this thing. Do you have someplace you can go?"

"Yeah. My brother's," I answered.

Detective Jenkins offered to give me a ride there and waited while I packed a bag. I wasn't paying much attention to what I was stuffing into the giant rolling duffle bag. I gathered some clothes, some toiletries, and my laptop together and then exited my room. A feeling of numbness had washed over me.

The detective spoke to me about the case as we drove the few blocks to Bash's building. I wasn't listening, but I did catch on that the chances of holding anyone responsible for the posting were close to zero.

She gave me her card as I exited the car and told me to call if anything else happened. Otherwise, she'd be in touch with any updates for me.

Josie let me into Bash's apartment. The boys were still at rehearsal. She took one look at my face and then bustled off to make us some tea while I rolled my duffel into Bash's room. I shot off a text to let Jill know what was happening. Hopefully, she wouldn't blame me like Martina had.

Over tea and lemon cake, I explained to Josie what was happening. She was disgusted and concerned all at once. "I'm glad you came here, Kaylie. It's not safe there for you anymore. Let me text Sid and Bash and tell them to come home now."

"No." I stopped her. "I'm safe here. Just give me some time to process all of this before they get home. I'm not sure how they're going to react. This is all just so crazy."

"It is," she agreed. "Who would do something like this to you?"

Tears welled in my eyes. "I don't know."

After our talk, I told Josie I was going to lie down for a bit in Bash's room. Before I went, I picked up Kody to cuddle and say hello. I bounced him a bit on my shoulder and just to add to my horrible day, Kody vomited all over me. He regurgitated foul-smelling baby formula that coated my neck and shirt. There were even some watery chunks in my hair.

"Oh, Kaylie! I'm so sorry." Josie rushed over and took Kody from my arms.

I examined my sopping wet shirt. "Wow. This has not been my lucky day."

She was looking over Kody. She put a hand on his forehead. "He seems no worse for the wear. Guess his bottle just didn't sit well in his tummy." She turned to me. "Oh, honey. It's all in your hair. You're going to smell like curdled milk."

"Ugh. It stinks already. I'm just going to jump in the shower and wash off. Luckily, I packed some clothes, so it's not a big deal. Plus, a nice hot shower might help me relax a bit."

Josie patted my arm. "You take your time, honey. You could use some relaxing."

♫♫♪♪

The state of the bathroom was surprisingly clean. I'd been in here before, mostly during parties, and it'd been pretty gross. Maybe Josie had a hand in keeping it cleaner.

I placed the clean towel I found from the linen closet at the edge of the sink next to the pile of clean clothes I'd chosen from my suitcase. While the water heated, I stripped off my puke-covered clothing. When steam started rising, I slid open the glass door of the shower and stepped under the hot spray.

I'd rinsed the baby puke off my skin and out of my hair. I could only find a generic men's shampoo, which boasted a rich, hydrating formula. Without conditioner, it was bound to look a little wonky when it dried, but there was nothing I could do about that.

Next, I studied the body wash options. One appeared to be super cheap, so I skipped that one. The next was an 'invigorating bergamot and pear essence'. I squirted a bit in my palm and tried it. It smelled nice — crisp and slightly musky, but not overbearingly masculine. The last bottle boasted a 'blend of distiller's spice, white oak, and single-cask bourbon'. I almost passed it up and went back to the bergamot and pear, but in the end, my curiosity won out.

As soon as the creamy body wash hit my palm, I realized it belonged to Sidney. Now I knew that those dreamy masculine scents surrounding him were a stunning combination of bourbon and oak. In no time at all, I was lathering the soap all over my body, luxuriating in the heavenly smell that reminded me so much of Sidney.

The hot water relaxed my tense muscles. I was safe for now. I'd have to move out of the apartment because I'd never feel safe there again, but I knew Bash would help me out financially. He'd help keep me safe, too. I'd stay here tonight and maybe for a few days until we could work out a plan.

That meant sleeping in the room next to Sidney's. Would anything happen between us? Was I sure I could handle it if it did?

I tried to think objectively about my situation with him. I still had a massive crush on him. My body ached just thinking about him. Could I steal a few nights of bliss from him and then move on? Or would I be risking heartbreak? Most importantly, would he ever stop looking at me as Bash's little sister and see me as the woman I was?

I closed my eyes and imagined him in the shower with me. It wasn't hard; his scent already enveloped me. Thinking about Sid's skin rubbing up against mine made me shiver. As I rubbed the suds of his body wash across my chest, I imagined it was his hands touching me.

It was his finger that was slowly circling my nipple. I felt an answering surge of heat in my core when I squeezed the stiffening peaks.

I tweaked my nipple several times while my right hand trailed slowly down my stomach. The ache in my pussy demanded attention.

The soap on my fingers made everything so slippery. My fingers circled my clit over and over until it was swollen with need. I slid a finger through my folds, dipping further back toward my opening.

The ache was building quickly, but it felt so delicious that I forced myself to continue slowly. I thought of Sid's fingers as I'd seen them so many times sliding over the strings of his bass. I imagined his talented and lightning-fast fingers working over me instead. Touching me everywhere.

I let out a moan. It felt so good. I dipped a finger inside, slowly sliding it in and out. Yes, Sidney. Fuck me harder. I added a second finger. I went deeper. Harder. Faster. But, it wasn't enough.

I tugged at my nipple but groaned with frustration. My other hand left my breast so that I could play with my clit while I was finger fucking myself. My finger circled the nub desperately, looking for release.

The intensity of pleasure was acute and quickly building. I let out a long, drawn-out groan as I pumped my fingers in and out. I was climbing higher and higher. Almost to the top. I tipped my head back as the first spasms rocked my body. The orgasm cascaded through me like an avalanche.

My fingers were still buried deep inside me as I came, but my other hand moved from my sensitive clit to play languidly with my breasts. A smile curled my lips. Fuck, that was satisfying.

I savored the bliss for a few more seconds before I removed my fingers and slowly opened up my eyes.

That had been a great fantasy. Because it almost looked like...

Sidney was standing right there. In the bathroom.

Watching me through the glass door.

But he was no fantasy.

From his expression, there was no doubt.

He had seen everything.

Mortification so deep and so primal swept over me. I thought I would die.

Chapter 24

Sidney

I DIDN'T KNOW WHAT to do. It had been 45 minutes. Kaylie was still locked in the bathroom and my balls were still aching as much as they were 45 minutes ago. The ache hadn't subsided while I took care of Kody and got him to sleep. How could it, when I couldn't stop thinking about what I'd witnessed?

I'd never seen anything so fucking erotic in my life. Hell, I watched my share of porn and even had women perform all kinds of crazy sex acts to impress me, but none of that had come anywhere close to turning me on the way that watching Kaylie had.

She was completely crushed by embarrassment, and I wasn't sure how to make it better. I should have bolted from the bathroom the second I realized it wasn't Bash in the shower, but one glimpse, and I was enraptured with lust. Seeing her like that was like a goddamn wet dream on steroids. I hadn't been able to turn away, and that made me an asshole.

Why hadn't Josie mentioned that Kaylie was here before she left for the day? Fuck, I should have knocked, but I assumed it was Bash and guys didn't worry too much about being naked. I made an honest mistake barging in there, but what had been unconscionable was not immediately leaving.

Now Kaylie was traumatized. I was as hard as a steel pipe, and she was hiding out in the bathroom. Was she going to stay in there all night?

I got up and tapped on the bathroom door. "Kaylie?"

Her voice was muffled. "Go away."

"C'mon. You can't stay in there all night."

"Yes, I can."

I couldn't suppress a smile. God, she was so cute. "It's not that bad. C'mon out. Let's talk about it."

She groaned. "I never, ever want to talk about it. Ever! And I don't want to see you. Go into the kitchen, so I can get out of here. I'll get my suitcase from Bash's room and then leave."

Her suitcase? Was she planning on staying here? Shit, I couldn't let her leave without discussing what happened, but she was stubborn. She'd hide in there forever if I didn't agree. "Fine, I'll go into the kitchen."

I stepped away from the door, but instead of heading toward the kitchen, I crept into Bash's room. I sat on his bed next to a large duffel bag filled with her clothes.

A few minutes later, I heard the bathroom door crack open. When she was satisfied the coast was clear, she scampered straight for Bash's room.

Her eyes opened wide when she saw me. "You tricked me!"

A smile curled my lips. "I had to; otherwise, you'd be in there all night."

Her face was flaming red. "Sidney, I'm warning you; I don't want to hear One. Single. Word."

"I think you're overreacting."

"Oh, really!" She huffed, throwing up her hands. "That was the most excruciating, humiliating thing in the world. I'll never be able to look you in the eye again without knowing exactly what you saw me doing."

Somehow, I had to fix this. I knew that if I let her leave in her current state, things between us would never be the same. She'd pull away. I had a gut feeling that how I reacted right now was critically important, but how did I fix this? On an intellectual level, I understood how vulnerable she felt that I'd seen her like that. If there was some way...

A thought popped into my head. I briefly worried that I was letting my dick do all my thinking, but pushed that aside. If there was any chance of remedying this, I had to take it. "What if we evened the score?"

She narrowed her eyes. "What do you mean?"

I reached over my head and pulled off my T-shirt. Her eyes opened wide, but I didn't miss how they trailed over my chest and down my abs, soaking everything in.

I placed my hand on the button of my jeans. "You better leave now if you don't want to see anything else."

I slowly pulled down my zipper. She was rooted to the spot. Before she had a chance to bolt, I slid down my jeans and pulled them off, along with my socks.

Just my gray boxer briefs remained. My dick was throbbing, but I paused for a second, hoping she'd stay. Her eyes bounced between the bulge in my underwear and my face.

Seconds later, I was pulling off my boxer briefs. I didn't want to scare her off, but my need for relief was so great that I fisted my dick and gave it a stroke.

Her eyes had gone cloudy and her lips were slightly parted. Fuck, she was so beautiful. "You like what you see, babe?"

She didn't answer, but she certainly didn't look away.

I gave my cock another long stroke. "Because I liked what I saw earlier. I really liked it."

Her eyes shot up to my face.

"What you were doing — it was so sexy. It made my cock so unbelievably hard. You have nothing to be ashamed of, Kaylie. You have a beautiful body."

Her breath was coming a little faster now as she watched me pumping my fist over my dick.

"It was hotter than any of my wildest fantasies about you."

Her eyes locked with mine again, and her mouth fell open. I was playing with fire, but it was too late to stop.

"Look what you do to me." I stroked myself while she watched. "When I was watching you, I wished it was my hands running over your body, Kaylie. I wished my tongue was where your fingers were. I wanted my tongue fucking your pretty pink pussy."

She swayed slightly and let out a strangled gasp.

Did I take things too far? Give away too much? "I've been fighting this attraction I feel for you for a long time, babe. I'm not sure I can hold out much longer."

She stood so still I thought maybe she didn't hear me. My chest squeezed when a slight frown crossed her lips. I'd fucked up. She was about to put a stake in my heart by running away from me. I'd just made everything a thousand times worse.

She looked up at me, blinking a few times, but then back down to what I was doing. She took a tentative step. Towards me. Not away.

A few more quick steps and then she sank down to her knees in front of me, pushing my hand away.

"You don't—" The words died as soon as her lips surrounded me.

It felt so fucking amazing. Her tongue swirled around the head of my cock while her hand wrapped around its base. I watched in awe as she took my length into the wet heat of her mouth, pushing me all the way to the back of her throat.

When I was buried deep, she looked up at me with wide eyes. I wanted to imprint that visual onto my brain forever. She pulled back almost to the tip, sucking hard, and then swallowed me again.

I nearly lost my mind. A groan of pure ecstasy rumbled in my chest. I grabbed a handful of her hair in my fist, not knowing if I wanted her to stop or keep going.

"I'm not going to last," I hissed. "You should—"

Fuck. Instead of stopping, she worked her mouth over me, sucking harder and faster. Her free hand slid up my thigh and then cupped my balls. I was about to explode.

I thrust into her mouth. Fuck. I couldn't help it. My whole body shuddered. One more thrust and I was coming. My eyes rolled back, and I grunted like an animal, but she kept her mouth on me, milking every last drop.

When my cock settled down, I realized my hand was still twisted in her hair. I gently eased her off my dick and then lifted her to her feet.

"Holy fuck, Kaylie." I pulled her against me and wrapped my arms around her, not wanting to let her go just yet.

She buried her face in my chest for a few seconds and then looked up at me with those green eyes that made my stomach flutter. "I want…" She looked away.

I grabbed her chin and directed her gaze back to me. "Tell me what you want."

Her eyes were still lust-filled. She swallowed nervously. "I want you."

My dick was already twitching. "Are you sure?"

She bit her lip and then nodded. "I've wanted you for forever, Sidney Anderson."

My stomach see-sawed and my chest tightened. I sucked in a breath to steady myself. Her words did something to me, but I didn't want to examine what the hell it meant.

Instead, I captured her lips with my own. The kiss was bruising. I had a lot of pent-up need and not just physical need. My mind was screaming for me to think of the repercussions of what I was about to do, but when Kaylie responded to my kiss with a hunger to match my own, those nagging thoughts were swept aside.

Without breaking our kiss, I leaned down and scooped her up into my arms in one motion. Her tongue was still dueling with mine as she curled her arms around my neck.

I carried her out of Bash's room and into my own. I was on a mission to show her how much I wanted her. I'd make her orgasm until she couldn't even remember her own name anymore. Fuck, the things I was going to do to her.

I peeled my lips from hers and then placed her on my bed. For a brief moment, I thought about my discarded clothes laying on Bash's floor. I wanted to close my bedroom door in case Bash came home unexpectedly, but then I might not hear Kody if he woke up. There was too much thinking going on, but then Kaylie peeled off her shirt and I was once again mindless with need.

I didn't waste any time. I stalked over to the bed and crawled up her body until I was directly over her. She trembled, and I froze. "Kaylie?"

Her arms wrapped around my back and pulled me down against her. "Please don't leave."

"I won't, babe." I brushed my mouth against hers, feeling her soft hands running over the skin on my back.

My tongue traced along the seam of her lip, but then she opened for me and I was back in heaven, showing her with my tongue exactly what I wanted to do to other parts of her. When I'd kissed her breathless, my mouth blazed a trail of feather-light kisses toward her neck.

A soft nip from my teeth wrung out a strangled whimper from her, so I did it again and then followed it by lightly sucking on the sensitive skin. I found several spots that made her squirm underneath me. I'd catalog those discoveries for later because I was impatient to get my tongue to other places on her body.

The hand that I wasn't using to prop my weight off her was already exploring her breasts. It had slipped inside her bra and was tugging at her hard nipple, eliciting gasps and groans of pleasure.

Each one of her needy sounds had my dick getting harder until my body was begging me to push inside her. It was a good thing I'd unloaded not even five minutes ago; otherwise, I wouldn't be able to maintain enough control to do all the things I wanted to do to her. I wanted to wring multiple orgasms from her. Make her scream my name. Ruin her for any other man.

A fierce possessiveness sunk into me. The desire to take her like a caveman was overpowering, but I needed to slow the fuck down or I'd scare her away. I slid off the top of her body to her side where I could lean on my elbow and devour her with my eyes. I unsnapped her red lacy bra and then wiggled it off her body. Her first reaction was to cover herself, but I grabbed both her hands in mine and pulled them over her head where I kept them captive. She had amazing tits.

She bit her lip. "What are you doing?"

My smile was lazy as my finger slowly circled around her pert nipple. "You are amazing. Beautiful. I just want to look at you for a moment."

She drew in a shaky breath. "Okay."

I watched as my finger trailed over her skin, dipping into the valley between her breasts, and up the soft swell of flesh to her other breast. She was squirming again when I softly tugged at her taut rosy tip.

"I'm going to take your pants off, and then your panties, until you're bare for me. And then I'm going to look at you. I'm going to get my fill before I get my first taste of you."

She was panting, her chest slightly heaving with every breath, but as I spoke, her eyes scrunched tightly closed.

Her face was flushed, a pink blush covered her chest, and her nipples were hard and standing at attention. There was no doubt that she turned on. Was she shy about me seeing her body?

"Kaylie, open your eyes." I waited until her stunning green eyes were gazing up at me. "Is that okay with you?"

She hesitated for a second. "Yes."

Fuck.

My feelings must have flickered across my face because she suddenly looked panicked. "Oh God, Sid, please don't stop. I'm sorry. I'm just a little nervous. Nobody's ever talked to me like that before. Please. Please."

Nobody's talked to her like that before? During sex? Did she mean dirty talk? Because on a scale of 1 to 10, what I had said had been maybe a 2. Not all that dirty. What the hell?

Her eyes met mine, and at that moment, I knew exactly what she wanted me to do. She didn't need to say a word. Her eyelashes fluttered as she tilted her head back, exposing the vulnerable curve of her neck. She looked so goddamn beautiful in my bed. Beautiful and innocent.

It hit me like a punch to the stomach. "Fuck, Kaylie! Are you a virgin?"

She winced. "No! No, I'm not a virgin. I'm just not that experienced. And, you're just ... And I'm so turned on right now. I need you. I just want you to ... God, I'm ruining everything."

Immediately, I let go of her hands that I'd held trapped over her head. Fuck. I didn't even know what to do. All the girls that I'd been with in the past were absolute maneaters. My profession attracted confident women who were no-holds barred when it came to sex. I couldn't remember one woman who ever was shy or virginal in bed with me.

I pulled my hand off her breast and took a deep breath. "We can take this slow, babe. I don't want to push you to do something you don't want."

She covered her eyes with her hands and groaned. "You don't understand. I want this." She removed her hands and looked at me. "I want this. More than anything. I've wanted it forever."

Two minutes ago, I didn't think anything could have stopped me from plowing into her. But now, I was hesitating. Doubts were creeping in.

Her hand wrapped around my dick, and she began to stroke me. Her touch was heavenly, applying the perfect amount of pressure and sliding up and down my length until I was clenching my teeth with need. She wasn't that innocent; she knew how to touch like an expert.

Pressing her body against mine, she whispered, "Please, Sid. I want this."

Her big green eyes were pleading with me again. My hand brushed against her cheek and then my finger tugged on the bottom of her plump lower lip. Fuck, I wanted her.

"Tell me what you want," I rasped out.

"I want—" She hesitated. "I want you to look at me. Naked. I want you inside me."

It felt like my dick was growing even bigger and harder under her soft ministrations. Her tongue darted out and licked the tip of my finger. Fuck, I felt that right in my balls.

"Dirtier, Kaylie. I'll only give you what you want if you tell me exactly what it is you want. The filthier the better."

Her hand stopped stroking me as she thought. "I want you to ... fuck me. I want you to look at my ... pussy." Her eyes grew glassy. "I'll spread my legs wide and you'll put your tongue on me. I want you to lick me with your tongue. Suck on my clit. Slide your fingers inside me and fuck me. And, then your big ... cock? Dick? Yeah, fuck me with your cock."

That was the most stilted dirty talk I'd ever heard, but fuck if it hadn't turned me on like no other. She sounded like a little girl trying out a new dirty word, but she definitely got an A for effort.

Her eyes darted to mine.

"I'm going to give you all that and more." My lips captured her mouth, and I gave her a preview of how damn thorough my tongue was going to be.

When she was breathless and moaning, my mouth moved to her breasts. I worked one with my hand while my tongue, teeth, and lips worked the other. My mouth rained kisses down her belly until I got to the waistband of her leggings.

I sat up so I could remove her leggings and panties, tossing them to the side. Pulling her knees apart, I then crawled between her legs. She looked exquisite. Like a buffet of my favorite treats laid out before me.

"I'm going to make you come so hard. I can't wait to taste you, babe." Pulling my gaze from her perfect pussy, I glanced up at her. "You're going to orgasm around my fingers the first time. Or maybe around my tongue. Only after that will you get my cock. You're going to be on top, riding me, so I can watch your face when you orgasm the second time. I want you to play with your tits while you're bouncing up and down on my cock."

I'd worked my dirty talk up to a 3. I didn't want to push it.

She was still watching me. "Yes," she replied with a breathy whisper.

I wanted to dive right in, but instead, I slid a hand up the silky soft skin of her right leg, following its path with my lips. Kissing behind her knee, I moved higher, slowly making my way up her inner thighs. I wanted to take it slow, but the scent of her arousal spurred me until my tongue was intimately exploring her.

I licked up and down her folds, parting her until I could nip at her clit. She was watching me with hooded eyes while she played with her tits. It was a breathtaking sight. I dove back in, feasting on her. I worked my tongue, relentlessly circling her clit before giving it a suck and then sliding it down to her opening where I fluttered in and out.

The sweet yet musky taste of her was driving me crazy and there was no doubt that I was driving her crazy. I knew she was close to the edge. She was crying out wildly now. Her hands were buried in my hair and she was bucking her hips frantically against my mouth.

My tongue found her clit again while my finger slid inside her pussy. My dick throbbed painfully; she was hot and tight and I couldn't wait to be inside her. I crooked my finger, stroking her G-spot like I loved to stroke my acoustic guitar.

She was screaming now, her thighs clamped around my head like a vise, her body writhing like it was possessed. Fuck, she was wild, but I didn't back down. My tongue flicked her clit over and over, while I slowly increased the pressure I used to rub her inside walls with my fingertip.

She shouted out my name, a few 'oh fuck' chants, and several unintelligible cries that turned to moans. I'd never seen or heard something so erotic. She was ready to explode.

I sucked her clit, and suddenly she gushed. Within a split second, she was spasming around me, around my finger, and around my tongue.

Holy shit! She'd squirted.

I'd made her come so fucking hard, just like I said I would. Fuck, I felt like Superman. There was nothing like making a girl squirt to stroke the ego. And, I didn't think it was possible to be any more turned on by Kaylie, but apparently, I was wrong. I ached to be inside her and claim her as mine.

While I was busy mentally high-fiving myself, her spasms had slowed and her whole body had started shaking. Was this the aftermath of an intense orgasm or was she cold? I pulled my finger out of her and slid up her body, covering it with mine to keep her warm.

I was on cloud-fucking-9 and about to kiss the hell out of her when I realized how stiff she was. She was trying to force her legs closed but my thigh was in between blocking her. Her head was turned away from me and her eyes were clamped shut.

"Oh, my God," she whispered.

I smiled. "You must have liked that a lot, babe."

"I can't believe I did that. I'm so sorry." She turned her body away from me, laying on her side.

Frowning, I scooted my body, flush against her length, so that I was spooning her. "Did you ever do that before?"

Her body went completely rigid. I almost couldn't hear what she said because her head was burrowing into the pillow trying to hide. "Pee in the bed? No. Oh God!"

I rubbed my hand up and down her shoulder. "You didn't pee. You squirted."

"What?" Her head popped up.

I chuckled. "Haven't you ever watched porn?"

"Not really." She shrugged. "At least not the kind where women are squirting."

I snuggled into her neck and kissed it. "Yeah. Well, you squirted. And it was fucking hot."

She turned onto her back and looked at me dubiously. "Are you sure? You're not just saying that to make me feel better? It felt like pee."

"It wasn't pee. Trust me, Kaylie. It tastes nothing like pee. It tastes like sex."

Her mouth opened wide with shock. "Oh, my God! You tasted it?"

My lips twitched, trying not to laugh at her. "Well, my mouth was right there. It was kind of unavoidable."

Her hands covered her face again. "I squirted in your mouth?"

I pulled a few strands of hair that were sticking to her face and rubbed them between my fingers. "You did. And it makes me feel like a million bucks. Like I did a fucking great job."

"You did," she said shyly. "I've never had an orgasm like that before. It was so … intense. Like I just lost control of everything and existed in a state of pure ecstasy. It was amazing. But what about you?"

I pulled her into my arms. "Me? I'm good. Don't forget that I 'squirted' in your mouth not too long ago. And that was amazing. Your mouth was like heaven, but I still want inside your pussy. Tell me you're staying over tonight?"

Her finger was tracing the tattoo on my chest. "I am. And I want you to, uh, fuck me, Sidney, but I think I need at least fifteen minutes to regroup. That was just so intense."

My fingers grazed up and down her sides. "I love it when you talk dirty to me. I'm going to — "

Kody was crying in the other room. His dinner-time naps were getting shorter and shorter. I sighed and reluctantly untangled myself from Kaylie's body.

I got up and headed toward the door. "Little stinker has bad timing."

Kaylie giggled. "Umm. You're still naked."

I ran a hand through my hair. "My clothes are still in Bash's room. Would you mind changing the bedsheets? There are some extras in the linen closet."

She grabbed the top sheet and pulled it up so that it covered her body. "Sure."

My dick was still hard and still hoping to sink into her. Sorry, buddy. It pulsed a few beats when I saw her staring at it.

"Pull down those covers and let me see you again."

After a few seconds of hesitation, she did.

My hand went to my dick. "Open your legs, babe. Let me see everything."

Christ. She looked like a damn goddess. Her dark hair was sexily tousled and splayed around her head in a crazy pattern, and her lips were red and swollen from my kisses. A muted pink color tinted her cheeks and along her upper chest. Her tits were perfect, natural, and large enough to fill my big hands, with nipples and areola a dusky rose color, which contrasted against her creamy pale skin. I'd always admired her long athletic legs, but this time her knees were bent and slightly splayed so that I could glimpse her glistening pussy.

Fuck! I wanted her so badly. I licked my lips and tugged on my cock wishing I could sink into her, but Kody let out another wail. I committed the vision of her looking like this to memory before I tore my gaze away.

Hurrying into Bash's room, I threw on my boxer briefs and jeans. I didn't bother putting on a shirt because Kody was starting to get worked up.

All the while I took care of Kody, I was thinking about Kaylie laying on my bed. We had just crossed a line.

And it had been fantastic. She made me feel so incredible. I'd never experienced sex like this before. We had a connection. Something deeper. I always knew it would be like this for us. I'd always suspected and maybe that's why I'd been so scared of it. One taste would never be enough. I needed more. I wanted all of her.

Maybe this was just all about sex for her. The thought sent a skittering of cold fissures erupting through my skin and ricocheting inside my veins. I wanted to make her mine, but I wasn't sure how she felt about me.

She emerged from my room about thirty minutes later, fully dressed, hair and makeup intact once again. She stared at my bare chest for a moment. "You should put a shirt on."

I crooked an eyebrow and joked, "Can't handle it, huh?"

Her lips turned down. "I called Bash and told him to come home. He's going to be here any minute."

What?

I kissed Kody on the top of his head as I tried to hold in the panic bubbling in my blood. Was she going to confess to Bash? Tell him what we just did?

What the fuck was happening?

Chapter 25

Kaylie

I was having a moment.

I can't believe I did that.

With *Sidney*.

My God, it blew away my every fantasy.

My head sunk into the pillow. So this was what euphoria felt like. An overwhelming satisfaction. Intense pleasure. Followed by profound happiness.

Amazing!

I snuggled under the covers that smelled like Sidney. I was still naked. In Sidney's bed. I bit down on my knuckle so I didn't squee out loud like a total dork.

When Kody's cries interrupted us, Sidney hinted that we weren't finished. I wasn't even sure I could handle anything more. I was still blissfully wrung out from the incredible full-body orgasm he'd given me. Something felt different within me. I was ridiculously high on Sidney.

This was only the second time I'd been in Sid's bedroom; the first time I hadn't been able to check it out properly. It was a small room, made even smaller with all the baby stuff crammed into it. Besides all the baby gear, small piles of Kody's folded clothes cluttered every free surface — on the dresser, the nightstand, and on the rocking chair. Plastic blinds covered the two windows on the side wall. The bed was seriously no-frills. It was a queen-sized mattress set resting on a frame with no headboard, comforter, or decorative pillows. There was one picture hanging on the beige walls — a framed print of a fancy-looking guitar.

The room had no personality, but I guessed guys didn't care too much about decor. It made me wonder if Sidney was planning on staying in this apartment to raise Kody. It didn't seem ideal for a kid. My euphoric buzz faded a bit when I thought about Sidney and Kody and what the future held. Where did I fit into the picture? Did I even want to fit into it?

I snorted with derision. What the hell was going on with me? Bash was right. I wasn't a casual sex kind of girl. One sexual experience with Sidney and I was already dreaming about our wedding. Jeez, I had to get myself together. I had so much shit going on right now in my life, I couldn't afford to flake out and let my heart get stomped on.

I thought about the last few days. If I were watching my life from afar, I'd have whiplash.

Just days ago, I'd been physically attacked. While it made me feel scared and vulnerable, I'd picked myself up, dusted off the fear, and moved on. I was proud of how strong a woman I was. Brave and bold. Not weak.

I'd attended my audition, even as my knee throbbed in agony and the dirty taste of my attacker's hand covering my mouth was still fresh in my memory. In fact, I hadn't just attended the audition, I'd killed it.

Even as a part of me wanted to cower away in fear, I stayed in my apartment that night. I didn't let Bash coddle me like a baby. I went to work. Everything was normal.

Up and down like a Yo-Yo. Fall down. Get back up.

The obscene phone calls were unnerving. I wondered if men even knew how much a nebulous threat like that could terrify a woman right down to her soul?

But the worry I had endured when I thought the phone calls were random turned out to be child's play when I found out what was really going on. Someone had taken the time to acquire my photo and personal information to post on a website asking people to rape me using the thin veil of pretense that I, personally, was posting with some kind of rape fetish.

Was it some kind of sick joke? Or was there deep, malicious intent behind it? Were they just trying to scare me? Or actually wanted me to get raped, or worse? Whatever the intent, it had stripped away all the bravery I'd been mustering since my attack and left me exposed in the crosshairs of looming danger.

Of course, I'd gone running to my big brother for help, but I couldn't deny that in the back of my mind, I was also running to Sidney. He was never far from my thoughts.

Then I let my guard down for just one brief moment. I couldn't explain it, but I'd felt completely safe for the first time in days. The shower had relaxed my tense muscles. I'd been surrounded by Sidney's scent, I was naked, and fantasizing hardcore about him. I still couldn't think about what happened without feeling that crazy dip in my stomach. I'd been caught by Sidney masturbating in his shower. Not just touching myself, but fucking myself. Oh, God!

I don't know how he did it, but Sidney somehow managed to soothe my utter humiliation. He said all the right things. Hell, he did all the right things. He'd pulled out his dick and had my mouth watering so that I instantly forgot how mortified I was.

I was back on that roller coaster again. I'd surprised myself by falling to my knees and sucking him off like a champion. It'd felt really sexy, and I'd actually loved it when he came in my mouth. It made me feel powerful that I could give him such pleasure.

When I realized that he was going to take it further, I vacillated between wildly aroused, painfully nervous, and nearly hyperventilating at the thought that my wildest fantasies were about to come true. He obviously noticed, because at one point he'd flat-out asked if I was a virgin. So much for the confidence-boosting blow job I'd given him.

I thought maybe I'd ruined everything, but I'd begged him to continue. It had led to the most sexually intense experience of my life. I don't know if it was Sid's mad skills or just the fact that it was him — more likely a combination of them both — but the eroticism had been off the charts.

The orgasm had been earth-shattering. It came from deep inside, hitting me like an unstoppable force and scattering bits of electrified bliss through every cell in my body. I could only surrender to the feeling, and it was pure bliss.

I lost all control. And I had squirted. Yeah, I read Cosmo from time to time, so I'd heard of it before but never could have imagined that happening to me. It surprised the ever-loving shit out of me. I still wasn't sure if it should mortify me, but Sidney seemed more than fine with what happened.

As much as I knew it was dangerous for my soul, I couldn't help but fantasize about a future with Sidney as I luxuriated naked in his bed.

The roller coaster had taken me way up that steep first hill, reached the climax at the top, and then plunged me down in a thrilling rush. Now I was waiting to see what the rest of the ride would bring. Would it be full of upside-down loops and thrilling twists and turns? Or would it be head-jarring, herky-jerky movements that turned the stomach?

My phone pinged from the floor. I scrambled off the bed and dug it out of the pocket of my leggings. The text message was from Bash. I'd forgotten that I'd texted him when I first got here. I'd asked him to meet me at his place because I desperately needed to talk to him. The text said he'd be here ten minutes from now.

I'd forgotten all about Bash. What if I'd missed his text? He could have easily walked in on Sidney and me. Where the hell was my brain? I scrambled out of Sid's bed and hastily threw on my clothes. I checked to make sure I looked presentable before I went to warn Sidney.

He was in the kitchen taking care of Kody. Shirtless. God, he looked so fine. He was loaded with muscles and tattoos. His jeans hung low on his waist, accentuating the treasure trail of hair that highlighted his washboard abs and had my eyes dipping lower. His cocky smile let me know that he'd caught me metaphorically drooling over his tight body.

I took a breath and shook myself out of my sex-induced daze. "You should put a shirt on."

His devilish smirk disappeared instantly when I told him I'd called Bash and he'd be here any moment. I took Kody from him while he went to get changed and to clean up any evidence of our sex tryst.

I frowned when he came back out, all covered up with clothes, but even clothing couldn't disguise just how hot he was.

"Kaylie, what's going on? Why did you call Bash?" His hand was absently rubbing his elbow.

"I'll tell you when Bash gets here."

He cringed and ran a hand through his hair. "Did you tell him?"

"What? No!" Why the hell would he think that? I decided to throw him a bone; though he'd be trading one worry for another when he found out what had happened. "Didn't you wonder why I came here with my suitcase?"

His eyes widened. "Oh, shit! Did something happen? Did that guy come back?"

"No, but I don't feel safe at my apartment anymore. I'm hoping it's okay that I stay here, at least for tonight. I haven't figured out what I'm going to do yet."

He pulled me in close for a hug. It wasn't an intimate hug, because I was still holding Kody, but it still had my stomach fluttering.

His lips brushed my skin as whispered into my temple, "Of course, you can stay here."

It felt good to be holding Kody and being wrapped in Sidney's arms. I was safe and happy, desperately trying to ignore my brain, which was flashing a warning sign. Don't get too caught up.

We broke apart when we heard the door opening. Still holding Kody, I followed Sidney out of the kitchen.

Bash rubbed at his chin. "What's going on, Kaylie? You've got me worried."

I took a deep breath and held it for a second. This was not going to be easy. "I've got to tell you something. Please promise me that you won't overreact."

His eyes ping-ponged between me and Sidney. "Now I'm really worried. Just fucking tell me."

First, I told them about the nasty phone calls. Their reactions didn't bode well for calmly hearing the rest of it. Bash was already pacing and clenching his fist. Sid's face had gone bright red from holding in barely suppressed anger.

It didn't help that twice in the middle of my telling them about the calls my phone rang with two different unknown numbers. I declined the call each time but noticed a few nasty texts popping up from those numbers.

"There's more." My voice sounded small.

As I explained the post that Detective Jenkins had found on the internet, both of their expressions grew increasingly dark. When I told them that my personal information had been listed, Bash reminded me of a rabid dog. His teeth were bared and his nostrils flared with anger. Sid was less angry and more concerned. His face paled, and he rubbed the back of his neck.

I explained some of the details the detective told me about the website — how they hadn't had any luck getting it taken down or posts removed because it was foreign and protected by big money or some hostile influential powers.

I let out a long shuddering exhale and then told them the worst part. "According to the detective, the post was written, so it sounds like I wrote it. It says that I have a rape fantasy and I'm begging strangers to fulfill my darkest fantasy by raping me. The rougher the better."

Bash's mouth dropped open in shock, and there was an audible intake of breath from Sid.

I glanced over at Sidney. His expression was pinched, and I could see a vein throbbing on his forehead. His muscles tightened like he was gearing up for a fight, but that was the main problem; there was no enemy to fight.

Bash's eyes were bulging with rage, his lips curled with disgust as he muttered a string of unintelligible curses.

I stood up and started walking around when Kody started fussing. "Calm down, Bash. Don't scare Kody."

He swung around and pinned me with a stare. "First off, you're not going back to that apartment. You can stay here until we find someplace else. Someplace with much better security."

I nodded, already coming to the same conclusion myself. I'd never feel safe again in that apartment.

He continued, "You can't go anywhere by yourself. I think you're going to need a bodyguard."

I knew he was going to go ballistic, but a bodyguard? "No, I don't need a bodyguard. I'll be safe here for now. No one knows I'm here. I didn't even tell my roommates where I'm staying, so coming and going from here won't be dangerous. No one could track me down."

Sid came and took Kody from me. "Kaylie, I think he's right. You need to take this seriously. Someone could track you down through your job and follow you when you get off. Who knows?"

I shot him an accusatory glance. Now they were ganging up on me. "I am taking this seriously. That's why I came here."

Bash could see I was getting agitated. "You did the right thing. Did you tell Mom and Dad yet?"

I sighed heavily. "You know they'll just insist I come home."

"That might not be a bad idea right now. You'd be safer there."

"Are you for real?" I whined. "I just had a great audition. It could be my dream role. A chance of a lifetime. I'm not leaving Los Angeles."

My phone began ringing. Unknown number. I was about to decline the call when Bash pulled the phone from my hand and accepted the call.

If I thought Bash's face looked scary when I was telling him about the website, what I saw cross over his face as he listened to whoever was on my phone was terrifying.

His jaw clenched and his scratchy voice sounded inhuman. "Listen real good, fucker. I'm tracking this number. I'm going to hunt you down and fuck you up so bad you'll wish you'd—"

The guy must have hung up because Bash let his hand drop to his side. "I can't believe this!" He was shaking with rage. You're going to need a new phone number."

"Yeah," I agreed quietly. "It's going to be a pain in the ass, but I can't take all these calls. I've already blocked nearly a dozen numbers, and it's not slowing down."

"Fuck, Kaylie! This is a goddamn nightmare."

Both of them were pretty worked up, but their male posturing wouldn't do any good. "The detective said that this would probably all calm down in a few days. The creeps would gravitate to the next victim."

"Kaylie." Sid's growl sounded like a warning.

Bash came over to me and wrapped me in a hug. "You're going to stay here until we figure something out. And you're not going anywhere by yourself for now. I'll make sure you're safe. I'm not going to let anything happen to you."

A flood of affection for my brother washed over me. I did feel safe and protected in his arms, but I knew it was only temporary. He wouldn't be able to protect me forever.

♫♫♪♪♪

I blinked. I just noticed that the credits to the movie I'd just supposedly watched were rolling.

After Bash had left, Sidney and I had eaten the meal that Josie had left for him in near silence. It was so awkward that I suggested we watch a movie when all I really wanted was to get naked with him and find out what he'd had in mind earlier, but I didn't know how to bring it up.

Sid had fed Kody his bottle through part of the movie, but now

Kody was sleeping on his shoulder and I was tucked into his side with his arm around my shoulder, holding me tight to him. I was overwhelmingly content in his arms, but now that the movie was over, I could only think of where I really wanted to be. Between the sheets with Sidney, exploring his amazing body while he did the same to mine.

How did I make that happen? And did he even want to anymore? He'd had plenty of time to think. Maybe he was regretting what we did now. Especially after seeing my brother and finding out how much baggage I now carried around with this doxxing issue.

He must have felt me tense. "Do you want to talk about it?"

"Which 'it' are you referring to?" I played dumb.

He rubbed my arm. "The phone calls. The website. I'm so sorry this is happening to you, Kaylie."

I was hoping he'd been referring to the giant elephant in the room — our hook-up. "Ugh, I'd rather not talk about it. I know I'm going to have to deal with it sometime, but I'd rather just forget about it for the night."

He nodded and then slipped his hand underneath my hair and to the back of my neck, causing a shiver to skitter along my spine. "Was there something else on your mind?"

I closed my eyes. "Maybe."

"Is it about what happened earlier? Do you regret what happened between us?"

My eyes flew open. Did he regret it? How did I answer him? My mind scrambled to think, but in the end, I could only speak the truth even if it revealed too much. "No, I don't regret anything. Do you?"

He scoffed. "Fuck, no. I want to do so much more. I want you, Kaylie."

A wildfire raged through my blood. "I want more," I whispered.

"Go wait for me in my room while I get Kody down," he ordered.

I went into his room and waited. I got more nervous by the minute. Was I supposed to undress? Pose on the bed? I didn't know. Did he like assertive women in bed? That certainly wasn't me, but maybe I could fake it. Or maybe he got off on submissive women? What if he was into kinky shit that I didn't even know anything about? All my insecurities came rearing to a head. I was shaking like a leaf by the time he entered the room.

He crossed the room and placed his hands on my shoulders. "What's wrong?"

"Nothing."

He studied my face. "Are you having second thoughts?"

"No. I'm just nervous," I admitted.

He wrapped me in his arms, my head tucked under his chin. "I'd never do anything to hurt you, Kaylie. If anything I was doing was making you uncomfortable, just say the word, and I'd stop."

My cheek rested against his chest. I swallowed hard. "I know. It's not that. I'm worried that I won't be enough for you. That I'm not what you're used to; that I'll be too boring in bed for you." I surprised myself by laying my insecurities bare, but I trusted him not to use them against me. I felt safe with him.

He tipped my chin up with his finger so that I had to look at him. "Kaylie, I don't want you to be anyone but yourself. I just spent the last five minutes thinking about all the things I wanted to do to you and look how fucking hard it made me."

He thrust his body against me, and I could feel his erection pressing against my stomach. I couldn't stop my hand from running over his hard length to feel for myself. He hissed at the touch.

His blue eyes had darkened to the shade of a storm-tossed ocean. "See what you do to me, babe? You've been able to turn me on like no other since that time in the closet when you were still just a teenager. One little kiss had me hard as a rock."

I gasped. "You felt it too?"

"Yeah." His thumb smoothed over my lower lip. "But you were Bash's little sister. I convinced myself I was just being a perv. But I can't get you out of my mind, Kaylie."

"Will you show me what you like?"

He growled. "I just want you to be yourself. Don't worry about sex being boring. Christ, you squirted in bed! You have absolutely nothing to worry about."

I tried to duck my head, but he wouldn't let me. "That was embarrassing."

"No, that was hot as fuck. I'm going to see if I can make you do it again and again. But not tonight. Tonight, there's no pressure. We don't have to do anything if you're not comfortable."

There was no way in hell we were doing nothing tonight. I was still nervous, maybe more of a nervous anticipation, but his words had put me more at ease. I knew he wasn't going to break out handcuffs and whips all of a sudden. He was taking things slowly for me, but it wasn't like I was a virgin. I'd had sex before.

I bit my lip. "Will you kiss me, please?"

A growl rose from deep inside his throat and then he was kissing me, crushing his mouth to mine, his tongue thrusting deep. This was not a tentative kiss. It was full of passion and the feelings it evoked only ever came from Sidney. I was so caught up in the kiss that when he broke away, I was surprised to realize that I was laid out flat on his bed with him hovering over me.

He pulled back. "I could kiss you all night long."

"Will you take off your clothes and kiss me?"

He groaned. "I'm not sure I can control myself if I do that."

My hands started lifting the hem of his T-shirt. "I'm counting on it."

He gave me a sexy half-smile. "You're the boss."

He tugged his shirt off and then his fingers flew to the zipper on his jeans. He paused for a moment.

My hands were busy running over his warm skin while my eyes took in everything. His broad shoulders. His tats. His amazing body. When he didn't move to take off his pants, I stopped my exploration. "I'm the boss. Take it all off, Sidney."

He smirked. "So bossy. I like it." It took him about ten seconds to remove the rest of his clothing, and then he stood before me, gloriously naked.

"What's next, boss?"

He stood still as I looked him up and down, especially down. As cheesy as it was, I may have licked my lips by accident.

"Next, you should take off my shirt."

I knew he was letting me take the lead so that I'd feel more comfortable. What I didn't know was if I'd be able to dictate exactly what I wanted step by step.

I didn't have long to worry. He removed my shirt and stared at my chest for a beat. I was wearing a simple black bra with no padding or push-up effect. My boobs weren't even looking their best, but Sidney was staring at them like he was about to devour them.

His lips brushed over the pulse beating wildly in my neck and then slid lower. He only held himself in check for a moment, then he was completely unrestrained. His tongue slid under my bra, even as his hands unhooked it from the back. His mouth worked over my taut nipple, laving and sucking, while his fingers tweaked and plucked at the other one. I felt each stroke and nip of the teeth right between my legs until I was writhing uncontrollably underneath him.

I was panting when he lifted his head. "Fuck, I need that pussy. Kay, babe, tell me it's mine."

Why was he stopping? "Yes. It's yours." I'd say anything to get him to continue.

He pulled up onto his knees and then worked my leggings down my legs and off my body. I was left in black boy shorts, but Sidney removed those just as quickly.

He'd already seen me naked, so why was his heated stare making me so shy?

He moved his body between my knees and then placed my legs, one by one, over his shoulders. "I've got to taste you again."

The ache between my legs grew molten with need. I watched his head dip lower and then my brain scrambled when his tongue and lips began exploring. He wasn't gentle or delicate. He was relentless. His tongue endlessly circled my sensitive clit, and he used his teeth to heighten the sensation.

His lips slid through my juices, skillfully moving from my clit to my entrance, where it thrust inside before starting over again, never once losing that overwhelming building momentum. The scratchy feel of his stubble and the vibrations against my most intimate parts when he grunted in satisfaction only ratcheted up the pleasure.

I was past the point of caring that my hips bucked without control, that my pussy thrusted against his mouth, seeking release. I was mindless, with a singular focus on the intense bliss exploding between my legs.

Sidney did not gently coax an orgasm from me; he pulled it out forcefully. It didn't just happen passively. It was a spectacular event, sending me soaring and crashing at the same time. It was primal and a little scary. Out of my control.

He looked up at me from between my quivering legs, his lips coated with the evidence of my desire. He said something to me, but I wasn't back on Earth yet.

Sid crawled up my body, hovering slightly above me, and pressed his mouth against mine. Our tongues tangled together, but I wanted all of him. I wanted to pull his body against me, but my arms wouldn't cooperate.

He pulled away from me, and I immediately missed him. My limbs were like rubber, but my arm reached out for him. It took me a few seconds to realize that he was rolling on a condom. An answering flare of need pulled at my core.

"Hurry, Sidney."

He chuckled lightly as his eyes slid to mine. "What do you want, babe?"

"I want you inside me." I slid my legs open. "Deep."

"Kaylie." It was a soft whisper, muttered while he stopped for a long moment and looked me over like he was memorizing every last detail.

He was the biggest guy that I'd ever been with, but I was so wet and ready for him that he slid in all the way to the hilt in one hard thrust that took my breath away. Sid stilled and clenched his teeth for a moment.

My legs encircled his waist, locking him deep inside, while my hands began tentatively exploring his chest. Finally, he grinned down at me and then captured my lips for another toe-curling kiss, but this one was short. He pulled off and then began pistoning in and out of me.

I began to build up too quickly. When his thumb reached down to circle my clit, I slapped it away. He was rubbing against me just right, sliding against some secret part of me that had me seeing stars. It wasn't possible. I couldn't possibly withstand it.

All my whimpering and calling out his name must have clued him in, so he began pumping faster. When everything crashed all around me, an explosive crescendo of intense pleasure jolted through me, electrifying every cell in my body. Wave after wave crashed through me. This was a type of full-body orgasm that I'd never felt before.

I wasn't even sure how long it took me to come down from it. Sidney was resting on his elbows, keeping most of his weight off me, staring into my face.

He slid a lock of my sweaty hair off my face. "That was beautiful. You are beautiful."

I bit my lip. "Did you even … finish?"

Sid laughed, and the sound warmed my insides. "Fuck, Kaylie. I came like a champ, and your orgasm milked my dick in a way I've never experienced before. That was incredible."

"Really? You're not just saying that?" I guess I needed his reassurance.

"You could bring me to my knees with that pussy, babe." He gave my lips a quick peck. "You're an absolute goddess."

Post-coital bliss had settled over me and Sid's words of praise amped up the emotions. The experience we'd just shared felt like more than just sex. It felt spiritual. I knew that was a dangerous thought, but I wasn't about to talk myself down from this amazing high just yet.

Sid pulled out and took care of the condom, and then he was back, gathering me in his arms. I tried to stay awake so that I could revel in this wonderfully sated feeling of pure bliss, but I dozed off quickly instead.

I awoke when Sid was gently trying to untangle himself from me. I was sprawled out half on top of him, not wanting to let him go.

"Go back to sleep. I've got to go get Kody."

Reluctantly, I let him go and then rolled over, so that I was lying in his spot and within seconds, sleep was pulling me back under.

I don't know how long Sid was gone. I was half-awake and

half-asleep still, but I think he'd just crawled back into bed with me. His body rested along the back of mine until he was fully spooning me. I sighed contentedly and wiggled back even further into his arms.

His arm was slung over me, his hand splayed across my stomach. I drowsily felt those fingers moving slightly like he was plucking at his guitar. It felt so good.

Those magic fingers drifted higher until he was palming my breast. His roughened fingers skimmed over my skin, mapping the outline of my breast and then circling inward until they traced my areola. My nipples tightened into two hard nubs as he softly tugged at them.

He played with my breasts like that for what seemed like forever. There was no hurriedness in his movements; he seemed content to take his time, but every tweak and pluck was causing an answering pulse deep in my pussy. It wanted to be stroked with the same attention.

When his hand finally worked its way down, his fingers dancing over my stomach and lower still until they slid toward the jackpot, I heard a sharp intake of his breath. I was drenched for him. I could even hear how wet I was as his fingers slid through my folds, back and forth.

Just as he'd touched my breasts, he explored every millimeter of me between my legs. He lazily circled my clit with excruciatingly slow strokes, dipping into my center over and over. It was so sensuous. So languid and hot.

Neither of us spoke a word. I just laid there, unmoving, and enjoyed his hands on my body, bringing me up higher and higher until I was panting for more and unconsciously pushing my ass into him seeking more. I felt the hard length of his cock pressed against my ass cheeks, but he was ever so patient. His muscular arm had me trapped against him as he tortured me with his talented fingers until I was sure I was going to implode.

I whimpered when his fingers left me. He lifted them to his mouth and I could hear him suck them clean. The thought crossed my mind that I wanted to suck on those fingers, but I kept quiet not wanting to break the spell that had woven around us.

Sid reached between us and guided his cock to my opening. He slid into me like he belonged there. It was as if it were a missing part of me. My pussy had been aching and bereft until he filled it up.

He brushed my hair to the side and kissed the hollow right where my neck met my shoulder while he slowly slid in and out of me. His hands fluttered between gently teasing my breasts and softly stroking my clit.

The feeling was exquisite. A sustained state of euphoria that went on forever. My orgasm was slow and deep. It snuck up on me. I gasped when it rushed over me like an errant wave. Heat blossomed as it continued on and on.

Sid's strangled response to it was like he wasn't expecting it yet either, but my clenching muscles forced him to tip over the edge, too.

I lay in his arm, limp and boneless, for a long time. He finally got up to take off the condom, but then he was right back against me, spooning me. This time his hand rested between my legs, molding me, as if in possession.

I turned my head slightly toward him. "When is Kody's next feeding?"

Sid grunted. "Probably at five."

"Mmm." I covered his hand with mine. "I can't wait."

Chapter 26

Bash

I don't know how Diamond Dick managed it, but getting the world-renowned Vance Beaufort to produce *Okay Babe* was epic beyond belief. The man was a recluse who never once attended any award ceremonies despite racking up a record number of prestigious music industry awards. I'd searched the internet looking for a picture of him but came up empty. To say he valued his privacy was an understatement.

I wasn't sure what to expect when we met him, but whatever my thoughts were about the man, I'd keep them to myself. We'd spent hours in the BVR offices signing NDAs that were so exhaustive and airtight that our lawyers explicitly warned our careers and our lives as we knew them would be finished if we so much as let one tiny nugget of information slip — even to a priest on our deathbed.

A few hours ago, the limo that had picked up Sid and me for

a three-night stay at Beaufort's private recording studio had rolled through the gates of the ginormous Malibu mansion that we were now chilling at. Ghost and Knox were already there when we arrived, Ryder arrived about 40 minutes later, and Donovan wasn't expected until tomorrow morning.

A business-minded woman in a navy pantsuit greeted us shortly after we arrived. She informed us that all the techs we'd requested for our session were busy setting up our equipment in the studio, but we were to relax for the evening. We were briefly shown around the artist's wing of the mansion and told to make ourselves at home.

The place was impressive. Each of us had our own bedroom and bathroom for the stay. Everything was decorated with style and elegance; it screamed money and luxury. The bathroom was insane, but what I loved the most about my bedroom suite was the incredible ocean view and the private balcony. I wondered if all the guys were lucky to have this stunning view, but with a house this big, yeah, they probably did.

After gorging ourselves on the generous spread of food that was prepared for us, we congregated in the large room with the coffered ceiling and the pool table. A fully stocked copper-topped bar with impressive wooden beams, carved panels, a tin ceiling, and cozy lighting was sunken into an alcove that ran along one side of the room. About ten barstools stood lined up in front of it, each one looking like they were worth more than my car was. A personal bartender stood waiting behind the bar to take our orders.

Ryder had turned on the gigantic TV on the other side of the room and tuned into a Lakers game, but no one was paying too much attention to it. The wall at the back end of the room consisted entirely of glass. It was too dark outside to see the ocean beyond, but the landscape lighting beautifully showcased the large infinity pool, the outdoor fireplace, the gazebo with the hot tub, and lush greenery that was anchored by dozens of palm trees.

Besides this room, our wing consisted of a theater room, a man cave/gaming room, a music room, a library, a gym, and a solarium. Each room was furnished richly and decked out to the nines. The most impressive was the music room which contained a baby grand piano as its centerpiece with dozens of other expensive instruments that we were 'free to experiment with' gracefully filling the space.

While Knox and Ryder racked up the balls on the pool table, I headed to the bar to get some drinks for us.

The bartender stepped forward when he saw me approach. "What can I get for you, sir?"

"Three single malt scotches. One neat and two on the rocks."

He pulled a bottle from the shelf. "Mortlach 20-year-old."

I nodded and scanned the bottles on the shelf as I waited for him to pour. The shelves contained only premium quality liquor — top-shelf and extremely expensive. I had no doubt the Mortlach would be outstanding.

While I was waiting, the glass wall at the end of the room began to retract, creating one huge indoor/outdoor living space. Ghost held up a remote control. "Fuck, that's cool."

I collected our drinks and dropped off two of them with Knox and Ryder who'd begun playing pool. Sid was sitting on a huge leather couch so I headed over to join him.

"You sure you don't need a drink?"

He looked up from his phone for a second. "I'll grab one soon. I'm good for now."

Sid was subtly trying to position his phone screen out of my view, but I'd already seen what was on it. The fucking nanny cam. We'd only been in the limo for about ten minutes before he was checking up on

Kody. I wanted to shake some sense into him and yell at him to stop obsessing about Kody every minute of the day, but I bit my tongue.

Instead, I slapped him on the back and spoke calmly. "Bro, we're in Vance fucking Beaufort's sick crib. This is once-in-a-lifetime shit. You don't want to spend it on your phone. Live a little. Kody's in good hands."

Sid reluctantly pulled his eyes from the phone. "Yeah, he is."

Kaylie had agreed to watch Kody while we were recording here. Josie would still watch him during the day, but Kaylie had taken off from work at my insistence. Without someone there to escort her back and forth, I didn't think it was safe for her. I was surprised that she'd so readily agreed to be confined to my apartment, but she said she needed the break. She was banking heavily on this acting job to come through, so she hoped her days working at the department store were numbered, anyway.

What was happening to my sister with that vile website doxxing her was all kinds of fucked up. It kept me up at night. I'd done everything I could think of to try to get that post down. I spoke with the band's social media team who was very experienced in getting unsavory pictures and posts about us pulled. They'd tried to work their magic and when they couldn't, they referred me to a specialist company. I dumped a ton of money on the company to keep people from finding the posting of Kaylie through search engines, but bottom line, anyone could find it if they went directly to the website. And apparently, that fucking website had a large following, but luckily a majority of its traffic came from outside the United States.

After changing her phone number and abandoning her apartment, Kaylie hadn't had any more encounters. That didn't mean the threat still didn't exist, and I didn't want her to let down her guard. The posting about her was still up on the internet and it only took one psychopath to put her in danger.

That's why I didn't want to rock the boat about her staying at my place. Truth be told, Kaylie staying at my apartment where Sid could keep an eye on her was the only thing stopping me from going totally insane. It still weighed on my mind that I'd promised her I wouldn't tell our parents what was going on. She insisted she wait until she got confirmation from that acting job. The production company had all but told her she had a role with them. I felt like a giant dick, but I hoped she didn't get it. What would happen if she was in the public eye? Shit like this would only be a hundred times worse. I'd never be able to keep her safe.

How long would she be content hiding out there, though? And how long could I keep foisting her on Sid? Sure, he was getting free babysitting. Kaylie was the only one besides Josie that he trusted to watch Kody for the three days that we'd be here. And Kaylie had insisted on making herself useful by helping with Kody. It made her feel better about invading Sid's space even though I still paid half the rent.

I hadn't told Kaylie, but I'd gone apartment shopping for her. Even if she had roommates to lower the costs, everything in her price range was absolute shit. The places that had doormen, better security, and were located in nicer neighborhoods were extremely expensive. I could afford to help her out, but I knew she wouldn't take any of my money.

I could only think of one solution, buying my own place and having Kaylie move in with me. According to Donovan, after this single dropped, we'd all be rolling in the dough. The album and the tour were going to exponentially increase that amount. The money guys like Diamond Dick and Beaufort had all but guaranteed it would happen.

I should have gotten a better place before. I'd made enough money from our last tour to do it, but I'd been hanging onto the status quo.

I liked my life the way it was before, but no matter what I did now, I couldn't get it back. Everything had changed.

It was past time to find a nicer place to live. I'd be able to afford a large place with ample security for Kaylie. Her name wouldn't be listed on any of the paperwork, so no one could trace her. She could use a PO box for her mail, so she was never linked to any address.

It was a perfect plan, but I'd been dragging my feet on making it happen. I felt guilty because I wasn't sure that I wanted to live with my sister. I loved her and wanted to keep her safe, but that didn't mean I wanted to live with her. Fuck, I liked to party and hook up with women and I didn't need my sister around to witness that. Besides, I wasn't all that sure that she'd want to live with me either.

As much as I told myself that it would be nice to get a bigger and more upscale place to live, I knew I'd miss living with Sid. He needed more room with Kody, our apartment was near bursting with all the kid's stuff, and I didn't really want to live with a baby. So, everything pointed in the logical direction of moving out.

But that just made me feel depressed. It represented the end of an era with Sid. Things had changed, but I wasn't ready to accept that yet. I still hadn't broached the subject of moving out with Kaylie, so for now, I was relieved that she was content hiding out in my little apartment.

Grimacing, I took a sip of the smooth-as-silk scotch. I didn't want to think about all the shit swirling around in my head. I'd worry about it later. For now, I was with my band and we were about to spend the next few days making music. We'd be back on the road touring soon and then everything would be perfect.

My hand was squeezing my glass hard. I relaxed my grip and then took another sip. Kaylie was safe for now. Tonight, I was going to enjoy myself.

Across the room, I watched Ryder sink another ball in the pocket and then checked my phone when I heard a text notification. It was from Lars, my drum tech.

Lars: Drums are all set. Sounds killer.

I texted back a quick thanks in reply. A few seconds later, I got a new text from him.

Lars: Acoustics in the studio are sublime. This place is wicked. See you in the morning.

I briefly wondered where the techs were staying and if I should invite them to hang out with us, but then I remembered all the confidentiality agreements Beaufort made us sign and decided not to.

Was I going to spend the entire night watching Sid on his phone? I stood up abruptly, and announced to the room, "All we need is music and some girls."

Ghost stopped meandering around the room for a moment. "I've found four remote controls so far, but none of them are for music. There's got to be a sound system in here."

The bartender beckoned to Ghost, and I headed over to the pool table to watch Ryder kicking Knox's ass. Knox was the worst pool player I knew.

A few minutes later, dark techno music filled the room, drowning out all our trash-talking around the pool table and the ambient noise from the basketball game on TV. Ghost liked his music loud. The volume was cranked up and the steady beat pulsed through my veins. Fuck, the sound practically made me hard in my pants. Listening to intense rhythms like that was pure sound porn for me. It made me want to fuck.

When Knox lost, I played the next game with Ryder. Sid finally got off his phone and grabbed a beer from the bar for himself before joining us. We were well into the second game when the girls arrived.

Five of them. All stunning. All in tiny dresses with towering fuck-me heels. My eyes were drawn to two of the girls who were blondes. One had a spectacular rack, but there was something about the other blonde that called to me. Maybe it was the hint of innocence on her face, the girl-next-door look. I knew I wanted to stake my claim on her before anyone else did.

These girls were down to party. An hour later, the drinks had been steadily flowing. Someone had lowered the volume of the music enough that we could talk without damaging our vocal cords. The claim on my girl, Ingrid, was thoroughly staked, and she hadn't wandered too far from my side since. She was cute and demure; the anticipation of fucking her later left a pleasant buzz in my veins.

I was having a good time hanging out with Sid, but I couldn't help but notice that he kept rebuffing the girl that had been hanging around him. Maybe he wasn't into her? I looked her over with a critical eye. There was nothing wrong with her. She was attractive with plump, pouty lips, and a nice body.

Maybe he wanted to do the double-team thing? I wasn't averse to sharing my girl with him. We hadn't done that in a long time. I gave him the signal, but he merely cocked an eyebrow and shook his head slightly.

He leaned into me and spoke low so no one could hear him. "I'm not feeling it tonight. I think I'm going to head up to my room."

"Alone?" I couldn't keep the surprise out of my voice.

"Yeah."

I disentangled myself from my girl who was clinging to me like a koala. "Ingrid, could you and—" I gestured to the girl next to Sid.

"Candi," she supplied.

"Right," I continued. "Would you and Candi get us some fresh drinks?"

"Sure." She giggled and then linked arms with Candi before they headed over to the bar.

I studied Sid. "You haven't gotten laid in weeks. Or has it been months? Since Kody showed up anyway. I understand why. You've got to prioritize him, but he's with Kaylie right now. He's okay and right now you've got your pick of gorgeous girls. What are you thinking, dude?"

"No, thanks." His eyes briefly flicked to the bar. "I'm not interested in a bunch of hookers."

That was harsh. "What do you mean, hookers?"

He shrugged. "High-priced hookers are still hookers. They're getting paid to keep us happy. That doesn't turn me on."

My eyes widened with shock. "I'm pretty sure there's no stipulation that they have to sleep with us. For fuck's sake, there not hookers."

Sid's jaw clenched. "They all have stripper names. They're paid."

"Ingrid isn't a stripper's name," I replied.

"Candi, Tiffany, Crystal, Amber. All stripper names."

I was getting angry. "What's the difference between fucking these chicks and fucking the groupies that hang out after the shows? It's not like these girls aren't into it."

"I'd rather not." Avoiding my stare, he took a long sip of his beer.

I was stunned speechless. What the fuck was going on?

I looked around the immense room. Ghost was on the couch, a girl on either side of him. There was some kissing and groping going on. I could see one of the girl's asses hanging out of her short dress as she draped herself half on top of him.

Ryder was just stepping away from the bar. He unhooked himself from Candi who'd just approached him and gave me a curt wave. He was leaving. I'd never seen him even look at another woman after Talia. He was always polite, but firm when turning them down.

Now Sid, too?

I wasn't about to let Sid's moral lecturing ruin my night. I turned from him and made my way back to sweet Ingrid.

Knox must have noticed Candi pouting. "Get your ass over here, Candi. If Ryder and Sid are leaving, I'll take two of you."

Candi giggled and joined Knox and the dark-haired girl he'd just been feeling up in the corner.

I could tell that Knox was close to being wasted. He started stripping off his clothes. "Time to check out that pool. Get naked, ladies," he bellowed.

Candi squealed and began shimmying out of her dress. One of Ghost's girls jumped up off the couch and started doing the same. Ghost got up and followed the group out to the pool.

I looked at Ingrid. "Want to go swimming? Or go in the hot tub?"

"No."

"Where do you want to fuck? Here or in my room?" I wasn't sure why I even gave her the choice.

"Either," she answered.

As much as I tried to ignore Sid's words, they had sunk into me. This girl wasn't into me. She didn't know me at all.

"Let's fuck here." I didn't want her in my space and certainly didn't want her to spend the night. I'd fuck her here and then leave. Or maybe I'd fuck her and then fuck one of her friends, too.

One of the girls, the one originally with Knox, wandered back inside from the pool area. She frowned. "I don't want to ruin my hair. Can

I join you?"

Fuck. Sid was right. We were all just as fucking interchangeable to them as they were to us. I'm not sure which set of us was worse.

"Yeah. Why the fuck not?" I answered her. I turned to the bartender. "Make my next drink a double."

Chapter 27

Sidney

I DIDN'T THINK IT'D be a rinky-dink operation, but when we stepped into Beaufort's studio, we couldn't help but be impressed. Our techs were already there waiting for us and the guitar tech, Benji, introduced us to the sound engineer used exclusively by Vance Beaufort.

He was an older dude in a bandana — kind of like Willie Nelson without the braids. He liked to work using a scratch track, so we recorded that while we waited for Beaufort to show up.

We were generally shooting the shit with the sound engineer, who'd worked with some of the top musicians in the world during his long career when Beaufort strolled in.

I wasn't sure it was him at first, because this guy looked like a fucking meme. He was chubby with a spare tire around his waist, dressed in an ugly-colored maroon velour tracksuit. His head was balding, so he combed his remaining hair upwards in feather-like shoots so that he looked a bit like the Little Caesar's pizza guy.

A girl hung on each arm, and one trailed behind him. They all wore identical outfits, some kind of glittery silver bra and boyshorts set with shiny metallic gogo boots that went up to their knees and lots of jewelry chains wrapping every which way around their bodies.

He stopped and shook hands with each of us, knowing all of our names beforehand, and then disappeared into the control room, telling us we'd start laying down the drum tracks in ten minutes.

What the hell? This was the famous Vance Beaufort? I crooked an eyebrow at Ryder, and he just shrugged. Bash got settled in behind his drum kit and started warming up.

The sound engineer, Marty, just smiled patiently. "He's the best in the business. You won't believe the magic he'll weave through your song. You won't recognize it when he's through."

Ghost scoffed and shook his head.

Marty continued, "*Okay Babe*. I listened to it with Beaufort a dozen times. Doesn't sound like Ghost Parker's usual material?"

"It's not," Ghost answered. "Sidney wrote it."

"Is that so?"

Knox, who was staring into the control room, absently slapped my arm to get my attention. "What the fuck is going on?"

I followed his gaze. Beaufort was sitting in a chair behind the mixing desk, facing away from us. Two of the girls were walking in circles around him.

Marty snickered. "That's his prep ritual. The girls play musical dicks. Whoever's left sucking his dick when the music stops wins. I don't know what the fuck they win. Never asked. But the other two get mighty salty when they lose."

We all looked around at each other, at a total loss for words. So far, this had been the craziest recording session we'd ever done, and it hadn't even started yet.

Less than five minutes later, two of the girls stormed out of the booth, one of them in tears, and left. Beaufort's voice piped in over the speakers. "Let's start with the drum track."

I had to pay more attention to the drum track than the others, so I settled in and observed Bash. He'd played perfectly and yet Beaufort had him repeating it over a few times. Then Beaufort subtly changed the essence of the rhythm and had Bash do it all over again. The drum track was the backbone of the song, so very critical, but Beaufort's dogged persistence seemed almost obsessive-compulsive.

Beaufort wasn't any easier on me. After I finished, we took a 20-minute break for lunch, and then Ryder, followed by Knox, were laying down their tracks. Beaufort knew the sound he wanted from us, and he made us do it over and over until he was satisfied. I heard so many variations of that song that I couldn't imagine how the final product would turn out once Beaufort mixed it all together.

We'd never spent so much time recording one damn song. Beaufort called it a day, and we hadn't even gotten to the vocals. Donovan, who'd shown up at the studio around mid-day, joined us for dinner.

We were all pretty wrung out after dinner and only wanted to relax, so when Donovan called a band meeting, we balked. Our compromise was to conduct the meeting in the hot tub with lots of alcohol.

Donovan protested, "I'm not going to stand around a hot tub in a 3-piece suit and watch your sausage party."

Knox began stripping down to his boxers. "No, you're going to get in and join us, mate."

The hot tub would feel nice after our long day. Besides, it was fucking huge. We could all fit in there without any sausages crossing paths. I followed Knox's lead and soon we were all chucking off our clothes. Apparently, Ghost had gone commando today, so he took some ribbing after flashing us his dick, but he didn't give a shit. Bash took the corner seat to my right and tapped his beer against mine.

"Fucking fine," Donovan conceded. He delicately stripped out of his suit and placed it carefully over the back of a lounge chair so it wouldn't wrinkle.

It took him about ten minutes to get us all to settle down and listen to him. "Okay, let's talk about the paperwork you all signed last night. Did any of you actually read it?"

I had briefly skimmed all the legalese, but I'd trusted Donovan when he'd presented it to us. That was what managers were for.

"I didn't think so." He sighed. "It boils down to the rights to *Okay Babe*. Sidney agreed to split the rights so that all six of you are considered joint authors."

"Six of us?" Ryder questioned.

"Yeah." Donovan nodded. "Beaufort gets a stake. It was non-negotiable. He's taking a small royalty. Mr. Diamond lobbied hard for Candace Collins to get similar treatment, but I held firm. She retains the right to perform and record *Okay Babe* either solo or with a band. She is also allowed to promote the song in any form. However, she is only receiving a flat fee for this recording, no royalties, and the six of you, including Beaufort, will receive royalties from any money she makes off it."

Ghost looked as confused as the rest of us. "Who the fuck is Candace Collins?"

Donovan took a sip of his beer. "Diamond Dick's newest pet project. Some up-and-comer pop princess. She'll be doing backing vocals for *Okay Babe*. I guess you'll meet her tomorrow."

"Oh fuck. Really?" Ghost looked disgusted.

"Next thing." Donovan moved on quickly before he had to hear us complaining. "I emailed you all a copy of our pre-tour promotion schedule. Dates and times are still tentative. You're all expected to attend any L.A.-based event and there's a handful set up in New York City. If any date doesn't work for you, for a really good reason, let me know as soon as possible.

"Most of it is for interviews and photoshoots, but there are several live performances scheduled. You'll be performing with Candace Collins. I've met her; she's really hot, but she's only 17 years old. There will be no one here fucking her under any circumstances. That's non-fucking-negotiable. Does everyone understand?"

Jesus Christ. I kept quiet while some of the guys muttered. Ghost rolled his eyes heavenward. He looked pained by this whole thing.

"Tour is coming along. BVR is aware of your situation, Sid. They're going to need a decision from you soon. BVR put me in touch with a tour manager that's experienced dealing with musician's kids coming on the tour. That's an option. You can also do a partial tour or drop out, but we'd need to get a fill-in for you either way. Whatever you choose, BVR wants you to participate in all the pre-tour promotions."

My stomach was churning with acid. "Don't the kids that go on tours have their mothers taking care of them?"

"There's a well-known country artist on tour right now with her baby. It's doable. Obviously, you're going to need someone to help take care of him. Someone you trust. You need to start thinking about that. I'll give you the tour manager's number, so you can find out how it would work."

Donovan kept talking about the tour, asking the guys if they had any tour riders to request, but I could barely listen. My heart was pounding in my chest just thinking about it. What the hell was I going to do? I was so mixed up about everything. It was a topic that I'd been avoiding for weeks.

"BVR is throwing tons of promotion at this. The release schedule for *Okay Babe* is aggressive. I was told that the money would start rolling in quickly. You're going to be shocked. They told me to get you guys prepared. I suggest you all find financial planners to get guidance about the money. Don't be stupid about it."

Ryder spoke up. "Is there any chance this is all bullshit? That the song will bomb and the tour won't sell out?"

Donovan tipped his beer bottle. "Is there a chance that Santa Claus is real? I don't know. But the kings in this business say this is a sure thing. So, don't spend the money before it rolls in, but fellows, I think we made it."

We all clinked our drinks and drank to it, but no one looked completely convinced.

Donovan continued. "This tour is going to be different. The tour manager has already been signed and there will be a dedicated assistant manager for Sid if he brings Kody. The stage setup is being designed right now. It's bigger and more elaborate. The crew size has tripled. You'll have a PR person from BVR assigned to you, a stylist who will be on tour, and a photographer who will tail you around for a few weeks. This is the big-time, boys."

We remained silent as we were trying to take it all in. Fuck, my head was spinning, and it wasn't from the three lousy beers I'd had.

"BVR anticipates that you'll each need your own security. They're setting that up. If it's deemed unnecessary, we can adjust, but they seem to think that all five of you will get lots of attention.

"You won't be able to go out in public without being hounded. You'll need to consult with security before you go anywhere. They're going to have more experience with this than you. They'll be meeting with you individually to go over the details. It'll be easier for security to keep you safe if they drive you, so treat them well. They'll be your shadows."

"This is all starting to sound a bit ... intense." Knox voiced what we were all thinking.

Donovan ran a hand over his face. "Once the single drops, it's all going to start coming at you quickly. BVR warned me to get you ready. Remember, being filthy rich also comes with a lot of perks. It's not all bad."

I stared into the frothy bubbles made by the hot tub jets. Two doors were before me. The crazy, fucked-up life of a rock star with all the trappings. Or the quiet life of a single dad. They couldn't be further apart.

"Is that all?" Bash chopped at the water with his hands.

"One other thing I want to mention." Donovan looked at each of us in turn. "Remember that everything you do in public can and will be recorded and probably used against you. You're living in a fishbowl now. And — " Donovan glanced at me quickly and winced, then looked away — "You need to be careful with women. Lots of paternity issues are going to pop up that we'll have to deal with. Women will be coming out of the woodwork, claiming you fathered their children once you guys are rolling in the money. Now, more than ever, you need to be careful. Keep it wrapped up, always. And it might not just be women gunning for the bucks. It could be relatives or friends."

He paused for a moment and then added. "Even Skull Crushers." That one was for Ryder. "Don't try to deal with it yourself. I'm here to give guidance and if I can't help, I'll find someone who can."

It all sounded like a big fucking hassle. Maybe I wasn't ready for it all.

He turned to me again. "Sid, you need to talk to a lawyer in case Kody's mama comes back looking for money. I'll give you a number. She may not want Kody, but she could use him as leverage. You need to get your paternal rights locked down so you're not susceptible."

The blood in my veins turned to ice. This whole situation was a fucking nightmare. Suddenly, I wanted to bail on Ghost Parker and forget about the whole thing.

"Any questions?" Donovan looked around the circle.

The guys started grumbling. Knox stood up and started climbing out of the hot tub. "I've got to take a piss."

Bash followed him. "Yeah. It's fucking hot in here." He stepped out and then cannon-balled into the pool.

Everyone started getting out, but I couldn't move. My thoughts were swirling. What was I going to do?

The past week living with Kaylie had been heaven. We'd felt like a family. Bash was coming around a lot to visit. It wasn't that he didn't trust me with his sister; I think that he did. He shouldn't, but he did. I felt bad about that, but not bad enough to stop. Bash just wanted to hang out with her more. And me being there was a bonus.

Normally, I would love to hang out with him. I was even having fun with him here at Beaufort's mansion. It was a bit like old times, even though I missed being at home with Kody and Kaylie.

It was getting awkward when he stopped by the apartment, though. Both Kaylie and I would count the seconds until he would leave. Then we'd rip each other's clothes off as soon as the door shut.

She was more comfortable in the bedroom now. She was opening up. Showing me what she liked. She was so damn responsive to me. If I wanted, I could get her off in seconds. Prolonged G-spot stimulation led to incredible orgasms for her and even made her squirt most of the time. She looked at me like I was a god when I did that.

Fuck, I was getting hard thinking about it and I had to tuck myself back in my loose briefs. I'd never grow tired of being with her. Sex was even better now. More meaningful.

We had to tell Bash what was going on soon before he found out on his own. We couldn't keep it a secret much longer. Why should we? This wasn't a one-time fuck. It was an actual relationship. We hadn't labeled anything, but there was no doubt in my mind it was a relationship. The first one I'd ever had. I wanted to be with her. I thought about her constantly. She was my everything. I called her every spare second I could. Half the time, I pretended I was calling to see Kody. I missed him, too, but it was a good excuse, so Kaylie didn't think I'd gone totally insane.

The bottom line was that I wanted Kaylie in my life. Permanently. The realization hit me like a ton of bricks. I was sure about it; I had fallen head over heels in love with her, though I didn't say the words out loud.

I still had my hand on my junk, trying to keep the beast contained, when I looked up and realized it was just me and Ghost left in the hot tub. I was grabbing my junk, and he was naked. Great.

He lifted his chin in question. He could clearly see my hand through the water. "The fuck?"

How did I explain my giant boner? "Just thinking about someone."

"Kaylie?"

"What the fuck?" I frantically looked around to see if anyone had heard. "No!"

He lifted his arm that was extended along the top of the hot tub, and I realized he was holding a blunt. Where the hell did that come from? He took a drag. "You're a shitty liar. You fucking her?"

I kept my voice low. "Jesus Christ, Ghost! Bash would fucking kill me."

His eyes squinted. "That's not a 'no'."

"Fuck off," I growled. "I didn't say that."

"She's a sweet girl. Nice tits. Tight ass."

I was seeing red. I almost stood up and knocked his teeth in.

Ghost laughed. "I thought so."

I forced myself to relax. He was messing with me. "Whatever you're thinking, keep it to yourself."

"I'm thinking forbidden love. Years of a burning desire for the little sister who was completely off-limits." He took another drag. "Unrequited love that you've recently found out isn't so unrequited, is it?"

I shook my head in denial. "You don't know anything."

He chuckled. "It's all in the song."

A pang of nerves erupted in my gut. He knew.

"Is there anything going on or are you still worshipping her from afar?" He was watching me intently.

Fucking Ghost didn't miss anything. It was pointless to lie. "I've been fucking her non-stop. And I don't want to stop."

He nodded.

Fuck, this was bad. "How did you know? Do the others know?"

"I've been writing lyrics for a while now. It's kind of my expertise." His cocky gaze turned sympathetic. "It's not very hidden, Sid. That shit's going to be blasting all over the world in a few weeks."

"Fuck," I uttered.

He shrugged a shoulder. "Knox knows. Pretty sure Ryder, too. Bash doesn't, but he'll figure it out, eventually. Maybe tomorrow when I lay down the vocals. Especially if Beaufort changes it around to the way I'm assuming you originally wrote it. It flows much better that way."

"Fuck, I'm dead." I was staring into the swirling water.

"You could just say I added all the raunchy lyrics," he offered. "I would have changed the chorus. That would have helped, but the suits were adamant we keep it unchanged."

I looked up at him. "You really hate the song, don't you?"

"It's not something I would write." He took a long pull on his blunt. "Doesn't mean I hate it. Just had to do a little ball-busting to keep my artistic conscience clear."

I tilted back my beer bottle and finished it.

"We're all going to hate it soon. We'll be playing it for every appearance. With some pop princess. Every fucking encore. You'll hate it, too."

I smiled. "Yeah, I hate hearing you singing those words. It's like you're singing to her. It pisses me off."

"Ah fuck, Vicious. She's like a little sister to me." He smirked at me. "You've got it bad for her, huh?"

"I fucking do."

He leaned back and stretched out both his long arms along the top of the hot tub. "And Bash is letting her shack up with you?"

"He trusts me."

Ghost grunted. "You want to settle down with her? Like Ryder did with Talia?"

I was tired of holding it all in. "I want to fucking marry her."

His eyes widened. "Fuck. Is that what she wants?"

"I don't know." Frustration knocked into me, leaving me breathless. "She's young. And I've got Kody. At first, I thought she was just rebelling against Bash; she told me she just wanted to have a casual fling. But it feels so much deeper."

He stood up, exposing his junk to me. I looked away as he climbed out of the hot tub. "You've got a lot to work out — the tour, your girl, Bash — and you've got to do it soon. This shit is going to start to unravel, and then you're really fucked."

He picked up his ratty jeans and slid into them, still soaking wet. "Let me know if I can do anything to help."

Chapter 28

Kaylie

THE CALL I'D BEEN waiting for finally came. I don't know how I held in my reaction while I was still on the phone, but as soon as I ended the call, I let out a huge whoop of excitement.

I ran out of Bash's bedroom, where I'd retreated with my phone and found Sidney on the floor with Kody. They were doing tummy time. Sidney was lying on his side, his head propped up on his hand, as he made encouraging noises to Kody. I was so exhilarated by my news that I launched myself at him. Sidney ended up flat on his back with me on top of him. My hands rested on his solid chest while my knees straddled his hips.

"You won't believe it!" I declared.

His hands ran up and down my thighs. "Hell, Kaylie, you're giving me a boner in front of Kody."

I scooted my ass down until it was resting gently on him and gave him a little grind. We were fully clothed, but this position was giving me some wicked thoughts. "Don't distract me. Guess what?"

He tucked a piece of my hair that had escaped behind my ear. "What, beautiful?"

I took a quick second for myself to squee internally that he called me beautiful and then launched into my news. "That was the production company for the sitcom. They just finalized the lead male role and the lead female is down to me and one other girl. They want us both to read with the actor to see which of us has better chemistry with him."

"Wow. That's great, babe."

I felt his cock hardening beneath me. "The best part of it is that even if they chose the other girl for the lead role, they all but said they'd offer me the part of the sister. We look enough alike to be sisters and they like us both, so it's just a matter of who gets which part. The sister character is a series regular. They said she'll be in almost every episode. I'm going to be in a TV sitcom! Can you believe it?"

He smiled up at me. "I can believe it. You've worked so hard for this."

His smile sent little flutters to my heart. This man did things to me. Copying a move he pulled on me every so often, I captured his hands and entwined his fingers with mine, and then brought them to either side of his head, pinning him down. Of course, I wasn't strong enough to hold him down, but he played along. My heart raced as I lowered my lips to his and I felt the warmth of his mouth against mine. A spark ignited inside me, something wild and uncontrollable that soon had me melting into his embrace. It didn't take long before he dragged me under his spell.

I was so intoxicated by him that I didn't even notice Kody crying until Sidney was laughing under me. "You're having your evil way with me, woman, while Kody's fussing. I think he's done with tummy time."

I climbed off him so he could tend to Kody. "Sorry, I didn't notice."

Sidney swooped down and picked Kody off the floor and stroked his back until he calmed down. "I'll take a rain check on what we were just doing. As soon as he's asleep, I want you to show me exactly what you were going to do next."

My eyes swooped down to the outline of his hard dick tenting his sweatpants. I may have licked my lips. "Mmm. I can't wait."

I laughed when Sid grumbled and adjusted himself.

While he was taking care of Kody, I grabbed my phone and started looking through social media. With the situation with that website, I'd cut way down on the posts that I made. I no longer made any posts about where I was located or what I was doing. I'd gotten a glut of friend requests after that website had posted that rape fantasy crap, but I never confirmed any of them. So far, it seemed like my social media accounts weren't affected by it. After checking through everything, I tweeted and updated my feeds with the latest news about the acting role.

A few replies of congratulations were already coming in from my friends. I felt a buzz of excitement. This was it! After years of endless workshops and networking and auditions, it had finally paid off.

Sidney was in the kitchen with Kody. I snuck up behind him and wrapped my arms around his waist. "I'm so excited! Let's celebrate!"

"What did you have in mind?"

I leaned my head against his back and breathed in his scent. "Let's get dressed up and go to a fancy dinner. With champagne! Maybe to a club afterward where we can dance and get crazy."

He tensed up beneath me. "Babe, I'd love to, but you know I can't."

I'd been so hyped up that I forgot about Kody. I stepped back from him, trying to mask my disappointment. "Can't we get a babysitter?

Just for tonight?"

Sid spun around, a frown marring his handsome face. "It's too late to find someone I trust, Kaylie. I'm sorry. We could celebrate here, though? Josie's dinners aren't fancy, but I'll see if I can get some champagne delivered. And after Kody goes to sleep, we'll celebrate naked." He ended his sentence with a wicked grin.

"Sure. That sounds nice." I smiled weakly. "Let me just get changed out of my work clothes."

I went into my brother's room and began changing into some comfortable sweatpants and a T-shirt. Sitting down on the edge of the bed that I'd never slept in, I rested my head on my hand. What was I doing?

I'd been living with Sid for about two weeks. Two weeks that had seemed like an absolute fantasy. A dream come true. I'd gotten much closer to Sidney, and we were having sex whenever Josie or Bash weren't around and Kody was sleeping. It had added up to a lot of sex. Amazing, toe-curling, out-of-this-world sex.

I'd even bonded with Kody. Sure, he'd always seemed like a cute kid, but being solely responsible for him when Sidney was away recording Ghost Parker's new single brought us closer. I could see how Sidney was head over heels for him.

Sidney couldn't just drop everything and go out; I understood that. He was a father and that came with a ton of responsibilities. I don't know why I felt a little pouty about it. We'd probably have a better time at home, anyway.

Maybe I felt off-kilter because Sidney and I never discussed our relationship. If you could even call it a relationship. We just kind of shacked up and started having sex. I couldn't claim him as my boyfriend. None of our friends or family knew what was going on between us.

Really, I wasn't sure that we had anything beyond the sex. I knew what I wanted, but I had no idea what Sidney was thinking. I was a dreamer. After loving Sidney for years and now spending so much time with him and Kody, I started seeing the three of us as a family. I couldn't help it.

And that was delusional.

We were more like roommates with benefits. A huge crimp had been put into Sidney's lifestyle when Kody came along. Partying every night and hooking up with random women was no longer doable for him. I was the next best thing. He wasn't shirking his responsibilities with Kody and still getting laid every night.

I knew I was treading water. Sooner or later, I was going to get my heart broken, but I just couldn't pull away. I'd take whatever scraps Sidney threw my way.

In the end, our celebration was far from fancy. We were both dressed in casual sweatpants and tops, and Kody sat on Sidney's lap as we ate Josie's beef stew. Sidney got us a bottle of champagne. It wasn't anything fancy, but it wasn't prosecco.

After dinner, Sidney broke out his acoustic guitar and serenaded us while I danced with Kody. The looks we exchanged had my heart fluttering in my chest. If I wasn't careful, I could convince myself that he had feelings for me.

When Kody went to sleep for the night, Sid grabbed the half-full bottle of champagne and whisked me into the bedroom. He spent a torturous amount of time drizzling my body with champagne and then licking it off. Only when I was out of my mind with frantic need, did he give me the orgasm my body craved so desperately.

I was sticky, head to toe, so Sidney carried my sated body into the bathroom and pulled me into the shower with him when the water was steamy. His hands lathered his divine-smelling bath soap onto every inch of my skin before he got to his knees, parted my legs, and gave me another mind-blowing orgasm.

My legs were rubbery, so I leaned against him as he toweled me off. He pulled me up into his arms as if I weighed nothing and brought me back to his bed.

I was folded up in his arms, drifting off to sleep. "That was some celebration. Thank you."

"Anytime, babe. You deserve it."

I knew that I'd remember our celebration forever. It wasn't fancy, but maybe it was even better than going out? It was low-key, but there had been a lot of laughter and some very memorable sexy times.

I snuggled against Sidney. A thought flashed through my mind right before I fell asleep — I'd be devastated if I ever lost this.

Chapter 29

Sidney

THE ONE DAY I wanted rehearsal to end early was the day that Ghost insisted we tirelessly work on a song that I thought we'd already nailed down to perfection. Next week, we'd be back at BVR's recording studio to lay down the last two tracks of our album. That was the last piece waiting to fall into place before a tsunami of activity overwhelmed the band. I was dreading it.

But, none of that was on my mind right now. I needed to get the fuck out of here. It'd taken me two days to plan everything. I'd never been on a date before — sure I've been out with women, but I never considered it a date. I'd been out to dinners, events, and activities with a woman accompanying me, but those occasions had come about spontaneously and were always one-and-dones. None of those women were special to me. I'd never actually planned a real date before. So, yeah, I think I was going on my first date.

After I'd seen the disappointment flash in Kaylie's eyes when she wanted to go out and celebrate her landing an acting role the other night, I felt like shit. Even more, I was scared that she'd come to her senses and drop me like a hot potato. Why would she want to be stuck with a guy like me? I'd never taken her out to wine and dine her. I really hadn't done anything to show her what she meant to me.

Admittedly, I didn't know how to treat a girlfriend. Growing up, I had no role models to emulate and my friends were all a bunch of degenerates when it came to women. Except for Ryder, none of the guys I knew were in relationships.

It had never been an issue before because I'd never really cared. Now, I was nervous that my lack of experience was going to bite me in the ass. I didn't know how to be a good boyfriend, but I was pretty sure that locking my girl in a tiny apartment with me and my infant son and fucking her like a sex addict whenever the kid was asleep wasn't in the 'How to Woo Your Girl' manual.

I couldn't turn to anyone for help, considering Bash still didn't know about us, which was only one of about 5,000 other things that were currently weighing me down. So, of course, I turned to the internet.

My plan was perfect. If I could get out of here on time. And subtly convince Bash to let me pick up Kaylie from work without sparking any suspicions. Then I had to make it through L.A. traffic in a fairly reasonable time. If all that came together, I was still only halfway there to pulling this off.

No wonder I was fucking nervous.

I almost groaned out loud when Ghost told us all to start again from the top.

Bash crashed his stick down on a cymbal. "Dude, it's Friday. Some of us have fucking plans."

Thank fuck someone spoke up!

Ghost stared hard at Bash for a few seconds and I held my breath waiting. This could go one of two ways.

"Yeah, we're good." Ghost didn't say anything else; he just strolled out of the room. The rest of the band began gathering our instruments and cleaning up for the day. It was hard to tell if Ghost was being a dick or not, but I didn't care. I had other things on my mind.

I took a super long sip from my water bottle waiting for Bash to come out from behind his drum kit.

Finally, he came over and slapped me on the arm. "He would have had us working on that song all fucking night."

"Yeah, I've got to get back to Kody." I felt bad about the lie, but there were more coming, so I sucked it up. "Thanks for letting me take the car. I've got to pick up that baby shit."

Holding my breath, I waited for him to ask me what I was getting. I'd spent twenty minutes trying to flesh out this lie, but in the end, Bash didn't give a shit.

I rubbed the back of my neck. "Yeah, so, since I've got the car and I'm going to be shopping over there, I might as well swing by and pick up Kaylie when I'm done. That way you don't have to make the trip."

The questions I had fake answers for never came. He was too interested in starting his Friday night. "Man, that'd be great. If you don't mind? Tell her I'll catch up with her tomorrow."

"Sure."

I felt the smile tugging at my lips as I watched Bash hurrying out the door. That had been way easier than I thought.

I turned around and bumped my arm into the guitar that Ryder was holding. He was appraising me with raised eyebrows.

I cleared my throat and then asked, "Big plans tonight, Stroke?" It was something I might have asked him hundreds of times before, but it suddenly sounded awkward.

Knox stepped around us and called out, "Later, mates," before leaving the two of us alone in the room.

Ryder crossed his arms over his chest. "Not very good plans, considering you stole my girlfriend for the night."

Right. I forgot he would know about that. "I needed a babysitter. Josie won't stay past five o'clock."

"So, I'm guessing you have big plans for the night? And, you just so happen to be picking up Kaylie on the way?"

A thousand denials sprang to mind, but I could tell that he already knew. "Ryder..."

"What the fuck are you doing, Vicious? This is going to blow up in your face. Are you fucking her?" He didn't look angry, just concerned.

"I don't know what I'm doing." I rubbed my face. "But, I have real feelings for her. It's not just about sex."

"Holy shit," he muttered.

"I know. I'm just so overwhelmed with everything — Kody, the tour — but this shit with Kaylie, it just feels so right."

Ryder shifted his guitar on his shoulder. "Bash is going to find out, eventually. Shit, I'm not sure how he's so damn blind. And, yeah, that fucking song ... You've got to tell him, dude."

Fuck! "I want a real relationship with her, so I know I have to tell him and convince him I'm good enough for her. But, it's not just me. Kaylie wants to keep it a secret and I'm not even fucking sure if she wants anything other than sex with me."

Ryder stared at me like I had two heads. "So you're just fucking your best friend's little sister and you don't even know if she wants more?"

"It's complicated." I winced at the expression. "I've got Kody, and she's still so young."

"You need to talk to her. Get on the same page. You can't have any type of relationship if you're not honest with each other. Maybe you're just caught up in a haze of good sex."

My denial was fierce. "I told you it's not just sex! I've been burying these feelings for years—"

"Yeah, I've heard the fucking song."

I groaned. "That fucking song." Shaking my head, I thought of all the problems it could create. I wasn't prepared for any of this.

I continued trying to convince him. "Listen, I'm taking her on a date tonight. It's the first time I've ever been on an actual date. This is real to me, man. I want her to be my girlfriend. Exclusively. And not in secret."

He slapped me on the shoulder. "Wow. I never thought I'd see the day. Well, good luck, Sid. I hope it all works out."

"Thanks."

He took a step toward the door but then turned around. "And don't stay out too late tonight."

This dating thing was so complicated. I frowned. Was there some kind of implied curfew for first dates that I wasn't aware of? "Why not?"

"Because I don't want to be up all night waiting for my girl to get home. I'd rather be fucking her."

After Ryder left, I headed to the bathroom with my duffel bag to get ready for my date. I changed out of my jeans and T-shirt into some date night clothes, tamed my hair, refreshed my deodorant, and added a spray of cologne to my chest. It felt strange to wonder if Kaylie would think I looked nice.

The drive to the department store where she worked went smoothly. I even found decent parking not too far from the front entrance.

She still had 15 minutes left on her shift, but after texting back and forth with her, she ended up getting someone to cover for her while she snuck out early.

I got out of the car and walked to the front doors of the store to meet her. Suddenly, I was insanely nervous. What if she didn't even want to go on a date with me?

Kaylie's eyes widened when she caught sight of me. "Whoa. You look ... different. Did you have to do some promotion stuff today?"

"Um, no." I grabbed her hand and interlocked our fingers and started leading her to the car.

She looked surprised for a second but then smiled up at me. Thank fuck. I'd never displayed affection for a woman in public unless you included groping a woman that I was planning to fuck after a show or in a bar.

I liked holding Kaylie's hand. The gesture was so innocent, yet it made me feel like I was walking on air. I wanted the whole damn world to know that this woman was mine. Ryder was right; I had to talk to her. Tonight, I'd make it clear that I wanted her to be my girlfriend.

When we reached the car, I walked her around the passenger side to let her in. She raised an eyebrow but didn't comment.

I was trying to act like a gentleman — like the perfect boyfriend — but none of this stuff came naturally to me. And, every step of the way, I felt nervous as fuck. I'd never felt nervous with a woman before and now I was sweating bullets about holding Kaylie's hand.

After I got the car out of the tight parking space, I reached for Kaylie's hand again, my hand hovered in the air for a few excruciating seconds until her hand finally met mine. I wrapped her tiny hand in my own and felt instantly better.

We didn't talk. My mind was too busy racing a hundred miles per hour to make small talk. I noticed that she stole some shy peeks my way several times, but she never said anything.

We must have been ten minutes into the trip when we hit the

highway. She sat up straighter. "Sidney, we're going the wrong way!"

"We're not going home."

She looked over at me. "Where are we going?"

"I'm taking you out."

"Out?"

"Yes, out. On a date."

"On a date?"

I laughed. "Is there an echo in here?"

"Where are we going?"

I saw a flash of worry in her eyes and it made my already nervous stomach twist. Did she think this was a bad idea? Did she not want to go out with me? Maybe, she'd just wanted to go out and celebrate the other night but didn't necessarily want to go out with me one-on-one.

On a date.

Fuck!

"It's a surprise." I lifted her hand to my lips and kissed her knuckles.

The next few minutes of silence were uncomfortable. I was second-guessing everything. Cursing my own stupidity in my head. Mentally freaking out.

She interrupted my freak out. "You're wearing khakis and a button-down. I've never seen you in khaki pants before."

I peeked over at her for a quick second not knowing what to say.

She continued, "And is that gel in your hair?"

My brow furrowed.

She leaned in closer to me and made some sniffing sounds. "Is that cologne I smell?"

"Uh, yes?"

She pulled her hand away from mine and then crossed both arms over her chest. Concerned, I took a quick glance away from the road and saw her lower lip sticking out in a pout.

Fuck. I used my finger to flip her lower lip playfully. "What's wrong?"

She took a deep breath. "You look so nice for our first date. And look at me!" She pulled up her leg and showed me her tennis sneakers. "I'd never wear these shoes on a date."

I laughed. "Is that why you looked worried?"

"Yes. And I'm a little nervous," she admitted.

"Do you want to go on a date with me? I can always turn around —"

"No!" she cut me off. "Don't you dare turn around. Of course, I want to go. What about Kody?"

I relaxed my shoulder muscles and reached for her hand again. "Talia's babysitting. Tonight it's just you and me."

Her hand slipped into mine.

We were obviously heading toward the coast, so along the way, she made a few guesses about our date. It wasn't until we were pulling up to Marina del Rey that she guessed correctly that we were going on a boat.

I led her to where the captain had told me Emerald Rose was docked. She was an impressive 37-foot classic wooden sailing yacht that I'd chartered for a private sunset sail. The professional crew who was there to take care of the sailing and preparing the gourmet meal that I'd arranged, greeted us at the dock.

Kaylie squealed with delight. Her eyes were glowing when she wrapped her arms around me. "This is such an amazing surprise, Sidney!"

I'd been wanting to kiss her ever since I'd picked her up at the department store, and with her looking at me like that, I couldn't wait any longer. I pulled her against my lips, enjoying her body pressed against mine, as I swallowed up her every whimper and moan while

I kissed her senseless.

We had an audience, so I reluctantly dragged my lips from hers. I grabbed her hand and then helped her onto the boat.

The captain greeted us. "Mr. Anderson. Miss Archer. Welcome aboard Emerald Rose. Looks like smooth sailing tonight, you're in for a treat. Please let the crew know if there's anything you need. We're here to make sure your evening is unforgettable."

One of the crew, Steve, led us over the teak deck to a sunken area tucked safely under the boom, where marine-vinyl lounge seating surrounded a small table laden with a floral centerpiece, a cheese platter, and a bucket of chilling wine.

Steve poured us each a glass of wine. "Folks, we'll be setting sail any minute. Please, stay seated until we get underway. Once the mainsail is up, feel free to explore."

I tucked Kaylie under my arm on the bench seat where we could watch the crew work as we sipped our wine and munched on the food. We slowly navigated out of the marina and soon we were in open water where the crew began working on unfurling the sail. One crew member began raising it by hand, but at a certain point, the captain began cranking a winch that was on the mast. They worked together like a well-oiled machine and in no time the boat was racing through the water powered by the wind.

Kaylie had taken a few videos of the crew working, but then she turned her phone camera to me. "Do you mind if I get some pictures of us? I won't post them or anything."

I fucking wanted her to plaster them all over, but I didn't say that. Instead, I grinned. "Go crazy."

She snapped a few of me and then slid in next to me so she could get the two of us together. We spent the next hour enjoying the food and wine while music softly played in the background. If I had to listen to romantic music, I wanted to hear a guitar, so of course, I chose something called 'relaxing and romantic guitar love songs'. While it wasn't something I'd listen to daily, it really set the mood.

When the sky began to light up with the setting sun, I grabbed a few pillows and then led Kaylie to the bow of the yacht, where we could observe the spectacular sight. Steve brought us each a flute of champagne and then offered to take a few photos. We posed for a bunch and then he told us he'd take some candids as the sun dipped - that we should just ignore him and enjoy the sunset. I reclined on the deck against the pillows and then pulled Kaylie down to nestle between my legs and against my chest.

The colors spread out across the sky, bursting off the streaky clouds in stunning pinks, golds, and yellows and reflecting off the water in deep orange and red. Sometime in the past hour, the sun had gone from a blazing yellow to a deep blood red as it descended in the sky.

She shivered lightly.

"Are you chilly?"

"No." She was holding onto my forearms which were wrapped around her. "You're keeping me warm."

We watched nature's show in awe as we sipped our champagne. There wasn't much to say in the face of such beauty.

She suddenly wiggled out of my arms, put down her champagne glass, and stood up. "Dance with me?"

I stood up and pulled her into my arms. We were swaying to the guitar music and the gentle movement of the yacht. I couldn't help but remember the last time we danced together. I chuckled softly.

Her head was leaning on my chest, but she looked up at me when I laughed. "What?"

"I remember the last time you asked me to dance. Do you?"

Her brow wrinkled. "At the Backstage bar?"

I nodded. "Yep. You told me how hot I was. Both of me."

"Oh, God." She ducked her head in embarrassment. "Wait, both of you?"

"You were seeing double." I snickered. "I believe you said it was 'double the pleasure'."

She bit her lip. "Stop! You have to be kidding! I would never say that."

I tapped a finger to my head and grinned. "It's all locked away up here. That's exactly what you said. Then you forced me to kiss you."

Her mouth fell open. I loved teasing her. Before she could protest, I leaned down to kiss her. What started out as a sweet, romantic kiss quickly turned into a revved-up makeout session. I had to pull away before my dick poked its way through my khaki pants.

She was gazing up at me with her wind-tossed hair, kiss-swollen lips, and a rosy flush staining her cheeks. Her gorgeous green eyes were shining brightly. I'd never seen her look so beautiful. "This is so perfect, Sidney."

"It is."

"You do realize we're sailing off into the sunset together." She giggled. "Literally."

My heart sped up. Everything felt right about this moment. About this girl. About us. "I guess that's a good omen."

The sun behind her was just about to kiss the horizon. I spun her around and folded her back into my arms. "The sun is setting. I don't want you to miss it."

A few minutes later, it had sunk below the horizon, stealing most of the breathtaking colors from the sky with its disappearance. We lingered for a few minutes, not wanting to break the spell, but eventually, Steven invited us below deck for dinner.

A table took up much of the small space that had a classic wood interior. Nautical oil lamps were mounted to the walls and cast a romantic glow to the room. The table was covered in a white linen tablecloth and set with two place settings. A few candles flickered in the middle of the table, adding to the ambiance.

I helped Kaylie settle into her seat and then I sat across from her. Steve removed the metal cloche from each of our plates revealing a pan-seared salmon filet with roasted vegetables and a scallop and asparagus salad. I held my breath until she enthusiastically voiced her approval. I'd had to guess between salmon, duck, or lamb as to which Kaylie would prefer and I'd asked the chef to choose the wine to go with it. When I took my first bite, I knew I'd made the right call with everything. It was magnificent.

Kaylie was in a great mood, telling me stories about some of the crazy customers from work. I could tell she was a bit buzzed from all the alcohol, so I reminded her to drink water, too.

When dessert was served, a sinful-looking slice of chocolate cake with fresh cream and berries, we decided to bring it up to the deck to eat.

It was darker than I expected when we got up top. There were only a few navigational lights lighting up the deck, but the moon was just beginning to rise and its soft light made the water sparkle around us. The breeze had gentled, so that we could hear the rhythmic sound of waves lapping against the hull.

We made our way to the bow and sat down against our cushions and ate our dessert. The cake was as tasty as it looked; I finished it in minutes. Kaylie took her time, enjoying every bite.

She only had a few more bites left when she put down her fork. "I can't eat another bite. I'm completely stuffed. Can we wrap it up and bring it home? It's so good!"

I laughed and then scooped the plate out of her hand and finished her leftovers in two bites. "No need to waste it."

She took a deep breath. "I'm going to have to do an extra workout for that, but it was worth it."

Raising an eyebrow, I smirked. "I know how we can burn some extra calories."

She looked up at me and squeaked out, "Here?"

"No, not here, silly." I chuckled. "Later."

"Oh, okay." She looked a little sad, and it had me amused.

I pushed the empty plates aside and then laid down on my back, propping a pillow under my head. I patted the deck next to me. She scooched in beside me, her head propped up on my arm.

I turned my head to kiss her cheek. "The stars are starting to come out."

"It's so beautiful. This has been so amazing, I don't want it to end," she whispered.

I was savoring every moment because I didn't want it to end either. I'd planned all the romantic stuff for her, but it turned out that I had enjoyed it just as much. The night had been absolutely perfect.

We lay quietly watching the stars while the yacht headed back to the marina. Way too quickly, the crew was lowering the sails and preparing to dock.

After the crew said their goodbyes to us, I discreetly tipped Steve over and above the gratuity I'd already prepaid, since he was the one who was serving us all night and because he'd given me the link where I could find all the photos he'd taken of us.

Kaylie fell asleep in the car on the way home. Her hand was resting in mine and I'd never felt more connected to her. I had wanted to discuss our relationship and make sure we were on the same page, but after the night we'd just had, it seemed so insignificant. We'd had our first date, and I'd fucking nailed it. I was already thinking about our second date and what we could do.

Not once had I looked at the nanny cam to check on Kody. I was happy to be going home to him, but I was happier that Kaylie was with me and would sleep in my bed tonight. Damn if I didn't feel like the luckiest bastard in the world.

Chapter 30

Kaylie

ALL WEEKEND I DISSECTED the new breakdown material I'd received about the TV sitcom and the two roles I could be cast to play. I memorized the new sides and practiced reading through them hundreds of times until I knew every nuance of the script. I felt it deep in my soul.

Between readings, I'd researched the casting director, the creator, the showrunner, the director — any person I could connect to the project — to get an insight into what they might be looking for in an actress.

I was as prepared as I could be, nervous and excited all at the same time. As a very sweet gesture, Sidney had delivered breakfast in bed to me this morning. Unfortunately, it remained mostly untouched because I was too full of anxiety to eat.

After breakfast, Sid presented me with a beautiful bouquet of roses and whispered his encouragement to me before Bash arrived to pick me up.

He'd already stolen my heart. But seeing this romantic side to him — the best first date in the world's history, the flowers, breakfast in bed — left me walking on air. He was everything I ever wanted and more.

Sid had even respected my need to prepare for the audition and gave me plenty of space to work over the weekend. He kept his distance during the day, but as soon as I finished, he'd pamper me. And the nights? Together, we were on fire.

When Bash picked me up, Sid stayed hidden in the kitchen. I didn't expect anything crazy, like a kiss in front of Bash before I left, but one last 'good luck' would have been nice. He'd kept his distance from me whenever Bash came around. I guess I couldn't blame him, but I didn't like it. As soon as this audition was over, I was going to talk to him about telling Bash our secret.

I didn't want to be a secret anymore. Sidney and I were both adults, and we could make our own decision. Now that I knew we weren't just a 'casual sex' fling, I wanted to claim Sidney as my boyfriend to all our friends and family.

I'd been tiptoeing around my growing feelings for Sidney, but after our date, I could no longer deny it.

I was in love with him.

It wasn't just a continuation of my teenage obsession. Yes, I'd been infatuated with Sidney for a long time, but this time, I'd fallen in love with the person he was — the amazing father, the intense musician, the caring friend, the sexy rock star, and the passionate lover. I'd keep my revelation quiet for now, but I knew exactly what I wanted — to become a permanent part of Sid and Kody's lives.

I didn't want to be late, so I had to stop daydreaming about Sidney, but that was hard. Bash was waiting for me by the door, so I had to leave without seeing Sidney again. As we walked to the car, I updated my social media, posting that I was on my way to the final audition on all my feeds, and added some hashtags: #audition #actinglife #wishmeluck.

Bash grinned at me. "You ready for this?"

"As ready as I'll ever be."

"You promise you'll take a cab straight back home when it's over?"

"Yes," I huffed. "But you can't keep me on lockdown forever, Sebastian. Nothing's happened since I changed my phone number. Everything died down just like the detective said it would."

We arrived at the car and both climbed in. I gave Bash the address where the audition was being held to put into his car navigation, and a few seconds later, we were pulling out.

Bash flipped down his sunglasses. "Kaylie, you can't let down your guard. And you definitely can't move back into your apartment."

This wasn't the conversation I wanted to have just before the biggest audition of my life. "I know that."

He rubbed his chin. "I've been looking at apartments. Sid needs more space for Kody, and I need to get out of his hair. I can afford someplace nice now. I found some sweet places with lots of room and great security."

My eyes widened as I stared at him. "I didn't know you were planning on moving out?"

He nodded. "The tour dates are going to be announced any day now. We'll be gone for almost a year. If we're selling out everywhere, it'll get extended beyond that. It would be perfect if you stayed there while I was on tour."

My mouth fell open. "You want me to move into your apartment?"

"You'd be doing me a big favor."

It wasn't a horrible solution if he really was looking to move out, but it wasn't what I'd been hoping for. Somehow, I'd got it in my head that I could stay with Sidney. "Why would you get a new place if you won't even be here?" My eyes narrowed. "I see what you're trying to do."

We stopped at a red light and Bash looked over at me. "Kay, who's going to look after you while I'm gone? You can't go back to your old apartment, and I'd be worried sick if you moved into some new crappy place in a dangerous neighborhood."

"Right now, I can't afford some swanky place, Bash." I really didn't want to be living off my older brother's money, either. I decided to put a little feeler out about what I was thinking. "Maybe I could just stay where I am now? In your room. Maybe we can both put some stuff we don't need for now into storage, for the time being, just to make a bit more room?"

The light turned green, so Bash hit the gas. "Without me or Sid around, that apartment isn't that safe, and it's too damn close to your old address. Besides, I doubt Sid is going to want to hold on to it when we go on tour. I'd rather ditch it, too. We've outgrown it."

"Wait! Sid's going on tour?" I'd been staring out the side window, but my head whipped around to look at him. What the hell?

"Of course he is." He said it with certainty. "The new single is about to drop any day. Then we're going to do a fuckton of promotion and then we're off."

"What about Kody?" I forced the words past my lips.

Bash shrugged. "Kody's going to come with us. We're getting a special tour manager that knows how to organize having a baby on tour. Sid will have to find a new nanny, I guess. He'll probably need someone younger this time. Maybe one of those au pairs. I hope he finds someone hot since she'll be always hanging around." Bash was tapping on the steering wheel with his fingers. He was completely relaxed as he obliterated my every dream for the future. "There's some famous country star that's touring with her baby right now. I think Sid talked to her tour manager to find out how it works."

I couldn't believe what I was hearing. Sidney was planning on bringing Kody on tour? Why did I assume the band was going to get a tour replacement for Sidney? Why did I think we were going to spend the next year living like a family in his little apartment when, in reality, he was leaving soon? For an entire year. And he hadn't said a thing to me.

I was reeling.

Why didn't he tell me?

He was just going to leave? With Kody?

We never talked about the tour at all. Just like we never talked about us. Because there never was an 'us'.

I had naively assumed something that wasn't the case. Just like Bash had warned me about so many times. I couldn't handle casual sex. My heart got too involved. And since it was Sidney, my personal kryptonite, my heart had gotten involved at lightning speed. Sidney was probably enjoying all the sex and free babysitting. After all, hadn't I declared to him at one point that I only wanted casual sex with him? He had never promised me anything.

Now my heart was going to get crushed. Not just crushed, but shredded, ripped out of my chest, stomped on, and destroyed beyond repair.

Tears burned at the back of my eyes. "Bash, I can't worry about all this right now. I've got to focus on my audition. We'll talk about where I'm going to live later, okay?"

"Yeah, okay. You're sure you don't know how long this thing is going to last?"

According to the GPS, we would be there in five minutes. I had to get away from him before I burst into tears. "No, but I promise I'll call a cab. I'll be fine."

He turned his head and smiled at me. "You'll call me when it's over and let me know how it went?"

I avoided his gaze. "I will."

Finally, we pulled up to the curb in front of the building. Bash leaned over to hug me. "Don't worry about the apartment shit right now. We'll work it out. You just go kill it, okay?"

"Thanks, Bash."

♪♪♪♪♪

This was the second time I'd been on an important audition when I was emotionally spinning. I guess all my preparation was paying off because I sensed I was doing pretty well.

The actor cast as the husband was very professional and easy to work with. I couldn't tell if we had screen chemistry, but our timing was in sync and our interactions came off smoothly.

I was giving it my all in my readings for both roles, the wife and the sister. There was a panel of five people watching the three of us perform a scene, and then we'd switch up the roles and do it again. Sometimes they gave direction, but usually, they left it up to us to interpret the script.

Landing the sister role would be amazing, but I was so close to the big prize that I couldn't pretend that I didn't want it badly. After arriving, the three of us were taken into a meeting room where the producer went over the shooting schedule, asked for any conflicts, and outlined the scope of the commitment since none of us had worked on an acting project this huge before.

It was an enormous commitment, but I would throw myself into it wholeheartedly when Sidney left me in the dust to go on tour. I'd need something to focus on instead of my lifeless, mangled heart.

We were mid-scene when a young blonde woman unceremoniously rushed into the room and approached the casting director. Surprised by the unexpected interruption, I stuttered through my line but managed to continue the scene.

When my 'husband' was speaking his lines, I glanced over at the casting table out of the corner of my eye. The casting director and the executive producer were scrutinizing something on the blonde woman's phone. They were frowning, and then one of them looked up at me. Shit, I got caught watching them instead of acting.

Thank goodness I hadn't missed my line. My 'sister' was speaking, and I answered her properly, but my mind was semi-occupied with what was going on. The phone got passed down to the other three executives, and I swore I heard an audible gasp from one of them.

At this point, I could tell my co-actors were also distracted, and the whole scene was slowly going to hell. One of us missed a cue, so we ad-libbed a bit. It didn't seem to matter because no one was watching us anymore. Their eyes were glued to whatever was on that phone.

The producer, holding the blonde lady's phone, abruptly stood up and then the other four followed his lead. He vaguely gestured to us. "Take five. Something has come up. We'll be back in a few."

None of the five looked at us as they left the room. The blonde lady, who was close on their heels, threw a sneering, triumphant look our way before she too departed.

"What was that all about?" the male actor, John, asked.

"I have no clue." Gina sniffed. "We were all doing great. I hope something didn't change with the show. That would be my luck. Just when I get my hopes up!"

I nodded in sympathy. "That would suck. Maybe it was just a pre-production emergency. Who knows? Should we run through our lines while we wait?"

The other two nodded in agreement. It was better to work than worry about what could potentially be happening.

We started from the top with the scene we'd just been working with. It felt like the three of us had a good rapport and I even cracked a smile at one of John's corny jokes from the script. We sounded natural together.

After about 15 minutes, we gave up on the readings and began talking about ourselves and our previous acting experiences. We were chatting amicably when the five people who held our careers in the palm of their hands returned, and they did not look happy.

Why did it feel like all five of them were casting hostile looks my way? It was probably just an illusion, but a tornado of nerves gathered in my stomach. I was sure, though, that one woman was staring at me with raw contempt.

The executive producer cleared his throat. "CDX Entertainment is a company that prides itself on its family values. The material we produce reflects those values and we expect our employees, on every level, to always uphold those same core values. Unprofessional, immoral behavior will not be tolerated."

The three of us remained mute, but I saw John nodding his head.

"Kaylie—" He looked right at me and sniffed like I was the lowest scum of the earth. My stomach sank to the floor. My legs felt like they might give out.

"It has come to our attention that your social media presence does not represent the image that CDX Entertainment wishes to project. We no longer wish to pursue a further relationship with you. I'd also like to remind you that you've signed a confidentiality agreement about this project. You are not authorized to disclose any information about it to anyone, in person or on social media. Not now and not ever. Do you understand?"

My veins turned to ice water. I couldn't move. I couldn't speak. I couldn't even think. I was numb. What was happening?

Gina inhaled sharply and whispered, "Oh my God!"

The casting director stood up and walked over to me when I hadn't moved for close to a minute. She took my elbow and began pulling me toward the door. "Thank you for your time, Miss Archer. I would appreciate it if you left your audition materials here."

I stopped in my tracks. "There must be some mistake—"

The corner of her lip tightened, and she scoldingly peered at me over her reading glasses. "Did you not just post on social media about this audition before you got here? And you hashtagged CDX Entertainment?"

"I did, but—"

She didn't let me finish. She began physically guiding me out the door by the arm. "Leave willingly with me now, Miss Archer, or I'll call security."

Holy shit! My mind was spinning. The lady was trying to frog-march me right out the door. I remembered to grab my handbag, which I'd left behind the admin's desk, and then within seconds, she had efficiently ejected me from the building.

I stood outside the building on the sidewalk in a daze. People rushed by me, busy with their day, while I tried to figure out what the hell had just happened.

I didn't even remember hashtagging CDX Entertainment, but would it have been so bad if I did? Had that gone against the confidentiality agreement? Even if it did, it hardly seemed like the egregious professional and moral failing they were making it out to be.

Had they all been gathered around that blonde woman's phone looking at my stupid post from this morning? Gasping in horror?

Nothing made sense.

A man hurrying down the sidewalk jostled me and realized I was blocking pedestrian traffic. I began walking slowly as I tried to clear the fog from my brain. I pulled my phone from my bag and switched it off of silent mode.

Some text notifications popped up. Not many people had my new number yet. The texts were all from my roommate.

> **Jill:** You crazy bitch!
> **Jill:** Are you for real?
> **Jill:** Are you trying to tell me something? Lol. I am not into pussy.

I had neither the time nor the energy to figure out what she was talking about right now.

I was about to go look up exactly what I'd posted earlier and check what hashtags I'd used when my phone rang.

It was my brother Brent. He was the middle child, nearer my age than Bash, but Bash and I had always been closer to each other. Not only did we share similar coloring and features, but we both had the same artistic temperaments. Brent was far from artistic; he was the analytical sibling.

For a moment, I thought about ignoring Brent's call, but he never reached out to me. We spoke about twice a month, but only when I called him. Even though I was in the middle of what felt like an existential crisis, I answered.

"Hey, Brent. What's up?"

"Kaylie…" His voice sounded weird. Strangled, almost like he was struggling to speak.

"Is everything okay?"

"I, uh, I got your post. About the audition." He sounded off. Maybe we had a poor connection.

"Brent, I can't talk right now. I didn't end up getting the part anyway, so I'm kind of bummed out." I tried to ditch him without being rude, as I was in no mood to chat.

"Kay," I heard a hard exhale. "Was that really your audition tape?"

Audition tape? My heart started to beat double-time; something was wrong. "What do you mean?"

Between the agony-laced words that Brent forced out, a mention of an audition tape, and the inexplicable humiliation I'd just faced at CDX, a dark and heavy feeling of dread seeped into my very bones.

He hissed. "You sent me a DM on Facebook asking me to look at your audition tape for the new role."

"No." My hands started shaking so badly, I almost dropped the phone. "I didn't DM you. It must have been somebody else."

"Fuck! It was you, Kay. It was … bad. I didn't know. I stopped watching as soon as I realized…" He sounded panicked and he'd said 'fuck'. Brent never cursed.

My brain scrambled to think. I'd never made any weird audition tapes. None that would make Brent sound like that. The most embarrassing tape I could think of was this stupid cheer routine me and a girlfriend had made in high school. I'd always been super careful with what I put on social media.

I took a deep breath and tried to calm down. This was just some kind of mistake. "Brent, what was on the tape?"

I hadn't realized, but at some point, I'd stopped walking again and people were shooting me annoyed glances as I took up the center of the sidewalk. I moved out of the way until I was leaning up against the outer brick facade of a residential building.

"Brent? Are you still there?"

"Fuck. Fuck. Fuck! You didn't send me a DM?"

"No," I denied.

"Then someone must have hacked into your account. Does anyone have your password?"

I ignored his question. "What was on the audition tape? Tell me."

"Fuck, Kay. You were ... naked."

"What?" I gasped. I was truly shocked. I'd never taken any videos of myself naked, and I'd never let any boyfriends do that. "That can't be."

"I only saw it for a few seconds. But it definitely looked like you." His voice sounded raw.

I opened up my app and signed in. It took me a few tries because now my whole body was quaking. In a few seconds, I was looking at a list of DMs I'd sent. A quick scan revealed that I'd sent about ten DMs this morning. They all said, 'Take a look at my audition tape for my new role!!' There was a video attached to each.

"Oh, my God, Brent. I see the DMs, but I never sent these."

I pressed play on the video.

The video was in color, but the lighting was low. I knew right away that it was me. The footage was surprisingly clear, not grainy at all. I was lying back, half-reclined against the headboard of the bed. I was naked. And I was following Charlie's every command. He wasn't in the video, but I remembered exactly where he was standing, strategically off-camera. In the video, I was looking at him, not at the camera that must have been hidden somewhere to his left.

I stopped the video because I recalled that night in vivid detail. Our sex life had never been particularly wonderful, but that night, Charlie had goaded me into doing something I didn't really want to do. He'd told me to do some dirty things to myself and I had. And, all along, he'd been secretly filming it.

I was about to vomit. My legs suddenly couldn't support my weight and I sunk down the wall until I was just sitting there on the filthy sidewalk.

"You still there, Kaylie?"

A keening wail burst from my lips. "Brent," I choked out, "The video."

"Kay, listen to me. Someone has your password. You've got to change it right now before they do anything else."

I couldn't focus. I hugged my knees to my chest and began rocking back and forth. "Oh, my God, Brent! Who else saw that video? There were lots of DMs!"

"Don't worry about that now. First, let's get that password changed, then we'll take care of the videos. Can you do that? Change the password?"

"Yes."

Brent kept encouraging me while I went through the process of changing the password. The authentication code came right away, so I got it done within a few minutes.

"Good job, Kay," he spoke soothingly. "Do you use that same password for any of your other accounts?"

"Um, yeah, I use it for..."

Tears began streaming down my face. This couldn't be happening to me. I'd never shared my password with Charlie, but he must have seen me use it one time.

I frantically swiped around on my phone until I was on Instagram. My heart plummeted.

The video was posted on my page with tons of hashtags. And it was already getting likes and comments. I read through the hashtags with horror. #howigotthepart #audition #selflove #castingcall #actinglife #actress #cdxentertainment #sexsells #xrated #yummy #porn #imallthat #likeforlikes #vidoftheday #love #like4like #girl #repost #like #ootd #explore #catlover #workout

Brent was calling my name over the phone, but I had to lean to the side to dry heave a few times. As soon as I was done, I was too frenzied trying to delete the post to listen to what he was saying. I got it deleted quickly, then I began to work on changing the password for this account, but it was difficult with shaky fingers and eyes blurry with tears.

I finally heard what he was saying. "Are you at home?"

"No." I wiped the snot that was mixing with my tears with my sleeve.

"Where are you?"

I glanced up from my phone. People walked by; no one was paying any attention to me. "I'm on the sidewalk."

"Let me call Bash to come get you."

"No!" I shouted. "God, no. I don't want him to know about this! I don't want anyone to know about this."

"Kaylie, you're in no state to be alone right now." I could hear how concerned he was.

I took a shuddering breath. "I'm waiting for the code to change the password. These are the only two accounts with this password, but I've got to check my other social media."

"Can you call a cab to take you back home?"

I couldn't go back to Sidney and Bash's apartment. Not after this. "I can't go back home. I'm going to go to a friend's."

"Okay. That's good." Brent agreed. "I'm going to get the next flight out there. I'll help you figure this all out. We'll fix everything."

"Don't tell mom and dad."

He paused for a moment and then agreed. "Okay. Stay on the phone with me until you get to your friend's place."

I felt like I was sleepwalking through a nightmare. Somehow I made it through the next few hours of my life, but I'd done it in a thick fog while humiliation and shame left me near catatonic.

Chapter 31

Sidney

TODAY WAS OUR LAST rehearsal before we recorded the two remaining songs for our album. We'd record them both tomorrow, but we had the studio reserved for Wednesday also, in case we ran into any issues. We were scheduled for a full-day photo shoot on Thursday and then Friday began the hardcore churn of pre-tour promotion.

I was running out of time about making a tour decision. A hybrid plan hadn't fully manifested but was slowly creeping its way into my thoughts. I wanted the best of both worlds, so I needed to come up with a solution that allowed Kody to come on tour part-time, and then I'd bow out for the other part, so I could devote all my attention to him at home.

I questioned whether I had what it took to be a full-time stay-at-home dad, but I thought I could do it. I hadn't mentioned it to anyone, but I wanted to explore songwriting. Maybe start playing the keyboards again? Everyone had made fun of the song I'd written, but BVR was laying heavy odds on it becoming an enormous hit. I was sure I had more of that creative energy left in me.

And Kaylie factored into my plans as well. I wanted to show her that Kody and I could fit seamlessly into her life. Once we were out in the open about our relationship, we could go out on more dates. I planned to show her that what we had wasn't just about sex — great sex was just a spectacular bonus. Neither of our career choices was traditional, but that made us uniquely suited for each other. And I'd show her that I wasn't looking for a partner just so they could take care of Kody. I planned on shouldering the majority of that responsibility myself. I'd never put Kody's care in the way of her ambitions.

At lunchtime, there were still no messages from Kaylie. So, I sent her a quick message, hoping that her audition was going well. Throughout the afternoon, I kept peeking at my phone whenever I had the chance. By the time we finished practice at 4 o'clock, there was still nothing.

I was surprised the audition was going all day, but Kaylie hadn't known how long it would take, so I wasn't too worried. On the way home, I picked up a bottle of champagne in case Kaylie wanted to celebrate like we did last time. I felt my dick stirring when I thought about how I licked tiny champagne bubbles off every inch of her skin.

Josie left when I got home. I waited about an hour before I ordered from the Colombian grill down the street that Kaylie loved. The food was delivered, and it sat.

And sat. Until it was cold.

I was getting worried. She wasn't returning my texts or my calls. It was almost 8 o'clock.

Finally, I broke down and called Bash.

"Hey, Kaylie never showed up here after her audition. Did you hear from her?"

There was a lot of background noise. It sounded like he was out somewhere, maybe at a noisy restaurant. "Oh, I forgot to tell you that she texted me. Kay didn't get the part, and she's pretty upset, I guess. She wanted some time to herself to rethink some things in her life. She's with a friend and she's going to stay there."

I was floored. She didn't get the part? Either part? She must be devastated. "She's not coming home tonight? I mean, here?"

"No."

"Who's she with?"

"She didn't mention, but she promised she wasn't alone." A woman called out to Bash in the background. "I've got to run, brother. I'll see you at the studio tomorrow morning."

He ended the call.

Stunned, I sat silently for a few minutes. Why wouldn't she come back here? I hoped she wasn't worried that I'd think any less of her for not getting the part.

Shit, I wanted to be there for her. I wanted to comfort her. A slither of misgiving crept up my spine. Why hadn't she turned to me? She'd gone to a friend, instead, to avoid me.

By the time I went to bed, I'd left her a handful of voicemail messages and texts, letting her know that I'd heard she didn't get the part and I wanted to talk to her. I didn't know the exact thing to say; I was no poet, but her returning silence left me uneasy.

That night, I slept like absolute shit. I missed having her in bed with me. I woke up to a gray cloudy day that promised rain. We didn't have too many of those days in L.A., so it felt like an extra slap in the face.

The studio session was uneventful. I came home and took care of Kody.

Kaylie still hadn't called. Nothing. I got that she wanted some space, but I was getting worried. She could have texted me at least; given me something. Maybe I was slightly angry, too. I wasn't the bad guy. Why was she avoiding me?

The next day, we had to go back into the studio to finish up. The guys were all joking around and in a great mood. It pissed me off. Sensing my sour mood, they left me to my brooding self. They assumed I was worrying about finalizing my decision on whether to go on tour.

We wrapped up our session early, so I got home around 3 o'clock in the afternoon. I knew something was wrong the moment I walked into my apartment, but I couldn't put my finger on it.

When Josie left, I tried to relax, but even Kody couldn't keep my anxiety at bay. I was walking on eggshells waiting for something to drop. Something horrible.

I put Kody down on his activity mat for some tummy time while I sat next to him. I reached for the copy of Bass Player magazine that was sitting at the top of my mail pile on my coffee table. Maybe it could distract me.

A white business-sized envelope addressed to S. Anderson lay underneath the magazine. I froze. There was nothing else on the envelope except my address, no company names, no logos. This was the only mail I'd ever received that only used the initial of my first name. It was less than a week ago that I'd filled in my information just like that to retain as much privacy as I could.

I knew exactly what was in that envelope.

I'd been a wreck when I'd sent in the kit. How the hell could I have forgotten all about it? Well, when Kaylie had disappeared with no warning and my world turned upside down, I guess I'd forgotten all about the paternity results.

As soon as Donovan had mentioned that Kody's mother could

stroll back into his life and start making demands, especially once she heard we were making a lot of money, I knew I had to protect him any way I could. It was time to find out the truth.

So, why was my heart galloping like a stampede of wild, angry horses?

I took a few deep breaths and glanced over at Kody. He was pretty content sucking on his hand, so I didn't have any excuse to delay. Before I could chicken out, I tore open the envelope and withdrew the papers.

The first page looked like a standard form letter. I quickly pushed it aside. Immediately, I could see the second page contained the results. There was a table with a few rows and columns containing random numbers. My eye scanned to the bottom of the page.

Highlighted in a box, it said 'Probability of Paternity: 99.9998%. A statement underneath read: The alleged father cannot be excluded as the biological father of the tested child. Based on the analysis of STR loci listed above, the probability of paternity is 99.9998%.

It was slightly confusing, but I was pretty sure this just definitively determined Kody's paternity. There was no doubt.

My hands shaking, I quickly flipped to the next page. It looked identical to the last page — the same chart with the random numbers. I assumed it was a copy until I noticed the 0% in the highlighted box.

Fuck! I had submitted two samples. A swab of my cheek and some of Bash's hair from a brush.

This page read: The alleged father is excluded as the biological father of the tested child. This conclusion is based on the non-matching alleles observed at the loci listed above with a PI equal to zero. The alleged father lacks the genetic markers that must be contributed to the child by the biological father. The probability of paternity is 0%.

I broke out into a cold sweat as I looked more carefully at the chart headers. Underneath 'alleged FATHER' was listed one letter as identification: V. That was me.

Kody was not my son.

My world shrank into a tiny little black point and imploded into nothingness. I heard the blood rushing through my ears and felt dizzy.

I'd known this was a possibility all along, but deep in my heart, I'd thought that Kody was my son. We had a bond that only a father and son could have. I loved him and the thought of losing him...

I was sinking.

Drowning.

Tears coated my cheeks. The last time I'd cried was when I was seven years old and my mother didn't show up for another visitation. I'd decided from then on I'd never let another thing hurt me like that ever again.

What the fuck was I going to do? I couldn't give him up. I couldn't let anything bad happen to him.

Panic was slithering through my veins. A cold sweat broke out on my brow and my heart was beating fast in terror. The room was suffocating. It was closing in on me.

I'd been close to tipping over the edge of panic. The only thing that eventually pulled me from the abyss was when Kody started crying.

I blinked a few times and then picked him up. He laid his head on my shoulder and stopped crying. I kissed the top of his head and I rubbed his back soothingly.

Somehow, I was able to comfort Kody, when I wanted to rage. Scream. Break shit.

What kind of world was this? How could this be happening? I wanted to puke.

What was I going to do? Should I keep this from Bash? For Kody's sake? Or was that just me being selfish?

What the fuck would Bash do when he found out?

I started pacing back and forth trying to contain the overwhelming devastation I felt.

Fuck!

I needed Kaylie. I needed to talk to her. I needed her strength and compassion. But, she'd run out on me.

I stopped in my tracks.

Something had been bothering me since the moment I'd walked in the door today. I looked around the room. Kaylie's shit was gone.

Holding Kody against my chest, I swallowed down the lump in my throat and strode into Bash's room.

All her stuff was gone.

She'd moved out.

Kaylie was gone.

Chapter 32

Kaylie

WHAT DOESN'T KILL YOU, makes you stronger.

I remember belting out that Kelly Clarkson song when I was a young teen. What some people might not know, is that the quote came from the famous philosopher, Friedrich Nietzsche.

Who was I to disagree with a famous philosopher, but I was certain that I wasn't any stronger.

I'd always believed that I was a strong woman — mentally, emotionally, spiritually, or whatever — but sometimes you didn't really know until you went through something devastating. I thought I'd be able to dust myself off and stand right back up telling myself over and over not to let that asshole, Charlie, win. Unfortunately, reality didn't actually square with the perception I had of myself. I hadn't bounced back. In fact, I was worried about my extreme reaction. Shaking it off like it was nothing wasn't going to work.

I was in hiding. I'd convinced Brent not to tell anyone what happened. Sure, some of my friends and acquaintances had seen the video, but many had not. I'd been able to delete the Instagram post pretty quickly, but not before it had been re-posted. Those damn hashtags helped posts go viral, and I would be fighting them for years. It was like playing whac-a-mole.

Good thing my parents weren't big on social media. Brent wanted me to come clean to our parents about what happened, but I just couldn't. Instead, I convinced him to tell my parents that he'd sent them a virus over Facebook by mistake. He told them he could 'remove it' if they gave him their passwords. My parents were very trusting and Brent never lied. With their permission, Brent went into their accounts, deleted the message with the video after confirming that neither had opened it and then instructed them to change their passwords.

He also did that successfully with my grandfather's account, but not so with my aunt's. She was one of the people who had seen the video. My Aunt Linda had promised Brent that she would not speak to my father about it. She said she'd give me some time, but she wanted to speak with me, eventually. That was one of about five horrible conversations that I still had to have.

The other DMs had been sent to mostly high school friends, to my roommate Jill and to Bash. A few of my friends had gotten in touch with me after seeing the video. I actually sent them a 'form' email briefly explaining what happened, asking them to delete the video, and telling them that I was still devastated by it and not comfortable talking about it yet.

Jill had seen the video and her reaction had been that it was no big deal. She was pissed at Charlie but didn't think I should let it get to me. Okay.

Bash was one of the ticking time bombs I didn't know what to do with. He wasn't big on social media, so I was sure he hadn't seen it. Yet. It was sitting there in his account and he wouldn't fall for the virus scam like my parents did.

Brent thought I should proactively ask people who hadn't reached out to me that received the DM to delete the video without watching it. I thought that would only serve to make them watch it. So, I waited, paralyzed, for the ticking time bombs to detonate.

The problem on Instagram was trickier. The video had been re-posted and the salacious nature of it had it spreading quickly. Without Lacey stepping in, it would have quickly gone out of control.

When I'd collapsed on that dirty sidewalk outside the audition, I felt like I had no one to turn to. I'm not sure why I called Lacey. Maybe I thought she wouldn't judge me so harshly about the content of the video.

She hadn't asked any questions which was a good thing because I didn't even have the ability to form sentences when she came and picked me up from the sidewalk in her crazy-ass high heels and power suit that showed off tons of cleavage. I'd never seen a woman in a business suit looking so incredibly sexy, except maybe on the set of that new *Dynasty* remake.

She climbed into the backseat of the fancy car with me. She told the driver to take her home, and it turned out that she lived in a multi-million dollar downtown penthouse.

Spinning around in the impressive space, I took in the breathtaking views out of the floor-to-ceiling windows. I finally found my voice. "I didn't know you were rich."

She shrugged. "It's mostly Daddy's money. And, I work at my Dad's company."

"Who's your daddy?"

She laughed. "I'll tell you, but it's a secret. You can't spread it around. And, if I tell you, you have to tell me what's going on with you. Deal?"

"Okay." I felt a bit ashamed that I'd never asked Lacey anything about herself. I'd known her for a couple of years. She hung out with my brother and the band. I had her pegged as a typical groupie.

Lacey began pouring some fancy-looking drinks into crystal glasses. "Bourbon sour. Sip slowly. It looks like you need it." She handed me a glass. "My father is Max Clements, owner and CEO of Castle Music."

My brow furrowed. "Your last name isn't Clements."

"Nope. When I started working for my dad, I didn't want anyone to know we were related. The cat's kind of out of the bag at Castle, but I still go by my mother's maiden name." She sat down on the modern white sofa and gestured for me to join her.

I plopped down at the other end of the couch. Lacey's confession had made a bunch of things click into place for me. "That's crazy, Lacey. Castle Music is the label that signed Cold Fusion. Are you the one responsible for getting Ghost Parker the hottest opening act slot in the country? The guys don't even know, do they?"

"No, and that's the way I like it." She swirled the ice around in her drink. "I'll tell you the entire story sometime, but right now, I want to know what happened to you. We had a deal."

I had just gotten to the part about the video being posted on my social media accounts when she stopped me. Her whole demeanor had changed. Gone was my friend and in her place was an absolute shark. She put down her drink and grabbed her phone pressing a few buttons to make a call.

"Good afternoon, Lacey." I heard the woman's voice on the other end.

"Myra, I need to speak to Corrine Michaels from SRI Solutions immediately. Only Corrine, don't let them pawn me off on one of her employees."

She hung up the call and then turned to me. "Kaylie, I'm sorry this happened to you. Tonight, we'll drink and commiserate over it, but right now we're working against the clock. We've got to act now if we want any chance of stopping this from spreading like wildfire. Corrinne's team is the absolute best in the business. They'll scour the internet and start filing take-down orders. They'll run down every re-post and hashtag. But, you've got to give me access to your accounts."

I was almost too numb to even care at that point, but Lacey sounded like she knew what she was doing, so I left it all in her hands.

From that moment on, Lacey took over and got me through the worst of it. The experts attacked the social media angle while Lacey took care of me. She used my phone to text Bash so he wouldn't worry, and I spent the night at her place. The next day, she sent a car to pick up Brent at the airport. And when I made my decision to run away from L.A., she organized a moving company to accompany me and Brent to my apartment to help pack up my belongings and place them in storage.

That afternoon, when I knew Josie would take Kody out for his walk, Brent and I snuck into Bash's apartment and gathered all my things. Brent knew nothing about me and Sidney, so when I broke down in tears, he just gave me a hug and told me everything was going to be okay. Brent didn't even ask me about all the baby stuff that was in Bash's apartment until we were on the flight back to Georgia.

I'd been in Georgia, hiding out at Brent's place for a few days. The official story was that I was disappointed about not getting the role and I needed some time to regroup. My mother was starting to get antsy for me to visit. I was running out of time, but I didn't want to see pity on her face when she looked at me.

And, I was still freaking out about the video. Everything was still so very raw. I felt like I'd just had a leg amputated, Lacey had applied the tourniquet and stemmed the flow, and now I was just praying I wouldn't slowly bleed out.

I wasn't sleeping well. My eyes were heavy, and my head ached from long nights of trying to coax myself into sleep. I was depressed and bone tired. The lump in my throat tightened as I thought about the video that had ruined everything, a video that left me feeling powerless and ashamed, shivering like a puddle of goo. I'd even lost faith in my career choice. I hated L.A. and everything about it. Every time I attempted to venture outside Brent's house, crippling anxiety clawed my insides, like a sinister force trying to drag me back inside. It felt hopeless.

And, I'd lost Sidney; even though, I'd never really had him. That was even worse than everything else. I climbed back under the covers. Brent was at work; he'd never know if I decided not to get out of bed today.

Chapter 33

Bash

I was so done with this photo shoot. We were on our fourth outfit change and despite what our new stylist said, each damn outfit looked nearly the same as the last. The new PR person from BVR, Trudy, was micromanaging the shoot until I thought I might snap. Without her constant input, this entire process would have gone ten times quicker. By late afternoon, even the photographer was getting grumpy dealing with Trudy's excessive attention to every fucking minor detail.

This pre-tour stuff was going to kill me. I just wanted to be on the road with my band, filling arenas, and bringing the house down with our music.

If I thought I was in a shitty mood, Sid was in a black pit of despair. He'd been a mess all week. When the stylist suggested another change of clothes, Sid practically ripped her head off. After Sid's outburst, she wisely decided our current outfits were good enough.

All day we'd been at this, and I had so much to do. I didn't have much time to figure out Kaylie's living situation before the tour started. She wasn't too keen on talking about it, and I knew she was going to be stubborn about taking my money.

I'd been calling her, but she wasn't answering my calls. I knew she was upset about not getting the role, but she was taking it a bit too far. Chicks and their emotions. I never understood it.

She needed to pick herself up and try again. She was still young. When I was 23, our band was going nowhere fast. Downward Spiral had all but collapsed. If we'd sulked at every roadblock, we wouldn't be where we were now. I knew that acting and music weren't exactly the same, but each relied a bit on skill and talent and more heavily on luck, timing, and networking. But luck needs you to be in the game for it to work its magic.

I begged her over text to call me back. I still didn't want her walking around the city alone because I was still worried about that fucking website. She was physically attacked, and I had the impression that she was feeling confined by the safety measures and would eventually let down her guard.

I was uneasy with her ignoring me and we still had to figure out this apartment thing, so I began bombarding her phone. Finally, this morning, after I left a few voicemails, Brent called me back and left a message. Kaylie was staying in Georgia with him. He told me that she needed some time to herself and that I should back off a bit.

What the fuck? What was she doing with Brent? I guess she needed to get away from L.A., but for how long? I had to figure out this shit, her living arrangements, quickly. It was just another damn headache for me to deal with.

To top off all the Kaylie drama, now Sid was acting funny. The news about being able to take Kody on tour with us should have made him happy. It was the perfect solution. Yet, he was a fucking mess. Everyone noticed. I wondered if he was having second thoughts about even going on tour. Fuck! I needed to talk to him. He would regret it for the rest of his life if he quit the band now.

I'd help him through it. He was probably worried about the logistics of touring with a baby. With the right help, it would all work out and then everything would be back to normal. Mostly.

The shoot finally ended, but Sid raced out before I could talk to him. What the hell had crawled up everybody's ass lately?

I decided I was going to go straight to the apartment to talk to him. Maybe I'd stay awhile and help with Kody. Since Kaylie was in Georgia, I could stay at home for one night. It'd been too long since Sid and I had hung out.

I felt strange about letting myself into the apartment without knocking, but it was still my place, too. Josie was in the kitchen cleaning dishes.

"Is Sid home?"

She turned off the water and spun around. "Well, if it isn't the little drummer boy. Hello to you, too."

"Hello, Josie. How are you today?" I rolled my eyes, so she was sure to detect my sarcasm.

She wiped her hands on a towel. "I'm peachy. Sid looked like he needed the fresh air, so I told him to take Kody out for a walk."

I nodded. He was with Kody, so I knew he wouldn't be out too long. I'd stay and wait.

"I made baked ziti and meatballs for dinner. Why don't you stay and eat? I think he could use the company. He seems lonely without Kaylie around."

I raised an eyebrow. It wasn't like Josie to be so civil to me. "I think

I'll stay here tonight. Give him a hand with Kody."

She patted my arm as she walked by me. "That would be nice. I'm going to head home now. Dinner's in the fridge."

After Josie left, I wandered over to the couch to sit down and wait for Sid to get home. Was he lonely, like Josie thought? Or was something else going on with him? I was determined to find out tonight.

I sat down on the couch and reclined my head against the cushions. My booted foot landed on something that made a crinkling noise. I bent forward to look and saw a piece of paper sticking out from under the couch. I gave the paper a cursory glance as I picked it up and tossed it on the coffee table.

The twisty logo on the paper reminded me of something medical. It took a few more seconds for my curiosity to get the better of me. I leaned forward to read the name of the company:

> DNA Answers.
> Quick and Confidential.

I grabbed the letter off the coffee table and began reading it. It was addressed to S. Anderson and thanked him for his trust and confidence in using DNA Answers for his needs. It explained how the test results were for informational purposes only and would not stand up legally in a court of law. A legal paternity test was available...

I stopped reading. Sid had gotten a paternity test done on Kody. Why hadn't he told me? I quickly skimmed the rest of the page, but it was more of a sales pitch for other products from the company. Where were the results?

I guess I could just wait until Sid came back and ask him. Instead, I knelt on the ground and looked under the couch for more pages.

Nothing. I sat up and felt around under the couch cushions and came up empty.

Could Sid's bad mood have something to do with the results? And it bothered me that he never mentioned it to me. Fuck, we'd really drifted apart these past few months.

Sid wouldn't leave the results lying around. Before I examined my motives too closely, I stood up and strode toward Sid's room. I wasn't going to search through his shit, but...

His room was messy. Messier than usual. Plus, a ton of Kody's crap had migrated to his room. We really needed more space. I took a few steps into the room and saw the two papers on top of his nightstand.

Something in the back of my mind was screaming at me not to look, but I didn't listen. In two seconds, I was holding the results in my hands. My eyes flew down the columns filled with random numbers that made little sense to me until I saw the number outlined in a box at the bottom of the page. Probability of paternity: 99.9998%.

I let out a puff of air. Sid was Kody's father.

The first column of numbers was allele sizes for CHILD (K). The second column was for Alleged FATHER (B). My heart began to thunder in my chest.

I flipped to the second page. Another chart with allele sizes. CHILD (K) again, but Alleged FATHER (V).

I knew what it meant. Since Sid and I both had the same initials, SA, he'd used Vicious and Bash. The probability of paternity on the V page was 0%.

I flipped back to the B page. 99.9998%.

Kody was my son.

I put the papers back.

And ran.

♫♫♪♪♪

The first thing I realized when I woke was that I couldn't breathe. Quickly following that, I felt the excruciating pounding in my head. Then, in a flash, I remembered that I was Kody's father.

He was my son.

I groaned as the magnitude of the discovery about Kody's paternity soaked into my addled brain. Damn, someone was yanking on my dick, and shit, my groaning only encouraged them to yank harder.

Fuck! My face was buried in a ginormous set of tits and the woman who owned the tits was stroking me so damn hard — like she was trying to get my dick to spark a flame.

I pulled back my head, searching for some much-needed oxygen. God help me, I was buried deep, but finally, I gulped in some air.

"Sweetheart, what's your name?"

"Lydia."

"Can you ease up on my dick, Lydia?"

She slowed down. "You rather have my mouth on it again?"

Ignoring the pounding in my head, I half sat up and looked around. "Do you know what time it is? I'm probably late. I have to get out of here."

She shimmied her boobs back near my face. "You got a wife you have to get back to?"

"No, I'm not married. I'm a ... dad." Tentatively, I tested the words on my tongue. "I've got a kid I have to get back to."

Her hand jumped off my dick lightning-fast and she slid away from me as if I'd just admitted to an active flare-up of genital herpes. "Oh jeez. You're a dad? How nice! You know, I forgot. I have this thing I have to do. I'm sorry. You'll have to go."

I guess being a single dad wasn't that attractive to the ladies. In this case, it suited me just fine. "I'm leaving. Do you have any aspirin? My head's killing me."

She chuckled. "I'm sure it is. You were so wasted last night. Let me get some."

She walked across the room, naked and without a hint of shame, and I watched because she had an unbelievable body. As she headed off into the bathroom, I found my clothes scattered on the floor and slipped them on, then I opened my phone and ordered a car to pick me up. When Lydia came back into the room, I handed her my phone to input her address while I took the aspirin she offered.

Still naked, she walked me to the front door. Before I left, I looked her up and down slowly. I was a dumbass to turn down a fuck with a girl who rocked a body that luscious, but I was already late for the morning round of interviews that were scheduled for Ghost Parker.

"Did we have a good time last night?" I asked.

She was twirling her hair, impatiently waiting for me to leave. "You were a shit lover. I sucked your dick until you got off and then you passed out."

Okay, then. At least there was no chance that I'd knocked her up. I jogged down the four floors of her building, each step reverberating in my head. Thankfully, I only had to wait a few minutes for the cab to arrive.

I sat back while the car whisked me away from the big tits and towards a bunch of angry people I'd let down. Donovan was burning up my phone with angry texts and the PR girl had called and left a handful of messages that I didn't bother to listen to. The last thing I needed today was to be interviewed.

And I wasn't sure I could handle seeing Sid without some kind of meltdown. He was my best friend, but I had no idea where I stood with him anymore.

"Hey, buddy." I leaned forward. "You mind if I change the destination?"

The guy shrugged. "It's going to cost more."

"That's fine." I gave him the new address, and within seconds, he was changing directions.

I stood outside my apartment door, almost too afraid to enter. Suddenly, this seemed like a bad idea. My head was feeling slightly better, but my emotions were still jumbled. I took a deep breath and entered.

Josie was holding Kody, and she turned to the door in alarm until she saw me. I felt guilty for scaring her; I should have knocked.

She scrunched up her brow. "What are you doing here? Aren't you supposed to be doing some Ghost Poker promotion crap?"

"Parker. Ghost Parker," I mumbled.

I couldn't take my eyes off Kody. He was my son. I wasn't sure what I was feeling at that moment, but it was overwhelming. A startling surge of intense emotions. Fuck! It almost knocked me off my feet.

"You look like shit and smell like an ashtray." She wrinkled her nose. "And cheap perfume."

I barely noticed what she said. My entire focus was on Kody. I took a step toward him. "Can I hold him?"

Josie hesitated, but I still couldn't pull my eyes from my son to see what her expression held. "Why don't you take a shower? I was just about to make his bottle. You can feed him before his morning nap."

I just nodded. She took him into the kitchen, and I stood staring after them. I shook off my daze a few moments later and took a quick shower.

After I dressed, I headed back to the living room. Josie handed Kody over to me. I'd held him in my arms lots of times over the past two months, but this time, it felt different. He snuggled into my arms and it pulled at something deep in my chest.

Even though he'd scared me to death when he showed up, I'd come to love him. I loved him as Sid's kid, just as I'd love any of Sid's future kids. But he wasn't Sid's baby. He was mine. He was my son. And, shit, I did love him. I'd already fucked everything up, but I'd do whatever it took to protect him from here on out.

I sat down on the couch and positioned him in my arms to feed him. Josie handed me his bottle and waited to make sure I wasn't feeding him air before heading back to the kitchen.

I stared at Kody's face while he sucked down his bottle. He looked up at me while he drank. I'd never experienced such naked emotion so viscerally. It left me breathless. I had to hold back a sob.

Kody's eyes drooped as he got near the end of the bottle, but even as he nodded off to sleep, he kept watching me. After I pulled the nipple from his lips, he slept in my arms while I stared at him. I was absorbing every bit of him that I could and making promises to him in my head.

Josie came over to the couch about 15 minutes after he fell asleep. "Why don't you put him in his crib? I made some breakfast for you. I'm guessing you didn't eat this morning?"

My stomach rumbled at the mention of food, but I didn't want to give him up. Reluctantly, I got Kody situated in his crib and then found Josie back in the kitchen. A plate of bacon and scrambled eggs was on the table.

I sat down and dug into the food. "Thanks, Josie. This is good."

She sat down at the table across from me. I waited for a snarky remark, but she remained silent.

I glanced up at her. "Did you know?"

She looked at me with pity. "Not until this very minute. Sid told me it was a possibility, but I never heard anything after that."

My fork tapped against my plate nervously. "When I was here yesterday, I found the paternity results. I'm Kody's father. I don't know why he didn't tell me."

Josie had tears in her eyes. "This must be a tremendous blow to him. I thought it was all about ... well, never mind. He must be devastated. Please don't be angry with him. Just give him some time."

This was the most monumental thing that'd ever happened to me in my entire life, but in the midst of it all, I was worried about Sid. "I'm not angry with him. I'm ... sad that our friendship has been affected, but most of that is my fault. Sid's more than my best friend; he's like a brother to me. I've seen how he's been this past week. I'm worried about how this is affecting him, too."

She reached across the table and patted my hand. "What are you going to do?"

"I haven't digested everything yet. But I'm going to do whatever it takes to be the father Kody deserves. He's my first priority." I looked down at my plate as I admitted the next part. "If you'd asked me that question when Kody first showed up, my answer would have been different. I owe Sid everything for protecting and loving Kody when I was too stupid or irresponsible or whatever the hell I was. Sid gave me the time I needed to get my head on straight about this."

Josie was watching me intently while I choked out my confession. I swallowed past the lump in my throat and gazed up at her with watery eyes. "Kody is my son and I'm going to take care of him, but he will always be a part of Sid's life. I would never take that away from either of them."

A single tear escaped Josie's eye, but she quickly wiped it away. "You'll do just fine, Sebastian. Kody's a lucky little boy to have you both in his life."

Chapter 34

Sidney

I HOPPED INTO THE car that was waiting to take me home. The only thing stopping me from heading to a bar and drinking my troubles away was Kody. But if it wasn't for the little guy, I'd still be stuck doing those fucking interviews. Donovan knew I had to get home to Kody and wouldn't do any promo work after 4 o'clock, and yet he'd tried to guilt me into staying.

Trudy had lined up a full schedule of promo shit, balls to the wall until the tour started. These first few rounds of interviews were with 'friendlies', reporters who had good relationships with our label and would ask the 'right' questions. Unfortunately, the right questions seemed to involve me much more than usual. It was all driven by the label, but I was asked repeatedly about writing *Okay Babe*.

They constantly referred to the song as a mega-hit when it wasn't even released yet. Was everything in this world completely manufactured bullshit? They asked me every fucking thing about it, over and over, including who my inspiration for the song was. I made up a bunch of artistic-sounding nonsense, but the topic was like a kick in the gut to me. Kaylie and her sudden disappearance were open wounds that were still festering.

It was the first time I'd ever let down my guard with a woman and I'd gotten burned. Badly. I thought Kaylie was different. I thought she saw something good in me that even I didn't see. God, it hurt. I hadn't felt this much despair since I was a little kid. Back then, I'd numbed myself to ever feeling that kind of pain again and I'd just have to do it again. Numb myself and never make the mistake of giving someone the power to hurt me like that ever again.

If that wasn't enough to make me want to give up on everything, then I found out Kody wasn't my son. Kody, who was the only thing keeping me going right now. I loved him with all my heart, but he wasn't mine to keep.

It was torture. Everybody always left me. It felt like I was fated to end up alone and miserable in this world. I didn't deserve any better. My own mother didn't even want me.

The car pulled over to the curb, and I started with a jerk when I realized we were in front of my building. I'd been in a daze of self-pity the entire ride home.

I opened the door and started heading inside the building. Kody was Bash's son. The words had been repeating in my head like a vicious taunt for days now.

I had to figure out what I was going to do about that soon. I had to tell him, but I kept thinking up excuses not to.

Bash never showed up today. It was totally irresponsible. Knox said that he didn't sleep on his couch last night. No one could contact him today and he wasn't calling anyone back. Even me. I'd tried him a few times. I left texts and messages. He was probably out all night partying and then sleeping it off. Maybe he'd decided to start the weekend early and was already partying again. He'd probably forgotten about all his obligations. Or he didn't care.

And that worried me. Kody needed a stable person in his life. Someone who would put him first. Would Bash be a good father to Kody? Would he even want to try?

By the time I made it to my door, I had almost convinced myself that I shouldn't tell Bash the truth, but deep down, I knew my reasons were more selfish than I pretended.

I opened the door. The first thing I saw was Bash holding Kody. Misery hit me like a ton of bricks. They looked so natural together. This was the first time I'd seen Bash with Kody since I found out, and it left an ache in my chest to see them together. Fuck! It didn't seem fair to have to endure so much sorrow.

A lump of grief lodged in my throat. The image of the two of them cemented my decision. I knew in that instant that I couldn't hide that Kody was his son from him. Whatever desperate justifications I was trying to use to hold on to Kody were just excuses. Telling Bash was the right thing to do for Kody and that was all that mattered.

"Where's Josie?" my voice was raspy with emotion.

Bash looked up at me. "She left hours ago."

"You've been watching Kody this whole time?"

"Yeah." His answer was simple.

I closed the door and took a few steps into the room. "You missed the interviews."

Bash flipped Kody around so he was holding him facing out from his chest, supporting his bottom. I'd never realized how comfortable Bash had gotten with him before, but he did some babysitting for me from time to time. "They didn't need me. They don't give a shit what

I say."

I frowned. "Donovan and Trudy wanted us all there. The whole band."

"I know. I had a lot on my mind."

"You want me to take him?" I held out my arms in offer.

"No." He shook his head. "I've got him."

There was that churning in my stomach. Just seeing him with Bash was choking me up. Fuck, I wanted to run into my room and sob like a little kid. I couldn't do this.

Bash lifted his chin. "Why have you been so upset lately? Is it because of the tour?"

My throat tightened as I swallowed back the emotions threatening to spill over. "I'm worried about Kody. I have to do the right thing for him, even if it isn't the best thing for me."

He was watching me with those intense fucking eyes, just like Kaylie's. "Sid, you are closer to me than my own goddamn brother. I'll always have your back. I'd do anything in this world to help you out."

Fuck. I swept a hand through my hair. I had to tell him. "Bash, I did a paternity test on Kody. He's not my son." My lip quivered. "He's yours."

I expected him to freak out. Deny it. Walk out the door.

He didn't even flinch but remained calm. "When did you find out?"

I wasn't sure I could stand any longer. I dropped onto the couch. "Monday."

He sat next to me with Kody on his lap. "Why didn't you tell me?"

Bracing my elbows on my knees, I dropped my head into my hands. "I was upset, and I didn't want it to be true. I guess I'm a big asshole. Kody and I had a real connection. I honestly thought he was mine, and I didn't want to lose him."

"Fuck, you're not going to lose him, Sid."

I kept going. "I was scared how you'd react. That maybe you wouldn't want him, but I was more scared of losing him. I'm a selfish dickhead. Are you mad at me because I kept it from you?"

Kody started fussing, so he stood up and started pacing with him. "No, I'm not mad. I gave you good reason to be worried about my reaction. Like I told Josie earlier — and I meant every word of it — I owe you everything. I wasn't ready to be a father when Kody showed up and you saved me from making the biggest fucking mistake of my life. You protected Kody when I didn't. What you've done these past few months, I could never repay you."

So, that was it. Bash and I were still solid. I took comfort in knowing that I'd stepped up to make sure Kody was safe and loved like every child should be, but Bash was his dad and he was ready to step into that role.

It was a happy ending. So why did I feel such overwhelming grief? Tears stung my eyes and my vision blurred. I wanted to answer Bash, but I couldn't speak because I was two seconds from breaking down in front of him. As I slowly rose from my seat, intent on escaping to my room, my footsteps felt heavier than usual.

He caught my shoulder to stop me. "Sid, I want to be the best father I can to Kody, but I hope you'll always be a big part of his life — like a second dad or, better yet, his favorite uncle. I love you, man."

"Yeah." That was all I could say before I fled to my room. Fuck, this hurt so badly.

Chapter 35

Kaylie

I'd been holed up in Brent's house for two weeks now. Except for going to the therapist, I hadn't stepped foot outside. Brent was worried, and that's why I'd agreed to see the therapist. Actually, he'd blackmailed me into going.

When he asked me to pick up a few items at the grocery store while he was at work last week, and I physically couldn't get myself to get past the front door, he grew concerned. I couldn't even go to the mailbox without thinking everyone who saw me would know about the video. It was completely irrational. I knew that, but that didn't seem to matter.

Brent saw I was only getting worse as time went by. He threatened to involve my parents if I didn't agree to see a therapist. It was the only way he could think of to force me to go. I wasn't averse to getting help; I was just a complete wreck at the thought of being seen out in public.

The horrific audition repeated in my head like torture. Those scathing looks the production company had been shooting me that I'd brushed off as my imagination? Well, they really had been looking at me. Judging me. After seeing that utterly humiliating video.

And that was how I thought everyone was looking at me. With judgment and derision, while I was stripped bare. With my therapist, I'd equated it to the 'Shame' scene from the Game of Thrones where Cersei was stripped naked and paraded through the city while villagers threw rotting food at her and chanted 'shame' over and over.

He accused me of being melodramatic. Fuck him. I accused him of having no empathy.

My therapist, Robert, and I had a hate-hate relationship going on, but after three visits, I was seeing tiny slivers of guidance that I could use. I thought about 50% of everything he said was utter bullshit. He questioned every statement I made. He even questioned my feelings. We fought for most of the session. One time, I stopped mid-rant and accused him of purposefully picking a fight with me. He merely arched a brow and scribbled something in his notes before he replied, "I'm toughening you up." Of course, that pissed me off some more.

Frustrated that he wasn't acknowledging the level of my humiliation, I insisted that only another woman could understand. Like with everything else, he challenged me on that statement.

Did I think men didn't have the capacity to feel deeply? Did I believe that every man would act unaffected by a situation similar to what I was enduring? Did I know that there were cases of men so hurt and humiliated that they'd taken their own life because they could no longer endure the pain? Did I think every woman would be crippled by debilitating anxiety if they went through what I did?

Damn, this man drove me nuts, but he wasn't wrong. It wasn't a male / female thing. Individuals reacted differently. He asked me if I knew a woman who would have brushed off the video if she were in my shoes. Of course, I thought of Lacey. She was always so confident and in control. He told me to use my acting skills and start modeling my attitude after Lacey. How I reacted after a major trauma was very important to my recovery and he was busy trying to re-wire my inner beliefs.

I was gaining some little nuggets of insight, but I still broke out into a cold sweat and wanted to roll up into a ball and hide away when I thought about that video. Robert said that the physical threat to my safety from that 'rape fantasy' posting, which I now believed was Charlie's doing as well, and my unresolved breakup with Sidney contributed to my extreme reaction. The only good news I could grasp in all of this was that he was fairly certain that a few weeks of intense therapy (3-4 sessions a week) was what I needed. He didn't feel this was going to be a long-term problem for me.

I was sitting on the couch thinking about all this stuff when Brent came home from work. Another day had gone by and I'd accomplished nothing. I'd meant to make dinner, but I hadn't even showered.

Brent glanced my way. "How're you doing today?"

He was treating me like an invalid and I couldn't blame him. I made the effort to get off the couch. "Good. I thought I'd make some stir-fry for dinner?"

"Sounds good. I got a call from Mom today."

My heart started pounding. "And?"

He was studying me. "Family meeting tomorrow afternoon. She wants us both there."

"I can't go."

Brent sighed. "She knows you've been here for a while. I can't keep putting her off forever, Kay."

I was chewing on my fingernail. This was a problem. "Did you tell her?"

"No," he denied. "But she's got to be wondering why you're avoiding her. I get it, Kay. But Bash is coming, and she wants us all there. If you don't go, I'm not sure I can keep shielding you from her."

"Bash is coming here? Why? Does he know? Is he going to tell them?" I started feeling light-headed.

Brent must have seen me spiraling. He walked over to me and put his arms on my shoulders to brace me up. "I haven't talked to him. Maybe he's just visiting before his tour starts. I'll be taking the afternoon off work. I'll swing by here and pick you up. Make sure you take a shower."

"I don't think I can do it," I whispered.

He squeezed my arms in reassurance. "Kaylie, we're your family. We all love you. Even if everyone finds out, that will never change. Remember what the therapist said about fatalistic thinking? Don't go there."

I huffed. "I don't know why I tell you anything!"

Brent laughed. "You tell me because you need to vent. I've never seen you as worked up as you are when you get home from those sessions."

It was crazy that I was making any progress. "He does it on purpose, too. I haven't figured out why, though."

He gave me a hug. "Well, I like seeing some of your old fire coming back."

♫♫♪♪♪

We pulled up to my parent's house, the house I grew up in, while panic swirled around me. Brent squeezed my hand. He'd spent the entire ride over trying to reassure me.

I really was a mess. Remembering what my therapist told me, I summoned my inner Lacey and stepped out of the car.

My mother was overjoyed to see me. She wrapped me in a hug and wouldn't let go. Instead of relishing the moment, I only felt immense relief. She didn't know.

My mother was a Christian woman, not preachy or self-righteous, but kind and compassionate. She would support me one hundred percent if she knew what I was going through, but I didn't think I could withstand knowing how disappointed she would be in me for acting like I did in that video. I wanted to avoid that at all costs.

The visit was going well. My mom didn't ask me anything about my career, thank God. Brent must have convinced her that it was the reason for my absence. Instead, she was talking a lot about what she and Dad had been up to.

Bash arrived about an hour later. We all grew quiet when he walked in the front door holding a baby carrier. He had Kody.

I couldn't hold back. "What is Kody doing here? Is Sidney here?"

"No." That was all he said. He knelt down and began unbuckling Kody from his carrier.

Bash picked Kody up and then began stroking his back soothingly as he looked around the room at our confused faces. "Mom and Dad, this is my son. Your grandson. Dakota. We call him Kody for short."

A stunned silence filled the room.

For the first time since it happened, I forgot all about the damn video. My mind was grasping for an explanation. Was this a joke? How? Wait, what?

My dad prompted Bash for an explanation. "He's your son?"

Bash took a deep breath. I could tell he was nervous. "Kody showed up at our door about two months ago. There was a note from his mother. It said that 'you' were the father, but it didn't say if 'you' meant me or Sidney. And the note wasn't signed. Neither of us knew for sure who the baby belonged to."

"What?" I gasped.

Bash whipped his head around to face me and flinched. "I'm ashamed about it now, but I panicked. I wanted to call the cops or social services or anyone to take the baby. Neither of us knew anything about caring for a baby. I denied the baby could be mine, but Sid's instinct was to protect Kody."

Oh my God. Kody was Bash's baby? I was his aunt? And what about Sidney?

Bash continued, "Sidney claimed Kody as his own child to keep me from washing my hands of the whole thing, and I went along with it. I thought Sidney would eventually come to his senses. But instead, Sidney got attached to him. He fell in love with him. He was a great dad to Kody. And in those couple of months, I got to know Kody, too. I became more comfortable around him and felt an attachment to him growing, even as I worried it was pushing Sid's and my friendship apart."

My mom pressed her hand to her mouth. "So, Sidney has been caring for him all this time?"

"Yeah, he has."

Brent was staring at Kody. "So, why do you suddenly think he's your son? What happened?"

"Sidney got a paternity test. He had his reasons, and they were to protect Kody. Obviously, we found out that I'm Kody's biological dad. And I'm ready to step up to the plate and be the father that Kody deserves." He looked over at my parents. "I hope I have your support."

My mother looked taken aback. "Of course, you have our support!

We love you and we love our grandson. Oh, my goodness, I'm a grandma! Can I hold him?"

My mother gushed over Kody while my dad slapped Bash's back and pulled him in for a hug. There was no question of my parent's support. I'm not even sure why Bash was so nervous.

Everyone was going gaga over Kody. I stayed sitting on the couch. Bash noticed and sat next to me.

"What about Sidney?" I asked quietly.

Bash frowned. "I'm not going to lie — he's devastated. I'm not sure how to help him get over it, Kaylie."

Barely suppressing the irritation that crept into my voice, I said, "I don't think it's something you can casually get over."

Bash couldn't meet my eyes and I felt bad for snapping at him, but I knew that this must have ripped Sidney's heart to pieces.

About an hour later, my mother was ushering us out the door. She insisted that the three of us siblings go out to dinner and catch up so that she could get a chance to know her grandson.

It took a lot of work for her to get Bash to leave Kody in their care. She insisted she raised three kids; she would be fine with him. Bash gave her tons of instructions and showed her all his stuff: his pacifier, his bottles, his diapers, his favorite toy. Finally, my mother shooed him out the door.

Bash handed her his keys. "I'll leave my rental car here. It has a car seat, in case there's an emergency."

We piled into Brent's car. Brent backed out of the driveway. "Where to? The Blue Anchor?"

Bash shrugged. "That's fine."

"No," I said, a little too emphatically. "Let's just go back to Brent's place."

Brent turned to me. "You'll be fine, Kay. We're both here with you."

Bash spoke up from the back seat. "What's wrong with The Blue Anchor?"

I didn't want Bash digging any deeper. "Nothing. It's fine. Let's go there."

The Blue Anchor was the local pub, but there probably was very little chance of running into anyone I knew. I could do this. I'd just summon my inner Lacey. How pathetic was it that I needed to muster all my courage to step into the local pub? I really had to work on getting better.

The waitress brought us to a booth. It felt like every pair of eyes focused on me, but I'd made it. I hid behind my menu while Bash and Brent were talking about Kody. Even though I wanted to, I couldn't follow the conversation because I was feeling panicky.

I peered around the bar. Did that guy just look at me? My hands began shaking.

The waitress took our drink order and scurried away. I asked for whatever the boys ordered because my mind was in a panicked frenzy. That guy was definitely watching me, his eyes searing through my soul as if he knew every bit of my shame. He'd seen the video, and he was leering at me like I was naked. His malicious laugh echoed in my ears as he whispered something to the other guy, and I knew they were talking about me. Suddenly, his phone came out of his pocket. I shrank down in my seat, certain he was looking for the video.

I was trying to control my shaking, which was getting worse, and I whimpered. Brent and Bash both looked at me.

"Kaylie, what's wrong?" Bash asked.

"Fuck," Brent muttered. He wrapped his arm around me. "Kaylie, you're okay. You're safe with us."

I felt tears on my cheeks and my teeth began to chatter. I was losing it.

"We've got to get her out of here. C'mon, Kay. I've got you." Brent helped me out of the booth while Bash threw down some money on the table. They ushered me to the car and fifteen minutes later, we were back at Brent's house.

I curled up into a ball on the couch. I declined a beer, but both Brent and Bash popped one open.

Bash sat down on the couch by my feet. "What the fuck is going on, Kaylie?"

I looked over at Brent, who sat on the chair across from us, but he remained quiet. He wasn't going to bail me out of this one.

"Is it something to do with that fucking website? Did something happen to you?"

"Kaylie," Brent implored, "Bash just got done telling us something that took a lot of courage for him to do. No one is judging him. You need to tell him. He loves you, just like I do. He wouldn't think less of you. I promise."

Bash's mouth dropped open. "What the fuck, Kay? Of course, I love you. You can tell me anything. God knows I've made mistakes. Big fucking mistakes. Please."

So, I told him. About Charlie. About the video and how it was posted on my feed and blasted out into the internet. How it was DM'd to my friends and family. How Brent had seen it. I tried to explain how humiliating it was, but I don't think he fully understood until Brent described the issues I was having that stemmed from it.

Bash was quiet through most of it. At one point, his face had turned bright red, so I know he was holding a lot back.

"I want to kill that fucking bastard."

I plopped back against the couch cushion. "Bash, that won't help. Please, just stay away from him. He still has the video."

Brent tapped on his beer bottle. "I don't think he'll be a problem anymore. A law firm sent him a very intimidating letter. I read it. It threatened him with legal action if the video should pop up anywhere. It was made clear that the video was obtained criminally without consent from the victim and any use of it would be met with criminal and civil prosecution. The lawyer I spoke to said it was an extremely effective deterrent."

I picked at the pillow on my lap. "You spoke to a lawyer?"

Brent nodded. "Lacey wanted my okay before they sent it."

"Lacey?" Bash's brow creased.

Brent answered. "Yeah. Lacey's been taking care of everything like a champ. She hopped on it right away and she's been monitoring it nonstop. The few minor problems that have popped up, she's taken care of. She recommended this lawyer for sending cease and desist letters and to keep Charlie under control."

I didn't even know half the stuff Lacey was doing for me. I guess I hadn't acted like I could handle it yet, so Brent had been shielding some things from me. "Aren't lawyers expensive?"

"Don't worry. Even though Lacey insists on not taking any money from me, I'm forcing the issue. I've got it covered."

Shaking my head, I sighed. "I don't want anyone spending all this money on me."

"Jesus Christ, Kaylie!" Bash groaned. "For once in your life, let us help you."

Later, after Bash left and Brent went to bed, I called Lacey.

"Kaylie? How are you?"

"Surviving," I joked lamely. "I hear you've been talking to Brent?"

"I just wanted to know how you were doing." She paused for a moment before adding, "I didn't want to bother you."

My throat tightened, and I pressed my lips together. I wanted to be truthful with her, but it was still too raw to dig into just yet. "I'm not ready to talk about anything yet, but I'm going to a therapist to work through my issues. But Brent told me tonight a little about everything you're doing for me. Thank you. You've been an amazing friend. I hope I can return the favor someday."

"Just get through this and come out stronger. That's all I want."

That was typical of Lacey. Maybe one day I'd tell her that I used the sheer strength and confidence I saw in her character as my inspiration for getting stronger.

"There's one more thing you could do for me."

She didn't even hesitate. "What is it?"

I blurted it out. "Check up on Sidney for me."

"Sidney? Why?"

I told her about Kody but asked her to keep it on the down low. "I know finding out that he wasn't Kody's father must have shattered him."

Lacey's voice softened. "Why don't you call him?"

"I can't." My voice cracked. "Please, will you do this for me?"

"I'm not sure what I can do, but I'll try."

I tossed and turned all night long, my sheets becoming a knot at the foot of my bed. But this time, it wasn't thoughts of the horrific video that kept me awake — instead, I was agonizing over Sidney.

Chapter 36

Sidney

I was alone. Bash took Kody to Georgia to meet his family, and he was staying there for a couple of days.

The thought of no longer having Kody by my side caused a sharp pain to slice through me. The emptiness of the apartment felt unbearable, and I wondered if I would ever be able to fill the void. Fuck, I missed that little guy. I even missed Josie's company these past few days. Losing Kody left an agonizing hole in my heart.

It had grown dark out, but I hadn't gotten up to turn on any lights yet. It was almost pitch black in my apartment, but I didn't care. What did it matter?

My phone pinged with a text. No one texted me anymore. I'd turned down offers to go out so much that eventually, they'd stopped coming.

Mildly interested, I glanced at my phone.

Lacey: Meet me for dinner?

I thought about it for a few seconds, only because I was hungry. And lonely.

Me: Nah, I wouldn't be great company.
Lacey: please?
Lacey: I can bring dinner to you?

She could be persistent. For a brief second, I entertained hooking up with her, burying my misery in her. I thought about it and quickly discarded it. Didn't interest me.

Me: I'm not interested in hooking up. Sorry, Lacey. It's not you. I'm just in a shit mood.

The three dots danced for a few minutes. I'd probably pissed her off, but I didn't have it in me to be tactful right now.

Lacey: Um … I'm not interested in that either. I'm just interested in spending time with a friend.
Me: Just dinner?
Lacey: Yep. Let's meet at Cantrell's at 7?
Me: Ok

If I didn't get out of here, I'd go crazy. And I had to eat. She'd given me just enough time to jump in the shower and get there.

She was already sitting at a table sipping a glass of wine when I arrived. I gave her a peck on the cheek before I sat down.

She scrutinized me up and down. "You're looking good."

I'd thrown on some clothes without paying much attention, but whatever. She looked a little different from how I usually saw her — a bit more toned down, with less makeup on and less skin showing. It made me relax a bit.

I ordered a beer and then sat back. "I was surprised you texted me."

She eyed me over her wineglass. "I heard about Kody. I wanted to check that you were okay."

Hardly anyone knew. Bash didn't want anyone to find out until he told his family. "How the hell did you hear that? The guys in the band don't even know yet. Unless ... unless it was Ghost. Somehow, he knows everything. Did Ghost tell you?"

"No, I don't talk to Ghost that much." She answered without answering.

"Did Bash tell you?"

"No." She took a sip of wine, avoiding my eyes.

I had no idea why she was being so secretive. I guess I was going to have to pull it out of her. "Jesus Christ, Lacey. Who the fuck told you?"

The waitress arrived with my beer. "Are you ready to order yet?"

"Yes," Lacey answered, even though I hadn't even glanced at the menu yet. The dinner she ordered sounded pretty good, so I ordered the same.

The waitress left, and I sat back in my chair with my beer. "Well?"

She was fiddling with the napkin on her lap. "Kaylie. Kaylie told me. She was worried, and she asked me to check up on you. I'm not sure she wanted me to tell you that, though."

"Kaylie?" I sucked in a breath. "You talk to Kaylie?"

"Yes. We're friends."

A thousand questions raced through my head, but I just drank my beer and stared hard at Lacey. But she didn't say anything more. I should have known she wouldn't break; she was tough as nails.

I gave in. "So, she's in Georgia?"

"She's staying with Brent."

That was new information. "Why isn't she staying with her parents?"

She raised a brow as if issuing me a challenge. "I don't know — why don't you ask her?"

I scoffed. "Maybe I would, but she's not answering any of my calls or texts."

She grimaced. "I'm sorry." Christ, she felt pity for me.

I pushed on with my questions. "Is she staying in Georgia? For good?"

Her lips turned downward. "I'm not sure she even knows that, Sid."

I grunted in reply and took a big swig of my beer. This seemed pointless.

Lacey began twisting a lock of her blonde hair. "Look, Kaylie hasn't confided in the extent of your relationship with her—"

It was time to shut down this conversation. "As far as I'm concerned, we have no relationship."

She persisted, "Well, I mean, how far any relationship between you two got..."

"For fuck's sake, she ran off to Georgia without even telling me. Packed her shit while I was at rehearsal and then she was gone. She cut me off cold. What's there to analyze?" I was getting a bit agitated; what the fuck was this? I wasn't about to confide deep, dark secrets to Lacey.

"She's going through some ... stuff. It's not my story to tell, but it's not about you."

"Is it because the audition didn't go well? And she didn't get the part?" I threw up my arms in frustration. "I get that it's upsetting, but she didn't even care enough to talk to me. She just took off without a word."

She was pleading with me to understand with her eyes. "It's not that simple."

My hand dug through my hair. Talking about this was driving me crazy. "Listen, I don't know what the fuck is going on with her, because no one has told me anything. Not you, not Bash, and definitely not her. But she treated me like I meant nothing to her. Like I was a good fuck that she walked away from without a backward glance. She scratched an itch with her big brother's friend when he'd explicitly told her to stay away from me. Like it was some kind of taboo thrill to defy him. Maybe it's fucking karma coming to kick my ass. God knows, I fucking deserve it."

Her voice softened in tone. "That's not it. She needs to talk to you and tell you everything, but she's not ready yet."

"It all sounds like a bunch of bullshit, Lacey," I bit out through clenched teeth.

She hesitated a moment as if weighing her words, but then she sighed heavily. "I can't tell you anything more, but I do know she cares about you."

I laughed bitterly. "She has a funny way of showing it."

"Sid, please just give her some time."

This talk hadn't left me feeling any better. In fact, it'd pissed me off. "Maybe it's already fucking too late."

The waitress who came with our entrée saved me from any more of Lacey's cryptic babble. I'm sure the meal was great, but it tasted like sawdust to me.

Lacey wiped the corner of her mouth with her napkin and then addressed the elephant in the room, despite my obvious dark mood. "You don't have to tell me if you don't want, but how did it turn out that Bash is Kody's father? I thought Kody was left with a note saying you were his dad? It doesn't make sense."

Lacey was a lot of things, but she was extremely loyal and she could keep her mouth shut. I knew she was going to find out eventually, so I told her. "I'll tell you the story, but we don't want it to get out in the media. We want to protect Kody."

She looked me directly in the eye. "I would never hurt Kody. Or any of my friends. I'm not a gossip, at least not with things that matter."

"I know that, Lacey." She'd just proven that by not telling me anything about Kaylie.

My explanation about Kody was brief, just the facts of what happened.

Still, her eyes looked teary when she said to me, "You didn't even know if he was your son and you did all that, Sid? You took on the enormous job of being his father? That's just so amazing and selfless. You're an incredible person. I admire you."

I wasn't comfortable receiving such praise, especially for something that I didn't consider extraordinary.

My shoulders slumped as the acidity of anger flooded my veins. The words tumbled out before I could stop them, my hurt evident in every syllable. "And just like that, he's gone — just like someone else I cared about who disappeared from my life without a trace. It's just the universe playing a really cruel joke on me."

"I'm sorry." Her eyes were shiny with tears. "Can I do anything to help?"

I stared down at my half-empty glass of beer and took a deep breath, trying to ward off the feeling of embarrassment creeping up my spine. With a heavy sigh, I drained the last few drops from the pint glass, set it back down on the tabletop, and leaned against the chair.

I didn't want her pity. "No. Don't worry about me, Lace. Our tour is starting soon. That's going to be my reset. I'm gonna go back to the old me where I party and fuck women without any attachments. I'll forget about Kody. I'll forget about feelings and emotions and all that shit. I'll drown myself in pussy and drugs and good old rock-n-roll."

She blinked a few times. "Oh, Sid. No!"

I flashed her a cocky grin. "Haven't you heard the news? I'm gonna be a big rock star."

Chapter 37

Kaylie

It'd been almost one month since Charlie had let loose the revenge porn that had changed my life. I was done hiding. Sort of.

My therapist, Robert, had helped me realize I hadn't done anything wrong to provoke Charlie's horrific behavior. It was most likely a result of a bruised ego when I rejected him after we broke up, combined with a fit of seething jealousy over my imminent acting success. He was a bartender struggling to break into the acting world, and my social media post seemed to trigger him.

It was a deficiency in Charlie's character that he'd violated my privacy by taping me in such a vulnerable position without consent let alone posting it for the world to see, but Robert focused on helping me deal with the emotional fallout I suffered from it. With his help, I was slowly taking back the reins of my life.

Although I originally questioned his methods, I could see now after a dozen or so sessions that they were working. He was mentally toughening me up while I was learning new coping skills to manage my stress. Most importantly, I was building an awareness of my thought patterns and how they affected me and also exploring my thoughts and actions from a different perspective.

Once I was able to venture out in public without turning into a puddle on the floor, we discussed the relationships in my life, the relationships with my parents, my brothers, friends, roommates, and romantic relationships. It was all very eye-opening to have uncomfortable truths about myself and others pointed out to me.

As I adopted healthier habits, I slowly improved. I still had my moments of insecurity, but I was finished living in the shadows. A few days ago, I started a new job cashiering at a local store. It was hardly my dream job, but I didn't want to sit around in Brent's house all day anymore. I wanted to keep busy and productive until I figured out what I was going to do with my life.

Now that I was on the other side of this monster that I'd been forced to face, I was ashamed of how weak I'd been. My brothers must think I was completely frail and feeble. I'd been incapacitated by it. Non-functional.

And Lacey? She must think so little of me. If this had happened to her, she wouldn't have let the video cripple her. She would have embraced it or used it to her advantage somehow. She would have had Charlie arrested, taken him to court, and held a press conference to belittle him and speak up for victims of revenge porn everywhere.

I closed my eyes and took a deep breath. These were the kind of negative thoughts I had to confront and not let take root. I mentally went through some affirmations to change the course of my wayward thoughts.

My phone rang, and I popped open an eye to see that it was Lacey

FaceTiming me. It was as if my mind had conjured her up. I thought about ignoring her call, but I was strong. Surprisingly, she had become a great friend. She didn't let many people see that amazing side of her.

She popped up on my screen. "How are you doing, Kaylie?"

"Pretty good." I could see skyscrapers behind her out the window. "Where are you?"

"I'm in my office at work." She lifted a pair of chopsticks and clicked them together. "I'm taking a late lunch. Do you mind if I eat while we chat?"

"No, that's okay." I brought my phone to the couch and sat down.

"You're dressed! And you brushed your hair. That seems like a good sign."

I groaned. The last time we FaceTimed, I must have looked like a wreck. "I just got back from an appointment with Robert. We're going to start cutting back on the visits. I'm venturing out into the world without thinking everyone is staring and pointing at me now. I even got a job. Don't ask, it's not glamorous, but I'm interacting with people all day and it's been okay."

"That's great! You even sound better." She speared a bite of her lunch with a chopstick and popped it into her mouth.

"I had my doubts about Robert, but things are turning around for me. Don't get me wrong, we still fight about half the session, but I'm starting to understand his methods."

She finished chewing and pointed her chopstick at the screen. "You know, I think I could use some therapy. All that fighting, it sounds so hot. Do you have fantasies about Robert?"

"Um, no." Gross.

Lacey got this devious look on her face. "I'd dress in a super short skirt with no panties, so I could flash him while I talked about my daddy issues. Maybe he would spank me for being so naughty."

"Oh, my God, Lacey. Robert is old enough that he could be your daddy. He's got these glasses—"

I couldn't even finish before she cut in. "An older man with authority. Commanding. Mmmm. Is he like that therapist on Greyson's show? What's his name?"

The therapist on *Devious* was this ripped, sexy dude who somehow managed to take off his shirt in every scene. Pure eye candy. I snorted. "He's hardly like that guy. Robert's got nerd glasses, a pudge, and curly hair that's starting to bald. He looks like the mailman from Seinfeld."

Lacey frowned. "You're ruining my therapy fantasies."

I chuckled and shook my head at her antics. It was nice to joke around again.

She slid her food to the side and leaned forward on her desk. "So, I just got the new report from SRI Solutions. Everything is pretty quiet. There's been a few postings of the video, but mostly overseas stuff. It's nothing to worry about and they are on top of everything they find. Those attorney letters we sent out seemed to do the trick. SRI is actively monitoring all those flagged accounts and there's been no activity."

Robert told me it wasn't helpful for me to be constantly scouring the internet, so I'd left it all in Lacey's hands. She'd done an amazing job. I was lucky because hardly anyone in my position had the resources to fight this like I did. "Brent tells me you've been fighting him over paying the bill. I know it's got to be huge. Please let him pay it. I hope I can pay everyone back someday for all this trouble I've caused. Between that and the therapist's bills..."

Lacey brought her face closer to the screen. "Kaylie, don't even think about that right now. Just concentrate on yourself. The money is nothing to me. Honestly."

Her kindness left me feeling vulnerable, but thanks to Robert, I was able to express myself graciously. "Thanks, Lacey. Did I ever tell you what an amazing friend you are?"

Did I just see her flinch?

She looked a little uncertain. "About that. Kaylie, I do consider you my friend. I don't have many girlfriends. There's my backstabbing posse, but that's not the same as a real friend. I know something is going on between you and Sidney, and everything I told you about me and Sidney at the baby shower was true. There is nothing at all between us, but I left out something that I feel I should tell you. Full disclosure and all."

Just hearing Sidney's name had my heart racing, but I could tell I did not want to hear whatever this was. I cringed. "If it's details about the threesome you had with him and my brother, forget it. I don't want to hear any of it."

"I just want you to know the truth, Kaylie. This all happened years ago when they first moved out to L.A. I hardly even knew you then. After the threesome, I hooked up with Sidney again one time. Without Bash." She slumped back in her chair and stared off to the side as she told me. "I tricked myself into feeling some kind of connection. I'd thought I'd sensed his loneliness, but I think I was just projecting. Anyway, I brought him up to my penthouse. I never bring men there, but yeah, I was caught up in some stupid fantasy. We had sex, and I was so happy, but he snuck out in the middle of the night. I confronted him about it the next time I saw him. He told me he felt nothing for me."

I sucked in a breath. I could clearly see that this was painful for her to tell me. Sidney had hurt her, and he probably didn't even know it. "That was kind of harsh of him."

She looked directly at the screen again. "I appreciate a man who doesn't play games. He was being direct. Better that than stringing me along."

"Why are you telling me all of this?"

She tapped a finger on her desk. "Well, first, I want to be completely honest with you. I value our friendship. And, second, I think he's in love with someone else and he has been for a very long time."

I felt like burying my face in the pillow. "And you're saying that person is me?"

"Remember when you asked me to check on him? I asked him to dinner over text and the first thing he said was that he didn't want to hook up." She laughed self-deprecatingly. "He's already rejected me enough, but he had to add that one for good measure."

"I don't understand. What does that have to do with me?"

"I haven't seen him out. He's not tethered down to Kody anymore, but he isn't going out like he used to. I did some reconnaissance, and he's not hooking up with women. Neither is Bash. The two of them are like monks."

Despite my uneasiness with the subject, a laugh burst from me. "Do I even want to know how you did this reconnaissance?"

She waved her hands around as she was talking. "I did it for you, babe. I had to cozy up to Ghost. He's hot as hell, but it's strange. I've never set my sights on him. When he puts his focus on you, though, wow. Intense. I bet he's phenomenal in bed. I might be interested in getting a taste of him. You wouldn't turn down a roll in the hay with him, would you?"

My reaction was immediate. "Ghost? Ew. He's like a brother to me."

"Aha!" she shouted like she'd caught me in a trap. "But you don't think of Sidney as a big brother."

"I'm not sure what you're trying to prove, Lacey. You know I have feelings for Sidney. After the baby shower, things progressed between us. We were sleeping together. Regularly. And, yeah, I fell hard. But, you know Sidney. He was just fucking me while he had Kody to take care of." I started getting more and more agitated as I talked. "He was going on the tour. With Kody. For an entire year! And he didn't even tell me. I had something totally different planned in my mind. But Sidney doesn't get attached to women. You've experienced it yourself. I don't know why I thought I was different."

"Kaylie!" she gasped. "You were sleeping together regularly? You are different. I'm pretty sure he loves you, Kay."

My shoulders sagged, and my heart felt like lead. "I thought we had a real relationship. He even took me out on a date. A very romantic date. But I must have read too much into it."

"No, you didn't. Have you heard Ghost Parker's new single? The one they just released last week?"

"No."

"You must have!" she exclaimed. "It's playing everywhere. Unless you're living under a rock."

I made a face. That's exactly what I'd been doing.

She hurried past her gaffe. "Ugh. Anyway, you have to listen to it. It's flying up the charts. Castle has been tracking it internally and the numbers are amazing. Somehow Diamond Dick got Vance Beaufort to produce it. This song is gold and BVR knew it. They've been throwing a fuckton of money at it."

"Good for them," I muttered.

"Sidney wrote the song." She was breathless with excitement. "It's called *Okay Babe*. And it's about you."

I blinked a few times.

She watched me carefully. "Sidney is still hung up on you. But, he's really confused about what happened. He doesn't know anything about the revenge porn. Think about it, Kaylie. From his perspective, you just ran away from him without saying a word. He's been devastated."

Robert was always trying to get me to look at things from other perspectives and to stop locking myself rigidly into my own conclusions as the only correct ones. Now Lacey was telling me the same thing.

"He's devastated because of Kody," I reasoned.

She looked at me expectantly. "Yes, that crushed him. He's going through a lot. But we were also talking about you. He made a flippant comment that he didn't deserve happiness. He expects people to leave him. I think he's been hurt before."

I knew about his past. He'd opened up to me. And, with my own problems and my own insecurities, I'd wound up hurting him too. Like a coward, I'd left without even talking to him. I'd only been trying to preserve my heart and my sanity, but from another perspective, I'd abandoned him.

"Kaylie, I think you should reach out to him. Tell him what happened. At least give him something to hang onto."

My head was spinning. Had I been mistaken? "But what about the video? I don't want him to know."

Lacey looked exasperated. "Please don't let that damn video get in the way. It's not even that bad."

My eyes flew to the screen. "Did you watch it? The whole video?"

"I did. Just to see what we were dealing with and really, Kay, it's not that scandalous." She held up her hands placatingly. "I get how you're embarrassed and don't want your parents or your brothers to see it, but it's pretty tame. You look sexy and all, but it's a little boring. I don't mean to offend you. But every single guy you know has seen stuff that's a thousand times racier than that. Don't let the video stand in your way, Kaylie."

I'd talk this over with Robert, but in my heart, I knew she was right.

That damn video was finished ruining my life. "Thanks, Lacey. For everything you told me. I've got a lot of thinking to do."

She nodded with relief and then gave me a big smile. "And, Kaylie? Listen to the damn song."

Chapter 38

Sidney

We were in New York City, doing a round of promotions. Today, it would take all day, even though we only had about five minutes of the actual taping of our 'live' performance that would air on the late-night show, but it was pretty exciting. A few technicians had set up our instruments on the set across from the stage where the house band played, and we'd already conducted a quick sound-check before the audience had arrived for the taping.

The stylist whisked us away after that and examined what we were wearing before pulling out new clothes for us. Somehow she deemed that Knox and Ryder had to change their entire outfits, Bash and I only had to change our shirts, and Ghost could wear his own clothes. When the stylist tried to remove Ryder's leather cuff from his wrist, he put his foot down. It was a gift from Talia, and he wasn't taking it off. Bash, Ghost, and Ryder all had to be freshly shaved, but Knox and I were allowed to keep our scruff. Mine was a few days old, so I was surprised when she said I could keep it. I had no idea what she was looking for, but I changed into the new shirt she gave me without an argument.

One by one, we wandered out of the dressing rooms and headed to the green room where we could stuff our faces with the spread from food services. The show host, a British dude by his accent, came into the green room to introduce himself to us and chat for a few minutes. The first guest on the show, a comedian, was also hanging out. He seemed like a good guy. The second guest was an actress we hadn't seen yet. We would go on toward the end of the show. The host would do a quick interview of the band, cut to a commercial, and then we'd perform *Okay Babe*.

We already knew the questions they would ask, and they'd be directed at Ghost and the backup singer, Candace. I didn't have to say anything, so I just sat back and took in the entire experience.

The stage manager, a woman named Cindy, was popping into the green room more and more as we got closer to show time. She poked her head in again. "We've got all the band here? Ghost Parker?"

The man who'd introduced himself as Candace Collin's manager spoke up. "Candace, the backup singer, is still in the dressing room getting ready."

"Right." She looked down at her tablet. "She's got 15 minutes, then I need her in here. Where's Eloise?" She looked around the room and then rushed out.

Bash strode over to where I was sitting on an overstuffed couch and handed me a cold beer before joining me. "A lot of sitting around for only performing one song."

I took a drink. "Yeah, but this is pretty big. The song is getting a lot of exposure. Did you hear that Ghost left the hotel this morning without security and nearly got mobbed by fans and even some paparazzi?"

Bash hadn't been hanging out with the band. His parents had flown up from Georgia to watch Kody while he was doing the promo stuff. When we were done, instead of hanging out, he went back to his hotel to be with Kody. Already, I was like an outsider.

I shouldn't complain. Bash was doing a good job being a father to Kody. Already he'd given Kody more than I could — grandparents and extended family. And he'd encouraged me to remain active in Kody's life.

Bash ran his hand over his thigh, which was bouncing up and down. "Fuck. I didn't know that. Hopefully, it's just Ghost who takes the brunt of it. I'm a little worried about being out with Kody and that happening."

"Yeah, make sure you talk to the security guys. Knox and I went out this morning. They took us out a back exit and no one bothered us. Ghost waltzed right out the front where there was a crowd gathered because I guess word went out on social media that we were staying at that hotel." I was trying to reassure him, but I wasn't sure it worked.

He scowled. "I guess we're going to have to get used to it."

Cindy rushed into the room. "We're live people. Everyone stay put from here on in. Mr. Hagel, you're on in 10. I'll be back to get you in 5."

I glanced at the monitors and watched for a few minutes as the host began his monologue.

"So this is where the party is!" A female voice yelled.

Candace, our backup singer, entered the room. Or should I say stumbled into the room? She looked high. Or drunk. Or both.

She was wearing a bright blue sequined dress that showed a lot of skin and a glittery pair of towering heels. Whether it was the height of the heels or just her being drunk, she looked like a baby deer just standing for the first time. She staggered around the room, groping and grinding up against every guy she fell into.

She was rejected by Ryder, Ghost, then Knox before she stumbled over to the couch and gracelessly dropped between Bash and me. I smelled booze on her breath and her words slurred when she commented on the food spread.

I slid her off the edge of my lap and moved over to the far end of the couch. Bash jumped up and walked away.

Ghost practically growled. He turned to Candace's manager. "She's wasted. She's not going on with us. No fucking way."

Her manager didn't look happy. "She was only alone for 30 minutes, tops. I don't know how..." He looked at his watch. "We've got about an hour before taping. She's not that bad. I can sober her up. She has to go on. There's a contract."

"She's not going on," Ghost said through clenched teeth. "Where's Donovan? She will not fuck this up."

Knox nodded his head in agreement. "She's a wreck. Donovan's on the phone. I'll go find him."

He left to find Donovan, and I shot up from the couch when Candace started inching my way.

When the stage manager popped her head into the green room, all hell broke loose when everyone started arguing about the situation. Nobody was paying attention to Candace, whose dress had ridden up and was unwittingly flashing the entire room. Not my problem.

My phone vibrated in my pocket and under normal circumstances, I'd probably have ignored it. I fished it out and checked who was calling. I had to do a double-take.

It was Kaylie.

My heart started racing, and that made me mad. Not once had she contacted me since she'd run off to Georgia. If I were a stronger man, I'd ignore her call. But, I couldn't.

I answered as quickly as I could. "Kaylie?"

The room was so loud and chaotic, I could barely hear her. I knew I was only adding to Cindy's headache as I headed out of the room just as Donovan and Knox came rushing in.

"Hold on," I said into the phone. "I'm trying to find someplace quiet."

"Where are you? Sounds crazy." I could hear her much better out in the hall.

"We're in New York City taping for a late-night show. Didn't you know? Your parents are up here with Bash and Kody." I settled against the concrete wall at the end of a quiet hall. I had no idea where I was and I didn't want to stumble onto the set by mistake.

She paused for so long that I wondered if the call had gotten disconnected. "I haven't been paying attention."

Okay, that kind of hurt. "Kaylie, why are you calling now? You took off and ignored all my calls. I got the message."

She sniffled. "Something ... uh, something happened. And I didn't handle it well. But I'm trying to work through it now."

My frustration was growing. "Was it because of the audition?"

"Not exactly, but sort of." She sniffled again, and I wondered if she was crying.

"Was it something I did?" I hated this guessing game. I wished she'd just fucking tell me.

She paused and then answered weakly, "No." It wasn't convincing.

I leaned my forearm against the wall and rested my head against it. "Kaylie, I can't do this right now. They're probably freaking out that I'm missing right now."

A small sob sounded over the phone. "Oh God, I'm screwing this up. My therapist said I need to be more open with you, but we never talked about our feelings."

"You're seeing a therapist?" What the hell was going on with her?

"Yes."

My voice was vibrating with anger, but I kept it low so no one would hear. "How about this for openness? I wanted an actual fucking relationship with you. You and I went on the first date I'd ever been on in my life and I thought it meant something. And I wanted to tell your brother that we were together and he'd have to deal with it. Fuck, I thought we were starting something good, Kaylie. But, no, we didn't have a chance to talk about it because you fucking ran away."

She gasped. "You're mad."

My frustration boiled over. "I am fucking mad! I don't know what the fuck is going on with you. I don't know what happened or what I did wrong. You're gone and you're seeing a fucking therapist, that's all I know. I asked Bash if you were attacked again, and he said you weren't, but he knows something. I just don't know and I don't have time right now. I've got to go." My voice cracked at the end of my rant.

"Wait!" She sounded distressed. "I want to tell you everything; I'm just scared, but I'll do it. I know you have to go right now, but will you call me when you have some time? Call me anytime, day or night. I'll be waiting. Please, Sidney?"

I hated all this emotional shit. That was one reason why I avoided relationships, but I'd call her. Just hearing her voice had me longing to see her, to hold her. My feelings for her, whatever the fuck they were, hadn't lessened any.

"I'll call. Goodbye, Kaylie."

I hung up and headed back to the green room.

The taping went off without a hitch. We performed *Okay Babe* without Candace, and that would be a hard pill for her to swallow once she sobered up and found out how badly she'd screwed up. I ignored all the drama and tried to focus on the performance that millions would watch, but my mind kept drifting back to Kaylie.

After the show, Bash invited me out to dinner with his family, but I declined. Bash had moved back into our apartment again, so I still got to spend a lot of time with Kody. Instead, I went out with the guys even though we had an early morning start with two big interviews with syndicated morning radio shows. We followed our security team's suggestions and ended up in a private section of a popular club that worked to accommodate us.

Less than twenty feet away sat a world-famous actress and her entourage. A few of those women came over and joined us. It was surreal to realize that we were quickly catapulting into fame just because of the song I'd written about Kaylie, the woman who was driving me insane. I should be enjoying the attention of these women, but instead, I was busy thinking about Kaylie.

We were several drinks in and my mind was just beginning to relax. Ryder tapped my leg with his boot and I looked up. Knox and Ryder were standing up, looking down at me expectantly. I must have missed what they asked.

"We're going to go meet Emma. You in?" Ryder asked.

"Nah, I'll pass."

They shrugged but then followed the girls back over to Emma's VIP section.

Ghost sat down next to me and handed me a new drink. "She can come the fuck over here and meet us as far as I'm concerned."

That got a chuckle out of me.

He leaned back. "You and Kaylie good?"

I jolted at the mention of her name. "Why would you think that?"

"You answered the phone and said, 'Kaylie', then you rushed out of the room. I figured you might be back with her. Plus, you're completely uninterested in all the babes that have been all over you tonight."

Nothing got past him. "That was the first time I'd talked to her since she took off for Georgia. And, it didn't go great."

"Why not?"

I tossed back half my drink. "She won't tell me what the fuck happened that had her running away, but apparently Lacey knows all about it. Bash, too, I think. I'm not sure all this emotional shit is worth it."

"Lacey knows?"

"Yeah," I answered. "Suddenly she's best friends with Kaylie."

Ghost nodded as he stared off into the distance. "That explains it."

"Explains what?"

He smiled slyly. "At first, I thought she was trying to get into my pants, but she's never done that before with me. I patiently waited until she finally showed her cards. She was subtle as fuck, but she wanted to know about you and who'd been warming your bed lately."

I grunted impatiently. "Lacey knows damn well that nothing's happening between us. I was clear from the start. She asked me out to dinner 'as a friend' and I spelled it out again, just to make sure."

Ghost lifted an eyebrow. "And what did you talk about at dinner?"

I thought back. "Kody. And Kaylie."

Ghost nodded. "That's because she's on team Kaylie. And Lace is a good person to have on your team. She was scoping things out for Kaylie, whether Kay asked her to do it or not. This means Kaylie is still into you, dude. The ball is in your fucking court — if you want it."

I set down my glass and sighed wearily. "You took several huge leaps to reach a conclusion that I'm not sure is linked to reality. Kaylie bailed on me."

"You two need to start communicating better," he muttered. "Christ, my therapist would have a field day with you."

"You have a therapist?" Was I the only one who didn't?

"For years." He shrugged. "We all have our issues."

"Kaylie said she's seeing a therapist. I have no clue why, though."

Ghost leaned his head back against the couch and stared up at the ceiling. "I think I know why Kaylie took off. Didn't she leave for Georgia right after that audition where she didn't get the part?"

I grimaced. "Yeah. I never saw her after that. She packed her shit and left while I wasn't home. She didn't even tell me she was leaving."

"Yeah." He pulled at his lip. "It makes sense."

"What does?"

He sat up straight. "I shouldn't tell you, but I will. You're such an insensitive brute that you'll fuck it all up if I don't."

I threw up my hands. "Just fucking tell me. No one else will."

"The day of her audition, Kaylie made a post about it. She posted a video and said 'Look at my audition tape' or something like that. I almost passed it by, but I noticed a few of the comments. They were strange. Curious, I watched it."

"And?" What the fuck did her audition tape have to do with anything?

"I'll tell you, but you need to keep your cool, man. Don't go all Vicious on me."

Why would I go crazy? A bad feeling washed over me. I gritted my teeth. "What was it? Tell me."

He was silent for so long, I wanted to strangle him. Finally, he spoke. "It was a tape of Kaylie. Just Kaylie, but it was a sex tape. I don't think you need to know anything more."

I couldn't speak. My mind was racing to understand what Ghost was saying.

He took a sip of his drink. "It didn't seem like something Kaylie would do. Someone did it to fuck with her. Probably an ex-boyfriend. It got re-posted a bit, but then it disappeared. You need big bucks to get something like that scrubbed that thoroughly, but it'll always be out there."

"Was it ... bad?" I croaked.

Ghost squinted. "It wouldn't bother some girls that much. But, Kaylie, yeah, she'd be devastated knowing that a lot of her friends had seen that."

"Fuck." I dragged a hand down my face. "I didn't know she was going through all that. Why wouldn't she tell me?"

He looked like he was going to say something, but then he just shrugged.

I pulled out my phone. "I've got to call her."

Ghost put out a hand to stop me. "No, don't call her in the middle of the night after you've been drinking. Wait till tomorrow after the interviews. Call with a clear head. You don't want to fuck this up any more than it already is, man. Trust me."

In the end, I decided to follow Ghost's advice, since I hadn't been doing too well on my own.

Kaylie had pushed me away when she needed me the most. I had to find out why and fix it. It was time to lay out all the cards on the table.

Chapter 39

Kaylie

THE DAY HAD FINALLY come. I had been simultaneously counting down to it with breathless anticipation while also dreading it.

Tonight was Ghost Parker's first show of the concert tour. Sebastian was behind the drums tonight, but then he'd take three months off the tour so that he could be with Kody before he joined up with them again. But tonight I wasn't here to see Bash.

Lacey and Talia, the only two people who knew I was there, stood on either side of me as we stood in the VIP section just in front of the stage. The opening band had been playing for about 30 minutes now. I was finally feeling more comfortable.

I'd worried about going out in such a large crowd. Sure, over the past few months, I'd made lots of progress. I was out in public all the time now, going to bars with Brent and his friends and working in a busy store, dealing with customers all day. But a rock concert was on a whole new scale.

I'd scanned the crowd several times, but no one was looking at me. All eyes were on the stage. Besides, I was in ripped jeans and a black lightweight hoodie while Lacey looked like a teenage boy's wet dream and Talia looked like a very lucky rock star's girlfriend. I'd seen lots of guys checking them out, but nobody's eyes lingered on me. It was a relief.

About two months ago, Sidney called me back after I'd reached out to him. I told him everything. It was a long and difficult conversation where I laid bare my weaknesses, my inadequacies, and my fears without sugarcoating anything to make myself look better. I hadn't come through the whole revenge porn mess unscathed, but dammit, I think Kelly Clarkson was right. I was stronger.

Sidney and I had spoken every day on the phone since then, tentatively rebuilding our relationship. I wanted to take things slowly because I was still working on myself. He was a good listener and shared a lot of things about himself with me.

The band's schedule was jam-packed with promo before the tour started, but it gave me time to reset. As predicted, *Okay Babe* was an enormous success. The boys are all getting mobbed in public because their faces were plastered all over the media and the song had been playing nonstop. Needless to say, the tour sold out quickly, so BVR was busy adding a European leg for next summer.

If our relationship was as strong as I thought it was, it would survive the year that Sidney was on tour. But I didn't want it to have to. I wanted to be with him. I had a plan to make that happen, and I was pretty certain he'd be on board with it. Our communication skills were much stronger now and I no longer had any doubts about how he felt about me.

I was so excited to see him; I really didn't know why I waited so long. Grabbing Lacey's arm, I leaned in so I could shout in her ear. "I need to see Sidney. Now."

She arched a perfectly manicured eyebrow. "I thought you wanted to surprise him after the show?"

My bottom lip poked out in a pout. "I don't want to wait."

She laughed. "Let's go find your man!"

Lacey, Talia, and I were backstage within a few minutes. The sound of the concert was muted enough that we could talk, but it was still loud.

"Are we lost?" We were wandering around the maze that was backstage.

Lacey stopped for a moment. "I haven't been here in a long time. I think the dressing rooms are this way."

"Kaylie?"

I whipped around. Sidney was standing in the hall behind us. He looked freaking amazing. His face broke into a wide smile.

I took a few steps toward him and then broke out into a jog before I launched myself into his arms. He whirled me around. It was like the quintessential reunion scene from a cheesy movie, but I loved it.

Until Sidney stiffened up and let go. It was a good thing I was hanging onto him like a monkey or I could have dropped like a sack. I slowly slid to the ground.

Bash was heading our way. He pulled me into a hug. "You came to see me? You're the best, Kay."

I pulled away from him. "Um, no. I came to see Sidney."

Sidney looked panicked. He took a step backward.

Bash smirked at him. "I know, you asshole."

I wrapped my arms around Sidney's waist and laid my head against his chest. Sidney wrapped his arm around me.

Bash frowned slightly. "Kaylie told me weeks ago and read me the riot act. I won't interfere ... unless you give me a reason to?"

Sidney looked nervous. "Bash..."

Bash folded his arms across his chest. "Don't think I didn't know who you were sneaking off to your room every night to FaceTime with."

The tour manager abruptly ended our conversation. He manhandled the guys, rounding them up and pushing them toward the stage. Sidney snatched a quick kiss before he was dragged away.

The show was phenomenal. The energy of the crowd was off the charts. They performed *Okay Babe* as the second encore. The crowd knew it was coming, so the crazy energy expanded to insane heights.

Even though I'd listened to the song probably a hundred times since it was released, it was a little strange hearing Ghost singing the words that I knew were written about me, but I couldn't take my eyes off Sidney the entire time. And he definitely knew where I was even if he couldn't see me because I got a very suggestive wink from him. The entire show was like the world's longest foreplay and when it was over, I was on a mission.

The boys were amped up and sweaty when we caught up to them. The whole band was there, so suddenly I felt shy. Sidney didn't have an ounce of shyness in him, though. He pulled me to him and wrapped me up in his arms.

Bash couldn't keep quiet. He joked, "Jesus, I'm going to have to hear that song about my best friend fucking my little sister every day for the next 30 years, aren't I?"

The boys all snickered, and this time I tensed up.

Sidney chuckled. "They all know, Kay. We were the worst kept secret."

I looked around at my brother's band. No one seemed shocked or horrified. In fact, everyone looked pretty happy. Until Sidney laced his fingers behind my neck and planted a kiss on me. An intense and lingering kiss. With tongue. And full body contact.

Bash groaned with disgust and a few laughs rang out. Someone muttered, 'Get a room', but they all wandered away and left us to our own devices.

An hour later, Sidney was showered, finished with the 'meet and greets', talked to the press, had a beer, and ate some food. "Okay, let's go."

"Don't you want to stay for the after-party?" I asked.

"Nope." He began tugging on my arm. "We can be at the hotel in 15 minutes. I'll have you naked in 20 minutes. That's the only after-party I'm interested in right now."

Chapter 40

Sidney

I COULDN'T KEEP MY hands off her. We were sitting in the backseat of the black SUV driven by one of the new security guys assigned to us for the tour. The hotel wasn't far, but it seemed like it was taking an eternity to get there.

I was excited to be on tour with the guys again, but when Kaylie explained that she didn't think she could manage the large crowd of a rock concert just yet, I'd understood, but I was disappointed. The concert tour would be grueling and I didn't know when I'd see her in person again. I missed her so much.

Her showing up at the concert meant the world to me. It was the best fucking surprise. Being out in the open about our relationship made it all sweeter, and Bash was taking everything in stride.

First thing in the morning, we were flying out to the second show venue in Florida where our tour buses were waiting. If I only had

Kaylie until eight o'clock in the morning, I wasn't going to waste any time partying. I was greedy. I needed her all to myself.

Kaylie turned in my lap. "I've got a proposition for you."

"Oh really?" That sounded interesting.

"I've been thinking a lot about what I want out of life, and I've been talking with Bash. We've come up with a plan."

"Okay," I said cautiously. Life goals weren't what I'd been expecting to hear. I'd been expecting something a bit more X-rated.

Her hands fidgeted nervously. "Only if you think it's a good idea."

I tipped her chin up with my finger, so she couldn't avoid my gaze. "I'll support you in whatever you want to do."

She took a deep breath and then began spilling it. "In three months, when Bash joins the tour with Kody, I would come with them. I've already helped him find a babysitter who's willing to go on tour and watch Kody. She's from Australia and she's always wanted to see America. And she has experience watching kids. But I would be a backup, to help with Kody and give Amanda some time off here and there to see the sights.

"Bash is working on the schedule. He'll be flying and staying in hotel rooms with Kody more often than you guys, but he's going to get his own bus. The back bedroom would be modified for Amanda and Kody to use. And I'd stay on the bus with the three of them. And you could, too. If you wanted to. To see more of Kody."

I was stunned. "You're coming on tour with us?"

"Is it a bad idea?" She bit her lip.

"It's the best fucking idea I've ever heard." Holy shit, please let this be true. "What about your acting career, though?"

She was smiling. "I haven't totally given up on the idea, but I'm not sure it's what I want anymore. Actually, I've been working on an idea with Lacey for a charity. I'm going to raise money for victims of revenge porn or cyberbullying so that they can afford a company like SRI Solutions. We both have a ton of ideas and with Lacey backing it, I know I can help so many people. That's what I want to do right now. That, and be with you."

"Babe, I haven't been able to fully embrace being on tour this time because I didn't want to be away from you for so long. I knew we could do it, but this is so much better."

Everything was falling into place and this time I wasn't going to fuck it up by being a closed-off bastard.

"Kaylie, I love you."

Her hand flew to her mouth. "Oh my God, Sidney!" Her eyes filled up with tears. "I love you, too."

♪♫♪♫♪

Making good on my promise, I had her naked within minutes of walking into my hotel room. I knew that if I put my mouth on her and my fingers inside her, I could make her orgasm fast. And that's just what I did because I couldn't wait for one more second to plunge my throbbing cock inside her.

Sex was different when you were in love. It was more. A whole other component to it existed that I'd never known about before. There was a purely transcendental element that raptured the soul in ecstasy, which even surpassed the physical pleasure. I was hooked, and I needed more.

I made sure to slow things down for round two. Fuck, I loved this girl, and I was going to show her every which way that I could. It was time to change positions because I wasn't going to last much longer while she was on top, taking me hard and fast. I tucked her in front of the length of my body, spooning her so that I could ease in and out of her while my fingers alternated between playing with her nipples and her clit. The sounds that my fingers coaxed out of her were more beautiful than I could ever make on my guitars.

I whispered into her ear, "Someday I'm going to write another song for you, babe. But it's not going to be a dirty fuck song. It's going to be a love song. I think I've got the melody."

She gasped. "Is that what you're playing? I think it's going to be another hit."

When I knew we were both on the edge and couldn't hold back much longer, I pulled out and then climbed back on top of her. I wanted to see her face when I made her scream my name.

After we both came back down from our orgasmic high and cleaned up, she cuddled into my arms and began drifting off to sleep.

I gently nudged her arm. "Kaylie?"

She chuckled sleepily. "Again?"

"Can we talk?"

Her fingers began lazily drawing circles on my chest. "You want to talk? We've been doing nothing but talking for the past two months."

I reached over and turned on the table lamp so that I could see her. "I'm just so excited that you're going to be going on tour with me. Kaylie, it makes me so happy."

She lifted her head up to look at me. "I didn't want to be apart from you for so long. But I won't be there for the first three months. Bash wanted to spend some quality time getting to know Kody first."

Even three months felt too long. "Can you come to some shows? Maybe stay overnight a few times?"

Her hair tickled my chest as she nodded. "Talia and I already talked about it. She's been getting the schedule from the tour manager to find out the best times to visit when we'd have the most free time together or when you'd be staying in hotels."

"Come as much as you can." I leaned up and gave her a quick kiss on the lips. "Then in three months, you'll be all mine."

"Well, I will have a job to do." Her eyes were shining. She looked so content. "Bash is paying me. He insisted, but I'd do it for free. Me being there for Kody is really giving him some peace of mind. He's hiring a security guy just for us out of his own pocket. He'll drive us around as needed and make sure we're not harassed by fans or paparazzi.

My focus will be Kody, but Amanda seems great. I've Facetimed with her a bunch already. And Bash will be taking care of Kody whenever he doesn't have stuff to do. So when you're free, I'll be free. We'll have plenty of time together. But he told me, no sex on the bus."

Bash setting down a 'no sex on the bus' rule was the most comical thing I'd heard in a while, but I understood it. I wasn't about to go against his wishes. "Don't worry. I'll figure out a way to keep you satisfied."

"Did you know that Bash has a realtor searching for a house for him and Kody? In the suburbs? He wants a home base for when he's not on tour."

I felt a twinge of jealousy. "He did mention it, but I didn't know he started looking already."

Kaylie and I had spoken quite openly about what we wanted in our futures. She knew that I was committed to Ghost Parker, but that I wanted a family — children and hopefully the opportunity to take in some older foster kids who were often overlooked. Luckily, she was on board with all of that.

After my experience with Kody, I had the urge to get Kaylie pregnant as soon as possible. But, since we hadn't even gone on our second date yet, I knew I had to chill out. It was probably a better idea to get through this tour first.

"And Lacey is going to hire a virtual assistant for me while I'm on the tour to help me with the charity. We'll be working the next three months to get it up and running." She was so animated as she talked about the project.

"I'm so proud of you, Kaylie, that you're doing this."

Her face lit up. "We have so many plans. Initially, we're just going to raise money to help victims on the internet cleanup end. Like SRI Solutions did for me. Once we get that going, we'll fund lawyers willing to criminally prosecute this stuff for any victims willing to fight. Or sue civilly to hold the perpetrators financially responsible.

"Eventually, we're going to lobby for tougher legislation. We'll put pressure on DAs, judges, or law enforcement officials that go easy on these predators. We're going to lobby tech companies to get better control. We have so many plans."

I ignored her fingers, which were running over my chest and focusing on my nipples. Fuck, I was getting hard. "Wow, you've really thought this through. It sounds amazing."

She casually licked my nipple and my dick took notice. "The best thing is that Lacey is excited about it. She knows a lot of influential people. Musicians and celebrities and just plain old rich people. She's already secured corporate sponsorship from Crowne. It really feels like I might make a difference for the better."

Her hand began sliding down my abs. I sucked in a breath. "It sounds like you've found your passion. I know it will be a success, Kay."

Her hand slid lower until it wrapped around my dick and squeezed.

I closed my eyes. "Well, I'm glad we could have this talk, but I think it's over. I can't even think anymore."

"Mmm. I agree." She started sliding down my body. "No more talk.

Time for action."

It was music to my ears.

Epilogue

Bash

MY PALMS WERE SWEATY and my throat was dry. My lawyer leaned toward me and whispered into my ear, "This is it. What you've been waiting for."

I glanced over my shoulder at my friends and family who filled the two rows of the courthouse hearing room behind me. My mother gave me a reassuring smile.

The doors at the back of the room opened. A middle-aged woman who looked vaguely familiar entered the room carrying a stack of binders in her arms. She was wearing a beige boxy-looking suit, with her dark hair pulled up into a severe bun, and a brown scarf knotted around her neck. She barrelled up the center aisle and dropped her armload on the table set directly to our right.

"Who's that?" I asked my lawyer in a low voice.

She leaned toward me again, a small frown on her face. "That's the court-appointed advocate for Kody. She's the one that visited your apartment and checked up on Kody's welfare."

My eyes widened with shock. The woman who'd interviewed me about Kody had worn jeans and a sweatshirt. Her hair had hung down her back, and she'd been friendly and outgoing. I could hardly reconcile that image with the one that now stood ten feet from me. The woman, who I remembered was named Marla, looked over her shoulder at the packed seats of the courtroom and sneered. She hadn't once glanced my way.

My lawyer squeezed my arm to focus my attention. "Remember to address the judge as 'Your Honor'. This will be less formal than court proceedings you've probably seen on TV. Even so, you need to be respectful. Do not speak unless a question is asked of you..."

She continued on her spiel, but she'd already prepped me on this several times. My eyes drifted back over to Marla, who was writing furiously on a pad of paper in front of her. For some reason, she looked hostile, and that worried me.

The bailiff asked everyone to rise. I stood up and watched as the judge emerged from her chamber. She looked a bit like Judge Judy but with steel gray hair.

The judge sat in her chair behind the bench and then ordered, "Please be seated."

The bailiff approached the judge with a folder and then announced the case. The judge leafed through the papers for several long moments and then looked up. "Good morning."

I listened intently as the judge and my lawyer spoke back and forth about my petition. There were many legal technicalities involved, but what it all boiled down to was that I was Kody's father and I was petitioning for sole custody of him. I was asking the court to relinquish any rights his biological mother had over him and asking for a legal birth certificate to be issued for him.

The judge turned her focus to me. "Mr. Archer."

"Your honor."

She peered down at the papers in her hand. "You are the biological father of the child known as Dakota Archer. Is that correct?"

"Yes, your honor."

"And you have submitted results from a paternity test that was taken in accordance with the court's stipulations required to prove paternity. Is that correct?"

I nodded but then remembered to speak up. "Yes, your honor."

"I have reviewed the submission and am satisfied that you have met all the requirements, Mr. Archer. I have reviewed the results of the paternity test. Mr. Archer, the court recognizes you as the biological father of Dakota Archer."

I'd known this for a long time, so why did the simple proclamation from the judge cause such a big grin to spread across my face?

"Now, Mr. Archer. You have submitted that you do not know who the biological mother is. Can you explain that to me, please?"

"Um, yes." I cleared my throat, remembering how my lawyer had advised me to answer. "When he was about two weeks old, Kody was left at my door with a note that said I was his father. It wasn't signed. I haven't heard from anyone claiming to be his mother since then."

The judge put on a pair of reading glasses. "And what was the date that Dakota was left at your door?"

"Your honor," my lawyer jumped in, "that was on January 18 of this year. We have several witnesses that can attest to the date and the manner in which Dakota showed up."

"Thank you, Ms. Robbins. Now, I understand the note that came with Dakota was misplaced, presumably thrown away. Mr. Archer, can you recall what the note said?"

"Yes. It was very short. It said that I was the baby's father and asked me to take care of him. The mother was sorry, but she could not take care of the baby any longer. She said she was going out of town and her boyfriend didn't want to take the baby with them. That was all. There was no signature."

"There was another person who read this note also?"

I nodded. "Yes, my roommate Sidney read the note, too."

The judge looked down at the papers. "Mr. Sidney Anderson. And you've submitted a witness affidavit as to that."

My lawyer answered, "Yes, your honor."

"Mr. Archer," the judge looked up, "how did you react when Dakota showed up at your door?"

My lawyer had advised me to tell the truth about everything, but that it was best not to mention the part about Sidney thinking Kody was his baby. "It was a shock, your honor. Sidney and I worked together to take care of Kody. We got some help from friends because we didn't know that much about babies at the time. We went to the baby store and bought all the necessities to take care of him. And then my friends threw a baby shower for him a few days later. Josie, his nanny, started taking care of him when Sid and I were at work. It was crazy, but we quickly became a family."

The judge nodded. "Mr. Archer, have you done anything to try to determine the identity of Dakota's mother?"

My lawyer had prepared me for this question, too. "Your honor, Dakota showed up at my door out of the blue. I've tried to think back to who the mother could be, but I don't know. I was not in a committed relationship at the time."

"Thank you, Mr. Archer." She shuffled through her stack of papers.

I took the break in questioning to look back at my support group.

My parents, Kaylie, Brent, and Josie were sitting directly behind me. Behind them sat Talia and Lacey with all of my bandmates, except for Sid, who was outside the courtroom with Kody. Even Donovan, our manager, had shown up to support me. Their reassuring smiles did a lot to ease my nerves.

The judge looked over to the woman who I knew as Marla. "Ms. Munson, you have been appointed by the court as the special advocate for the child known as Dakota Archer. Is that true?"

"Yes, your honor."

"I have read through your submission to the court and I have read your recommendation. Will you please give the court an overview of your findings?"

"Your honor. I interviewed Mr. Sebastian Archer twice. Once over the telephone and once in person. I have also inspected Mr. Archer's residence, which is a 2 bedroom apartment in a seedy section of the city."

My body tensed. What the hell? I didn't live in a seedy part of town. And the telephone interview? I didn't even know I was being interviewed. We chatted for about five minutes when she called to set up the visit to my apartment. She'd been asking questions about Ghost Parker like any fan might.

She went on. "Mr. Archer is a member of a rock and roll band called Ghost Parker, which regularly goes on music tours around the country. The band goes on the road for months, up to a year, at a time. They are currently on a short break in the middle of a tour. Next summer, I believe, they go on a world tour across Europe and Asia, which could last well over six months."

My lawyer spoke up. "Your honor—"

The judge cut her off by holding up her hand. The judge's rebuke was biting. "Ms. Robbins, you had your turn. I'm listening to Dakota's special advocate right now. Do not interrupt again."

Fuck. What was happening?

The judge turned back to Marla. "And you believe this will have an impact on Dakota?"

Marla nodded. "How can it not, your honor? A concert tour features music shows, usually a new concert in a different city every night. They typically travel by bus to the locations. The lifestyle is well documented, your honor. I'm sure you've heard the term, 'sex, drugs, and rock and roll'? It's no place for a baby."

The judge's eyebrow shot up. "And that is why you've recommended the court remove Dakota from Mr. Archer's custody?"

I gasped as I frantically looked at my lawyer. My heart was pounding with adrenaline. I vaguely heard the reaction from the crowd behind me. It was a collective cacophony of outraged gasps and a few shouts of denial or surprise.

Just like in the movies, the judge grasped her gavel and then hammered it down. "Quiet! Or else I'll have the bailiff drag every last one of you out of here."

My lawyer's head bowed and her shoulders slumped. She wouldn't meet my eye. How could this all be going to shit? I wanted to stand up and start screaming out in my defense, but I bit my tongue.

The courtroom was quiet again. The judge ordered, "Continue, Ms. Munson."

"That's not the only reason, your honor. I have some pictures that were taken from social media. I can confirm that they were taken in the residence of Mr. Archer, the residence that Dakota lives in."

"Go on."

"The photos depict concerning behavior, your honor. Scantily clad women, drug use, sexual exploits, excessive alcohol usage ... I've identified Mr. Archer in several pictures, his roommate Sidney Anderson, members of his rock band — all of whom sit before you today dressed up in fancy suits."

A murmur went through the crowd behind me. My lawyer looked blind-sided. Like a deer in headlights. What the fuck! She had to do something, so I grabbed her hand to get her attention. I leaned in and growled over the commotion, "This is bullshit. We haven't had one party since Kody showed up."

The judge banged her gavel again. "Silence!"

The crowd quieted down. My lawyer finally spoke up, "Your honor-"

"Silence," the judge repeated. "I will take 15 minutes in chambers to review the photos Ms. Munson has provided before I return with my ruling. I wish you all to remain seated where you are. When I return, you will remain quiet throughout the entirety of the proceedings. This is your last warning on that front."

The bailiff moved to the front of the bench. "All rise."

I forced my body to obey and stood up. The judge left out the same door she'd entered.

Everyone immediately began to talk. My gaze slid over to Marla, the seemingly harmless woman I'd joked with at our only meeting. She looked my way, a sly smile stealing over her face.

Why the fuck was she doing this?

I swallowed down the insult I wanted to hurl her way and concentrated my attention on my lawyer. "What the hell is happening?"

She looked up at me. "We drew a bad judge. I'm sorry, Sebastian. There was no indication that the court advocate would do something like this. Please, let me think for a few minutes. I need to write down some points in your defense before the judge returns."

She sat down and began scribbling on her yellow legal pad. I turned around. Brent was trying to soothe Kaylie, who was crying. My mom's hand was covering her mouth. Josie had her hands on her hips like she was ready to give the judge hell. My bandmates either looked pissed off, completely stunned, or a combination of both. Everyone was a mess.

I sank into my chair and held my head in my hands. How could this be happening? My leg was bouncing and my fingers were tapping out a beat against my temples, but the rhythm didn't soothe me like it normally did.

I was scared. I was going to lose Kody, and it scared me to death. A twisted swirl of agony erupted in my chest.

Only about five minutes had passed when the bailiff announced, "All rise."

The judge was returning early. What did that mean? I glanced at my lawyer. I could see her skin blanch as she threw down her pen and mumbled, "Oh shit."

Fuck! How could I stop this?

Everyone rose until the judge said, "Be seated."

The judge pulled off her glasses. "I've reviewed all the materials, and I have made my judgment."

My lawyer stood up. "Your honor, if you would please—"

She got shot down hard again. "Ms. Robbins, do you want to be cited for contempt of court? If you do not agree with my judgment, then you will have an opportunity to appeal your case."

I felt my blood boiling. This wasn't justice. The judge hadn't given me sufficient time to present my case or defend myself against the accusations that the court advocate had smeared me with.

The judge looked my way. "Mr. Archer. Is Dakota present in the building?"

I had trouble speaking past the lump in my throat. "Yes. He's with my roommate, Sidney Anderson."

"Thank you. Bailiff, will you please ask Mr. Anderson to bring Dakota into the courtroom?"

"Yes, your honor," the bailiff replied.

I gripped the edge of the table hard. Please tell me this was not happening. A few minutes later, Sid entered the courtroom carrying Kody. His smile melted when he saw the shocked and nervous faces of my family and friends.

"Mr. Anderson, please hand over Dakota to the bailiff while I render my decision."

Sidney's eyes met mine with a heartwrenching look of pain. The bailiff took Kody from Sid's arms.

I had to look away, but my gaze slid past Marla just as she smirked with victory. How could taking a baby away from his father be considered a victory?

My head hung low as the judge began speaking. "As I have stated earlier, the court finds Mr. Sebastian Archer to be legally recognized as the biological father of the child known as Dakota Archer.

"At this time, it is unclear who the biological mother is; however, the court finds that the mother acted with intent to abandon her child. I order that if there has been no contact from the biological mother after 1 year from the date Mr. Archer took physical custody of Dakota, which will be January 18th of next year, the mother will have all parental rights terminated."

She looked up from her papers. "In the meantime, if the biological mother shows up, she is not authorized to take custody of Dakota Archer. She will have to petition this court to have any contact with him. She will be given a chance to explain her actions and reveal any mitigating circumstances; however, this court does not take abandonment lightly."

Kody fussed in the bailiff's arms and I longed to take him. Would he be immediately taken away from me? Would I even get the chance to say goodbye to him?

"Now, on to the issue of identification," she continued. "Because of the circumstances, we do not know if a birth certificate was issued for this child at his birth. Therefore, I am authorizing the state of California to issue a birth certificate under the name of Dakota Archer. Based on information from Dakota's physicians, the official date of birth will be listed as January 4, 2022. The father will be listed as Sebastian Archer and the mother listed as unknown. On the order of this court, this birth certificate will vitiate any other birth certificate for this child that is currently in existence."

Kody began squirming more. His face was turning bright red, and I knew what that meant. A few seconds later, he let out a whimper, which quickly turned into full-out crying. The bailiff rocked him in his arms, but Kody didn't let up.

The judge frowned. "John, why don't you hand over Dakota to Mr. Archer? I'm sure Dakota will be more comfortable with him."

I stood up and took Kody from the bailiff, and held him against my chest. What I really wanted to do was take him and bolt from the room. What if this was the last time I'd be able to hold him? To comfort him? My heart felt like it was filled with lead, but I patted Kody's back and made soothing noises in his ear until he settled down and stopped crying.

"Now on to the most important ruling in this case, which also happened to be the easiest. As to the custody of Dakota Archer, his biological father, Mr. Sebastian Archer, is granted sole parental custody, which includes both legal custody and physical custody."

I sunk into my chair, relief surging through me as a cheer went up behind me. Something so powerful bubbled up from my chest that I almost couldn't breathe. And, fuck, I was crying. I was standing in front of all my friends and family with tears streaming down my face. I'd never live this down, but what the fuck did I care? Kody was my son; I would protect and love him forever, and that thought filled me with joy.

The judge was still talking. "Your lawyer can help you get a copy of the order and the new birth certificate will be ready in a couple of weeks. Congratulations, Mr. Archer. Kody is a lucky boy."

"Thank you, your honor," I somehow managed to choke out.

"Court is dismissed. Ms. Munson, please approach the bench."

I turned to my lawyer. "What the hell just happened?"

She smiled big. "I think the judge saw through all the bullshit. I think I'm going to write a letter to Ms. Munson's supervisor. What she did was unethical, but let's talk about that another time. Now it's time to celebrate with your friends and family. Congratulations, Sebastian."

I wiped the tears from my face and laughed. Yes, it was time to celebrate.

Sidney

Kaylie wanted to see snow this winter. Real, honest-to-goodness, boot sinking deep into the white stuff kind of snow. Since neither of us skied, I skipped the pretentious ski slopes favored by celebrities and jetsetters and booked us for five nights at an exclusive resort in Montana.

I had my girl all to myself. The cabin was rustic-luxe; exposed beams and antler chandeliers were paired with plush throw rugs, cloud-soft bedding, radiant in-floor heating, and a romantic gas fireplace.

We'd already foregone the highly-rated restaurant and utilized room service in order to enjoy our privacy. Our meal had been outstanding, and the staff was really accommodating.

After dinner, we joined a few guests toasting marshmallows at the bonfire with the fur-lined seating surrounding it. Kaylie was slightly tipsy and decided she wanted to play in the snow. We were having a blast, but that only lasted about 15 minutes before she was freezing and ready to head back inside.

We returned to our cheery cabin with the blazing fire and stripped out of our wet clothes. There was a private hot tub a few steps from our back door and a copper bathtub inside with a gorgeous view of the snowy landscape and lake.

I pulled off my shirt. "Hot tub or bathtub?"

Her teeth were chattering. "It's freezing out there. I'm not going back out there tonight. Definitely bathtub."

I stripped down to my black boxer briefs. "Come in front of the fire while you undress. I'll start the bath."

After I started the water, I checked to make sure my order had been delivered — chilled champagne and chocolate-covered strawberries. I wanted to make tonight special.

My whole life had changed this past year. Boosted by the wild success of *Okay Babe*, our album went platinum and our tour was incredibly successful.

After *Okay Babe* had broken into the top 10 for a few weeks, Donovan had shown up with our royalty checks. He flipped out when it turned out that Bash had been the only one to take his advice and hire a financial planner. When he showed us the number on the check, we understood why. My eyes had almost popped out of my head.

That was only the first of dozens of checks and they were still coming. We'd made it. We were financially secure beyond what we'd ever imagined. Fame was harder to grapple with than fortune, especially for Ghost, who was taking the brunt of the attention. Privacy in public was a thing of the past. There was a huge learning curve in figuring out how to navigate our new world as true rock stars.

At the end of the tour, Kaylie and I had moved in together in a penthouse apartment that she'd picked out while I was still on the road. It had private underground parking, so we could get in and out without being disturbed, and great security. I felt better knowing Kaylie would be safe there.

Our new place was great, but we spent most weekends at Bash's house in the suburbs. We both liked to get out of the city, and we always loved to see Kody.

We were all trying to catch our breath from the last crazy tour, but BVR was already busting our collective asses to produce a new album and get back on the road. We were a huge cash cow right now and in high demand, so they weren't going to let up. Donovan was already talking about us getting back to our rehearsal space to bang out some new hits.

But who was I to complain? This was everything that I'd ever wanted and more. It was a lot of change in a short amount of time.

And things were about to change again.

I adjusted the water temperature and began lighting some candles all around the bathroom while the tub slowly filled up. Then I stepped into the bedroom and unzipped my suitcase that was stowed in the closet. Inside a zippered pouch, I rustled around until my hand closed around the black velvet box.

"Is the water ready yet?" Kaylie shouted from in front of the fireplace.

I opened the box and peered at the ring. "Nope, give me a few seconds, babe."

I stopped for a moment and took a deep breath, mentally checking to see if I was nervous. Nope. Not one fucking bit.

For tomorrow, I'd booked a ride on a horse-drawn sleigh through the countryside. I'd thought about proposing to her then, but I knew Kaylie would want our privacy. This was better. The first time I saw her wearing my ring, she'd be naked. Then, I wanted to make her feel so good that she screamed my name. Over and over. I was pretty sure the horse and driver didn't need to see or hear any of that.

I hid the ring in the bathroom, checked the water temperature one more time, added a bit of bath oil, and then headed out to get my girl.

♫♫♪♪♪

Kaylie was luxuriating in the tub. She looked so good, I almost skipped the proposal so I could join her in there.

She was eyeing the champagne that was chilling in a stand at the side of the tub and the tray of gourmet chocolate-covered strawberries. "Aren't you going to join me?"

"Not yet."

She made a pouty face. "Do I at least get a bite of that delicious-looking strawberry, or are you just going to torture me?"

"Patience, woman." I shook my head, but then caved in when I saw the disappointed look on her face. She loved her chocolate.

Lifting a strawberry off the tray, I brought it to her mouth for her to bite. I brushed her hand aside and then fed her each nibble until it was gone.

I chuckled to myself at how hard she'd tried to seduce me. She'd sucked my fingers sensually, played with her nipples, and then slid her hand between her legs, all the while moaning sinfully. Under normal circumstances, my plan would have been abandoned as soon as the finger sucking started, but tonight I discreetly adjusted the boner that was peeking out the top of my boxer briefs and backed away.

Grabbing my guitar from the corner of the room, I pulled up a stool and sat down by the tub. "I wrote a song for you."

She smiled. "Another new mega-hit?"

"This one's just for you, beautiful." I strummed the guitar. "It's called *Entwined*."

The song was my proposal. It'd taken me almost a year to write, and it only scratched the surface of the depths of my feelings for Kaylie, but it was heartfelt. It wasn't as catchy as *Okay Babe*, but it wasn't written for anyone but her. She was my one.

She wiped a tear from her eye when I finished. "That was beautiful, Sidney."

I had nothing else to say; my song had said it all. I put down my guitar and then swiped the ring from its hiding spot. In front of the tub, I got down on one knee and showed her the ring.

Her eyes widened in shock. She splashed some water out of the tub as she sat up so quickly.

"Kaylie, I want to be entwined with you forever. Will you marry me?"

"Yes, yes, yes!" she shouted. "A thousand times, yes!"

I slipped the ring on her finger and we both stared at it for a minute. I could afford something a lot flashier, but I'd been more modest because I knew that's what Kaylie would prefer.

"Do you like it? We could get something else if you don't?"

"It's perfect." She held out her hand. "Look, I'm so excited, my hand is shaking. How did I get to be the luckiest girl in the entire world?"

My lips curled up. "Well, it all started when you put your hand down my pants in a stinky closet."

"True." She splashed some water at me and then frowned. "Oh my God, why are you still out there? Get in here with me! It's time to celebrate."

She didn't have to ask twice. I slipped into the tub and we popped open the champagne so we could toast to our future.

It only took a good minute or two after that to get her screaming my name.

Kaylie

4 years later...

It was brutally hot in the sun, but I'd staked out my lounge chair in a nice shady area where I could watch the antics going on in the pool. Today, we gathered together at Bash's house for the one-year-old birthday party for my niece, Delilah. She was Bash's little princess.

The entire Ghost Parker extended family had turned out to celebrate. Ryder and Knox were horsing around in the pool with Tommy,

Tyler, and Alex from Cold Fusion and their older kids. Sidney was busy tossing Kody into the pool over and over again while Kody's neighborhood friends were taking turns jumping off the diving board.

Greyson and Ghost had just gotten out of the pool and were joking around as they toweled off. Luckily, I had my shades on so I could check them out with no one noticing. Then, Bishop got out of the pool. He was one of the security guys that the band had gotten friendly with. Several of them and their families were here as guests. Like many of the security team, Bishop was ex-military and had muscles on top of muscles. I tucked my tongue back in my mouth as I watched the drops of water streaming down his tanned chest.

I didn't know where to look first. It was hot guy overload. Most of these guys were dads, but there was not a dad bod in sight. I was getting a little hot and bothered. I blamed the pregnancy hormones.

Lacey snickered next to me. "Now I know what your 'O' face looks like."

I glanced over at her and frowned. Lacey was pregnant, only a few weeks behind me, yet she had a flat stomach. Not only did she look completely not pregnant in her string bikini, but she looked like a damn pinup model reclining sexily on her lounge chair. Her hair was put up in a cute ponytail, her makeup looked freshly done, her skin was tanned to a natural golden hue, and her nails were perfectly manicured and matched her bikini. Don't get me started on her boobs. She was well-endowed to begin with, so why did her boobs look even bigger when her stomach was still flat? She was even wearing cute, dangly earrings. Come on! And how come she wasn't sweating like the rest of us mortals?

I looked down at my baby bump. After I had the twins, I'd worked so hard to get back my figure. I'd succeeded, too. When I'd gotten pregnant again, this time my stomach popped so freaking early. It looked like I'd swallowed a basketball. The maternity bathing suit that had looked so cute on in the store, looked downright frumpy now.

I glared at Lacey over my sunglasses. "I don't know what you're talking about."

"Please," she snorted. "You're worse than Josie. She can't make up enough excuses to come out here and ogle the eye candy. At least she admits it."

Josie was hysterical. Sidney and I had pilfered her from Bash years ago, and now she was a nanny to our sons, Brady and Emerson. It was perfect because sometimes she came with us on the weekends so she could visit Kody and Delilah.

My parents, who'd moved to California to be closer to their grandchildren, were inside on baby patrol with Josie. Most of the babies and toddlers, including my two, were currently down for their naps, giving their parents a well-deserved break.

I looked around the patio. Donovan was holding a sleeping kid while he talked with one of the guys from the opening band at Ghost Parker's first major tour. That band had crashed and burned, but the guys had remained friends with two of its members. A few of the roadies were grouped together, talking to some of the guys from the opening band from the second tour. That band seemed to be taking off.

Brent was talking to Marie and Sadie. Trudy was chasing down Knox's toddler son, who looked like he'd swiped her cocktail. Livvy marched over to the sound system and turned off Ghost's playlist and put on her own. Southern rock started playing to all sorts of groans and protests, but soon everyone was enjoying it.

The party was in full swing and everyone was having a good time. The sliding door of the house opened, and Candace Collins walked out.

I side-eyed Lacey. "Oh God, who invited Candie?"

Lacey turned to watch the girl making her grand entrance into the party. "Supposedly, she's been clean and sober for almost a year now. Bash and Sid want to give her another chance. She's had a rough go of it."

I knew most of the story. Candace's parents had managed her career from an early age, and through shady business practices, pretty much stole all of their daughter's earnings. Candace had turned to drugs and alcohol and had driven everyone crazy on that first tour with Ghost Parker.

She had a lot of talent, but her personal life was a mess. Sidney and Bash were working together to form an indie record label. Taking on Candace Collins could be a genius move or their biggest mistake. Only time would tell.

When Candace caught sight of Amanda, the Australian nanny that watched Kody on that first tour, sparks flew. It looked like we were heading to a reality TV throwdown, complete with hair pulling and bitch slapping. Luckily, Bash came out of nowhere and pulled the two girls apart.

"What the heck was that all about?" I wondered.

Of course, Ghost knew. "Remember that guy, Ralston, from the first tour? Yeah, he was fucking them both."

"That was like 5 years ago? Wasn't..." I didn't finish my sentence because Sidney was heading my way. He'd just gotten out of the pool and he was looking mighty fine. Out of all the hot guys here, he was the only one that could get my body revving with just a look in my direction. I still lusted after my husband and the pregnancy hormones only seemed to enhance it.

He stood over me dripping a few drops of water on my leg. "The boys still asleep?"

I couldn't keep my glance from sweeping over his toned body. "Yeah. They should be down for about another hour."

"That should be enough time." He held out his hand to help me up.

I grabbed it and awkwardly stood. "Where are we going?"

Ghost rubbed his chin. "Let me guess. You're going to go play hide the salami while the boys are still sleeping."

Lacey snorted. "Kaylie," she warned. "Remember the last time you got the big D when you were preggers? You better be careful! You don't want your," — she made air quotes with her fingers — "water to break."

My face flamed red. "Lacey!"

Late in my pregnancy with the twins, when I was as huge as a house, my obstetrician told me no more sex when I reported that it had become uncomfortable especially because my husband was so well endowed. I may have been huge, but I was also very swollen and sensitive down there. Sidney had plenty of ways to keep me satisfied.

I was at 36 weeks, right in the range where my OB had told me twin pregnancies usually lasted when I thought my water broke. My OB sent us directly to the hospital. Sidney alerted all our friends and family that it was showtime. Most of them were already on the way to the hospital when we had to tell them to turn around; it was a false alarm.

My OB was puzzled to discover that my water had not broken. When she found out that I thought my water had broken when I'd had an orgasm due to G-spot stimulation, she figured it out.

I'd squirted again, but who knew that the quantity could be so much larger when pregnant? They didn't go over any of that in pre-natal classes.

Sidney had let it slip that my water had not broken after all and most of our friends assumed that I'd peed myself. He'd been valiantly trying to defend my honor that I didn't pee myself and he kind of gave away the whole thing. I'd never live it down.

"What?" Lacey smirked. "Ghost knows what happened. Ghost knows everything."

I turned to Ghost, pleading with my eyes for him to say he had no clue what she was talking about.

He held up his fingers and made a motion like he was shooting a water gun. "Squirt, squirt."

Everyone around me broke out into laughter.

"You people suck."

I saw Sidney wink at Lacey before he led me away.

♫♫♩♪♪

Sidney wanted to take a walk, but I didn't really want to. My feet were just beginning to swell when it got hot out. Sweat was dripping down my back. "Let's turn back. It's too hot."

He squeezed my hand. "We're almost there."

"Where?" He didn't answer but started leading me down the driveway of the house diagonally across from Bash's. "Why are we visiting the neighbors?"

"You'll see."

"As long as they have air conditioning," I said grumpily.

I balked when he took out a key and began unlocking the front door.

"They gave me the key. The owners are out of town right now."

I looked around the space as we stepped inside. "What are we doing? Feeding the cats for them or something?"

"Or something."

Sidney stood in the foyer and studied my face. "What do you think?"

The air conditioning had improved my mood, but I still didn't know what was going on. "About what? What are we doing here, Sidney?

"How would you feel about buying this house? The owners told Bash that they're putting it on the market soon. It's ours if you want it."

I felt a stir of excitement. "You'd want to live so close to Bash?"

"And Kody. And Delilah." He smiled. "The cousins would grow up together."

I threw out some objections. "What about the city? You love it there. And our penthouse?"

"We'll still be close enough to enjoy the city when we want to, but we don't have to deal with the traffic and the paparazzi or fans day to day." He pulled me into his arms. "And think about all the weekends we're here and you grumble when we have to leave. You love it out here."

I thought about my charity. "I could do all my Cyber Angels work just as easily from here, too. But, what about the band stuff?"

"You know that Bash and I have been thinking about working on our own projects, especially when Ghost Parker is taking some time off. Bash was thinking about building a soundproof studio in his pool house. This yard is pretty big. We could add a pool house or guest cottage out back behind the pool and use it as an office space or music room."

My eyes widened. "There's a pool, too?"

He tugged on my hand. "C'mon. Let's go check it out."

Oh my God, I really wanted this. "We can afford something so much bigger. It's kind of small. Are you sure you want this?"

I nodded as I took in the open floor plan. The great room had two-story windows that looked out the back. The kitchen was large and airy and finished as nicely as the one in our penthouse.

I ran my hand over the quartz countertop on the giant island. "It sounds like you've thought this through."

"I have." He turned me around and put his hand on my belly. "And our family is outgrowing the penthouse."

"Three bedrooms are plenty of room for now." The new baby was taking over the guest room, but that didn't bother me. We rarely had guests stay there now that my parents were living in California.

He was grinning at me lazily like he knew a secret. "It might not be for long. We got approved, Kay. We're going to be foster parents soon."

"Oh my God, Sidney. That's amazing!"

We'd discussed becoming foster parents for years, but we'd agreed that now was finally the time. Sidney picked me up and twirled me around.

I slapped at him. "Put me down, you're going to throw out your back."

"You're not that huge, yet." He smiled playfully. "You're still enjoying the big D as Lacey put it."

We toured the rest of the house, but I'd already made up my mind. I could picture our growing family living happily in this house. I was so excited when we agreed we were going to do it.

Bash was waiting for us when we returned. He hugged us both when we broke the news to him. Apparently, he was the one who suggested it to Sidney in the first place when he heard his neighbor was moving.

"I have something for you." Bash handed me an envelope that was bursting at the seams. "I opened up Delilah's birthday cards. You made about $86,000."

When Bash had said he wanted Delilah's party to be gift free — his princess already had everything in the world anyway — Lacey suggested we ask the guests to donate to Cyber Angels instead.

While some of our sponsors and donors had donated much bigger sums, the money that my friends and friends generously donated made me proud.

We were making a difference. We helped a 14-year-old girl who thought she was sending a topless photo to a teen boy that had befriended her online, only to learn that it was a middle-aged man. When the man deliberately used the photo to destroy her life and then the harassment followed her when the girl's family moved to another state, the girl became suicidal. When law enforcement couldn't offer much help, Cyber Angels pulled all our resources together to attack the problem at the source. And when Lacey was pissed, she was a force to be reckoned with. We had helped to turn that girl's story around and we saw the positive results of our work every day. With our resources, we'd been able to help lots of people when they felt completely helpless.

Sidney held my hand as we headed back out to the pool area. I looked around at all our friends and family. Everyone here had their own story, most were way more interesting than mine. I saw Greyson Durant, a huge Hollywood celebrity, holding his tiny baby. Now, that was a doozie of a story. Mixed up in there was Ghost with his always interesting life. And Knox, the way he met his wife was crazy.

But, those were all stories for another day.

Sidney was my soulmate, and I was so lucky that I got to share my life with him. My story might be bland compared to some of my friends, but it was the only story I wanted to star in. And it was only just beginning.

The End

Next in Series

Bad Boys of Rock
Book 3:
(Keep turning the pages for an excerpt!)

How to Date a Rockstar

Summer

After being burned one too many times, I'd sworn off men for good. And it was working. My life was finally on an even keel.

As soon as I saw him, I knew he was Trouble. I was instantly attracted to him and that pissed me off, so I decided to take my frustrations out on the arrogant stranger with the sexy Scottish accent. We clashed like thunder and lightning, and I was fairly certain I was winning our verbal battle until...

Surprise! My mother showed up. From across the country. And assumed that the sexy Scotsman was my boyfriend. The *fake boyfriend* I'd invented to get her off my back.

Knox
Fake dating the feisty and breathtakingly gorgeous Summer was no hardship. I played along for the sake of her mother, spending a weekend at a luxurious spa with Summer and her parents. Though Summer was fiercely determined to keep her distance from me, I was even more determined to get her into my bed.

My plan was to seduce her, but it turned out all along, she was seducing me. Despite my no commitment vow, I fell hard for the sassy lass. But when she discovered that I wasn't who I said I was, everything fell apart.

Grab your **backstage pass** to meet the boys of Ghost Parker and get ready for an electrifying tale of passion, betrayal, and the healing power of love. Turn up the volume and prepare to be utterly consumed by this rockstar romance — a steamy and erotic tale of mistaken identity, fake dating, and enemies becoming lovers. Lose yourself in this glittering story of deception, desire, and the redemptive power of love amidst the chaos of stardom.

Keep turning the pages to read an excerpt from
How to Date a Rockstar

Arabella Quinn Newsletter

Let's keep in touch!

Sign up for my newsletter and be the first to know about new releases, sales, giveaways, and other exciting news. As an added bonus, you'll receive a FREE ebook as my thank-you for signing up!

Arabella Quinn newsletter
https://subscribepage.io/ArabellaQuinn

Bad Boys of Rock Series

Who doesn't love the tattooed bad boys of rockstar romance? **Get ready to toss your panties on stage — it's gonna get wild!**

Book 1: How to Seduce a Rockstar — A mind-boggling case of mistaken identity sets the stage for a scorching hot romance between Ryder, the sinfully sexy guitarist of a famous rock band, and Talia, the unsuspecting woman who stumbles into his life. After the erotic encounter with the mysterious and sexy stranger in his bed, Ryder's world is rocked.

Book 2: How to Tempt a Rockstar — Forbidden desires ignite in this sizzling romance between Sid, the tattooed bad-boy bass guitarist, and Kaylie, his best friend's little sister. When a tiny bundle shows up at Sid's door, Kaylie reaches out to help as his world turns upside-down. As the lines between love and lust lose focus, they must weather the tempest of forbidden desire and hidden truths to see if their love can survive the ultimate test.

Book 3: **How to Date a Rockstar** — In this sizzling rockstar romance, enemies become lovers while secrets threaten to tear them apart. Knox, the lead guitarist with the irresistible Scottish accent, becomes entangled in a fake dating scheme with Summer to appease her meddlesome mother. When the lines between fake and real blur, Knox must confront his tragic past and face the truth that he's been battling. Can their budding relationship survive the harsh glare of the spotlight and the ghosts of the past that haunt them? Or will the truth shatter their hearts beyond repair?

Book 4: **How to Catch a Rockstar** — Passions burn hot when Ghost, the enigmatic lead singer of a popular rock band, becomes ensnared in a tempestuous love triangle between Remi, a woman who ignites his dormant emotions, and her boyfriend, whom he despises. As lust and hatred collide with betrayal, can the three navigate the treacherous waters of a passionate love triangle and find redemption amidst the chaos of stardom, or will their dangerous games leave them shattered? The only question is—who will be left standing when the music stops?

Book 5: **How to Marry a Rockstar** — Bash, the reckless and carefree drummer of a chart-topping rock band, is busy juggling fame, fortune, and fatherhood. Lacey, the sultry vixen, has been friends with Bash and his band for years. Their lives take an unexpected turn when one reckless night in Vegas changes everything, leaving them entwined in more ways than one. With their secret passions and insatiable cravings unleashed, they embark on a steamy friends-with-benefits arrangement with a side of untamed kinks.

Also By Arabella Quinn

BAD BOYS OF ROCK SERIES

How to Seduce a Rockstar

How to Tempt a Rockstar

How to Date a Rockstar

How to Catch a Rockstar

How to Marry a Rockstar

ROCK ME SERIES

Rock Me: Wicked

Rock Me: Naughty

Rock Me: Crazy

Rock Me: Sexy

ROMANCE NOVELS

My Stepbrother the Dom
Impossible (to Resist) Boss
Being Jane

THE WILDER BROTHERS SERIES

(small town romance)

Fake Marriage to a Baller
Luke – coming soon

Other Novels by Arabella Quinn

MY STEPBROTHER THE DOM

A sizzling stepbrother romance with a twist:

For years, I had the worst crush on my stepbrother, Cole Hunter. We used to ride bikes, skateboard, and go fishing together — now I couldn't even be in the same room as him without my pulse racing. One cocky half-grin from Cole would have my face blushing while my panties melted. It was insane — and completely humiliating.

It was a painful secret that I guarded fiercely. Cole was off-limits. *Forbidden*. If he knew how I felt, I would die of embarrassment.

I avoided Cole for years, until one wild night, when my best friend took me to a club. I thought I was going to see a grunge band, but it turned out to be a much kinkier kind of club. A club where anything goes, and well, things got a little crazy. Make that a lot crazy.

No one would ever know what I'd done, right?

Then I discovered who the man behind the mask really was...

IMPOSSIBLE (TO RESIST) BOSS

A sexy billionaire CEO. His headstrong secretary. And a computer file that exposes her most secret and dirty fantasies about him.

Lilliana

I hate my boss.

He's an inconsiderate and demanding tyrant. I hate his juvenile rules, his micro-managing ways, and his selfish and unapologetic manner. But most of all, I hate how insanely sexy he is — how all the women around him can't help but fawn all over him.

He's a wealthy, ego-driven maniac that has a new bimbo at his beck and call with the mere snap of his fingers. Despite these irrepressible naughty fantasies I keep having about him, I wouldn't stroke his ego for all the money in the world.

Jason Kaine

I may have found the one.

After years of fruitless searching, I've found the perfect secretary. She's scarily efficient, not afraid of hard work, detail-oriented, and best of all, she doesn't complain about my important rules. She's a dream come true.

So why can't I keep the image of her, deliciously naked and spread out invitingly across my desk, from invading my head? I didn't get to where I am today by being stupid. I've got plenty of willing women to choose from who understand my absolute no-strings policy.

Lilliana is strictly off-limits, but I see the way her eyes devour me. I see how her pulse pounds whenever I get near. I know she's ripe for the taking, but that would be disastrous for both of us. It might be the worst mistake ever, but something's bound to give.

About the Author

A RABELLA QUINN IS A *New York Times* and *USA Today* bestselling author of contemporary romance. When she's not busy writing, you can often find her clutching her Kindle and staying up way past her bedtime reading romance novels. Besides contemporary romance, she loves regency, gothic, and erotic romance — the steamier the better. She also loves thrillers, especially psychological thrillers. She saves reading horror for when her husband is away on business but doesn't recommend that. She averages about five hours of sleep per night and does not drink coffee. Also, not recommended!

ARABELLA QUINN NEWSLETTER
https://subscribepage.io/ArabellaQuinn

Excerpt

How to Date a Rockstar

Prologue
One year ago...

Summer

A little swoosh sounded on my phone. Disappointment flooded me as I stared at the text I'd just received.

> **Jack Hartman:** I can't make our lunch meeting. Something's come up. Reschedule?

I wanted to be angry with him. Complain to him. Whine a bit, maybe. Stalk by his office to see what was up. But I'd do none of those things because I was a professional and he was my boss. I hissed out a breath and typed out a reply.

Me: Sure

Meek. Compliant. Doormat.

No, I was strong. Confident. In total control of my emotions. Mature. Yeah.

It was well past noon and the office lunch crew had already left. I could probably text Jana and find out where they went, but I wasn't in the mood for that exuberant crowd today. I could hit the cafeteria, but that didn't appeal either.

So fast food it was. There was nothing like a greasy burger to lift a bad mood. I pulled my raincoat off the hook in my cubicle and grabbed my umbrella before I headed out the door.

I walked as briskly as I could manage in my high heels through the wet parking lot with my umbrella held over my head, thankfully blocking most of the rain. I passed by Jack's metallic gray Range Rover parked in its usual spot. Every time I went in and out of the building, I couldn't help but look for it.

Thirty minutes later, I was sitting in my car finishing up my super-value meal. It had cheered me a little, but my mind was still on Jack. I wanted to see him. Hell, I needed to see him. That's when the plan started to take shape in my head.

After cleaning my fingers with some hand wipes I kept in the glove box, I drove out of the parking lot and onto the highway. I passed by the Days Inn on my left, the one that charged $88 per night. Less than a mile down was a small strip mall that contained a liquor store. I picked out a bottle of champagne and bought two novelty glasses that had been on display near the register. I headed back to work and waited.

The day went on forever. I tried my best to concentrate on work, but I was constantly daydreaming about my plan. I was so distracted. At 5 o'clock, most people were packing up to head home for the night. A few had left even earlier. As was usual, by 6 o'clock the place was deserted.

I plucked my jacket — a beige trench coat that tightened at the waist with a wide belt and fell to mid-thigh — from its hook and strolled casually to the ladies' room, scanning the cubicles along the way. To my relief, no one was working late.

Inside the bathroom stall, I took off all my clothes until I was standing naked in my black stilettos. I slipped into the trench coat and tied it closed with the belt, forgoing the buttons. When I stepped back in front of the bathroom mirror, I felt uncomfortably exposed when I saw my bare legs sticking out from the coat, but realistically, anyone would assume I was wearing clothes, maybe a short skirt. I assessed my appearance critically to make sure no one could guess that I was naked underneath.

I freshened up my hair and makeup and then wrapped my clothing into a tight ball. I took a deep breath, trying to tame the butterfly riot in my stomach, and then headed back to my cubicle. All was quiet. I dropped my clothes onto my office chair and then slid the chair completely under my desk. That way, no one would see the small pile of clothes if they happened to walk by.

This next part was tricky. I didn't want to be seen carrying a bottle of champagne to Jack's office. How would I explain that? I decided to do a quick reconnaissance stroll without the champagne first. Jack's office was a corner office, down the end of a short hallway. Everything was quiet as I headed toward the hall. The only other office in Jack's hall, Ben Miller's, was empty. Across the hall, the conference room was dark. The coast was clear.

A few more steps let me see that the door to Jack's office was shut. That meant he was still there. Jack was always the last to leave. He was the boss, after all. Thank God. I would have felt stupid getting naked under this coat if he had already left for the day.

My body surged with giddy anticipation as I hurried back to my cubicle and pulled the champagne bottle and glasses out from under my desk. I suppressed a giggle as I imagined Jack's face when I opened my trench coat and let it drop to the floor in a puddle around my feet.

My strides were quick, and I could feel the heat of arousal between my legs as I went. I stopped in front of his door to take a calming breath. I wanted to look sexy, not desperate. None of the office doors had locks, and I knew I could just barge in and surprise him, but I didn't want to do that. We had a special knock that I used whenever we'd had an after-work rendezvous — knock, knock, pause, knock-knock.

My hand trembled as I raised it to the door and rapped lightly. A muffled sound came from within his office and I assumed he'd said something like 'enter'. I'd probably surprised him; he wasn't expecting me today. Emboldened, I opened his door, strutted inside with an extra swizzle in my hips, and then struck a sexy pose.

When I saw the look of horror on his face, I knew something was wrong, but I didn't quite know what it was. He was standing behind his sleek, modern office desk facing me, his arms spread wide and braced on the desk with his shirtsleeves rolled up and his tie askew. Two computer monitors on his desk blocked most of his body from my view, but I could clearly see the panic that sparked in his eyes.

I stood rooted to the spot for a moment. My brain was still trying to process something important here. What?

I heard something. Wet and sloppy. Slapping? No, sucking sounds.

My insides grew ice cold. No! This couldn't be happening.

The overhead lights were off, but there was still enough ambient light streaming through the windows that I could see some slight movement beneath his desk. I angled my head and bent down slightly, just enough to see the worn soles of a pair of red high-heeled shoes. Shoes that I knew belonged to Missy Peterson, two cubicles down from me — shoes that were attached to a naked body on hands and knees, wiggling ass jutting out toward me as she sucked off my boss. It was the exact position I had assumed several times in this very same office for the very same boss, who only a few weeks ago had told me that he loved me at the Days Inn.

The champagne bottle slipped from my hand. It exploded like an improvised bomb all over the floor. Small shards of glass flew everywhere like shrapnel and a puddle of champagne began expanding across the floor. The noise of the crash must have startled Missy. I heard her head crack loudly against the top of the desk, followed by a grunt of pain from Jack. Hopefully, she bit his dick off.

Adrenaline surged through me. *Fight or flight*. I stumbled a few steps backward toward the door, utterly shell-shocked. *Fight or flight*. I didn't even glance at Jack again. I had only one thing on my mind.

Flight.

Chapter One

Knox

It wasn't so unusual for me to wake up with a woman in my arms. What was unusual — extremely unusual — was that we were both fully dressed. I popped open an eye to get my bearings. I was crammed on a couch, my neck jammed against the armrest at an ungodly angle, in some unknown flat with a petite brunette on top of me.

My head was fuzzy, but thankfully, not pounding. The night before slowly came back to me. I'd been flirting with this girl — Sharon or was it Karen? — with sensational breasts that were almost too big for her slight frame. She'd heard my accent, the one that always became more prominent the drunker I got, and clung to me like glue for the rest of the night. For her benefit, I might have called her a 'bonnie lass' and thrown in a few extra 'ayes' and 'wees' into the conversation. My Scottish accent never failed to leave a girl's panties soaked. At least that had been my experience here in America.

At the end of the night, we'd ended up together. We were going at it hot and heavy on the couch, practically sucking each other's tonsils out, when she'd passed out with her hand down my pants. I never would have fooled around with her if I'd known she was that drunk. Since the party was over, I'd removed her hand from my raging hard-on like a gentleman and fell asleep with a case of blue balls. Not my most successful of nights.

It appeared to be mid-morning, but no one was up yet. I tried again to think back to how I'd gotten here or whose flat I was at, but I couldn't remember. I'd started the night out partying with Ghost, but he'd disappeared before I'd left the weird nightclub with Sharon.

Ghost was the frontman for our band, Ghost Parker, and I was the lead guitarist. Besides me, he was the only one left who still partied regularly; the others had all fallen over the last 18 months or so. Ryder was married and just had a brand new baby girl with his wife Talia. Sid, our bassist, had just gotten engaged to his girlfriend, Kaylie. Her brother, Bash, our drummer, lived out in the suburbs with his son, Kody. Two years ago, Kody had been abandoned on Bash's doorstep with a note claiming he was the baby's father. Bloody hell. If that wasn't close to a guy's worst nightmare, I didn't know what was.

So much had changed, but the guys in Ghost Parker were still my best mates here in America. I'd been living in the U.S. for almost six years already and had been playing with Ghost Parker for nearly five of them. We'd been on the road touring for the last year and a half, and then I had to travel back to Scotland to get my work visa extended. Now, we were all enjoying a much-needed break, while our record label was already making noises for us to get back into the studio.

We'd made a ton of money, mostly thanks to the hit single Sid wrote, so now was the time to enjoy it, but I didn't know how to do that. Buying a fancy house like two of my bandmates had, or even a penthouse apartment like Sid's didn't interest me. I was content in the same flat I'd lived in for years. A luxury getaway sounded appealing, but the band had just spent months traveling all over the world. They wanted to stay in L.A. so they could spend time with their families. Who would I even go with?

We hadn't been home long, and already I was feeling restless. I needed to be moving. Playing guitar. Keeping busy.

What I really needed was to get out of this flat and away from this girl before she woke up. It was a Saturday morning, but I had no plans. There was no practice with the band today; I had no commitments. Hours of nothing lay ahead of me.

I didn't enjoy sitting still. It gave me too much time to think.

Last Saturday, I'd spent it with my band family at Bash's house to celebrate Kody's second birthday. It was a crazy day, but surprisingly fun. It was great catching up with Ghost Parker's extended family. Even Josie, the nanny, was there. After Sid found out that he wasn't Kody's father — long story — Josie continued to watch Kody until Bash moved into the suburbs.

I'd been surprised to see Josie there, especially on such good terms with Bash. Back when Bash was living on my couch, he used to complain about her all the time. He had some kind of hate-hate relationship going on with her. According to Bash, she was some kind of militant grandma that had taken an instant dislike to him. Now they seemed like good friends.

A surprising feeling of nostalgia washed over me. I thought about the months before we left on tour. At the time, I wanted nothing more than to have my space back to myself, but now it seemed so empty. Before Bash had been living on my couch, Ryder had camped out there for about a month after he sold his house to pay off a loan shark, but he hadn't been partying every night like an animal. I'm pretty sure Bash had been fucking chicks on my couch and that was just...no.

That should be the first thing on my list of things to do: buy a new couch. Eighteen months had gone by and I hadn't spent much time in my flat during them. It didn't feel like much of a home anymore. I shook off my glum thoughts, telling myself that I just needed some more time to get used to being off tour again.

The tour schedule was brutal, but it had kept me busy. The longer I spent aimlessly floating around without focus, the more I felt like the walls were closing in on me. I had to keep moving — then maybe next time I could outrun whatever shite life wanted to fling at me.

Speaking of moving, it was time to split. I slowly maneuvered myself out from underneath the snoring girl on top of me. It wouldn't be too awkward if she woke up; it wasn't like we'd done anything, but I didn't feel like sharing a cab or making small talk with her. She sleepily resettled on the couch while I stretched my aching muscles.

I patted down my pockets, making sure I still had my keys and wallet, found my shoes and baseball cap, and then headed toward the door. I'd let my hair grow longer since the last round of promo photos were taken and I hadn't shaved since I'd gotten back from Scotland. That and a ball cap were my disguise.

We'd all gotten used to living with mobs of fans always wanting a piece of us, and we'd learned the hard way to follow our security team's rules while we were on tour. Now at home, we were all having to readjust to new rules. I'd been able to get around without security with various levels of success, depending on where I was and who I was with. Ghost wasn't having any luck. He stood out like a sore thumb.

I hit the sunny streets outside the apartment building feeling restless as I started my walk of shame. First off, I hadn't gotten any action last night, so that was pretty shameful. Second, I probably looked as shitty as I felt. I was rocking rumpled clothing, severe bed head (or was it couch head?), lots of itchy hair on my face, and a nasty drool ring on my T-shirt that circled my left nipple, compliments of Sharon. Looking like this, I didn't think I'd have to worry about anyone recognizing me.

My first order of business was to get some food; I was starving. A cup of coffee would help clear my head. Then I'd figure out where the fuck I was and get the hell home so I could play some guitar. I began scanning the shops, looking for sustenance as I walked down the sidewalk.

I walked about a block when I noticed a line of people spilling out the door of a shop across the street. The sign read Underground Coffee

Bar. Good enough for me. I crossed the street and got onto the back of the line.

I vaguely noticed the girl in front of me only because she was so bundled up. It was sunny out with almost no breeze; it must have been close to sixty degrees Fahrenheit. Hell, in Scotland we only got this kind of beautiful weather at the very height of summer.

Her outfit was classy. Immediately, I thought she was rich. I didn't know much about fashion — she had on one of those really long sweater-type jackets over some skinny pants and was wearing high-heeled short boots. But this girl looked ridiculous because she was wearing a knit hat and scarf with her getup like she'd been exploring the polar ice caps. I couldn't see her face, because her back was to me, but the long blonde tresses that spilled out of her knit cap looked pretty.

Because I was bored, I watched her, hoping she'd turn around and show me her face.

Five minutes later, I don't think the line moved an inch.

"What's the hold up here?" I spoke out loud.

I snickered to myself when I heard the thick Scottish accent that came out of my mouth. Yeah, after living in the States for six years, I could imitate an American accent pretty spot-on when I wanted to. My natural accent had definitely softened a bit according to my family back home when I recently visited, so this heavy accent that slipped from my lips was for show. I guess I needed a wee bit of attention.

She turned around, probably wondering who I was talking to. I wished she wasn't wearing sunglasses because I couldn't see her eyes, but I'd confirmed she was definitely pretty.

She gave a small shrug. "This place is always slow."

I had a feeling she was looking me up and down from behind those sunglasses. It only took seconds, but I must have come up lacking. She turned back around and returned her attention to her phone.

Well, shite.

I chuckled softly. "Is there a blizzard in today's forecast that I didn't hear about?"

She whipped around and pulled off her sunglasses. This time she eyed me up and down very obviously; unfortunately, zeroing in on my left nipple—or rather, the drool stain on my wrinkled T-shirt—and the words that read 'BLINK if you want me' across my chest.

Her eyes narrowed with disdain. "I'm not blinking."

Ouch.

The line moved, so we both took a step forward.

This girl was feisty, and I was bored. Yeah, I was going to mess with her a bit.

Something about her seemed familiar. Her eyes pulled me in; they were the bluest blue. Maybe she had colored contact lenses because I'd never seen eyes so bright blue. The hair poking out of her hat was long and blonde, her teeth were straight and super white, and her nose was just adorable. Not one blemish marred her skin and her lips were glossy pink with a pronounced cupid's bow on the top lip. Those lips … yeah, my cock twitched.

Then it hit me. She was one of the 'beautiful' people. The people I'd watched on television growing up in Scotland. I used to watch this show about some high school kids in America. The kids were all impossibly beautiful and rich with endless amounts of designer clothing, fancy cars, and impossibly white teeth. And the weather in America was always sunny and warm. It looked like paradise.

It was no wonder when I had to get out of Scotland that I ran to the U.S. It had always seemed like a fantastical wonderland to me. Reality had tamed that notion over the years. I'd toured through most of the states with Ghost Parker and had met an incredibly wide variety of people and experienced an amazing variety of weather and landscapes. America was fucking huge and not all the people were beautiful looking.

But this lass? She was the embodiment of the perfect American girl from that show I used to watch. They were a dime a dozen here in southern California, but a lot of them had shitty personalities to go along with their beauty. Entitled. Bitchy. Fake.

"Is the coffee good here? Is it worth this wait?" I muttered.

She didn't even glance my way when she answered. "There's another coffee shop a couple of blocks down. Maybe you should go there?"

I rocked back on my heels. "Well, aren't you just a wee ray of sunshine?"

She looked like she was ready to unleash an unholy torrent of curses upon me, but then she took a deep breath and shrugged casually before turning her back on me as if I didn't matter.

I wasn't going to let her ignore me. It was too much fun messing with her. "Such a sensitive lassie."

That did it. I heard her sharp inhale and then an actual gasp of outrage as she whipped around to confront me. "Did you just call me a dog?"

I wanted to laugh out loud, but I kept my smile lazy. "You're a lassie, aye? You don't look like a lad to me."

Her eyes narrowed. "Isn't there some leprechaun meeting somewhere you should be running off to?"

Fuck me. This girl thought I was Irish. This time, I couldn't hold back my chuckle. "Sorry to disappoint you, but that meeting was last night. But, I heard the Barbie club was meeting today. It should be right up your alley."

Her face turned bright red. She was so mad; she actually spluttered. I braced myself for what she was about to let loose when her phone rang. She paused, eyeing me for a long moment before answering her phone.

"Hey, Mom."

She turned away from me, her back toward the street. The line moved forward another step as she listened to whatever her mother was saying.

"No, I'm not at my apartment right now. I just stepped out to get a coffee."

I was blatantly eavesdropping but didn't feel the slightest bit bad about it.

"Yes. He took me out to dinner. It was lovely."

Was she talking about a boyfriend? Shite. Now, that was oddly disappointing.

"Mom! Don't be so nosy."

She glanced over her shoulder and our eyes met for a brief second before she looked away. She looked flustered.

"I told you, I don't want to jinx anything. Maybe you can meet him if we make it to the six-month mark."

She kicked at the pavement with her boot. "Has it been six months already? Are you sure? Wow, time flies, I guess."

I heard her sigh at least once as her mother launched into a long diatribe in response.

Finally, she replied, "Well, we'll see Mom. You know, his schedule is always so busy. There's no way he'd be able to take enough time off to fly out to Kentucky right now. Maybe this summer would be better?"

Her body language was tense as she listened to her mother again.

She sounded like she cut her mom off. "No. No, he's really good to me. He makes plenty of time for me, Mom. He's so sweet."

She lowered her voice so I could barely hear what she said next. "Yes, he's right here with me now. We're getting coffee."

I looked around. I hadn't seen her with anyone this whole time.

"Just down the street from my apartment."

Hmmm. Was she telling tall tales to her mother?

"No, I told you; he's just shy about taking pictures."

She stole a quick peek at me again. Sorry, lassie, this was good. I was listening.

"Argh. Yes, he's tall. About six foot two."

Another big sigh escaped from her pretty lips.

"Well, let's see. Light brown hair — a little on the longish side. Brown eyes."

Shite, so far, she could practically be describing me.

"Yes, he's fit and muscly."

Now I knew she must be describing me.

Her nervous giggle was so feminine. "Yes, Mom. You'd definitely consider him 'eye candy'."

Her eyes flicked back to mine again briefly before skittering away. I couldn't help the smug smile that spread across my face.

She was so engrossed in her phone conversation that she didn't see the woman barreling down the sidewalk, making a beeline straight for her. I'd felt the woman's eyes latch onto me from afar as she approached. The woman was blatantly looking me over while she spoke on the cell phone that was clutched against her ear. At first, I thought she might have recognized me from the band, but as she approached, it dawned on me that she was an older version of the feisty lass standing right next to me. The wee lassie was in for a big surprise.

I had a feeling that this was going to be highly entertaining.

Chapter Two

Summer

I cringed as I described my fake boyfriend to my mother. Dammit, I was shit under pressure and I might have just described the annoyingly sexy guy behind me in line at the coffee shop. I didn't mean to, but I took a quick peek at him. Yep. I'd described him to a T, including his delicious muscular physique. If I had met this guy in my sorority days, I'd have been thinking about dropping my panties for him; however, these were my 'I hate men' days, so sex was the last thing on my mind.

Who was I kidding? The guy was insanely hot. Sizzling. He oozed sex appeal. And if sex wasn't on my mind, why were my panties so wet right now?

I sighed. He was just the kind of guy I didn't need in my life. Didn't need and most definitely didn't want. My mom was still babbling on the phone with me about how much she wanted to meet my fake boyfriend. It was getting harder and harder to put it off. My lies were getting more preposterous every time I talked to her. *He's really shy about getting his picture taken.* Yes, I knew it was time to break up with my pretend boyfriend. He'd been a great buffer from my over-eager mom while it lasted.

My eyes swept over to the Irish guy in line behind me. Did I mention that he had an absolutely panty-meltingly sensual Irish accent? If I could just ignore the dumb stuff that came out of his mouth — he'd called me Lassie the dog, for God's sake — I'd be in heaven just listening to him talk. Now, if he'd only whispered some dirty things in my ear...

My brows narrowed in confusion. What was going on? He had a

smirk of epic proportions on his face. His arms were crossed. Smug. Satisfied. Like maybe he thought he'd won our little sparring battle? As if. No, that wasn't quite right. It was like he was about to witness the greatest show on earth. Or maybe it was that he was about to witness my downfall. Like I was about to get steamrolled. What. The. Fuck?

Then the steamroller hit.

Mother.

She was here. On the phone with me, but also right in front of me. In the flesh.

What. The. Absolute. Fuck!

"Mom?" My mouth hung open in shock.

"Baby!" She squeezed me in her arms in one of those warm, swaying hugs. "I'm so happy to see you. I've missed you so much."

"Mom, I've missed you, too. What are you doing here in California? Is Dad here?" I whipped my head around, searching for my dad.

My mom waved her hand. "He's busy hauling all our suitcases up to your apartment, but I couldn't wait, so I came down here to find the coffee shop and surprise you."

"Oh, wow." I bit my lip. "This is such a great surprise."

I had been vaguely aware of the sexy Irish guy watching our little reunion with interest. I really didn't want him to bear witness to the shitshow when my mom discovered my fake-boyfriend fib. The line had moved up so that we were almost in the door now. If I wanted to retain any shred of pride, I needed to get my mother out of there now.

But, of course, my mother was always two steps ahead of me. Before I could make a move, she turned to the hot Irish stranger and beamed at him. "You must be…"

I blushed. I winced. I opened my mouth to say … what? How could I stop this disaster in the making? Think, Summer. Quick!

"Scotty." He offered his hand to my mother.

"Scotty!" My mother was a hugger. Scotty didn't stand a chance. She enveloped him in a big embrace. "My daughter has told me so much about you!"

I snorted. I purposefully had only told her about three things in total about my fake boyfriend.

My mother took a step back from him and looked him over critically. "And she wasn't kidding!"

His smile lit his eyes. He was clearly amused. And he had two dimples, which were like my kryptonite.

Oh, My God. Shoot me now.

"It's nice to meet you, Mrs...." his voice trailed off.

"Oooh. You can call me Lara." She turned to me and squeezed my arm. "You forgot to mention that Scotty has such a lovely accent, sweetie."

Suddenly, Scotty was at my side. His arm wrapped possessively around me, and he pulled me flush against his hard body. "Sweetie, you didn't tell your mum where I'm from?"

How was I supposed to stop this nonsense? It was like a slow-motion train wreck. I swallowed. "Right. I can't believe I forgot to mention it. Scotty is from Ireland."

Scotty sniggered. "Oh, my wee bumpkin. How many times have I told you?" He actually kissed the top of my head. "I'm from Scotland."

My mother frowned. "Bumpkin?"

Scotty didn't hesitate. "It's a term of endearment in Scotland. She actually prefers to be called Lassie as a pet name, but I like to call her my wee bumpkin ... My Bouncy Bumpkin. Because she's so ... bouncy."

Bouncy Bumpkin? I was ready to knee him in the balls. "And I call him..." I could never think quickly on my feet. "Limpie Pie."

Mom scrunched her nose. "Limpie Pie?"

I held up my pointer finger and then slowly cricked it until it drooped. "It's an inside joke."

"Oh, I see." Mom gave Scotty the side-eye.

When he squeezed my side in warning, I flashed a pretty smile at him. His eyes narrowed into little slits and his teeth clenched. I guess I hit the target with that one.

Scotty turned on the charm. "That's just a joke, Lara. Don't worry. There's no problem there, I assure you."

Mom twittered like a bird. "Oh, well, that's a relief."

Yuck. This was kind of gross. Time to ditch this guy. "Well, Scotty, I wasn't expecting to see my parents today — what a surprise! So, I'll have to take a rain check on our plans. I'll, uh, call you later."

"Nonsense!" my mom exclaimed. "Your father would love to meet Scotty, too. I told him I'd pick us both up a coffee while I came to see you — our flight was so early. We can bring the coffee back to your apartment so your father and I can get to know Scotty better."

The hundredth lie of the day flowed from my tongue quite easily. "Oh, that would be nice, but Scotty has an important meeting this morning with his club. It's a heritage thing, you know, leprechauns and man-skirts and stuff. He can't miss it." I patted his biceps. "Isn't that right, Limpie Pie?"

The muscle in his jaw clenched. "I would like to get my coffee first, if that's okay with you, Bouncy Bumpkin?" He held the door open as we entered the shop. We'd finally made it inside.

The coffee shop was fairly chaotic inside. I asked my mom a million questions, generally trying to keep her busy and away from Scotty. I had no idea why he'd gone along with my crazy deception, and I didn't really care. As soon as I could, I'd whisk my mom away from here and never see him again. If I played everything right, my parents would never find out that Scotty was a fake. If they planned on staying more than a few days, an unexpected breakup with my fake boyfriend was in the cards.

Scotty stood behind my mother and me as if he was the next customer in line, which was exactly what he really was. He wasn't really paying that much attention to us anymore. For some insane reason, that disappointed me. I liked our crazy conversation and silly insults, and I certainly didn't mind getting attention from a sexy guy. But I knew I couldn't trust myself around men like him. And this one unquestionably looked like trouble.

While I was paying for the four drinks I ordered (I figured I owed Scotty a coffee for his trouble), I noticed my mom had cornered Scotty and was talking animatedly with him. I felt a moment of panic when I couldn't get over to them to run interference. What was she saying? What was he saying? I couldn't hear anything over the din of the crowd.

As soon as I could, I stepped over to my mom and locked arms with her, drawing her away toward the counter to wait for our order. When it was up, I handed Scotty's coffee to him and spoke to him pointedly. "I know you need to get off to your meeting before you're late."

He had a naughty glint in his eye. "Can't keep the leprechauns waiting. Thanks for the coffee."

"No problem."

My mother gave him a big hug. "I look forward to getting to know you better, Scotty."

He nodded to my mother and then flashed me a mischievous smile. Before I could take my next breath, we were kissing. He caught me by surprise, so I didn't have time to turn my head to reject him. He captured my lips thoroughly with his and lingered a few seconds longer than a chaste goodbye kiss should last. Both my hands were filled with coffee, so I couldn't even shove him away.

Sweet holy hell! The kiss left me breathless. Buzzing and fluttery.

Aching in a place that felt long dormant. I couldn't even move.

His answering smirk was all-knowing. "Later, my wee bouncy bumpkin."

I was too gobsmacked to put him in place with a sarcastic retort, and then suddenly he was gone. He flitted in and then out of my life like some kind of sexy apparition. What the hell?

My fingers traced my lips. The simple kiss couldn't have been that good. I was just so sexually repressed right now from swearing off men like a nun. And that 'no man' plan had worked out well. Life was orderly. Even. Successful. In a few days, I'd forget all about the drop-dead gorgeous stranger who'd pretended to be my boyfriend for a hot five minutes. And I'd forget about that kiss — the no-tongue five-second lip contact that had my lady bits clenching with need.

How to Date a Rockstar

Printed in Great Britain
by Amazon